Now I Can See The Moon

Bonar Ash

*To Joan,
from Bonar Ash,
aka Gillie Shilson*

Lutestring Press

© 2022 **Bonar Ash**

The right of Bonar Ash to be identified as the Author of the Work has been asserted by him in accordance with the Copyrights, Designs and Patents Act 1988. All rights reserved.

No part of this publication may be reproduced, stored in a retrieval system, or transmitted, in any form or by any means without the prior written permission of the publisher, nor be otherwise circulated in any form of binding or cover other than that in which it is published and without a similar condition being imposed on the subsequent purchaser.

All characters in this publication are fictitious and any resemblance to real persons, living or dead, is purely coincidental.

Barn's burnt down —
Now I can see the moon.

Mizuta Masahide

Chapter 1

Surrey, England
1955

THE THING ABOUT IZZY IS, SHE'S LIKE THE SISTER I never had. We have history.

When we were seven, as a big favour I allowed Izzy up into our attic, after months of forbidding her with the excuse that it was a special, private place to which she, not being an actual member of our family, did not have access.

After the accident in which my mother and my grandparents died, on fine nights when everyone else was asleep I would climb the stairs to the attic. Standing on a chair I would reach up on tip-toes to push back the dirt-encrusted sky-light so that I could lose myself in the night sky with its overwhelming stars. I would search the glittering mass, looking for answers. I wondered if Grandma and Grandpa and my mother had somehow got tangled up in them and were wandering about, wondering what on earth had happened and why they couldn't come home.

To pay me back for my sauciness, sitting cross-legged on the bed Great Grandpa had died in, Izzy told me a ghost story, and this was the story she told:

Three friends were staying in a lonely hotel in the country. The attic of the hotel was supposed to be haunted and no one would go up there, so to prove how brave they were the friends decided that two of them would spend the night up there while the third friend would lock them in so they couldn't escape. Then in the morning he would come and let them out.

Izzy whispered all this in her huskiest, spookiest voice and already shivers ran up my back and the hairs on my arms stood out, and she'd only just started.

It was January and dark outside. We had decided that after tea would be the best time for Izzy to visit the attic since she was almost always in our house at tea time, being partial to the Milk and Honey biscuits (her favourites, hoarded by Babe who looked after us, other females being absent), oatcakes and Battenberg cake which, now rationing had ended, were on offer. There was no electricity in the attic so we took torches which in my opinion were spookier than candles because when you switched them on all they lit up was the little circle where your torch was pointing, so your mind worked itself into a frenzy imagining all the awful things that were probably going on elsewhere. Especially when you were seven.

'In the morning,' Izzy said in her special, spooky voice, 'the friend climbed up the stairs to the attic and slowly ... slowly,' here she paused for effect, 'unlocked the door.'

I gasped. 'And?'

'And there,' said Izzy. 'Actually, at first, he couldn't see anything because of the dark. It was completely dark like it is now.' (We had turned off our torches.)

'Was it?'

'Actually he had forgotten his torch so he had to go back for it.'

'Oh no!'

'Yup. He had to go all the way back down to his bedroom and get his torch then climb all the way back up the stairs to the attic.'

'But he'd left it unlocked so the people could have escaped?'

'No, he very carefully locked it before going back down the stairs to get his torch.'

'So he had to unlock it again.' I could hardly breathe. My heart hurled itself against my ribs as though it was trying to get out.

'He did, he had to unlock it again. And when he turned the key it made a horrible grating sound in the lock which was all rusty with age. At first he couldn't see anything, even when he shone his torch right around. His friends seemed to have disappeared.'

'D-disappeared?'

'Well ... then he shone his torch right over into the farthest, spideriest corner of the attic ... and there they were.'

'Were they all right?'

Izzy lowered her voice even further, jutted her face forward and shone the torch up under her chin so she looked as scary as a pumpkin on Hallowe'en. 'They were sitting on the floor cross-legged, opposite each other.'

'Were they?'

Long pause, then – 'Each with his chopped-off head in the other person's lap.'

I screamed. Izzy began to laugh. Feet came pounding up the stairs and Luke threw open the door. 'What happened? Milly, stop that yelling. Izzy, what's going on?'

'Nothing,' Izzy said, still giggling. 'I told her a story, that's all.'

'What kind of story?' Luke stood there, simmering. He'd

only just moved in to our house as caretaker and problem solver and I expect he was having enough trouble with me as it was without Izzy making it worse.

Izzy slid off the bed and sat on the floor. 'Honestly, she's such a scaredy-cat.'

'Izzy,' Luke said in his Voice of Doom. 'Go home. Now.' He hardly ever used his Voice of Doom but when he did you sat up and took notice.

'Sor-*ry*,' Izzy said, rescuing her half-finished bag of crisps and scrambling to her feet. Not sorry a bit. 'Crumbs, what a fuss about a silly old ghost story.'

I followed Izzy down the stairs, feeling a fool because of Luke whom I still didn't know very well. He'd only been living with us a matter of weeks. On the landing, when Izzy had disappeared down the next flight, he hunkered down in front of me. 'Milly,' he said. 'Look at me.'

I looked. His eyes were warm and brown and very sincere.

I was shivering and shaking and overreacting as only I knew how.

'Sweetheart,' he said. 'I'm here now.'

It has always seemed to me that Luke knows by instinct exactly what you need. He knew that just as when you go to a stranger's funeral (Esme, one of the lodgers, told me this), your inexplicable tears are as much for other losses, other regrets, as for this person you hardly knew, so my panic and fear that afternoon were as much for the fog of half-truths and uncertainties I'd been stumbling about in since the loss of my family, as terror over the idea of two men sitting cradling each other's severed heads. What I needed was what he gave me.

Looking into my eyes, he held my spindly arms above the elbows in his warm, strong grip. 'You're safe now,' he said. 'As long as you need me I will never, ever leave you. That's a promise.'

I never forgot his words and the way he looked when he said them. They filled my sad, seven-year-old heart with the conviction that I could completely rely on him, and that come what may, Luke would always tell me the truth.

And then I went and spoiled it all by breaking away and standing on my head, because I was embarrassed and because I wanted to regain control of the situation. I hoped that Izzy could see but by then, like the will-o'-the-wisp she was, she was long gone.

Chapter 2

Ten years later

I HEARD THE MUSIC FOR THE FIRST TIME THAT NIGHT. I'd gone up to the attic because I needed to talk to my mother. I felt closest to her in the attic because that was where I kept the suitcase. It was a sort of reliquary, I suppose. It contained the few things of hers that I'd managed to keep hold of after the accident. Every so often I felt impelled to go up and look at them, smell them, touch them, try to pull her to me, to feel her presence near.

And that was when I heard it, the music. Faint but persistent, as though someone had left a radio on somewhere, it spiralled up from the orchard to the attic window far above. I frowned and looked at my watch, the Omega Luke had given me on my sixteenth birthday. Eleven o'clock. Who on earth could be out there at this time of night? The lodgers had gone to bed ages ago.

I pulled the old chair with a hole in its cane seat over to the window. It was wobbly but reasonably stable. I stood up on the wooden edges and struggled to open the creaky window. It was cold with the window open because even though it was the end of July I only had my skimpy blue top on, the one Izzy was always wanting to borrow. I began to feel annoyed with the window-latch because it wasn't really strong enough to hold the window up and the window was heavy and my shoulders were beginning to ache, and then I heard the music again.

The moon was full, floating on the vast ocean of the sky with the grandeur of a boat in full sail. The moon pulled me the way it always does with its unbearable loneliness, as if it's trying to tell me something but I can't hear what it's saying. Like when somebody dies and you're desperate to make them hear you and for them to say something back, only there's this vast distance between you, this impenetrable silence, overwhelming and powerful. And the silence always wins; it leaves you feeling exhausted and stupid for even trying. It's like whomever it is has escaped. There's a kind of triumph about it, as if they're thumbing their nose at you. Because however long you search, you won't find them.

(I was angry with my mother about this for a long time. I mean, why would she do that? Disappear beyond my reach, finally and completely. She had done that anyway, quite a lot, but this was the final straw. I was six when she died. I was seventeen now and knew better.)

I decided to go down and have a look. I closed the window and jumped down from the chair, dusting my hands on my jeans. The house was in darkness as I crept down the attic stairs; even Luke had gone to bed. He and Jean-Paul had been working their socks off to get Mrs Henderson's sideboard finished in time for her son's wedding. She was a returned client so they wanted to keep in her good books. At supper Luke had opened a rare bottle of wine to celebrate getting it done on time, but he was obviously shattered, he had a hard time suppressing yawns.

I pushed open the side door, which we never locked.

My feet scrunched on the gravel path. The moon was so bright it cast shadows and the night air smelt fresh and cool after the mustiness of the attic and the left-over smell in the hall of Babe's cottage pie. But no music. I veered off sideways and made for the orchard. When I got there I heard it again.

I moved in among the apple trees. It was darker under the thick spread of branches. I felt my way from tree to tree, searching, not knowing what for. I was scared, which was stupid, I mean I've practically lived in the orchard all my life. It's where Izzy and I built fairy houses in the tree roots when we were little after reading *The Mossy Green Theatre,* where I always escaped to when things went wrong, where Izzy and I spent half our time sprawled in the long grass with our Toffee Whirls and Nux bars, talking.

No music. Must have imagined it. It could have come from one of the houses surrounding ours, even though they were some way away beyond our sprawling, unruly garden. I'd go back in, go to bed as I should have done ages ago only I'd been worried about Izzy who seemed to have vanished. I hadn't seen her for the whole weekend.

And then it started again and I realised what it was. It was my mother's favourite Françoise Hardy song that she'd loved and played over and over again: *'Tous les garçons et les filles de mon âge se promènent dans la rue deux par deux ... Tous les garçons et les filles de mon âge savent bien ce que c'est d'être heureux ...'*

There were no words, only the hypnotic tune. The instrument could have been a flute, or a recorder. It was faint, but definitely there. I wasn't imagining it. The accompanying words, so familiar, rang through my head. My heart clenched. What was going on? I charged forward, my fear gone. 'Who's there? Izzy ... Izzy? Is that you?'

The music rolled on, insidious, relentless: *'Et les yeux dans les yeux ... et la main dans la main ... ils s'en vont amoureux sans peur du lendemain ... Oui mais moi ... je vais seul ... par les rues, l'âme en peine ... Oui mais moi ... je vais seule, car personne ... ne m'aime ...'*

The next moment the music stopped as suddenly as it had begun. I crashed through the trees, my heart thundering. I stopped and peered through the moon-splattered darkness, trying to make sense of what was happening.

Ahead of me a light flickered. I watched, unbelieving, as a bubble of light appeared from somewhere between the trees. It rose, so slowly that it seemed almost not to be moving at all, up, up until it vanished among the canopy of leaves overhead. I waited. The silence rolled in, questioning, vibrating with something – what? – until once again the orchard settled down as though nothing had happened. 'Izzy,' I moaned pathetically and sank into the grass.

Because it was her, it had to be, she'd set this up for some diabolical reason of her own. She was getting her own back because just before she'd disappeared we'd quarrelled violently about the affair she was having with Robert, who was married and of whom I disapproved. Not of Robert, *per se*, but of the situation. We were supposed to be going to university in September, in my case to St Andrews to read English Literature, in hers to Bath to read for a degree in architecture. She'd been mad to be an architect since she was ten years old but now she'd met Robert her brain had turned into mush and all sensible thoughts of her future seemed to have melted away under the hot light of his allure.

'Milly, is that you? What's going on? Are you all right?'

Oh brilliant, I'd woken one of the lodgers. Behind me, feet rustled through the long grass; the hem of Esme's nightdress whispered over fallen leaves. I struggled to my feet. 'Sorry, Esme. I came down because I heard something.' I turned to face her. She stood there, her long, bespectacled face pale and anxious. Her dark hair salted with grey, released from its usual bun, fell around her face, making her look younger. She was wrapped in a pink silk negligée. Esme's uncharacteristically exotic choice of underclothes and nightwear had long ceased to surprise me.

'What was it? An animal of some kind? It's probably Oranjello or Sapphy.'

Jello, a huge orange neutered tom, the bane of our other lodger Felix's life, was Esme's cat; Sapphy, a delicate, smoky grey tabby/Siamese cross, was the love of mine.

'Not a cat,' I said. I looked away, frowning. What could I say? If it was Izzy I didn't want to drop her in it. If it wasn't, well, I didn't know Esme's views on the supernatural, if that was what this was. She had always seemed the most prosaic of people, more like a librarian than a mystic or a romantic, but having said that, there was her choice of lingerie.

'Why don't you come back in and let me make you a cup of tea,' Esme said. 'It's time you were in bed anyway. Aren't you starting at Amy's soon?'

'Monday.' My heart sank. I'd forgotten all about it. I'd agreed to help out on a temporary basis, cleaning Amy Booth's house. She was a friend of Izzy's mother Juno, and her regular cleaner, Gill, was in hospital, having had some kind of accident: I didn't know the details. I'd been meaning to get together with Babe, our housekeeper, for a quick masterclass on the basics, but what with one thing and another I hadn't. Let's face it, I didn't know the first thing about how to clean a house.

I gave a last glance back into the trees. In my imagination that orb of light floated again and again into the branches above. As I followed Esme gloomily into the house I felt a tremor of foreboding, almost, of fear.

AFTER THE TEA, which I drank more to please Esme than myself – a good dollop of brandy would have been more welcome – I crept back down the stairs from Esme's room to my own, tiptoeing over the creaky floorboards past Felix's room. He's a light sleeper, and sure enough his door handle rattled, the door opened and his head appeared around the door wreathed in smoke from the cigarette he was holding.

'Excitements?' he said. 'Hello, young Milly, what's going on?'

'Nothing, Felix, I just went down to get a drink of water.' Music was coming from the old Grundig radio sitting on his chest of drawers. Someone was singing, something awesome and unfamiliar. I cocked my head.

He stood aside and indicated with the hand holding the cigarette. 'Maria Callas. *Vissi d'Arte*.'

'Golly!'

'My thoughts exactly. Well, goodnight, young Milly.' He bowed his head and withdrew.

Esme complained bitterly about Felix's nocturnal habits. 'Damn him and his endless baths,' she said. 'It wakes me up you know, Milly, the water rushing through the pipes. Niagara Falls. It runs right under my floor. I wouldn't mind if it wasn't two in the morning. The wretched man never sleeps. I wake thinking it's the flood come at last, which we're all waiting for, the way things are going.'

'Still at least he has baths,' I pointed out.

'I'd put up with the aroma. I need my sleep. There ought to be rules. I shall speak to Luke.'

Felix looked as though he never ate enough and would have been tall if he only stood up straight. His still abundant black hair was streaked, badger-like, with grey at the temples. His expression was furtive, which Luke said was probably shyness rather than un-trustworthiness. He was gentle and courteous, even when needled by Esme, and I privately marvelled that he'd managed to keep order at the boys' prep school where he'd taught History for so many years. Apparently he'd retired early on grounds of ill health, whatever that meant; he seemed perfectly okay to me. His blue eyes were shaded by bushy eyebrows and had a downward slant most of the time, but when he lifted his face and looked at you properly, they startled you with their innocent, intelligent light. I liked him a lot.

It was a mystery to me why he'd given up his lovely little thatched cottage in Leatherhead – there was a photograph of it on the wall of his bedroom – to come and rent a room in our house. He'd never explained, despite my promptings. There was a pastel painting, too, of a little girl about six which he'd volunteered once was a portrait of his granddaughter Leonie. That was as far as he'd go. Nothing about why he never seemed to see her now. It was maddening. I wanted to help. He often looked sad and I knew there was a story there.

IN THE MORNING I went up to the attic again. When I opened the attic door, the warm, stale air, heavy with ancient scents, greeted me like a pair of loving arms. Up here felt different from the rest of this old stone house. Everything here was more or less on its last legs: the springs in great-grandpa's brass bedstead had gone long ago, one or two even managing to poke up through the mattress. The bed sagged in all directions; even its long brass legs went different ways, like a dog being pulled somewhere it doesn't want to go. The old duvet thrown over the bed was stained and coverless, the cream paint on the old pine chest of drawers chipped and faded. Instead of a lamp, a candle sat on the rickety bamboo table by the bed and a folded piece of cardboard under one of its legs stopped the bed rocking on the uneven floorboards. The two small painted bookcases, one pink, one white, were crammed with children's books, mine and, much older, my mother Miranda's.

I reached under the bed, which lolled like a vast beached boat in the middle of the attic floor, and hauled out the old leather suitcase. I dragged it over to the skylight. Dust-motes danced around my head; I took a breath and blew and they flew off in all directions, glittering where a shaft of sunlight caught them, whirling around before settling down again. I dug down inside my tee-shirt and felt for the thin black leather cord that hung around my neck. I pulled it up and leaned forward to unlock the suitcase with the little key dangling from the end of it. As always my heartbeat ratcheted up. I could never be sure that when I lifted the lid I wouldn't be in for a shock – a seething mass of scorpions or a bloodied, severed head like in the ghost story Izzy had scared me witless with when we were little. Luke said I had an overactive imagination. Whatever, opening the suitcase was always a tense moment. I held my breath and peeped inside.

And it was fine, they were all there, my mother's things. I reached inside and touched the softness of silk. I lifted out a pale green petticoat and shoved my nose violently into it, inhaling desperately but in vain; all there had been of my mother – her sweat, her scent – had long since faded.

Hugging the petticoat against me with my elbows I

reached in again and lifted out a cardboard writing-folder with three sheets of pale pink scented paper and two envelopes tucked into its pocket and a pink rose on the outside. I lifted the folder to my nose and inhaled, fingering the corner where the grey cardboard showed through a worn place on the shiny outside. I wondered if things wore out with being taken out and looked at and would eventually fall away to nothing. Then there would be nothing left. I oughtn't to do this so often, I decided, just every once in a while from now on, perhaps on my birthday, and at Christmas.

There was a small pile of programmes clipped together. I pulled off the paper-clip and examined them one at a time, as if I hadn't done this a thousand times before, as if I didn't know them, every word, off by heart. They still might throw up some answers.

There was a programme for *Peter Grimes* at Sadlers Wells in June 1945 and one for *Sweet Yesterday*, a musical at the Adelphi Theatre. There was Ivor Novello's *Perchance to Dream* at the Hippodrome in April and ballet with the Sadler's Wells company – *Coppelia* with Margot Fonteyn and Robert Helpmann at the New Theatre in St. Martin's Lane.

It all seemed so exotic to me, even the names of the theatres. I imagined the lights in the foyer and the people gathering in their best evening clothes, waiting to go in, then the excitement of waiting for the curtain to go up. We hardly ever went up to London, there wasn't the dosh. I didn't mind a bit but it was nice to imagine my mother having fun and going to all these exciting places while she was waiting for her baby – me – to be born.

I dug in under her blue velvet evening cloak and found the return ticket to Waterloo, my mother's black and green mottled Waterman fountain pen, the empty scent bottle, the round black box that still smelt faintly of Max Factor face powder, the scarlet Revlon lipstick and the bottle of Revlon nail-varnish gone hard long ago. The nail varnish was the saddest thing; when I was little it had made me wonder what had become of my mother, buried in the churchyard at St Michael's just down the road. Had she gone hard too?

I folded the petticoat away and laid it back in the suitcase with a slight feeling of disappointment. My mother's possessions were gradually losing their power to charm, the way if you stare at a photograph too often you begin to forget what the real person looked like. They'd become unsatisfying, like the Vesta ready-made meals which Babe had tried out on me once or twice. Sometimes it even crossed my mind to give Luke back my mother's ballet shoes which he had given me when I was little, and throw the rest of the stuff away. Just not yet.

Nobody knew about the suitcase, not even Izzy. I could have told her once when we were younger but somehow I never had and now, when the distance between us seemed to be stretching like a piece of old elastic, it had become impossible.

I shoved it back under the bed, calmer suddenly as though through handling her things I'd heard my mother's voice. I couldn't remember what I'd called her when she was alive. Mother, I said in my head. Mummy. Mum. Mama. I must have called her something. Some of my friends called their mothers by their Christian names. What a waste, I never would have. 'Mother' has such a beautiful sound.

I wish I could hear you speak, I whispered aloud. Just one last time.

And somewhere in the air around my head, I heard a chime, a sweet chime like the sound of a silver spoon touching a crystal glass, and with it a swirl of music, soft as an exhaled breath. I listened, my heart thudding, longing for more, but nothing came.

I sat back on my heels and put my hand over my stomach which had gone hard as a drum again. I was worried about Izzy. Not just about her going missing but – suppose Robert's wife found out about him and her? And then suppose Luke got to hear about it? He would freak out. He'd think I ought to have persuaded Izzy to stop it. If only I could talk to him about it but he'd disapprove, I knew he would. Then I'd be torn between him and Izzy.

I couldn't confide in Pascale, my mother's old nurse who lived with us still and seemed to hate my guts. I hadn't a clue why she was so grouchy with me. I worried that it might have something to do with the memories that reared up sometimes like shabby ghosts out of the dark, usually when I was falling asleep, memories that seemed to be of bad behaviour on somebody's part.

Was it my bad behaviour? Had I done something really dumb that I couldn't remember, that made Pascale despise me so? I must have done something. Perhaps I'd suppressed it. People do that. I half longed, half dreaded to know what it was.

Chapter 3

Luke

As usual when I'd got myself steamed up, I needed Luke. I drifted into the kitchen. Babe had disappeared but Luke was sprawled at the kitchen table reading *The Times* and managing to smoke a cigarette at the same time, no mean feat and one which had on occasion resulted in the newspaper going up in flames. The kitchen smelt of coffee, toast and cigarette smoke. I went to the dresser and picked up the bread knife.

'Morning sweetie,' Luke said, relinquishing the paper and stubbing his cigarette out in the ashtray on the table. 'Got to go in this morning I'm afraid. Something I have to finish.' He gathered the paper together again, held it up and peered around it. Harold Wilson, pipe in mouth, looked quizzically out from the front page. He seemed to be looking straight at me.

'But it's Saturday.' I waved the bread knife at him. He shrugged and made a sorry face. 'Oh well,' I said. 'If you have to. Don't stop reading. I'll just get on.'

'I might just finish this section. If I can stomach the utter folly of the human race.' He shook the paper straight and disappeared behind it again. I wondered what the human race had done now. It was probably something to do with high-rise flats, or Dr Beeching. I smiled inside and cut a slice of Hovis, trying to even up the end of the loaf. Luke was perfect in every way but he couldn't cut the bread straight. *Hovis, the golden heart of a meal,* I quoted under my breath, dropping the slice of bread into the toaster. We'd recently started renting a television from the DER shop in the high street, and the advertising jingles got into your head and wouldn't leave you alone. *Go to work on an egg,* I found myself mouthing as I deposited a poached one on my plate. *A swinging way to start the day* as I poured milk on my puffed wheat.

Babe wandered in from her little sitting room next door. For as long as I could remember the room had been a depository for everything nobody knew quite what else to do with, but when Luke came he cleared it out and turned it into a cosy little room where Babe could sit and listen to the radio and do her sewing and knitting and generally get away from us all.

'Sir Alec's resigned,' Luke said to nobody in particular.

'Oh, I like him,' Babe said. 'He always looks such a gent. Why?'

'It's not entirely clear,' Luke said from behind the paper.

'Well, I think it's a shame.' She patted me on the shoulder. 'Milly, you haven't given me your green jumper. Don't look like that. You agreed.'

'You're not really going to unravel it? I love that jumper.'

'But you can't get into it,' Babe said. 'Don't be daft. If I unravel it I can knit you a bigger one. I've still got some of the wool somewhere. You can help me ball it up. How are you getting on with that skirt?'

I was making the skirt from a Vogue pattern and some

left-over curtain material Babe had produced but my heart wasn't in it. To be honest I didn't fancy going about looking like a flower bed, I'd rather stick to my jeans. I didn't want to hurt Babe's feelings though which meant acting enthusiastic. 'Fine,' I said. 'Great pattern. I'll get the jumper in a min.'

'I'm gonna wait till the stars come out,' sang Wilson Pickett from Babe's room, *'and see that twinkle in your eyes.'*

'No cereal today?' Luke said. X-ray eyes. The sun behind him shone through the long windows and his shadow loomed behind the translucent paper wings extended between his raised hands.

'It says in *Woman's Own* toast and fruit are better for you.'

The door from the hall opened and Pascale shuffled in, holding an empty mug outstretched before her like the cup at communion. She hobbled towards the sink, throwing me a reproachful look. 'You disturb Monsieur Luke.'

'Nonsense, Pascale,' Babe said, giving her a look. 'Jumper, Milly,' she said and went back next door.

My toast popped up. 'I have to eat, Pascale,' I said. 'I'm trying not to disturb him. Leave that, I'll wash it up.'

'Always you disturb.' Pascale hobbled back towards the door. 'Mind not to break.' The door closed after her.

I rolled my eyes. Luke, who on over-hearing this exchange had lowered his newspaper, frowned and seemed about to speak but after a moment's thought he changed his mind and lifted it up again.

Pascale was in her seventies but looked even older. It was partly the arthritis which had stiffened her joints and bent and twisted her fingers. Perhaps she looked old too because of the way she dressed, always in black from head to foot. Under her long skirts in the summer she wore ancient wooden clogs and in the winter stout Docs which Luke had recently persuaded her to wear. When she'd seen herself in the long cloakroom mirror for the first time in those boots she had very nearly laughed.

'And she hardly ever laughs,' I told Izzy. 'She does smile, sometimes, reluctantly. It's just that she never laughs. She never shows her teeth.'

'Maybe she hasn't got any.'

'She's got dentures. She just doesn't laugh.'

'I wonder if she's always been like that.'

I wondered too. Before my mother's death which had dimmed the light of Pascale's life (although not completely of course, because of Jesus), had she been the life and soul of the party? Had she laughed then?

If I really tried I could imagine that when she was young Pascale might have been beautiful. Her hair, still dark though heavily dusted with grey and pulled back into a tight bun at the nape of her neck, was abundant, her mouth, though soured now with life's sorrows might once have been sweet; her face, though wrinkled now like an old apple, might once when she was young have had an attractive roundness. Perhaps then she had known how to smile properly, even, unlikely though it might seem, to laugh.

I brought my toast to the long farmhouse table, sat down and reached for the butter dish. The butter knife stuck out from the roll of yellow butter like a dagger from a plump, round body. I pulled it out and stabbed it in again, hard.

WHEN I'D FINISHED my toast I left Luke to it and ran upstairs to fetch the jumper and my notebook, chewing pleasurably on a strip of Wrigley's I'd found in my jeans pocket. On my way down I passed Pascale rummaging in the airing cupboard on the landing, muttering. I couldn't think off-hand of anything in particular I'd done to bug her but you never knew with Pascale; it didn't take much. Perhaps it wasn't me for once, perhaps it was the sound of Esme's typewriter annoying her, clunking away behind her bedroom door.

Babe was standing at the sink in the kitchen running hot water into the washing up bowl singing along to Herman's Hermits. I couldn't imagine Babe without her Jupiter Six-de-Luxe transistor radio by her side or hanging from the end of her arm. It went with her everywhere.

'Every time I see you looking my way,' Herman sang cheerily from the draining board, *'baby, baby, can't you hear my heartbeat?'*

Babe was Barbara Anne Bellow-Eve, her name far too big a mouthful for anyone, hence the nickname imposed by me, aged eight. She had a voice that could open tins, eyes as soft as pansies and an uncomfortable relationship with her clothes which had a habit of slipping off her at unexpected moments as though trying to escape. Her bra-straps fell down and on the rare occasions when she wasn't wearing jeans it frequently snowed down south (petticoat showing, for those who don't know the vernacular) and there was often a generous amount of cleavage on view. Babe and her clothes seemed engaged in a constant struggle for domination.

'Greetings, music lovers,' I said cheerily. 'Didn't we do the washing up last night?' I frowned at the pile of dirty crockery.

Babe shook her head and squirted Fairy Liquid into the bowl. 'It got late. I'm much quicker anyway. You lot dawdle around and chat.' She looked at me, frowning. 'You be careful with that chewing gum, it'll wrap itself around your heart.' She picked a plate off the pile and examined it. 'Hardly worth washing,' she said. 'Never anything left on the plates anyway.'

This was true. We all went on like ravening gannets. It was partly because Babe's cooking really was far out. I sniffed hungrily. 'What's for supper?'

'Hello, my ol' mateys,' Brian Matthews boomed from Babe's elbow.

'You can't be hungry already.' Steam from the hot tap swirled around her head.

'But I am, that's the trouble. I'm always hungry. Oh flip,' I said, looking down at myself. I reached for a drying-up cloth. 'I only have to look at a doughnut to feel my waistband expanding. Izzy can eat anything and not put on an ounce. It's not fair.' I envied Babe her narrow thighs.

'Flippin' Nora,' she exclaimed when I moaned about this. 'Stop complaining. You can walk, can't you? There's many'd give their teeth for your legs. You be thankful.'

I felt like pointing out that then they wouldn't be able to eat.

Babe looked me up and down. 'Will you give over. It's only a bit of puppy fat. Everyone's much too thin nowadays.'

Babe thought this because all the people in this house were bean poles, me included, actually. I just liked hearing her scold, it gave me a safe feeling. Babe had lived with us since I was seven. She was brought in to look after me after my mother died in the accident and had been my rock ever since. Well, Luke was my rock too but a woman was different. Babe was like a mum even if she was only in her thirties still.

'It's Irish Stew.' Babe started plunging plates into the washing up bowl. 'Supper.'

'My favourite!'

Babe banged a saucepan down on the draining board. 'This needs a soak, mashed potato, sticks like glue. I thought I asked you to put cold water in it last night.'

'Sorry.'

Babe rolled her eyes and tightened her lips. I felt guilty. She was right, too often nowadays I fell below the standard I ought to be setting for myself. I wandered about dreamily doing nothing very much and forgetting to do things like filling saucepans with water. Perhaps it was my age.

'Blow me a kiss from across the room,' Kitty Kallen's sultry voice urged from the draining board. Babe joined in. *'Say I look nice when I'm not.'* Was there something you wanted, lovey?' She'd forgiven me already. I didn't deserve her.

'I needed to ask you about cleaning. I'm starting at Amy's tomorrow. And a Wagon Wheel would be ace.'

'You've just had your breakfast.' Plates started to stack up in the drainer. Babe's red curls jiggled on her shoulders as her arms described energetic arcs, her hands transferring plates from bowl to drainer. I started drying up like mad, just managing to keep up. I looked tenderly at Babe's wet hands, so familiar, large and slightly reddened and wrinkly with all the work she did. I knew I didn't help her enough, but it was partly because she was so efficient and she was right, she did do everything twice as quickly as the rest of us.

'I know. Why am I always hungry?' I leaned over and picked a green bean out of the colander sitting on the draining board, bit the end off and chewed.

'Give over, that'll taste horrible. That's it, leave the rest to drain, just make sure you're around to help with lunch. Celery soup. There'll be chopping.' Babe dried her hands on a tea towel and passed me the biscuit tin. 'Go on then. Help yourself. Right then. Let's have a look.' She hunkered down in front of the sink cupboard and opened the door. She began taking out cartons and spray-cans of cleaning materials and collecting them around her on the kitchen floor.

'I can chop.' I plumped down beside her on the floor, licking the chocolate off my Wheel. 'Can't believe I'm starting work tomorrow. I ought to have practised.'

'Hmm.' Babe sat back on her heels and looked around at the muddle. 'You could always practise on this house.'

'Aw, come on, I do help sometimes. Anyway, Amy's paying me and I want to buy some sandals. I saw a fab pair in the Sue Ryder shop ...' I took a closer look at Babe's face. 'Hey, Babe ... what's the matter?'

She looked at me sullenly. She was paler than usual and there were tiny wrinkles around her eyes I hadn't noticed before and dark smudges under them as though she hadn't slept well. 'Wedding anniversary,' she said gruffly after a pause. 'Always hurts, no matter how many years go by.' She reached for a bottle of Mr Clean and looked intently at the label as if it held the answer she was looking for. She sighed and put the bottle down. No answer there then. 'S'pose it always will.'

'Oh dear. I'm sorry.' I put my hand on Babe's shoulder. Babe's life before she came to Half Moon was a mystery to me but I knew vaguely that rather shockingly she'd been through a divorce. Her skin was warm through her thin blouse. I took a risk and said, 'You must have loved him a lot.'

Babe looked at me and the expression on her face made me feel small and ignorant, guilty and apologetic, all at once. I took Babe so much for granted. We all did.

'Still do,' she said crossly. 'Always will. Even if he did leave me. The bastard.'

'Bastard,' I agreed loyally.

Babe didn't even notice. Normally she'd have ticked me off for bad language. 'What? Oh ... cleaning. Let's see.'

Over our heads Dusty Springfield began to sing that she was *'Wishin' and hopin'.'*

'Aren't we all?' Babe responded. 'Where'd we get to?'

I finished off my Wagon Wheel and wiped my hands on my jeans. 'You were going to help me sort out what to take to Amy's.'

'Bucket of cold water if you ask me.'

'What?'

'Never you mind. Now let's see.' She looked around.

'Do we really use all this stuff?' I picked up a can of Mr Sheen and inspected it.

'Yes, *we* do.'

I picked up a carton of Ajax. 'This looks useful.' I looked at a can with *Glo-Coat* written on it. 'What's this for?'

'Floor wax. Good stuff that. Here.' Babe handed me an unopened packet of Dobie pads. 'And take some Janitor,' she said, passing over a green carton of something or other. 'And some Pledge.'

'She wants him to make something for her. Luke.' I put down Mr Sheen and picked up a bottle of Dettol kitchen surface cleaner. 'Won't she have her own cleaning stuff?'

'Hah! Wouldn't bank on it. Here, pass me that basket.' Babe tossed a tin of Handy Andy and a packet of dusters into the basket. 'Take some of these. And take some Bar-Keeper's Friend, you can't go wrong with that. And do a good job, mind. No brushing the dirt under the carpet.'

'As if I would. What do I use Bar-Keeper's Friend for?'

'Anything nothing else will get off. Work surfaces and things. You'll find out.' Babe hauled herself to her feet – like an old woman, I thought, watching her anxiously. She turned on the hot tap and started washing her hands. 'Oh well,' she said, above my head. 'Love. Who needs it?'

Well, I do actually, I thought.

Take a trip upon your magic swirlin' ship, sang the Byrds.

'I must be off,' Babe said. 'Got a pile of darning to do. Never known anyone get through his socks like Luke.'

'Give me some to do,' I offered. 'I rather like darning.'

Babe looked at me. 'All right then. Make sure you get it nice and flat. It's on the heel. It'll rub.'

'I'm brilliant at darning,' I said. 'You taught me so I ought to be.'

'Well, all right then.'

Luke was hauling on his work boots in the kitchen as I went through carrying my basket of goodies. He got up and strode to the back door. 'Bye sweetheart.'

'Bye, Luke. Have a good day.'

The outside door slammed and I stood for a moment, listening to the silence and perhaps for a repetition of the chime ... or the music ... something.

Nothing. As always, the house rang so hollow and empty when he was gone.

Chapter 4

The mother-daughter thing

'So how was it at Naomi's?' Juno said, stirring her coffee and looking across at Izzy who was toying irritably with the slice of bacon on her plate. Why do I bother? Juno thought, annoyed with herself, half-suspecting that trying to force-feed Izzy, clearly against her will, might be an attempt to assuage her own guilt at Mike's leaving.

Perhaps it was living with Izzy. Just looking at her hurt. That odd-coloured hair. Her long, thin body, just like Mike's.

'Oh, leave it, if you don't want it.'

'Sorry. Not hungry.'

'You're never hungry nowadays. Anyway – Naomi. Had a good time?'

'It was okay.'

Now she was looking embarrassed. It was like getting blood out of a stone. Why couldn't she have a daughter who wanted to confide? 'Her mum seems nice.' She hated the way her voice became placatory, almost pleading.

Izzy looked up. 'I didn't know you knew her mum?'

'I don't, not really. I mean we've met sometimes at school things.'

'She's away a lot,' Izzy said quickly. 'I mean, they are. They're not very sociable.'

'She seemed perfectly friendly when I met her.' She's ashamed of me, Juno thought. She doesn't want me crashing in on her social life.

'Oh, she is. I mean, they are. They're just busy, I expect.' Suddenly she was up. 'Gotta split.'

'Where are you off to now?'

'Things to do.'

'I thought it might be nice if—'

'Oh—' She lingered by her chair.

Juno shrugged. She picked up her coffee cup. 'Oh ... okay.'

'Sorry.' Izzy pushed her chair back.

'Stop apologising, it's fine. I know you don't have much time before starting college. You're bound to have things to do.'

Izzy gave her a searching look and turned away. That was it then. Izzy could hardly have made it more obvious that she couldn't wait to get away.

She left, slamming the back door.

Juno let out the breath she hadn't realised she was holding, slightly ashamed to discover that what she was feeling was almost entirely relief.

'Juno? It is Juno, isn't it? Izzy's mother?'

Juno looked up. She didn't want to be late for work. She'd been late leaving home because of wanting to have breakfast with Izzy and because Izzy had got up early and hogged the bathroom till nearly half-past. 'Yes?'

The woman, who had stopped and was standing smiling at her, was vaguely familiar but not immediately placeable.

'Esme. Half Moon House. I lodge there.'

'Oh, of course.'

'Such a lovely name, Juno. Are your parents lovers of the Irish dramatists?'

Juno hadn't the faintest idea what she was talking about. 'Well, they're dead now, but I suppose they may have been.'

'Well, good for them.'

'I'm afraid I'm running a bit late,' Juno said, glancing at her wrist and realising that she'd forgotten to put her watch on. Damn. 'You don't happen to have the time, do you?'

'It's five to nine,' Esme said, looking at her with an interested expression. 'Milly often talks about you,' Esme said. 'She's very complimentary about your singing voice. I understand you nearly made a career on the stage.'

Juno's stomach relaxed. 'Yes ... that was a long time ago. I met my – you know. Plans change.'

'Of course. I trod the boards briefly myself once upon a time. Only rep, of course, but enjoyable all the same.' She had a lovely voice, deep and melodious. Esme was looking at her with such sympathy that Juno's eyes suddenly and unexpectedly filled with tears. She looked away.

'Well, I must let you get on,' Esme said. 'Perhaps we might meet up for a coffee some time.'

'That – would be nice. I could ring you perhaps.'

'Do,' Esme said. 'I would like that.' She smiled pleasantly. 'Well, goodbye.'

She has such poise, Juno thought, walking rapidly on. Esme. That's unusual too. She's quite a bit older than me, but I wonder if we might be friends.

And she lives with them, she thought, her heart-beat

quickening. She unlocked the building-society door. She knows Milly. She knows Luke. Milly may even confide in her. She may know something.

I will ring her, definitely. Perhaps we can have lunch.

Chapter 5

Keeping up standards

AMY BOOTH, ANGELICALLY BEAUTIFUL AS SHE WAS, I thought, thundering about while trying not to panic, soon showed her iron fist, as for the third time she sent me back to re-polish the round, rose-wood table ('antique, of course, do be careful,') in the centre of the vast, square hall.

It would help, I thought, trying not to be too impressed with the house, if she didn't insist on standing over me watching my every move. The hall was full of gilt, and glass. Mirrors. Chandeliers. A red-carpeted staircase with a polished bannister rail rose loftily in the distance to the first floor. I slipped and slid in my socks across acres of the shiniest parquet I'd ever seen.

'You haven't done this kind of thing before, have you?' Amy said, watching me critically as I poured floor wax into the top of the floor-mop, as instructed. 'Of course Gill – she's my usual cleaner – is a marvel, an absolute marvel. So unfortunate that she had that awful accident. I was so relieved when Juno said you might be able to help while Gill's in hospital. I don't know what I should have done. Is that food I can smell in your knapsack? Is that hygienic? Do you always carry food about with you? Well, never mind. Leave it in the kitchen.'

Two hours had passed during which I had scrubbed, polished, vacuumed, mopped and scoured. After the first half-hour Amy, presumably deciding I could be trusted to get on with it by myself without breaking anything, had disappeared into the drawing-room and closed the door.

I'd had another nightmare the night before and was more tired than I should have been. I dragged the Hoover over to the staircase and sank down onto the bottom step for a little break. I went over the dream in my head. Familiarity never made it any better. I would surface from sleep, a weight of water dragging me down, my lungs on fire, desperate things pulling at my clothes. I knew that in a moment I would have to breathe in and then I would drown ... I lashed about, desperate, hopeless, and then, at last, a green light was slanting through the surface .... I struggled up ... and at last ... at last the air.

'Did I ever fall out of a boat?' I asked Luke once, when I was younger.

'No,' Luke replied. 'I would know, if you had.' He was sitting on my bed, his face pale and concerned in the lamplight.

He didn't come into my bedroom now, he hadn't for years, I suppose he thought it wasn't appropriate once I started properly growing up. I couldn't quite remember when he'd stopped coming and had got Babe to come instead. I'd minded a bit at first because I was so used to him and found him so comforting. I liked the clean smell of his shirt and the strength of his arms as he held me while I gradually woke, I liked the way he always seemed to be dressed then, in ordinary jeans instead of his work clothes and I liked his kind voice and his ruffled hair; often he'd been working late and hadn't yet gone to bed.

I sat with the Hoover at my feet and remembered the sanctuary feeling of my room with Luke sitting quietly with me, the pool of light from the bedside lamp, the silence, apart from the whirr of a daddy-long-legs lured in by the light, rustling against the lamp shade. There was something special about those times. I felt so safe, so cared for, for those few minutes. In the morning, of course, the secure feeling would have gone but while it lasted it was magic. I wished I could feel like that all the time instead of like a visitor from an alien planet who didn't speak the language. I always felt on the edge of things and as if I constantly had to earn my right to exist.

This wouldn't get Amy's house clean. I got up and lugged the Hoover up the stairs to the landing. The upstairs phone rang. Amy didn't appear so I picked up. 'How's it going?' Luke said.

'I'm at Amy's.'

'I know you are, poppet, I rang her number. How are you getting on?'

'She's a slave driver.'

A chuckle from Luke. 'Really?'

'I mean, I know she's impossibly glamorous, but ... Luke,' I lowered my voice, 'where is he? Her husband?'

'They're separated, I believe.' He sounded amused. 'I hope she can't hear you.'

'I'm upstairs. There's a phone on the landing. She's in the *drawing*-room.'

'Why d'you say it like that?'

'We-el. She's an awful snob.'

'This isn't like you, Milly. I thought we'd decided it was important to be kind.'

'I know but ... she's so surprised anybody can be a furniture-maker *and* a top-drawer gentleman. She simply can't get over it.'

'I think we'd better end this conversation.'

'Okay then!'

'See you later then. Be good.'

'I'm not a child, Luke.'

'Don't behave like one then. Bye.'

Do I? I thought, putting the phone down. Perhaps it was more grown-up to pretend you were cool with it when someone got right up your nose. More diplomatic, anyway. I needed this job.

Dear Luke, I thought, plugging in the Hoover. Sometimes when I thought about it I could hardly breathe, I felt so grateful, I'd told Izzy, that Luke had come to my rescue and saved me from Dr Barnardo's.

'Don't you have any relations?'

'Absolutely zilch, apparently. Luke was my only hope.'

When I let myself imagine whom I might have ended up with – someone like Amy? – I felt quite paralysed. But by a miracle it had happened to be Luke, and when I said my prayers which I did sometimes, I thanked everyone I could think of, usually God but sometimes the angels I visualised standing around my bed, wings extended in a guardian position. Not so much Michael, Raphael and Gabriel but girl angels. Clones of my mother Miranda, when you came down to it.

'Baubles, bangles and beads,' Amy sang out of tune, wandering into the kitchen as I was tipping the last bucket of soapy water down the sink. She stopped with an exclamation of surprise. 'Goodness! I thought you'd finished and gone home ages ago.'

'Mind my floor,' I said in best Mrs Mop tradition. 'I'm just finishing.' Surely I'd need to be paid, wouldn't I, if I was leaving? Perhaps I was only going to get my money at the end of the week. I was supposed to be doing three mornings. I stood at the sink, rinsing out the bucket and the sponge.

'You haven't been washing the floor on your hands and knees, have you? There's a proper floor mop you can use, you know, it's in the scullery.' She bent over and inspected a patch of floor. 'I hope you cleaned it properly.' She stood up. 'It looks all right, I suppose. Next time use the mop, there's a good girl. When you've put the things away come and sit down. You must be parched. I'll make us some coffee. I can't abide that dreadful instant stuff,' she said a few minutes later, indicating a chair and putting a cup and saucer in front of me on the table. 'And coffee tastes so much better in a china cup, don't you think? I do so dislike this habit of drinking everything out of those awful mugs. I mean it's all very well but one must have standards.' She sat down and reached for a tube of Sweet'N Low nestled between the salt and pepper pots. 'Now, Milly... Luke. Tell me about him. What a delightful man. A relation?'

I shook my head, frowning. Something hovered on the edge of my mind, something I'd forgotten but that I felt was important. 'His family lived next door when my mother was growing up.'

'And how does he come to be living down here? I'd have thought London – such talent. Awards, I gather.'

'Yes, he is frightfully good,' I said, thinking hard. What was it I was trying to remember? 'He's brilliant, actually.'

And I remembered. Babe had told me that when Amy had first moved into the village, Luke had asked her out and she'd turned him down. Gossip had it that she'd gone around telling everybody that she couldn't possibly go out with someone who was 'in trade.' In trade! The snobbery of it! And why had she suddenly changed her mind?

Of course. Awards. He was beginning to make a name for himself. Articles were being written about his artistry, his genius. Of course. She could think of him as an artist now, not just your common or garden carpenter. It all made perfect sense.

'But why—?'

'The thing is,' I said, trying not to show the disdain I was feeling, 'Luke and my mother practically grew up together. Then when my mother—'

'Ah yes ... tragic. Juno did say.'

My face grew hot with embarrassment. 'When I was born,' I rushed on, 'he promised my mother that if anything ever happened to her – I mean it can't have seemed likely, at the time – that Luke would—'

'A knight in shining armour.'

'Sort of ...' I sipped my coffee, my face burning.

'He must have been very young. How long ago was this?'

'She died ten years ago. He hadn't even finished his training. I stayed with Izzy and Juno for a year – the people next door. He came to live at Half Moon when he'd qualified.'

'Such a responsibility for him, poor man.'

I put my cup down, hard.

She frowned. 'Careful, you'll break it.'

I'll break you, I thought. Nosy cow. (Oh dear, mustn't, but she's so—) 'We have Babe to help. And Pascale has been around for ever.'

'She's the funny old woman who lives with you?'

'She was my mother's nurse. She's just never left. Well ... she's got nowhere else to go.' For a moment or two I visualised Half Moon without Pascale in it and the thought was so delightful that suddenly I felt like crying. I swallowed a mouthful of coffee and burnt my mouth.

'Fascinating. And lodgers too?'

'Felix,' I said when I could speak. 'And Esme.'

'What sort of age ... Esme, did you say?'

'Oh, she's quite old, I dunno – forty? Felix is older, he's retired. They're both lovely, we're very fond of them.'

Amy looked pleased. '*So* romantic. What a household! So bohemian.'

Bohemian?

'That adorable man, so good-looking. Always so kind and friendly. He's very popular in the village, you know.'

'Is he?'

'Oh *yes* ... and not because he's – well – becoming so celebrated, winning all those awards. Because he's a thoroughly nice man.'

Yeah, yeah.

'I'm determined to have him make something for me.'

'He said. I'm sure he'll be pleased to,' I said, putting down my empty cup. 'Only he's got an awful lot on at the moment.'

'He must come to dinner again one weekend. The last time was very short notice. Does he – I mean, would he expect to bring someone?'

I hadn't realised he'd been to dinner here. 'No,' I said. 'Unless you count me.'

She blinked. 'You?'

'Only joking.' I grinned. 'There's Babe, of course.'

'Babe?'

'You must have met Babe? She's our housekeeper. Sort

of. She's terribly pretty. Luke is awfully fond of her.' Put that in your pipe.

'Oh but – a housekeeper ...'

'She's more like family really. She came after my mother died. Pascale couldn't really cope with a baby – me – and then the lodgers and everything. The cooking, you know. My mother was a dancer, did you know? She always intended to go back to the ballet but well – the accident happened.'

'Tragic ... really dreadful. Babe, did you say?'

'She was a wonderful dancer, my mother. There are photos. Pascale sorted them all into albums. She adored my mother.' Now I had started I didn't seem able to stop. 'Luke gave me her shoes. They're tiny. She was small, not tall like me. I wish I could ask somebody about her. It was ten years ago, the accident.' My mother had been driving at the time. I didn't like to dwell on this point.

'But can't you ask Juno about her? I gathered from Mrs Murchison at the post office that she was close to your mother. I'm so very sorry,' she said after a pause, with what sounded like real sincerity, which made me like her after all and forgive her for being such an idiot.

I liked her even more when she gave me an envelope which when I opened it on the way home – I ran most of the way – actually contained two one-pound notes.

Old Flint was sitting leaning against the wall outside Waitrose, his legs stuck out across the pavement. There would be complaints. He was coal black from head to foot and his hair hung in a matted plait down to his waist and beyond. 'Wotcha, Milly.'

'Hello, Mr Flint. How're things? Are you hungry?' I swung my rucksack around and hunkered down. 'Cornish pasty. And a banana.'

He seized the food. 'You're an angel, Milly, that's what you are.' He wrenched open the paper bag and seized the pasty. 'Din' sleep a wink last night,' he said with his mouth full. 'Can't sleep indoors, see? Much better under my bit of canvas out on the common there. They won't have it. Keep trying to force me into that there night shelter. Smells in there and noisy ain't the word. Groanin'. Fartin'. 'Scuse my French, Milly. No privacy.'

'Oh, that's a shame. I thought they didn't mind in the summer. It's lovely and warm just now. Mind you, I do sometimes wonder how you're getting on when it pours.'

'I don' mind. Nothing wrong with a bit of wet. Don' like the cold, mind. I'm perfeckly willin' to sleep in the shelter when it's snowing. But not now, when the trees is all smellin' green and the bracken's thick. No. They can keep their shelter.'

'I s'pose they can't force you. We're making you a cake. Lemon drizzle, your favourite. For your birthday. I'll bring it next time. Well, better be getting along now.' I stood up. 'See you, Mr Flint.'

'See ya, Milly. Take care o' your pretty self.'

Juno, I thought, ambling home. Were they really good friends, Juno and my mother? But Juno's never said, she's never talked about her much and she knows, she *knows* how desperate I am to know about her. Why don't people tell you the truth? Why didn't she say?

Chapter 6

Love

'So on the whole,' Esme said, inserting a cotton bud gingerly into her left ear, 'you got on reasonably well.' We were in Esme's bedroom, Esme seated in front of her elegant dressing-table, part of the Edwardian bedroom suite she had brought with her when she came to live with us, and me idling against the window-sill, watching her put on her makeup. As well as the bedroom furniture, which gave the room an elegant and stylish, if slightly old-fashioned air, she had imported a lovely mahogany kneehole desk which I envied, and some rather nice artwork. I particularly fancied a pair of beautiful Kaoro Kawano woodblock prints.

Luke had provided both the lodgers with a small screened-off area with a gas-ring and a tiny fridge so they could make hot drinks and cook the odd snack between meals. I loved their rooms and wished I could have cooking facilities in mine, but unfortunately neither Luke nor Babe considered this necessary. Anyway, as Luke pointed out, I would be off to St Andrews in September, where I'd be able to be as independent as I liked.

Esme was still not dressed even though it was nearly

lunch time. She'd started work early on her next project – Esme translated romantic fiction into Esperanto for an independent publisher – and the time had slipped away. It was just the right time for a little break, she'd said tactfully when I knocked on her door.

I liked Esme. With her pepper and salt hair pulled back into a bun, usually quite a lot of it escaping from its pins, and her penetrating turquoise eyes, she looked severe but was universally kind although she did sometimes get snappy with Felix. This was partly because Felix disliked cats and said so, and also because of the bath situation.

I wondered if I could tell her I believed it was Miranda's ghost I had been aware of in the orchard that night.

'It was okay.' I glanced at Esme's profile. 'She's awfully pretty, Amy.'

'Do you like her?'

I shrugged. 'She's okay. A bit of a snob. She went on and on about Luke being "in trade" and yet obviously a gentleman. Honestly, like Trollope or somebody.'

'Ah, the class system alive and flourishing in sixties Britain ... oh Lord.' Esme leaned in to her reflection and plucked at a flap of loose skin under her chin. 'I'm starting to look like my father.' She sighed and tossed the cotton bud into the wastepaper basket. 'Oh well, it can't be helped. Go on about Amy.'

'She seems awfully gone on Luke.'

'Does she? Well, well.'

'Goes on and on about him. She wanted to know all about everything and made me a cup of coffee as a bargaining chip. She seems fascinated. She says we are *bohemian.*'

'Goodness me. She can't have seen much of life. I

expect Luke can cope. He must be used to women throwing themselves at him by now, don't you think?'

I frowned. 'Really? D'you think so?'

Esme gave me a smiling look over her shoulder. 'Come now, Milly.'

I shrugged. 'D'you really think? I suppose I'm used to him.'

'Indeed I do think. Anyway, that's Luke's problem. She'll have competition.'

'Who from?' I couldn't think of anyone else who seemed particularly smitten.

'No,' Esme said. 'I mustn't encourage you to gossip. Who was it who said we should be less curious about people and more curious about ideas?'

'Dunno,' I said. 'But it sounds like good advice.' I watched her assaulting her nose with face powder. It was fascinating watching other people put on their makeup. I'd only just started and didn't have a clue what I was doing. Esme didn't seem to use a base of any kind, just a bit of powder on her nose and the faintest possible trace of the wrong colour lipstick: it was much too dark, she'd have looked better with something softer and pinker, not so red. I longed to say something but it seemed unkind, especially as the lipstick was almost new. 'Esme,' I said. 'Were you ever in love?'

'Once ... a while ago.' She brushed some specks of powder off the dressing-table top. 'It was not appropriate. It was the wrong time.' She swept her makeup things into the top drawer. 'It's an illness, of course.'

'What is? Being in love?'

She nodded. 'It suspends all rational judgement.' She stood up from her dressing-stool, smoothing down her turquoise silk dressing-gown over her hips, and I followed her gaze as she looked away and up out of the window at passing clouds, at swooping birds, at the wind blowing the tops of distant trees. 'It's an enchantment. Which is all well and good but I did not cope with it very well. What I felt was so different, you see, from what I'd felt for my husband, and it confused me and made me anxious.' She moved over to the kettle. 'I suffered agonies of jealousy. I was unhappy ninety per cent of the time.'

'Oh shoot. Was the ten per cent – was it worth it? Did it make you happy?'

Esme picked up the kettle and stopped to think, her head on one side. 'Hard to judge. Happiness? No ... endless suspense ... a feeling of being intensely alive, but constant nausea and an inability to eat. I lost pounds. And always held within the excitement the certainty of sorrow to come.'

'Oh, Esme.'

'Folly, madness, self-destruction.' She took the kettle to the sink and turned on the tap.

(Was she serious?) 'Even if it's returned?'

'Even then. There are so often obstacles ... things are not always straightforward. By no means. He was not free, you see.' She sighed, watching the water flowing into the kettle. 'Ah well,' she said, straightening her shoulders, (I could see she was thinking, Enough, she's only young). 'He cast his spell upon me, he bound me to him with hoops of steel.' She switched the kettle on and turned around. 'Oh, Milly, you're crying. Don't cry. I'm so sorry.'

'I'm not. I'm not.' (I was.) 'It's just ... is it always ... I thought love was supposed to be wonderful ... something happy. But it isn't, is it? It sounds awful.'

But however awful, it was something I wanted desperately. Someone to love and to whom I could be everything, who would always be there for me, and me for him.

The thought came into my head that it would be wonderfully convenient if I were to fall in love with Luke. The problem was, I didn't love him. I mean, I did, of course. Luke was my friend, my everything, but love him romantically? Never.

I heard someone calling and leaned out of the window to see who it was. Jello, Esmé's cat, was standing in the gutter. He looked at me piteously. I looked down into the garden. Izzy stood there, gazing up at me, waving as if everything was normal. How could she, after ignoring me the whole weekend? I was really hacked off with her for giving me all this aggravation. I wriggled back into the room and gestured towards the window. 'Izzy's there.'

'Oh good,' Esme said. 'Off you go, then. Don't worry about Jello, he'll come in when he's hungry. I was about to leap forward and grab you by the ankles. You were at least six inches off the floor. Nice thin ankles, too,' Esme said. 'I notice them, you understand, because I am dissatisfied with my own which are of the English variety. Ah well, we are what we are.' She ladled tea into the little blue teapot-for-one, opened the cupboard door above her head and rooted for a teacup and saucer which she set down on a little tray, 'I've finished *Passion's Slave* so I'm well up to speed.' She bent to take a jug of milk out of her tiny fridge. Esme's work ethic was extraordinary, she got through at least two books a week.

I slid treacherously towards the door.

'Pointless to worry about one's ankles at my age of course,' she went on, pouring boiling water into the teapot. 'Once you reach forty you become invisible. Ah well. Off you go, dear.' She sighed and picked up the little tray and carried it over to the window. She set it down on a little table beside the basket chair with the blue cushion into which she sank every so often to take a little break.

Sometimes I wondered what it must feel like, being so old. Who would look at Esme now? She had been married but he had left her. He was in the Foreign Office and he said he could no longer stand her refusal to conform.

I arrived under the apple trees, puffing and tight-lipped. Izzy was sitting cross-legged under our favourite tree. She had on her Wranglers, purple shades and a white cheesecloth top with embroidery around the neck. She held out an opened packet of Spangles. 'Hey, bean. Help yourself.'

I took the next one which was red. Strawberry, my favourite.

All the same. 'So come on then, where have you been? You missed Dick Van Dyke.' I looked closer. 'Where did that top come from?'

Izzy leaned over and peered into her makeup bag, propped against a tree root. 'This? Robert gave it to me. And this. Look.' Smiling, she held out a small white box. I picked it up. '*Oh! de London*' it said on the front. Yardley.

'What's this?'

'Scent. Isn't it the most?'

'Robert too?' I gazed at Izzy and tried as hard as I could, as recommended by Henry Hamblin whose helpful book *My Search for Truth* I had come across in a second-hand book shop in Guildford a month or so ago, to imagine Izzy being showered with blessings and all kinds of good things. *'It is a great help if we have learned the art,'* Henry Hamblin says, *'of returning love for every wrong done to us. It is pride that makes us want to justify ourselves.'*

I tried to remind myself what Henry Hamblin would advise me to do in a situation where I felt hacked-off and resentful but my mind had gone blank. All I wanted to do was kick somebody, preferably Izzy who was looking as smug as Sapphy when she's eaten a mouse. She was practically licking her lips.

It seemed ages since the day Izzy had climbed over the gate into the orchard saying, 'Guess what, I won't be able to wear white when I marry now.' It took a few seconds for the penny to drop. Izzy jumped down, her hand came up over her mouth and then, unusually for her, she started crying.

That was sometime in May. She and Robert had found themselves standing next to each other in the queue at Webster's some weeks before and started chatting, Izzy in that sparky way she's so good at, and one thing led to another and before she knew what was happening, Izzy said, they were an item.

After she met Robert, Izzy was happy for a while but that didn't last long and recently she seemed to be miserable all the time. Not today though.

'Anyway, babe,' she said. Her eyes were sparkling. 'How's things?'

'Okay,' I said, plumping down cross-legged beside her. 'Had another nightmare last night.'

Izzy frowned. 'Bummer. Bad?'

I nodded. 'How long have you been back?'

'Lunch time. Sylvia was due back in the afternoon so he thought he ought to get back.'

Common sense had told me to expect this answer but her certainty threw me a little. 'Are you sure you didn't come back till today?'

She looked at me, frowning. 'How d'you mean? 'Course I'm sure.'

'You weren't home Friday night?'

'I was with Rob Friday night. I told you. Why?'

'Something funny happened. I thought it might be you messing about.'

'What? What d'you mean, something happened?'

'Here, in the orchard. Music. And lights. It was a bit strange.'

'What kind of music? It was probably Esme playing her recorder, come out to worship the full moon. She's peculiar enough.'

I looked through my crossed legs at the ground. 'Don't joke. I'm serious. Izzy, listen – it was that song my mum always played: the French one. Françoise Hardy. *Tous les garçons et les filles de mon âge* ... that one.'

'God, Milly, you're hearing things now.'

'No. I did hear it. Oh well, if it wasn't you ...' I slumped down sideways.

'It's this obsession you've got about your mother. It's obviously turned your brain at last.'

'It's not *funny*, Izzy. I was scared.'

'Milly. Lights? Music? Come on. Anyway, even if you did hear something, why would it have anything to do with your mother?'

'It was her favourite music. I know it was her. It's different for you, you've got a mother. If you hadn't, you'd be curious too. About what she was like. How she felt about you.'

Izzy rolled her eyes. 'She was your mother, Milly. Mothers love their kids. Therefore, she loved you. I don't know why you have such a problem with this simple concept.'

I didn't know either. It's just, something was rolling around in the back of my mind. Something I couldn't quite remember, and was desperate to. Like Felix when he suddenly forgot a word or a name he was looking for and wandered about muttering that he'd go nuts if he didn't remember the name of the general in charge of the Battle of Rutland. 'It's just, I can't remember.' I leapt up and strode about, kicking up dead leaves. 'And I so desperately wish I could. I wish I could be sure she even liked me. It's all very well for you, I know you moan about her but you know Juno loves you, she's always trying to make you eat and worrying about you.'

Izzy softened suddenly. 'Look, I don't mean to be unsympathetic. It's just your mother's dead, yeah? She's gone. You can't ask her.'

I came back and leaned against my tree. 'That's why I'm wondering if she knows it bugs me and that's why she's come back, to reassure me. To tell me herself.'

'Milly, that's looney-tunes. How d'you know you didn't imagine the whole thing?'

I sighed. 'You're probably right.' I set off trampling about again. How could I explain to Izzy that part of my problem with her and Robert was sheer envy? I could never trust anyone enough to get involved with them like that, I'd be too scared of losing them. Izzy had managed it even though her dad had gone off when she was little which I knew was a problem for her. Everyone's different, I suppose. I just felt, if I could be sure that one person, *one* person, had loved me the way Juno loved Izzy, I could kind of move on and stop looking back all the time.

'You've got to let it go. Or ask Luke.'

'He never saw her with me. Your mum did, a bit. The person who really knows is Pascale and she won't tell me anything. I've tried.'

'Oh God, Milly, I don't know. Perhaps you're right. Perhaps Miranda has come back to tell you to stop being such a silly bugger and move on.'

I rolled my eyes at her and laughed. Of course she was right. Time to move on. I only wished I could.

Oh well. 'Go on then,' I said, propping myself against the tree opposite. I hooked a fallen apple out of the nearest bit of sunny grass. It was a bit wormy but who cared? 'You might have told me you were going away for the whole weekend. I've been really worried. I even went over to see your mum. She said there wasn't a phone where you were.' An uncomfortable memory came into my head of Juno lolling against their kitchen door frame fiddling with the collar of her blue M&S pyjamas, obviously delighted I had no idea where Izzy was. 'I'm surprised Izzy didn't tell you, she's been full of it for days,' she'd said, her expression tinged with triumph. You're not the only friend she's got, it seemed to say. I'd looked into her defensive blue eyes and sighed. Juno seemed to have gone off me too.

I pressed the apple, warm from the sun, into the hollow of my cheek, breathed in its fragrance and closed my eyes. I wasn't going to ask again. If Izzy had something to tell me, she could damn well volunteer it. The little smile haunting her face was beginning to get right up my nose.

Izzy reached into her makeup bag and took out a bottle of nail varnish. She looked up at me sideways through her flossy hair, unscrewed the top and balanced the bottle of varnish carefully against a tree root. 'You're supposed to eat it, not inhale it. Sit down, for God's sake, I'm getting a crick in my neck.'

I slid my back down the tree trunk into the grass and bit into the apple. Fragrant juice spurted into my mouth. Izzy had started painting her nails the weirdest colour I'd ever seen.

'Aren't you going to ask me where I've been?' She bent her head over her nails.

'I'm sure you're going to tell me.' I chewed fiercely. Swallowed. It was nice here in the warm sun, with the trunk's rough bark against my back and the smell of the grass and the taste of the apple. I closed my eyes and pretended I was Sapphy doing her cat thing, just enjoying being alive.

'We went to his house.'

'But it was the weekend. Where was his wife?'

Izzy concentrated on painting the nails of her left hand. 'She was staying with some kind of aunt. We had the whole place to ourselves, Milly ... it was just – far out.'

'You went to their house?'

''Course we did.'

'You slept in their *bed*?'

'Where else would you expect us to sleep?'

'But suppose she'd come home! What would have happened?'

She slanted me a look. 'Don't be such a wuss.' She started on her right hand. 'She didn't, everything's cool, don't worry about it.' She was frowning now. Izzy hated being criticised. It spoiled the picture she had in her head of being a person who was always right.

We sat in silence for a bit until Izzy started giving off an atmosphere like an egg that had gone off and was about to explode. 'Oh, Milly, it's a wicked house,' she burst out, waving her hands about. 'You should see it, there's all this fab furniture and stuff and pictures and a grand piano, and the bed is a four-poster with tapestry curtains and everything.' She paused, peering at me.

Well, ring-a-ding-ding.

'Don't look like that,' she said.

Actually what I was thinking was that this reminded me of that bit in *Pride and Prejudice* when Jane asks Elizabeth exactly when it was that she decided she did love Mr Darcy after all and Elizabeth says, *'I hardly know when it began. But I believe I must date it from my first seeing his beautiful grounds at Pemberley.'*

She was still flipping smiling, her Chinesey eyes shining in her heart-shaped face, also glowing. In fact she seemed radiant with insane happiness.

People seem to think passion justifies everything.

'I know you don't rate him,' she said eventually in a small, disappointed voice, looking down at her nails.

'I never said I didn't rate him. I don't know him. I just haven't liked him making you so down for the last few weeks, that's all. Which you seem to have conveniently forgotten.'

'I'm not down now,' she said softly.

'Well, good-oh. What's changed? Except that you've just spent three days in bed with him.'

'Exactly. Anyway, we weren't in bed all the time.'

'Spare me the details.' Above our heads a bird burst into song. 'How are you going to feel when it all falls apart, that's what I want to know.' I leaned sideways and peered up through the leaves. I could see the tiny bird's orange chest vibrating as it sang. A robin, then.

'It won't.'

'I'll remind you you said that the next time you ring up in floods of tears.'

Izzy laughed. If only she wasn't so crazy happy. 'Look,' she said. 'I know I haven't spent much time with you so far this summer.'

'No sweat. Anyway,' I said, self-justifying, 'it hasn't been just this summer. You met him ages ago.' I nibbled around my apple core and pretended not to notice the pitying and frankly patronising look on Izzy's face.

After a moment she said, 'It was April.'

April Fool's day actually. Highly appropriate.

'Anyway it isn't just *it*, you know, me and Robert, there's more to it than that.'

'What then?' I threw the core away and wiped my hands in the long grass. 'Tell me one thing you've got in common apart from *it*.'

'Don't see why I should. It's none of your business.'

'You can't, can you?'

'Oh, *Milly*. Why are you being such a cow?'

'Moo moo.'

'What is wrong with you? Are you feeling left out because I've got Robert?' She waved her hands about to dry her nails, her forehead twisted in a frown.

I said, not looking at her, 'I didn't realise it was so serious, that's all. I just thought you liked him a bit.'

'I do like him a bit, I like him a lot, that's the whole point. I wouldn't be doing it with him if I didn't.' Her hands stilled in mid-air so that for a moment we could have been kids again playing statues. 'Jeez, don't look like that.' She started waving them about again. 'Oh man, I wish I hadn't told you now, I might have known you wouldn't understand. You're such a kitty-cat.'

'I do understand, I was just a bit surprised, that's all. And I'm not a child, thanks.'

'Anyway, it doesn't matter.' But I could tell by her face that it did. She reached out, her fingers spread, picked up the bottle of varnish and tucked it back in her makeup bag, not looking at me.

How could I explain? How could I show her the pit of desolation that opened up inside me at the realisation that for the first time in as long as I could remember I no longer came first in Izzy's life. I knew I was being unreasonable.

The feeling inside me seemed in an obscure way tied up with the music I'd heard, my mother's music, reminding me, not that I ever forgot it for long, of my motherless state.

I said carefully, after a pause, 'He's quite old, isn't he?'

'He's thirty-seven. That's not old.'

'Twenty years older than you. Anyway, I bet he isn't thirty-seven. Forty-two at least if you ask me.'

'Well nobody is asking you, so you can just – mind your own business.' She scrambled to her feet, her face all twisted up. She pulled a handkerchief out of her puffy sleeve and blew her nose. Then she dropped the makeup bag and it tipped over onto its side and everything fell out. She gave a little sob and hunkered down. In the slightly fraught silence I knelt down and helped her put it all back.

I relented. 'Oh, Izzy, don't be upset.' I tried not to show that I'd noticed she was crying. 'It's just I've been so worried. I didn't know where you were. I sort of guessed you were with him but I didn't know where and I thought, what would I say to your mum if you didn't come back?'

'Why wouldn't I come back?' She pulled a hanky out of her sleeve and blew her nose. 'You knew I'd come back.'

'He could have been a mass murderer for all I knew.'

'Robert? Give me a break,' she said more cheerfully, tucking the hanky back.

'I know it's daft. But I didn't know. And Juno didn't know either. She said you were staying with Naomi and I knew you weren't.'

'I didn't tell you because you'd have tried to stop me going and I knew I was going to go so I was pretty sure we'd have a row.'

'Instead of which we're having one now.'

'No we're not – are we?' She peered at me. 'Oh Milly, he's such a hunk. He's totally cool.' She relaxed back on her heels and looked away from me into the distance where presumably a vision of Robert hovered, blowing kisses at her.

She came to and looked anxiously at her nails to see if she'd smudged them. They were a kind of dirty blue this time, like liver when it's gone off. I wished she'd done them a cheerful colour like the green she sometimes did them, or silver or pink. 'Don't say anything, will you?' Izzy said. 'Especially to Mum. She'd have seven fits.'

'Doesn't she notice when you're out such a lot?'

'She thinks I'm with Naomi. She thinks we're best friends I see her such a lot. That I'm always around at her house. Ho hum.'

'She'll find out sometime.'

'Not yet. Don't you dare say anything.'

'As if I would.' I looked up and shivered. I felt cold suddenly. It looked like rain. The clouds had gathered after breakfast, grey and threatening but nothing actually happening. Phantom rain clouds.

'It's only till we've sorted something out. She'll only want to meet him and be boring because of him being married and stuff.' She wriggled around and struggled to her knees. 'Oh, Milly, he's miserable with Sylvia. She's awful to him, they don't sleep together or anything.' Her eyes shone with sincerity. 'What's wrong with him finding some happiness with me? It's not hurting anybody; in fact, it's a help, he says, it's probably keeping his marriage going, because he's so happy with me. It's better for the kids and everything.'

My mouth dropped open.

'And I won't – you know – I've – he took me to a place in London.' Her face was rather red. She bent her head and looked at her nails again and felt them gingerly. 'Dry,' she said. 'This new stuff's brilliant, it dries in two secs. Rob got it for me.'

I found my voice. 'He's got *kids?*'

'Two little boys,' Izzy boasted, as if it had something to do with her. 'Didn't I tell you?'

'No you didn't. You never said he had kids!' I don't know why I minded so much, but I did. I was incensed. Kids needed a mum and a dad. Izzy had no right. I was shaking with fury.

'What's the big deal?'

'But, Izzy!' How could she do that to two little kids? Get between their mum and dad like that. That was just so like, *gross*.

'Oh, I knew you'd be like that,' Izzy said, shedding her sophistication, her face clouding over.

'What did you expect me to be like? How old are they?'

'Paul's twelve and Adam's ten,' she said, perking up. 'They're sweet. He takes them for walks on Sunday afternoons and I've seen them in the park with him. Don't worry, Milly.' She leaned forward on her hands and peered into my face. 'You worry too much. His wife doesn't care about him, she concentrates on the children and he feels left out.'

I couldn't believe this was Izzy talking; she sounded completely brainwashed. She was so jazzed, she was behaving like the girl who'd discovered Miracle shampoo and found it had changed her whole life.

'So everything's cool then. Look,' I said, standing up and wiping my dewy hands on my shorts. 'I'm out of here. I have to go and give Sapphy her painting lesson. And I said I'd help Babe with lunch.' I turned away.

'We'll talk another time,' Izzy said. She scrambled to her feet, forgetting to be graceful. Her face was red again and she'd lost her radiance. My heart was really going at it now and there was a sick feeling in my stomach. In a moment Izzy would walk away. I stuck my hands in my pockets and pretended to look around for Sapphy who I knew perfectly well was lurking on the hen-house roof. We didn't have hens anymore but Sapphy could still smell them.

'See you later then.' Izzy bent to pick up a piece of cotton wool, blue-stained, half-hidden under a dead leaf. A heavy drop of water fell on my forehead. At last it was beginning to rain.

'Later, yeah?' I nodded, not meeting her eye, turned and walked away. The moment my back was turned I screwed up my eyes and pulled an excruciated face as though someone had just dug a fork into me, hard.

Why was I so upset? Was it because I felt that Izzy was moving away from me, would not always be around? What an idiot I'd been to imagine she would be. What with gorgeous Amy Booth's interest in Luke, Izzy and Robert's affair and my mother's slightly threatening manifestation, the future had suddenly become more unpredictable. Scary.

Now why had I thought Miranda's appearance threatening? What had put that idea into my head? And threatening to who? Whom. Me?

Chapter 7

Sometimes people just don't get along

IN THE QUEUE AT THE COUNTER AT WEBSTER'S, A VOICE behind Juno said, 'Afternoon.'

Juno turned. Babe was standing behind her. She tried to smile but it was an effort. Babe didn't like her. She never smiled properly when they spoke, it was more a twitch of the lips for the sake of convention, not because she meant it. Juno searched for something to say. At least Babe hadn't pretended not to see her; if she'd really wanted to avoid her surely she'd have joined another queue? But perhaps she hadn't seen her until too late.

She felt herself shrinking. Her father's voice said, 'For Christ's sake, say something, girl, don't just stand there like a moron.'

'How are you? How's ... um ... the family?' Oh. Mistake. Babe was no fool. She always looked at Juno with that slight edge of contempt as if to say, You're wasting your time, madam, he isn't interested in you.

'Blooming,' Babe said. 'As usual. Had to nip out for some cocoa. Used the last lot up on Milly last night. Had another nightmare, a beauty according to Luke.'

Two assistants were free. Babe moved to stand beside her at the counter. Juno blinked. 'Cheese,' she said to the assistant. 'Please. About four ounces?' She watched the girl carefully slice a piece off the enormous whale of cheese on the back counter. 'That'll do, that's fine.' She watched as it was weighed – exactly four ounces – and wrapped. Beside her Babe was buying sugar, flour, ham.

What else? Butter. She watched the assistant's gloved hands as she set the packet of Anchor down on the counter. A packet of suet and some paper hankies. A tin of pineapple pieces and one of Morton pears, Izzy liked those. A couple of tins of soup, a packet of Cheerios.

Babe had handed her money across and was fitting tins and packets into her basket. Babe wasn't a bit like a housekeeper, Juno thought resentfully, she went on as if she owned Half Moon. She was quite attractive. Juno wondered if Luke thought so.

'Cocoa is the only thing she wants after one of them,' Babe said.

She was still on about Milly's wretched nightmares. Honestly, Juno was sick of hearing about them. Even if she did have a pretty good idea of what lay behind them. Why on earth didn't Luke just tell the child and have done with it?

'It's a good thing you were there to help her.' Juno tucked her groceries in her basket beside the cabbage she'd bought from Stear's and stood uncertainly by while Babe accepted her change and turned away. Juno took hers and followed her to the door.

'Oh, it was Luke who heard her, yelling out the way she does. His room's nearer hers. I don't hear anything from my bit of the house. He came and knocked on my door so I could go in to her while he went down to the kitchen to make her some cocoa.'

And who took her the cocoa? Juno's heart was pounding unpleasantly. I hope Luke doesn't go into Milly's bedroom, not at her age. She's seventeen, for goodness' sake.

'There's something at the root of it,' Babe said. 'Mark my words. Awful, really.' She shook her head. 'The whole first six years of her life gone like that with nobody left who remembers her mum. Mind you,' she said, looking at Juno speculatively. 'It might help Milly if you were to talk to her a bit about her mother. That Amy Booth told Milly you were pretty close. I'm surprised you haven't.'

Juno looked down at her basket and tucked the packet of cheese in more securely. 'We weren't that close. Pascale is probably the person who knew her best.'

'Maybe.' Babe lifted her eyebrows and pushed open the door. 'She's not saying anything, is she? Milly has tried. Dunno what her problem is.'

Maybe it's the same as mine, Juno thought. If only you knew. 'Well, it's a shame,' she said, outside on the pavement. A car drove by, splashing her legs with water from the gutter. She stepped back. 'Milly's such a dear girl.' Good God, she thought, is that really what I think or did I just say that so Babe would like me? (She clearly thinks the sun shines out of Milly's bottom.) Do I actually think Milly is a scheming little minx and do I actually rather loathe her?

'She's a sweet soul,' Babe said over her shoulder. 'Can't help but love her, no matter how daft she is sometimes.'

'She's a darling,' Juno said.

Babe nodded and began to walk quickly away. Juno closed her eyes briefly and relaxed. What else? Bread. She walked along to the baker's and watched as the assistant wrapped her loaf in tissue paper and handed it across. There was no room for it in the basket so Juno tucked it under her arm. She's got lovely hair, Juno thought, walking rapidly back towards the building society, her heart beating unnaturally fast. *Babe*. Ridiculous name, she'd always thought so. That wave looks natural and it's such a lovely colour. If I had hair that colour I'd wear soft blues and greens and aquamarines, not that awful brown and pink get-up.

She doesn't make the best of herself, she thought, stowing away the butter in the tiny office fridge. There wasn't room for the cabbage because someone had stacked the fridge with perishables. She tucked her basket with the rest of her shopping under her desk. The cabbage would just have to take its chance; it wasn't all that hot today.

And unless she was the best actress in the world, it was obvious that Babe didn't have a clue about Milly's past. She felt a moment of triumph. Luke clearly hadn't told her anything. So they couldn't be that close, she told herself. Then she remembered that Luke hadn't seen much of Miranda after Milly was born. He'd known her as a girl. He knew her when she was pregnant. But after Milly was born he was away most of the time getting trained. That meant that he probably didn't have a clue, either. She sat down at her desk and let out her breath. She hadn't realised she was holding it.

Chapter 8

Family dynamics

'AM I LATE?' FELIX LUMBERED INTO THE KITCHEN AT supper time. Esme hovered by the window looking out at the masquerade roses struggling up towards the light through the luxuriant undergrowth. 'Not so fond of those myself,' Felix observed, glancing out of the window on the way to his chair. 'They don't seem able to make up their minds what colour they want to be. I haven't got to that bit yet,' he said defensively.

'What do you mean? What has the state of the garden got to do with you?'

I was laying the table and heard their exchange. I don't expect Esme meant to sound rude. I knew Luke had told Felix that if he helped with the garden Luke would cut down his rent, but of course I didn't say anything, Felix being a little sensitive about his lack of bread.

'You may not be aware that I help sometimes in the garden,' Felix said, his voice tight. 'It's rather much for Luke, with all his other commitments.'

Esme sniffed instead of answering. I wished she would reassure him. I was grateful to Felix. Only the other day I'd asked in all innocence if anyone knew where the secateurs were and Pascale had snapped, "Ow you not know? 'Ow long you live 'ere?' and a lot more besides. We were having tea around the kitchen table. Luke was out or she wouldn't have dared, I thought, blushing and humiliated, partly because Izzy was there.

'Here, lay off, Pascale,' Felix had said into the surprised silence. (It was as though a mouse had answered a cat back.) 'Gardening isn't one of Milly's pursuits, that's all. Why should she know where the gardening things are?' He looked around the table. 'Milly does other things,' Felix said.

'What sings?' Pascale retorted. Of course Felix couldn't think of a single thing. 'Well, she writes poetry,' he said.

'What poetry?' Pascale said.

'It's okay, Felix,' I said, putting him out of his misery. And Pascale was right, what did I do? My poems weren't for the light of day. Not yet, anyway. It was just something I did, like Babe cooked and Luke made furniture.

'Milly is a joy, just as she is,' Esme had said firmly, and that shut Pascale up. She spent the rest of the meal muttering under her breath to her dead husband André, who was visible only to her. We were all used to André and I was particularly partial to him since he was the only person who dared stand up to Pascale. From the sound of her side of their altercations he made no bones about criticising her black clothes, her cloggy shoes, even her cooking.

I walked around the table putting napkins beside people's places. They were being nice to each other: perhaps Luke had sorted out the bath problem.

'Right, everybody, sit down,' Babe said, lifting a pile of plates out of the Aga. 'Sorry for the hold-up but Luke isn't in yet. Evening, Felix.'

'Good evening, Babe.' Felix stood behind his chair and leaned on it heavily as though to stop it from flying away.

I put a napkin on Esme's side plate. 'One for you, Esme.'

Pascale tut-tutted under her breath.

'It's okay, Pascale. Mrs Landower likes me to call her Esme, don't you, Esme?' I put the last napkin beside Luke's place at the head of the table, arranging it with extra care on his side plate.

'Certainly, my dear.' Esme turned from the window. She gave Pascale a severe look and went to her usual place on Luke's right.

Pascale, oblivious, muttered something to André and plodded around the table to her place next to Babe at the other end.

'What was that, Pascale?' Babe paused in front of the Aga with the pile of plates held between her oven-gloved hands. I glanced around, ears pricked. I couldn't help being pleased when Babe got annoyed with Pascale. Things between them were sometimes interestingly volatile. Babe said it gave her the creeps when Pascale started chatting to André. Also, I knew it annoyed Babe that Pascale still interfered in kitchen affairs even though she was supposed to have handed it over to Babe ages ago. I was surprised Babe hadn't strangled her already.

'It is my hat,' Pascale said primly. 'André he say he not like.' She reached up with both hands and attempted unsuccessfully to straighten the fuchsia-pink straw hat balanced on her head.

'It's a really cool hat,' I said, then stopped, fearful of sycophancy. Also nervous; you never knew how Pascale was going to react to friendly overtures. 'Tell him we all think it's cool.'

'What is this cool?'

'It means it's fab. Pretty.'

'Why you not tell him yourself, then maybe he believe.'

'Where is he?'

'Where? Where he always, close by me, make himself a nuisance.'

'André, we all really, *really* like Pascale's hat.'

Pascale nodded approval.

'Well, now that's settled,' Babe said, 'can we get on? Do sit down, Pascale. You've been on your feet the whole afternoon. Get the serving-spoons, will you, Milly?'

'Should we start,' Felix rumbled, 'without Luke?'

Babe hesitated. 'It's not like him to be this late. I think we'd better.'

Esme put her elbows on the table and smiled around, looking over her glasses. Taking spoons from the dresser drawer I dropped one, fortunately back into the drawer and not onto the floor.

'*Tiens tiens,*' Pascale muttered as I retrieved it. 'Always so noisy. Always the clottering.'

'Sorry,' I said. Esme gave her a look and I put one of the spoons down beside the mat Babe's pie was about to land on.

'Rocking,' Felix muttered, lumbering off around the table. 'Rocking and rolling.'

'Now where's he going?' Babe said. 'Pascale, for heaven's sake will you sit down!'

'*Monsieur* Luke, he is not here.'

'We know that but we're dishing up. *Nous commençons,*' Babe said. '*Asseyez-vous.*'

Felix jiggled Pascale's chair encouragingly against the backs of her knees. Pascale lowered herself, batting André away with her left hand. '*Pas maintenant,*' she hissed. Felix tucked her chair in. He would never sit until all the ladies were seated. Me excepted of course. I looked at Esme, hoping she would award him a Brownie point for this old-fashioned courtesy but Esme was unrolling her napkin, studiously oblivious.

In the distance the front door slammed. The kitchen door opened and Luke put his head around. 'Sorry to be late. Just wash my hands.'

I hurried to help Babe who was bending down, knees akimbo, about to lift the big earthenware pie dish out of the Aga. 'What's up with him?' she said. 'Mind out, this weighs a ton.' She set the dish on the mat in front of the plates. 'I'll be mother today. Mutton Spicy pie, if anyone's interested. Come on, Milly, spit spot, let's have the veg.'

Luke came in as I was lowering the last vegetable dish onto the table. The edge of the dish jogged Esme's water glass which almost toppled over. Water splashed onto the tablecloth.

'Always so clumsy,' Pascale said under her breath. I bit my lip. Suddenly I felt tearful.

'Ooh goody, sprouts,' Esme said, darting Pascale a filthy look. 'I love sprouts.'

'Sorry, everyone,' Luke said. 'Got held up. Afraid I can't stay. Just pause here for a bit before I pop up and change.'

'Why, where are you going?' I said. Luke was wearing his old grey sweatshirt over a pair of ancient jeans. I loved the way he could lounge around at home with his shirt hanging out or wearing a sweater with holes in the elbows and still manage to look good. It was his leanness and the way he moved, as deceptively languid as Sapphy.

He pulled out his chair and subsided into it. He glanced across at Pascale's hat, looked across at me and rolled his eyes. I clamped my lips together and looked away. I knew he had seen the flash of tears in my eyes:

he'd bring it up later, he always did. He hated when I got upset.

'Everything in order?' Felix said. 'I was hoping we might have a game of chess this evening. You must give me a chance to even the score.'

'Sorry, Felix, got to go out, I'm afraid.' Luke heaved a breath and relaxed back into his chair. 'A customer dropped in and suggested I join her for supper later.'

'Who?' I asked.

'Your Mrs Booth. Amy. Wants to commission a chair.'

'She's not my Mrs Booth,' I said.

'It isn't the chair she's interested in,' Babe said, digging her spoon into the crust.

Luke rubbed his hands over his face as though to wipe the tiredness away. 'I won't dignify that remark,' he said.

Babe smirked and began handing out plates laden with pie. A heavenly aroma of lamb and apples filled the room, silencing everybody.

'Started your job there, have you, Milly?' Felix said. 'How did you get on?'

I groaned and passed Esme the potatoes. 'I'm working my socks off. I think even Babe would be impressed.'

Pascale threw me a cynical look. I knew just what she was thinking – I was useless at cleaning and Amy was a mug for paying me to do it.

'It's only till Gill comes back, isn't it?' Babe said. 'Probably only be for a week or two. Where is she, anyway?'

Felix cleared his throat. 'She's in hospital,' he said. 'She was – I think the word is mugged – on her way home from Mrs Booth's. She was quite badly – beaten up.'

We all looked at him in total surprise.

'How dreadful,' Esme said. 'Was she badly hurt?'

'A couple of broken ribs I believe. Bruising.'

'How do you know all this?' Luke said.

Felix looked at him, frowning. 'Well, Gill is my daughter, isn't she? Mrs Booth informed me.'

There was a bit of a pause while we all took this in.

'She's your *daughter*?' Esme said. 'And she goes out cleaning? Wouldn't she prefer a more suitable occupation?'

'It's perfectly suitable. And she doesn't have to do it, she likes it,' Felix said, looking bruised. 'Look, it's all perfectly all right. We'll say no more about it, if you don't mind.'

'I didn't know you had a daughter,' Esme said.

Felix took out his handkerchief and wiped his nose. 'There's no reason why you should.'

'Ah, Felix,' Luke said. 'I recollect now. You did tell me. It was through Gill that you heard about the room here, am I right?'

Felix nodded. 'We remain friends, although separated. It doesn't have to be a blood bath.' He tucked the handkerchief away in his jacket pocket.

'Of course not,' Luke said. 'And you're quite right, it's nobody's business but your own.'

'Well,' I said, 'Amy says she's a simply marvellous cleaner. And I'll do my best so it's nice for her when she comes back.'

This produced another mutter from Pascale. Esme thanked me for the potatoes and Luke passed me the beans. He winked at me. My heart lifted. Who cared if Pascale was foul to me when there was Luke?

Chapter 9
Heartache

Juno plunged her hands, knotted into fists, deep into the pockets of her skirt. A light wind had blown up and was moving the branches of the tall trees beyond the orchard so that the light streaming from the windows of Luke's house seemed to be blowing and moving, flickering like candle flames.

Something had to be done. She'd run into Amy Booth again in the town and she'd gone on and on about Luke. The woman was obsessed. She'd invited him to supper this evening, she said. And she'd asked him to make her a chair. Well, the bloody woman was lucky she could afford it. What Amy wanted she would make sure she got, and at the moment what she seemed to want was Luke.

Inside the house they would have finished supper by now. Babe and Milly would be clearing away and later on the light would go on again in Luke's room, the last one on the right on the middle floor, and if he was at home instead of at Amy's he would be taking off his watch and undressing, folding his clothes away neatly or draping them over the back of a chair – because he was a tidy man, everything he did was composed and neat and thoughtful – and then he would shower and climb into bed and as he always did, fall instantly, exhaustedly asleep. Juno closed her eyes. Oh, Luke.

Her lips tightened. She opened her eyes. She mustn't soften. Softness was not part of the plan. She was done with all that. Luke had hurt her feelings and her pride. Now he must pay.

Hardened in heart anew. Now where on earth had that come from? It was from a poem she'd read somewhere. *Hardened in heart anew ... But glad to have sat under ... Thunder and rain with you ... And grateful too ... For sunlight in the garden.* That was it: Louis MacNeice. And she had been grateful, she had adored every moment of the brief affair with Luke, which was why when the end came the pain and humiliation had cut so deep.

In MacNeice's poem, hearts were being hardened in preparation for the onset of war, rather than revenge, but in a way that was quite appropriate. This felt like war.

Carmena drifted into Juno's head and in her imagination Emily's voice rose, sweet and strong. Emily her star pupil, coming on in leaps and bounds, which was more than could be said of most of them. Juno shook her head in exasperation, remembering how hard she had practised in her own student days. Emily was one of the very few who seemed the slightest bit motivated to practise between lessons.

Still the music surged through her head:

> *Dance and song make glad the night,*
> *Hark, the castanets are sounding light ...*

After the car accident that killed Miranda and her

parents, Milly had moved in with Juno and Izzy for nearly a year. Pascale, it was decided, was too old to cope with a six-year-old and after all, Milly and Izzy were the same age and best friends. Juno agreed to take Milly in for as long as it would take for Luke to finish his training and sort his affairs out.

Juno closed her eyes again and gave herself up to her memory of seeing Luke walking up the path to her front door, the day he came to collect seven-year-old Milly and take her home to Half Moon House.

She remembered standing on the doorstep looking up at him, the scent of lilac all around them and the light spring wind blowing her hair around her face, brushing her cheeks like kisses, soft and cool.

Ah, now rings a voice I know from every voice apart,
Thro' the orange grove he hastens.
He is coming, oh my heart!

Still, all these years later, tears filled her eyes. Luke, she thought. You were so tall, so beautiful. I fell in love, there on that doorstep.

She felt herself softening, her resolve weakening. No. No. She brushed the tears away. All that was over. She hated him now. Their affair had lasted only a matter of months until, abruptly, he had ended it.

In moments of rare self-examination, Juno knew why he had ended it: he had sensed her growing obsession with him. He had tried to tell her that he liked her and enjoyed her company, but that he did not, could not, love her. The affair had been a mistake, he said. It would be best to nip it in the bud.

Contributing to her almost overwhelming regret was the

realisation that if she had only managed to play it cool, if she'd pretended that her feelings were not so deeply engaged, the affair might have gone on a lot longer. But for whatever sensible, indeed compassionate reason, he had ended it, still he had hurt and humiliated her and she had not forgiven him.

She sighed. Izzy still hadn't come home. She was getting more and more secretive, almost as though she had something to hide. Juno remembered with a thrill of dismay Izzy's parting shot after breakfast that morning. She'd left the kitchen in a bad temper, saying she was going over to see Milly, then a moment later the door had opened and she'd put her head around. 'I forgot to say,' she said, grinning. 'You're not going to believe this. Milly thinks there's a ghost haunting the orchard, and she thinks it's her mother. Can you believe that?'

Juno put her hand to her head. She felt dizzy. It was partly Izzy's mercurial change of mood and partly – 'Miranda?'

'Yah. Milly thinks she's come back to tell her something. Isn't that the funniest thing you've ever heard? She's obviously gone around the bend. I mean whoever heard of a ghost coming back to tell you something? It would have to be something life or death important, don't you think?' She left again, chortling. 'Life or death,' Juno heard. 'What a hoot!'

The colour had drained from Juno's face. She'd sat for a long time staring at the Aga, her heart going into overdrive.

Chapter 10

All good things are wild and free

PERCHED HIGH UP ON THE LANDING I CLOSED MY BOOK and looked down into the shadowy hall. The front door flew open and Luke came in, his mackintosh whirling on a blast of rainy wind. He leaned his shoulder against the heavy door to close it, lifted off his broad-brimmed Stetson hat (my last Christmas present) and sent it skimming towards the hat-stand where it hit one of the hooks, shuddered and settled.

He looked up. 'Still up?' He shrugged off his mac and strode over more sedately to hang it up. It struck me suddenly that it was as if, on coming in, the exciting possibilities of life outside the home had been extinguished at a stroke; one final flicker and then – gone. Was that how he felt?

Is it me? I thought with a pang. Am I a burden? The thought really flipped me out.

'It's late,' Luke said. 'Couldn't you sleep?' He looked so cool. I loved it when he wore his dinner jacket. It was completely different from how he usually looked, i.e. dungarees and covered with sawdust.

'I thought it would be nice for you to come home to someone up,' I said. 'Instead of all of us crashed out.' And to make sure she hasn't swallowed you up, that woman, hook, line and sinker.

'That was kind.' He came and stood at the foot of the stairs. 'I can still smell Babe's mutton spicy pie.'

'That sounds as though you're still hungry. Didn't she give you enough to eat?'

He shrugged. 'She's an excellent cook.'

Bet she wasn't half as good as Babe.

'She says you're getting on very well with the cleaning. She seems pleased.' He came and clasped the carved ball on the newel post at the foot of the stairs and looked up at me.

My fingers tightened around the thin, hardback copy of Walter de la Mare's poems that I'd found that morning in the attic, shoved into one of the whitewood bookcases beside my mother's copies of E. Nesbit and Alice. I tried but failed to read the expression on his face. My mind was torn between my delight at seeing him and trails of the midnight garden with its scents of nicotiana and stocks where I'd been wandering among all the tangled greenery reciting the poem I'd learned last term:

Is there anybody there? said the Traveller,
Knocking on the moonlit door;
And his horse in the silence champed the grasses
Of the forest's ferny floor.

My socks were soaking. I wondered whether the relief I was feeling was partly because there had been no more music coming from the orchard. Perhaps I really had imagined it.

I pulled my faded pink cotton nightie down over my

knees. Babe had made it for me years ago – years – it was far too short for me now, out of a remnant found in a bin in the January sales at Debenhams.

'Do you think she's pretty, Mrs Booth?'

'Exquisite. A bit done up.' Still hanging from the newel post he leaned away and tipped his head to one side, his eyes half-closed. It occurred to me that he might possibly be slightly blitzed. He let go of the post then and ambled about a bit, tall and restless, his hands in his pockets, then he turned back and stood looking up at me, legs apart, his face in shadow.

If only I could see his eyes I would know what he was thinking. I didn't know why I was so ambitious for him not to particularly like Amy Booth; I just was. Perhaps it was just me bogarting. I mean I didn't want him for myself, so why did it seem like such a big deal?

'I'm glad you don't wear all that paint and powder on your face.'

I did, a bit, but he hadn't noticed. 'I'd better split now,' I said, reaching for the bannister.

Luke's eyes strayed to the grandfather clock standing against the wall by the study door. 'Midnight! How long have you been sitting there waiting?'

'Hardly any time at all, jeez, no.' I stood up briskly. I didn't want him to think I was like one of those slutty women in those forties black-and-white movies who hang around in the kitchen in their dressing gowns, fags hanging out of their mouths, nagging their men for staying out late having drinks with their mates.

Luke pulled open the study door, waved and disappeared.

That was that, then. I stood up and pulled the old silk kimono tightly around me. Waves of comfort engulfed me.

It had been my mother's kimono and it was as if my mother herself had wrapped her arms around me and hugged me, tight.

There it was again, that glassy chime. I looked up. 'Mother?' I said in a low voice. 'Is that you?' My breathing came shallow and fast. I listened hard, my heart thundering, but no music followed. What was happening? Why now?

I was more and more convinced that my mother was trying to tell me – or warn me – about something. But what?

Chapter 11

You can always tell a good man

'Tea.' Esme put her head around the door as I galloped across the landing the next morning on the way back from my walk. 'Would you like some? I'm not quite up. Come and chat while I do my hair.'

I sprang backwards onto the bed and shouldered off my rucksack.

'Have a go at re-stringing these,' she said, sitting down at her dressing-table. I caught the paper bag she tossed over to me. Good catch. Miss Jenkins (games) would be proud of me. 'Lapis,' Esme said. 'So have a care.' She picked her cup up and sipped.

'I met a man on the common today,' I said, spilling the beads into my lap.

'You didn't speak to him, I hope,' Esme said, picking up her hairbrush.

'I was warbling away, you know, the way you do when you're alone. There's a deer that comes sometimes.'

'What, you mean it listens? You are funny, Milly.'

I shrugged. 'It seems to. Unless it's just so surprised it can't move. It's rather sweet. I'd like to try and tame it. The man I met was walking his dog. We stopped for a chat. He said he wished he could sing and I said, well, why don't you go and see Juno.'

Esme turned right around. Even her legs. 'Milly, you didn't!'

'Why not? She'll teach him to sing.'

'Did you tell him where she lives?'

'I did, actually.'

Esme shook her head and turned back to the mirror. 'You really shouldn't have, you know. He might be dangerous.'

'No ... he was nice. A bit of a hunk. And he has a cool dog, a red setter.'

'Well, that's all right then.'

'You can tell a lot from a dog.'

'I'll take your word for it.'

'His name is Jack Marmalade – or something.'

'Oh Milly, you really are hopeless. You look at everyone through rose-coloured glasses. Not everyone is good, you know. Believe me.' Esme started to brush her hair, then stopped and put down the brush. 'Speaking of which, what is it with Pascale?' She glanced at me through the mirror. 'Has she always been so ... hostile ... with you, I mean? If you don't mind my asking.'

I felt my face redden as I bent my head over the brilliant beads. I shrugged. 'As long as I can remember. No idea why.' I picked up a bead and examined it. 'What a fabulous blue.' I dropped it back in the bag. 'Well, she's right, I am 'clomsy'. And when she gets cross with me it makes me worse.'

Esme looked thoughtful. 'I suppose it can't be much fun to be old and widowed with not much to look forward to, but all the same she does profess to be a Christian.' She picked up her comb, looked at it and put it down. 'Although as regards faith, hers does appear to be genuine. She never seems to question it, whatever horrors may assail her imagination, if indeed horrors ever do. Perhaps that's her problem, perhaps she has no imagination.'

I chuckled, threading a bead onto the broken string. 'Felix says, how can you possibly believe in a loving God after watching the news.'

'Well, I rather mistrust people who claim to be in touch with Divine Presences.'

'She's definitely in touch with André.' I looked up, wondering if this would be a good time to tell her about the weird happenings in the orchard.

'I wouldn't call him a Divine Presence, would you?'

'Hardly. He's just old André.' Perhaps not.

'Mind you,' Esme said, 'as far as Divine Presences go, it often amazes me how unworthy the recipients of their attention so frequently seem to be.'

'Oh cool, there it is.' Head down I rummaged around for a dropped bead, squashing a yawn. I'd slept badly.

'She's a strange fish,' Esme said, starting to put up her hair. 'In a world of her own half the time.'

'She's old. She's been here for ever. My grandmother was fragile after my mother was born so Grandpa brought Pascale over from Brittany to look after the baby.'

'Miranda.'

'Yup. My mother. Grandma and Grandpa met Pascale when they were on holiday. She was looking for a job so ...' I shrugged. 'André came over soon after and stayed as a sort of handyman. He did the garden as well. He died of cancer when I was a baby.'

'Her husband?'

I nodded. 'She adored him. She was really bummed when he died.'

'It unnerves me the way she talks to him as though he's actually there.'

I giggled. 'I like the way he tells her off. Nobody else would dare. She gets quite upset, for her. She's mostly quite calm. She leaves everything to *le bon Dieu* and gets on with it.'

'But André isn't there, he's dead.'

'Not to her, he's not.' The ridiculous idea came into my head of my mother and André communing in the orchard.

Her hands now dealing with the top of her head, Esme's beautiful blue-green eyes peered back at me in the mirror through arms angled like a Balinese dancer's.

Esme's eyes, she had recently told me, were the only feature in her forty-year-old face that gave her any reassurance. Everything else, she said, was either dropping, softening or wrinkling.

It must be just awful, I thought after one of these conversations, to be forty.

'You seem tired, Milly.'

'I had another bad dream on Sunday night. Haven't caught up yet. The drowning one this time.'

'There are others?'

'Oh crumbs yes. Horrid. Shouting and darkness and being alone and scared, but I wake up before finding out what of.'

'How awful for you. Do you really not know what's behind them?'

'No idea.'

Esme lowered her arms and turned her head this way and that, her hand mirror raised to reflect the back of her head. 'That will have to do.'

'I ought to go, Esme,' I said, bundling the beads back into their bag. 'I'm meeting Izzy later and I've got stacks to do getting ready for September. Can I do these later?'

'Of course, there's no need for you to do them at all. It was just something for you to do while we talked.'

I slid off the bed. 'I want to ask Juno about my mother. I hadn't realised they were friends but Amy says they were quite close. Juno's never mentioned it. Maybe she thinks it will upset me if she talks about my mother. People don't always realise that actually that's just what you want to do, talk about them. Especially if you can't remember a thing about them.'

Chapter 12

Some people just make you feel small

PULLING INTO A SPACE IN THE NEW SAINSBURY'S CAR-park Juno's heart sank when she realised too late that she'd parked one car away from Amy Booth. Amy was stacking hessian bags in neat rows inside the boot of her smart grey Mercedes. That meant she'd done her shopping, thank goodness, so they wouldn't be dodging each other all around the store, and Juno wouldn't have to disguise her complete ignorance of the new system. She'd get hopelessly lost, she knew she would. How on earth were you supposed to cope with no assistants to help you find what you needed?

She lurked in her car, hoping she wouldn't have to get out till Amy had gone. It had rained hard on her walk home from work and she'd forgotten to take her umbrella so her hair had disintegrated into a mass of frizz. She'd jumped straight into the car to go shopping, banking on not running into anyone she knew.

It would have to be Amy; she was always so ridiculously well turned out, not a hair out of place, and she had a snooty way about her that made you feel worse than ever. Juno couldn't pretend not to know her because they had attended the same charity lunch a couple of weeks ago and she'd found herself sitting next to Amy. They'd had quite a long chat, even though Amy had spent most of the lunch sucking up to the woman sitting opposite who happened to be married to an M.P. and knew people she claimed to be in the Cabinet. Juno had only gone to the lunch because she'd felt flattered to be asked.

Oh God, Amy had seen her. She was always looking around to see who was admiring her, even in Sainsbury's car park, for crying out loud.

'Hel-*lo*,' Amy said.

Bet she puts on that plummy voice, Juno thought. She climbed reluctantly out of the car and went to the boot to collect her shopping baskets. 'Sorry about my hair. I got rained on.' Why was she apologising?

'The weather's awful, isn't it? I'm so thankful I can get away with this simple style. I go to Hair Art, you know, they're frightfully good. I always have Belinda.'

I'm sure you do, Juno thought. There was no way in the world she could afford Hair Art.

'Do you have a permanent?'

'Yes.' Juno slammed the boot shut. She was aware of Amy looking at her critically.

Amy sniffed. 'In my opinion a really good haircut is much less trouble.' She wheeled her trolley around to the front of the car. 'Thank goodness that's over,' she said over her shoulder, pushing her trolley over towards a parking bay under the steps. 'I hate grocery shopping, don't you? Nice lunch the other day, wasn't it?'

Juno trailed after her. Amy parked her trolley neatly and turned back. 'I was pleased you recommended Milly for me while Gill is away. She's proving to be quite a nice little worker.'

'How is Gill?'

Amy looked surprised, then vague. 'I haven't the slightest idea. I expect they'll tell me when she's ready to come back. I'm seeing a good deal of Milly's family at the moment, of course. Luke is making a piece for me. He's such a find. So unusual, a gentleman carpenter and such a charming man. You know them, of course.'

God, she was a snob. 'Of course.' We live next door, what does she expect? 'Milly and Izzy are great friends.'

'Izzy is your daughter?'

Juno nodded.

'You're on your own?'

'Izzy's father and I divorced a long time ago.'

'Oh, I am sorry.' She paused with her hand on the door handle of her Triumph Herald – Juno knew what it was because she'd always wanted one – and looked at Juno for a thoughtful moment during which Juno had to fight quite hard not to say, 'Luke and I are an item, of course. We are lovers.' That would wipe the condescending look off her face.

And once, for the briefest of times, it had been true.

In her heart of hearts she knew that it had only come about because of his loneliness and disorientation when he first came to live at Half Moon, and because of her own persistence. But it had happened. And then – and then, unforgivably, he had abandoned her. With no explanation. She felt her hands squeeze themselves into fists by her side and turned away to hide the rush of emotion flooding through her.

'I suppose you see quite a lot of them too,' Amy said, letting go of the door handle and leaning against her car, her arms folded.

Why doesn't she just go? Juno thought.

'It's such an interesting household, with those odd housekeepers, and the lodgers. Do you know Esme?'

'Yes, of course, she's awfully nice.' It was such a relief to be able to say this. So often with Amy you hadn't a clue about the bewildering number of people she brought into the conversation. That was part of the humiliation Juno felt in her presence: Amy hadn't lived in the village half as long as Juno but she knew far more people than Juno did. 'Felix is nice, too, but he keeps himself to himself rather.'

'I don't know him. I do like Luke though. I bought those special biscuits he likes, those Walkers shortbread ones, he loves those, for when he comes to coffee next. I'm having him to drinks this weekend to introduce him to a friend of mine who is interested in commissioning a piece. We must all do our bit to help,' she said, unwrapping her arms and opening her car door.

As if Luke needed her help.

'Well, must dash,' Amy said, inserting her narrow bottom onto the car seat, feet together. She swung her legs in.

'Me too. Goodbye.' Juno pounded up the steps and through the automatic door. She hadn't even needed to do a Sainsbury's shop, she'd only come here to avoid going home to an empty house and depression.

What was Amy doing buying Luke special biscuits and asking him round for drinks? She'd have to find out from Milly if something was going on.

Wish I'd stood up for myself more, she thought, irritated beyond measure, hauling a trolley out. She wasn't sure quite what she meant, or how she could have, it was just a feeling, the way she so often felt when with Amy. Second rate.

. . .

Juno pushed open the door into the Sue Ryder shop on the high street and nearly had her nose broken by a large woman shoving the other way. A squirming bundle of hair tucked in under her arm turned out to be a small, very snappy dog. Juno recoiled.

The woman glared at her. 'Don't be silly,' she snapped. 'Archie wouldn't do anybody any harm, would you, Archie? Look where you're going, can't you?'

'Sorry,' Juno said, backing into someone walking along the pavement. 'Sorry,' she said again, holding her aching nose. She stepped inside, her heart thumping with sorrow and temper. The room smelt strongly of air-freshener and unclean clothes. She pretended to look through the skirts suspended from hangers on a low rail. So rude, she thought angrily, her heart thumping. And it's my nose that got hurt. Not a word of apology. That door shouldn't swing both ways like that, it's dangerous.

'Why don't you do something about that door?' a calm, upper-class voice rang across the stuffy room on its owner's way out. 'It's an accident waiting to happen.' The door swung to behind her.

Why couldn't she be like that? She looked to see who was behind the counter. Oh. It was the tall, grey-haired woman who never smiled and always looked at you as though you were infested with lice and about to pinch something. What was she doing working in a place like this anyway? Surely they were supposed to be caring sort of people, not like her, always looking at you as though she despised you for being there in the first place. She looked through the size fourteen jumpers and tops, then gave up. Nothing here for her.

Walking back to the building society she felt she'd reached the nadir of her existence. She hadn't seen Luke, which had been the reason for coming this way in the first place. Sometimes he came back from the workshop in his lunch hour and dived into the Plough for a half and a sandwich. Once or twice she'd bumped into him and they'd exchanged a word. Trouble was she never knew which day he would choose.

You are not feeling sick, she told herself, pushing open the door into the office; it's just your imagination. Her father had always told everybody she'd got an overactive imagination. He'd said it not indulgently but contemptuously, the way he always spoke about her. He'd always made it clear that she'd been a huge disappointment to him. He'd criticised her for her fine hair, her teen-aged puppy fat, her self-effacement. Which was a bit rich since the reason she'd avoided him and kept her opinions to herself had been because she knew exactly what his response would have been – utter rubbish, you don't know what you're talking about. Especially if it was anything to do with politics or the role of women in society.

The stupid thing was he was hardly Dean Martin himself. He was a lowly civil servant working in the Ministry of Pensions. He hadn't even been good-looking when her mother had married him, and he'd let himself go, put on weight and quite often didn't even bother to shave at weekends. Her poor mother. No wonder she'd clung to Juno for moral support. Not that she'd been much use.

Pamela looked up from her packet of M&S sandwiches and her Agatha Christie. She never went out for lunch. 'What are you doing here? I thought it was your afternoon off.' She frowned. 'Are you okay? You look as though you've lost a pound and found sixpence.'

Exactly what her father used to say. 'Forgot my jacket.' She collected it from the hook behind the door. If only she could confide in Pam about how depressed she felt but she couldn't, they didn't know each other very well, they just worked together. If only she had a friend she could really talk to.

Like Izzy and Milly. Thick as thieves they were. Izzy had loads of friends. She spent almost as much time with that Naomi now as she did with Milly.

She wasn't going to think about Milly. If she started down that path she'd end up in the tiny office kitchenette, cutting her throat.

Don't be so ridiculous, Juno, she heard her father's voice. You always have to exaggerate everything. Don't make such a fuss.

She wasn't fussing, she was planning. The first thing she would do was get Milly around for coffee and have a proper chat, find out how the land lay. So her father could just butt out.

She felt a tiny frisson of triumph. Her father was dead. He couldn't get at her anymore. In that one thing at least, she had won.

Chapter 13

Acid drops

Izzy arrived in the orchard, swinging a Lennon's paper carrier bag, the little Braun transistor radio Juno had given her for Christmas dangling from her other hand. She plonked herself down in the grass and pulled out her makeup pouch. She had it with her all the time now. 'Don't like this colour,' she said, looking scornfully at her nails. She took out a bottle of nail-varnish remover and balanced it between some tree roots lumping up through the grass.

'Radio Caroline?' I said, collapsing cross-legged into the grass next to her, my back pressed uncomfortably against the tree, its trunk biting through my tee shirt into my spine.

'Good, isn't it?' Izzy said. 'You can listen all day if you want to.'

'I've got Babe,' I said. 'Hers is on all the time.'

Izzy had started scrubbing off her nail varnish with remover and a piece of cotton wool.

Like a complete unknown, Bob Dylan sang. *Like a rolling stone ...*

'I had a chat with Esme this morning,' I said. 'She told

me she had a love affair. When she was married.' I wanted to see if I could get Izzy to be interested for one minute in somebody who wasn't herself. 'Doomed,' I said. 'The affair. From the sound of it.'

'What's it to you?' Izzy said. 'She's only the lodger. It's only old Esme.'

'You shouldn't be mean about her. I like her.' I flicked a dead leaf off my knee and watched as Izzy started to paint her nails a pale, silvery green.

'I don't *dis*like her but she clucks away like an old hen.'

'No, she doesn't. She only does it with you because you make her nervous. She knows you think she's boring so it makes her be like that. When she's with me she's perfectly sensible. Interesting even. Poor Esme,' I said, tipping away from her sideways into the grass. 'She isn't beautiful, not like my mother was.'

'I wish you'd stop going on about your bloody mother.'

'Why are you doing those again anyway?' I asked with my back to her.

'Rob decided he didn't like that colour after all.'

'Blimey, what a slave driver.'

Izzy was in a foul mood today. It was bound to be something to do with Robert. I sat up again and watched as she put away the bottle of nail varnish and began smearing green eye-shadow over her left eyelid.

While I give to you and you give to me, Bing Crosby sang, *true love, true love ...*

'I love that idea,' I said, wanting to provoke her. 'True love. There's one person meant for you and you just have to go on looking till you find them.'

'That's looney tunes,' Izzy said, rubbing her eyelid.

'D'you think?'

''Course it is.' She started on the other eye. 'There can't just be one person who's right for one other person. What if one of them is Icelandic and the other one's Chinese, for God's sake? The human race would die out in five minutes. 'Struth, look at that. A grasshopper jumped right into my eyeshadow. It's got green stuff all over its feet now.'

'At least it's green,' I said, bending over to look.

'Gross,' Izzy said, peering down.

'Is it okay?'

'I dunno. Go on – shoo! Get off!'

'Don't hurt it.'

'Of course I'm not going to hurt it. Oh good, it's gone.'

I shut my eyes and inhaled. The air smelt of apples. Somewhere a dog barked and through the open kitchen window came the sound of the Kenwood doing its stuff and the Beatles feeling fine. Babe was making a cake. 'You're going out with him again this evening, aren't you?'

'What do you think?' Izzy snapped shut the little box of eye-shadow and wiped her fingers in the grass. I looked at her sourly. Something only had to go the slightest bit wrong for Izzy to turn into a girl who seemed to be sucking a permanent acid drop. I watched in silence as she tumbled her makeup into her makeup bag and stood up. She'd changed out of her shorts and was wearing a clingy blue dress which showed off her tiny waist and small, high boobs. She looked gorgeous and alarmingly grown-up. I wasn't going to say so though.

I can't get no satisfaction ... sang the Rolling Stones.

A tremor of disagreement had arisen and hung palpitating in the air. I lay back and rested my head on my linked hands. I gazed thoughtfully up at the jigsaw pieces of sky visible through the apple boughs. I ought to have got used by now to Izzy being so secretive since she'd started going out with Robert but somehow I never could. I still longed for the mutual trust and confidence we'd had in each other as children.

Izzy stood up and poked me playfully in the ribs with the toe of her sandal. So that was all right then. Sort of. 'Well, see ya,' she said. 'Sylvia's got a French conversation class this evening, if you must know.'

'Have a nice time.' I sat up on my elbows and watched her walk towards the gate in the crumbling stone wall that led to the lane that separated our orchard from her garden. Izzy's walk seemed different from usual. Less jaunty and more kind of swaying. I watched as she hauled herself up onto the top rung (never the easy way for Izzy), turned around as she always did and waved. I waved back. Izzy jumped down on the other side and disappeared.

I felt sad. She was growing away from me. She seemed so much older, since Robert. Kind of burdened. Love, I thought, panicking slightly, who needs it? It seemed to bring nothing but trouble.

An hour later she was back. She put her head around the lobby door. My heart sank at the sight of her woebegone face. 'It's all off,' she said. 'He has to stay home.'

'I'm sorry, Iz. What happened?'

'What are you doing out here anyway?'

'Clearing up?' I looked around at the mismatched boots and coats hung up all anyhow. 'This place always gets into such a mess. Nobody can ever find anything. Come and give me a hand, tidying always makes you feel better.'

'It won't. She didn't feel well. She decided to stay home.'

'Then we'll have tea. Babe's made a cake. Cherry

almond, your favourite. Look at this,' I said, holding out a long, dark-blue overcoat. 'Felix's clothes all have good labels, Austin Reed and Jaeger and things. You'd never think it to look at him.'

'He does look a mess,' Izzy agreed more cheerfully. 'He looks like what he is, I suppose, a gent down on his luck.'

Felix was happy with his torn Viyella shirts with the turned collars and cuffs (was it Gill who'd been to all that trouble for him, I wondered?), his old jerseys with leather patches on the elbows, presumably to hide the holes, and his trousers all slightly shiny at the knees, his books of which he had about a ton, and his whisky.

'Doesn't Felix mind your poking about among his things?' Izzy asked.

It was pointless to react, because Izzy was obviously miserable about something (look at those crossed arms and That Face.) 'I'm not poking about. I'm tidying, it's different. I wouldn't go into his room, unless he asked me to. And he's not likely to do that, he never lets anyone in there when he's not there. His room is his castle, and most of the time the drawbridge is up.' I picked up a stray shoe and put it neatly beside its partner in the shoe rack.

Izzy came a step nearer. 'Milly, I've got to tell you ... I found some letters. Believe it or not, Mum's had them all this time. Letters from Dad. And presents. To me. To *me*. And she never told me. Come around in half an hour ... please come. I need you.' Her voice sounded funny. She had a strange expression on her face, a bit like when you don't feel good and you think you might be going to throw up.

I FOUND Juno in the kitchen. 'I'm not sure where Izzy is,' Juno said, depositing three bulging shopping bags onto the kitchen table. 'Give her a shout and I'll put the kettle on. What a day, it's so hot and the traffic was horrible. I'm exhausted.'

'I'll put it on.' I stood by the kettle waiting for it to boil while Juno unpacked her shopping.

Izzy walked in. 'God, not more bags,' she said. 'You've got drawers stuffed full of them. Why don't you use them? Hi, Milly.'

'I know, I always intend to take them with me and then I forget.'

'There's always an excuse with you,' Izzy said. I looked at her in astonishment. 'Where've you been, anyway? You've been gone ages.'

'I bumped into Amy in Sainsbury's carpark.'

'Did you get the cheese spread? That Dairylea stuff?'

'Oh, I'm sorry, I forgot. It was running into Amy, it drove everything out of my head.'

'Oh, typical. It's always about you, isn't it? That was the whole point of your going.'

'Well, hardly the whole point. And you could always go yourself.'

'Yes, but you said you were going.'

Juno looked at me. 'How are you getting on with the cleaning?' she said, for distraction purposes I imagined.

''S'okay. Don't know that I'd want it as a permanent job.'

'Ah, Gill,' Juno said, putting a packet of cheddar into the fridge. 'She's a marvel. Nice woman. Very efficient.'

'She'd need to be. Amy doesn't let you get away with a thing.'

'Not that you'd want to.' She smiled at me. She seemed to have decided to be friendly today.

Izzy gave a huff of frustration and slumped into a chair. 'I'm knackered.'

'Actually,' I said to Juno, 'Amy told me that you and my mother – she said you were really close. Is that true? It's just I never realised – you've never said anything, I mean, you never talk about her much.'

'Damn, I forgot the eggs,' Juno said, her head in the fridge. 'What was that? Oh – your mother. We weren't that close. What did you want to know?'

'Well – anything really.' I looked at Izzy, waiting for some crack about my obsession with my mother, but she said nothing.

Juno opened a cupboard door and put away a packet of tea and two tins of baked beans. She turned to face me and smiled. 'We used to talk about her quite a lot, when you were younger.'

'Really? I'd forgotten.'

'You can always ask me anything, you know that.'

'I'd like to ask you something,' Izzy said.

Juno looked at her, eyebrows raised.

'Why didn't you tell me Dad had written me all those letters?'

'I beg your pardon?'

'Oh, *Mother*. Don't pretend. I found them. All the stuff from Dad you've been hiding from me all these years. Letters. Presents.'

'Oh,' Juno said.

'Yeah, *oh*.'

'Do you make a habit of rummaging around under my bed?'

'Of course not. I was looking for something.'

'What?'

'My birth certificate, if you must know.'

'Whatever d'you want that for?'

Izzy shrugged. 'I just wondered where it was.'

'It's in my desk, not under my bed.'

'I know that now.'

'So you've been through my desk too.'

'Yes, I have. Never seen such a mess.' Izzy folded her arms and glared at her mother.

'You sound just like your father.'

'Was that why he left?'

'Oh, *Izzy,* don't be an ass. Of course not.'

'I've got to go,' I said, standing up.

'Sit down,' Izzy said fiercely. 'I want a witness. And don't you dare look like that, Milly Redmayne, you know nothing about it.'

'What are you going to do?' Juno said in an attempt at humour. 'Sue me?'

'Maybe,' Izzy said.

Juno, rather pale, sat down and looked out of the window, sighed, and looked as if she might cry.

'I really do have to go,' I said. 'This isn't anything to do with me.' My knees suddenly felt as though they might give way.

Juno took out a handkerchief and blew her nose. 'I'm sorry, Milly.'

'I bet you are,' Izzy said, her anger breaking out again. 'Now she knows what a bitch of a mother I've got. It makes me sick,' she said, rounding on me, 'the way you go on and on about your bloody mother. Just because she's dead and you don't know what she was really like. I bet if she was alive it would be a different story. You'd know what she was really like then.'

'Stop it, Izzy,' Juno said.

'Well she would. She thinks her mother was little miss perfect. Well, I bet she wasn't.'

'Milly, go now,' Juno said. 'Go on. I'm so sorry. Don't

worry about us, this happens sometimes, it doesn't mean anything.'

'Yes it damn well does mean something,' Izzy said. 'I never knew before what a liar you are.'

'Bye then,' I said, turning to go. It was obvious that Juno didn't want any more dirty linen washed in front of me.

Walking home, feeling sad for Juno and Izzy, I remembered that Izzy was good at lying as well, she'd never told Juno about all those meetings with Robert when Juno thought she was at Naomi's. Wasn't that just as bad?

Suppose it was me being lied to. Suppose my mother wasn't dead after all but had just walked out and was alive somewhere, just didn't want to see me.

Suppose they made me think she was dead to save my feelings.

I'd never forgive them. You've got to be allowed to make your own mind up. You've got to know what's real and what isn't. It isn't fair otherwise. There's got to be a fixed point somewhere, and that point is the truth.

But of course if it was my mother in the orchard then she must be dead, mustn't she?

Luke would never lie to me. I could ask him anything, he'd always tell me the truth, just as he always knew the right thing to do and the advice he gave me was always worth listening to.

I ran in at the back door. He'd be almost finishing work by now. He'd put his tools away tidily, the way he always did. He and Jean-Paul would brush the work-bench, screw tops back on cans and bottles and sweep up wood-shavings and dust.

Then he'll come home, I thought, comforted, and I'll see him again. I climbed the stairs, went into my room and shut the door. I sat down on the edge of my bed, reached for a pillow and held it against me, pressing it against my stomach, my arms around it, hugging it close.

Chapter 14

To kill a butterfly

I ROUNDED THE CORNER, HEADING FOR THE POST office. It was the lunch hour and the pavements were crowded, people weaving around each other like maypole dancers. There would be a queue in the post office as long as my arm.

I stopped. On the ground, near enough to the edge of the pavement to have remained so far miraculously uncrushed, a Red Admiral butterfly sat seemingly unaware of the moving forest of legs and feet missing it by inches. I crouched down and put my hand, palm up, beside it on the pavement. Obediently it crawled onto my forefinger and then onto my palm. 'I do hope I'm not hurting you,' I told it. I'd heard that human skin burns insects' feet like hot coals. The butterfly however seemed to be feeling quite at home. 'Come on.' I stood up again and continued on my way to the post office, the butterfly perched on my hand. 'I'd better find you somewhere green. You poor thing, what's the matter with you?'

'Oh look!' a passing woman exclaimed. 'She's got a butterfly on her hand!'

I turned on my heel. I'd find a side street and take it down to the little park that ran parallel with the high street. There'd be somewhere to leave it there.

The butterfly suddenly changed its mind and hurled itself drunkenly into space where it wheeled about in mid-air, flapping wildly, and made a crash-landing on the pavement again. I bent over it, frowning. There seemed to be something wrong with its motor skills. Could you take a butterfly to the vet? I held out my hand again and watched as the butterfly climbed trustingly back onto my palm.

I set off again through the crowd. I'd only gone a few yards when a trio of young lads approached, pushing each other and talking loudly, showing off. As they came level I saw that one of them was a girl, boyish-looking with short, rough-cut blond hair so fair it was almost white, dirty jeans and a black top with a slogan scrawled across it in what looked like red paint. *'When I'm good I'm bloody good,'* it proclaimed. *'But when I'm bad I'm better.'*

Ha ha. The funny thing was I was almost sure I'd seen the girl somewhere before.

The blow on my wrist took me completely by surprise, numbing my hand for a moment. The butterfly fell, wheeling helplessly to the pavement below, and the nearest and biggest of the lads, a boy of about fifteen, lifted his booted foot and stamped down on it, crushing it into the stone.

'Ugh!' he said, lifting his Doc and looking at the mess on the sole. His two friends burst into delighted laughter. Passers-by, most of whom had missed what had happened, skirted them warily.

'Oh!' I gave a horrified gasp. Rage and a childish desire to burst into tears welled up inside me. 'You – you moron! How could you?'

'Oo-ooh,' they jeered, dancing about, delighted by my reaction.

The girl dug me in the ribs. 'Watcha gonna do then, miss?' she said. 'Report us to the police?'

'Butterfly-killers,' snorted the smallest one, capering about. 'Wanted alive or dead.' He threw himself about, killing himself with mirth. I looked at them, my face burning, my eyes filling with tears.

'Oh come on,' said the girl contemptuously. 'It was only a fucking butterfly, for Christ's sake.'

'I know you, Micky Lamby,' said someone in the small crowd that had started to gather, attracted by the commotion. 'You're the lot goes around vandalising benches and spraying graffiti everywhere.'

'Get stuffed, grandma.'

'I'm glad I'm not your grandma, I'd be that ashamed I couldn't live with myself.'

'Come on Micky, for Christ's sake. It's only a sodding butterfly,' the girl said again, still looking at me.

'But why?' I said.

'Why the fuck not?'

'Why not,' I repeated.

'Are you all right, love? You look awful.' A kindly face, bushy pepper-and-salt eyebrows, thin hair stranded across the top of his head. Anxious blue eyes.

'I'm okay.'

'Don't take on. They're not worth it. Scum of the earth, that lot.'

That lot had moved away, laughing and jostling each other.

Scum of the earth. But each with a little bit of the divine in them, I reminded myself desperately. Henry

Hamblin. Jesus. You had to try to remember that. However well-hidden.

I was shaking. The crowd that had gathered began to disperse. A man turned and gave me a little wave before melting into the crowd. It was him, the man from the common, the man who wanted to sing. There was no sign of the dog.

I felt sick. I wanted Luke. I wanted to climb onto his knee the way I used to when I was little and feel his arms around me, holding me tight, keeping me safe. Only of course I couldn't, not now. I wasn't a child anymore. I almost smiled, imagining his reaction if I did. He'd shove me off and tell me not to be so silly.

Someone tugged at my elbow. 'Milly.'

I turned. 'Jean-Paul!' With his dark hair and olive complexion he looked out of place in this very English crowd. 'What are you doing here?'

His thin, handsome face was full of concern. 'What's going on? Hey, are you okay? Come on, I've got the Fiesta. I'll take you home. What happened?'

I couldn't speak. I glanced at the barely perceptible smudge on the pavement that had been the butterfly.

'Did they hurt you?'

'No ... of course not. It's nothing, I'm being silly.'

'I saw you talking to them. You want to steer clear of that Micky Lamby, he's trouble. Come on.'

The car was parked on a single yellow line. A traffic warden was standing beside it flicking over the pages of her block of tickets. 'Another minute and you'd have got a ticket.'

'Thanks, mate,' Jean-Paul said. He opened the passenger door for me.

'You're only supposed to load. And you left your keys in the ignition.'

'Lucky you're an honest citizen then. Anyway, it was a crisis.'

'What kind of crisis?'

'She hasn't told me yet.'

The traffic warden glanced at me, shrugged and moved off.

'I was on my way to the post office,' I told Jean-Paul, climbing in and shouldering off my rucksack. 'I'm supposed to be getting some air-letter forms for Luke and some stamps for Babe.'

'I'll get them. I'm on my lunch hour.'

'No, it's okay. I said I would. You'd better let me out.'

'I'm taking you home. You're white as a sheet.'

I sank back in my seat. I saw the butterfly whirling to its doom. It had happened so fast. It had been alive and then it was gone, just like that, for no reason. Perhaps that was why I was so upset. It was the suddenness, the narrowness of the line between life and death.

How narrow? My thoughts went back to the lights in the orchard, my sense that my mother was hovering around somewhere. But why now? She'd been gone ten years and not a whisper. And now this.

'What happened?' Jean-Paul climbed in and slammed the door.

It sounded idiotic when I told him, but he didn't laugh, he just listened and then he said, 'Little blighters, not a brain in their heads between them.'

'You know them?'

'Who doesn't? They've been making a right nuisance of themselves in the town this summer, up to all sorts. Personally I blame that Jonny Sullivan, he's older, ought to know better. The others just tag along. They hang around down by the river mostly. They'll get themselves into serious trouble if they don't watch out. Not a care in the world for anyone except themselves. Totally selfish ...'

'There was a girl with them.'

'Yeah. She and that Micky Lamby, they broke into the workshop a couple of weeks back.'

'Did they do any damage?'

He shook his head. 'Luckily we were both there. We'd stayed after work to do the accounts. We were in the office so they didn't realise there was anybody there and we caught them red-handed. Luke gave them a right wigging, I can tell you.'

'Did he report them to the police?'

'Nah ... you know Luke. Tried to make them see the error of their ways. Told them if they did it again they'd be for it. Were they grateful? Not on your life. He got a mouthful of abuse once they were out of range and running.'

'That's awful.'

'No harm done.' He cleared his throat, looking straight ahead. 'Milly, um, I've been meaning to apologise for all that stuff at Christmas. I'd had a bit to drink. Dunno what came over me. I was upset, my dog just died.'

I began to shake with laughter, tried to stifle my giggles and failed. I put my hand up to cover my mouth.

'What's so funny? Luke was so furious I thought I'd got the sack. You know I've always liked you, Milly. My heart just got the better of my head.'

'I'm sorry,' I said when I could speak. 'I'm terribly sorry about your dog. I didn't know you had a dog.'

'Well, I haven't now.' He was looking at me sideways, half-smiling. 'You're not mad at me then?'

'Course not.' I calmed down and took a breath. 'It's flattering really, it's just, I'm sorry Jean-Paul but I don't feel that way about you. I like you a lot, but not like that.'

'I know.' He sighed. 'It's just you're so beautiful, Milly. You've no idea. I hug my pillow at night—'

'Stop!'

'Sorry?'

'Don't wanna hear it.'

'Sorry. I thought if I could just – if I could make you understand how I felt—' He glanced at me. 'How I feel.'

'I do realise,' I said. 'Only I just don't feel that way myself.'

Perhaps if I said it often enough he would believe me. It occurred to me that I felt no pity at all for poor, suffering Jean-Paul. I'm a horrible, hard-hearted person, I thought. I don't care a bit that he's suffering over me. It's ridiculous. He's much older than me, he must be at least twenty-two. 'Why are you called a French name when you're not French?' I asked, to distract him.

'My mama was French. She scarpered when I was a bairn.'

'A bairn?'

'A nipper. Dad's a Scot. Glasgow. Have you had any lunch? Food, that's what you need. Have a dig in my backpack, there are some sandwiches in there somewhere.'

'I wouldn't dream of eating your sandwiches. Thanks anyway, though. I'll have something at home. Thanks for the lift, Jean-Paul, you're so kind. Dunno what I'd have done, I felt so peculiar.'

'Shock, I expect. You're too sensitive, Milly. Soft, like him. Like Luke.'

'Luke's not soft.'

He glanced at me. 'He's got a heart as big as a house. He just looks tough.'

I would tell Izzy but she would probably think I was being an idiot making such a fuss about a butterfly. Luke wouldn't though, he'd understand.

I thought about the girl. Perhaps that was why that Micky person had killed the butterfly, to show off in front of the girl. If only I could remember where I'd seen her before. I could see her face as if it was right in front of me: thin, hard and unforgiving, her pitiless blue eyes glaring at me as though she despised me, hated me even. Then, out of the blue, I remembered.

Chapter 15

So much easier to pretend

IT WAS OBVIOUS FROM THE SLOW DRAG OF IZZY'S footsteps through the dead leaves and dry grass that something was wrong.

I knew better than to ask her what it was. She took up a stance leaning against a tree, half-turned away. She said, 'I saw his wife today.'

For a moment, my mind still occupied with the butterfly, I couldn't remember whom she was talking about. Then I said, 'Are you okay?'

She twisted the peace symbol bracelet Robert had given her around and around on her thin wrist. She said, 'They were going into Boots.'

'Did they have the children with them?'

She shook her head. 'They've got an au pair, I think. Anyway, they were on their own.'

'Perhaps they were at someone's house. I mean it is the holidays.'

'Jeepers, Milly, who cares about the kids, I saw his *wife*, don't you understand?'

'Sorry.'

Izzy abandoned the bracelet and sat down suddenly, her legs crooked up and her elbows resting on her knees, her forehead leaning on her hands. 'I feel so funny, so sort of ... I don't know why I was imagining someone so much older.'

'What was she wearing?'

'Capri pants,' Izzy said indistinctly. 'White. And a blue blouse, really pretty with lacy kind of sleeves. And she's got this fab hair, chestnut sort-of, shoulder-length with flip-ups. Really neat. I've always wanted hair that colour.'

'Izzy.' I put out my hand but didn't quite dare touch her.

'She's nothing like I imagined. Not from what he said. She's *pretty*. Beautiful, actually. Spiffy-looking.'

'Were you close enough to see her properly?'

'I was behind them, walking along the pavement. I didn't realise it was them and then suddenly there they were. When they turned to go into Boots I got a good look. Suppose I'd been coming the other way! I suppose Rob would have said Hi, I mean I could just have been somebody he knew. I expect he'd have made something up to tell her. Suppose he'd pretended not to know me ... I'd have felt even worse, it would have been awful.'

'But it didn't happen, Izzy.' She was even better at making up worst-case scenarios than me.

'But suppose I meet them again. We have to talk about it, me and Rob, we have to make a plan about what to do, what to say. It's nerve-wracking, living in the same town. I wish we didn't now. I wasn't bothered about her before, she didn't seem real somehow, but now I'm going to worry all the time. We can't go on for ever like this, can we? Maybe he thinks we can.'

'Do you want him to leave her?'

From the look on Izzy's face you'd think I was the biggest idiot in the universe. 'What do *you* think? Oh, Milly, he had his hand on her waist, you know, as if she belonged to him, as if he liked touching her. It wasn't – it's not like he said. They went in through those double doors they've got, you know, and he was holding one half-open with one arm and kind of ushering her in with the other. They looked so kind of – belonging. How could he be like that with her after all the things he's said to me?'

'Well, he wouldn't want to make her think—'

'He told me he loved me, Milly. He's always saying he loves me.'

'Well, he probably does. D'you know how long they've been—'

'Dunno, about fifteen years I think. Oh, Milly, I feel so awful.'

'You could stop seeing him.'

'What? Not awful because of *her,* dumbo.' She climbed to her feet and flung herself away. Her back was turned but I just knew the kind of scornful, hurting expression she had on her face. 'I couldn't care less about her. Because of him, because he goes back to her and pretends that nothing is different. It makes me feel I don't exist. What about *me?*' She turned around. Her face was all red and dissolving like a tomato that's going off. 'And don't you dare start moralising at me. I know he's married and I don't care. I didn't force him to have an affair with me, he did that all by himself. If his wife is so stupid that she doesn't suspect anything then that's her problem, it's nothing to do with me.' She stabbed at the ground with the heel of her trainer like a bull in an arena. 'And now I'm going in to wash my hair.'

Now was not the time to tell her about the butterfly, or anything else. I bit my lip. 'When are you seeing him again?'

'He's going to phone. Perhaps I'll tell him I don't want

to see him again. I don't know, I haven't made up my mind.' She set off towards the gate.

Even the backs of her legs looked miserable.

AFTER LUNCH Izzy rang sounding a lot more cheerful. Everything was okay, Robert had rung, she was going out to tea with him. 'Come down, Milly. I don't know which blouse to wear, come and give me some advice. I have to look nice. I'll bring both the ones I like.'

We had a fashion parade in the orchard and I told her I liked the white muslin one with the little blue polka dots best. She'd wear it with her blue capris. She was pretty hyped up and I couldn't help wondering how long she was going to be able to cope with this level of tension.

'Jeez, is that the time?' she said, bending over to peer at my watch. 'I said I'd see Rob at the end of the road at four. She's gone up to London to meet a girl-friend so he's taken the afternoon off.'

'It's ten to.'

'I'd better go.'

'You seem okay now.'

'Yeah. I mean, it was a bit of a shock seeing them together – you know.'

''Course.'

'We're going out to tea like a proper couple. I'm with Naomi if Mum rings or anything, right? Although she won't.' She rolled over and sat up. 'She doesn't love him, you know.'

'You said.' I flicked a tiny curling leaf off my shorts and smiled at her. 'Have a great time. Will you be back in time for Dr Finley?'

''Course. Wouldn't miss it. Oh, Milly.' She tipped

forward on her hands and knees. 'I'm crazy about him. Looney tunes. I'd marry him like a shot.'

'What happened to the budding architect?' I clicked my fingers at Sapphy, who was pouncing on shadows, but to no avail. She stalked off on more important business. Traitor. Just when I needed her.

'I know. Sad, isn't it? I don't care a hoot about all that now. I think if things were more settled I could concentrate on working ... I mean, they sent me all that stuff I'm supposed to be looking at but nothing seems important except him.'

I thought of that thing some poet said: *'Man's love is of man's life a thing apart; it is a woman's whole existence.'* Lord Byron? I was horribly afraid it might be true. We didn't seem to have changed since Jane Austen.

'I used to really want to achieve things,' Izzy said. 'I wanted to have a career and be independent: now look at me. I wish I could do something about it. It's maddening just having to wait and see what his wife will do next.'

'Is that how it is?'

'That's what it feels like. Or the kids. He said the other day, maybe when they're older, but how much older? How long does he expect me to wait? It's not going to be any easier to break up when they're older, in fact, it might even be worse.' Izzy was now chewing her lip uncertainly.

'Does he realise how you feel, about him being married and everything?' I concentrated on picking bits of lichen off a fallen twig. A tiny spider ran onto my leg, over my knee and into the grass again. A blackbird burbled peacefully over our heads. The scent of new-mown grass drifted in from next door's garden. I couldn't help noticing the contrast between the peacefulness of our surroundings and the soap-opera turbulence of Izzy's emotions.

Izzy sat back on her heels, balancing herself on her finger-tips. 'I think he thinks I'm okay with things the way they are.' She looked down at her knees. 'I'm so good at pretending. I'm always so cool with him, as if I couldn't care less.'

I frowned. 'Why?'

She shrugged. 'Dunno. I sort of feel it's what he wants, for me to be cool and not care very much.' She was starting to look miserable again. 'Trouble is, it's difficult to keep being like that. It's not how I really feel at all.'

'Don't like the sound of that.' I hadn't meant to say anything, it just popped out. 'It isn't good for you, all that mind-body separation stuff. You should tell him the truth, then at least you'd know where you are.'

'What d'you mean?' Izzy stood up, brushing down her skirt. A look of panic passed over her face. 'I can't possibly. Not yet, anyway. It might scare him away.'

'But if he says he loves you.' I stopped. 'Sorry.' But it wasn't real, was it, if Izzy was having to pretend all the time?

'Perhaps I should tell him.' She turned away. 'I'll think about it. See you then. What are you gonna do now?'

'I need to sort out Sapphy's stuff ... she's done another stunning painting. Honestly that cat will be in the Royal Academy before you can say Three Blind Mice. In fact that's the title of one of her paintings. I've put it in the shed to dry.'

Izzy giggled. 'Clever old Sapphy. I'll come over tomorrow and have a look. Sorry I can't stop now. See you later then.'

'Love ya, babe.' I watched her walk away.

But I was so afraid Izzy was cruisin' for a bruisin'. Heading for a fall.

. . .

I KNOCKED and put my head around Felix's door. 'Hi, Felix. Babe says supper in five minutes.'

He was sitting at his desk smoking and staring into space. Veils of smoke hung about the room.

'Are you okay?'

He roused himself. 'I'll be down in two shakes. I don't know, Milly: Edward Heath as our new Prime Minister? What d'you think, eh? Father's a carpenter, you know.'

I leaned against the door. 'Well, that's good, isn't it?' I'd never thought of Felix as a snob. I hoped he was just commenting.

'Bit of a change. Douglas-Home's an old Etonian, you know. First-class cricketer.' He began pushing himself up out of his chair. 'Don't worry, I won't be long. Can't be upsetting Babe by being late.' He smiled his sweet, sad smile, hauled himself to his feet and went over to the basin to wash his hands. He dried them and as he arranged the towel neatly over the rail, I saw that his hands were shaking. I hovered by the door, not sure whether to wait or not.

He stood for a moment staring across the room and following his gaze I noticed his eyes resting briefly on the photograph in the blue enamel frame on his desk. My eyes widened as I recognised the face. I was right. This was where I'd seen her before: the butterfly girl.

'My granddaughter Leonie. She lives with her mother, in Leatherhead actually, so not far away, but we've lost touch since her mother and I ... well, you know how these things are.'

I hadn't a clue but it was nice that he thought I might.

He turned on the hot tap again and picked up the soap. It slipped out of his hands and fell into the basin. He fished around for it and lathered vigorously. 'Didn't believe you could miss someone so badly. She was always my little girl. Just like to know how she is. You know. That everything's all right.'

He turned away from the basin, towelled his hands dry and gave his shoulders a little shake. 'Ah well,' he said, this time draping the towel over the edge of the basin. 'It's a lesson, isn't it? Not to get too attached.'

He turned towards me and I led the way, resisting the urge to dash back and hang the towel in its proper place on the towel rail. I closed the door behind us. Opposite, across the landing, Esme's door was closed too.

'Let's hope she's shut that dratted animal inside,' Felix said. At the top of the stairs he stopped suddenly and turned, almost cannoning into me. 'Better just—' He moved past me and went back and tried the door. He wasn't going to wash his hands *again,* was he? The door was firmly shut. Just checking, then. He sighed, turned again and set off slowly, lumbering down the stairs.

LATER THAT EVENING I sat two steps down from the upper landing, my book open on my lap. The familiar smell of beeswax furniture polish rose from the shadowy, lamp-lit hall.

A door handle rattled. Luke came out of the study. Faint strains of something classical seeped into the hall from behind him. He stood with his hands in his pockets, not looking at anything in particular. Pascale came into the hall from the kitchen passage, duster in hand, and started bustling about, lifting things up and putting them down again. She began to hum. I recognised *Jeanne Lorraine*.

'Hello Pascale,' Luke said after a moment or two, quietly so as not to frighten her.

Pascale jumped. '*Ah, Monsieur!* It is you, you make me a start. I am just put the house to bed.'

'Putting, Pascale,' Luke said gently. 'Putting.'

'Put-ting.'

'Have you seen Felix?' Luke said after a moment or two in which he walked up and down. Like a caged animal. *Tyger, tyger burning bright.* 'He's supposed to be coming down for a game of chess.'

'Maybe he forget.'

'Maybe. Well ...' He nodded and turned on his heel, hands still in his pockets. He strolled to the study door, looked around as though to make sure Felix wasn't lurking about somewhere in the shadows, and disappeared into the study.

Heavy footsteps descended the stairs from the floor above and Felix trudged past me, breathing noisily. 'Good evening, Milly. What do we have here?'

I lifted my book up for inspection.

'Can't see too well in this light,' he said. 'What is it?'

'Sorry. *Wuthering Heights.*'

'Ah, the great Emily. Are you enjoying her?'

I could hardly admit that the book gripped me to the extent that it gave me a pain in my inside. 'Very much, thank you.'

'Well, well. Read on. Or perhaps not in this light. You'll ruin your eyes, my dear.'

'Actually I'm kind of on my way up to bed.' Anyway that was an old wives' tale. It said on Woman's Hour it wasn't true.

He looked down at me kindly. 'Well, I am on pleasure bent and I'm late, so I'll bid you goodnight.'

'Goodnight, Felix. Sleep well.'

He turned right around and looked up at me. 'And goodnight to you too, young Milly. May all your dreams be pleasant ones and may you survive until the morning.'

'Cool,' I said, startled. 'It never crosses my mind that I might not survive until the morning.'

'Does it not? Ah, the confidence of youth. Well, goodnight.'

I wondered if he had been at the bottle again. I watched with interest as he reached the bottom of the stairs. Pascale was still fussing about below. She didn't seem to have heard us talking. She often didn't seem to hear. Of course she could be in the middle of a conversation with André; not all their conversations were out loud.

Felix stood on the bottom step, his long arms hanging by his side, watching as Pascale picked up one object after another and wiped it with her duster before replacing it carefully. He stumbled down the last step and moved towards her until he was standing close behind her. Still she didn't seem to realise anyone was there. I tensed. 'Pascale,' Felix burst out suddenly.

Pascale visibly jumped.

'What is it that makes you so absurdly content all the time?' he said. 'What is this amulet you have, this charm?'

Pascale turned around slowly and stood looking up at him reproachfully, her hands clasped in front of her at waist level. '*Mon Dieu, Monsieur,* for what you come behind and fright me like that? *Ah non, mais c'est beaucoup trop ça.*'

'I apologise,' Felix said. 'Not my intention to alarm you. Please accept my apologies, my dear madam.' He turned away, then back again. He reminded me of some large, lumbering animal, lost and sniffing the air for which direction to take. 'Wanted to ask you something. Now, what was it? Ah yes. Harrumph ... Hardly know anybody that's happy. No. Most people live lives of quiet desperation ... etcetera. But you – contented as a cushion all the time. I wish I knew your secret, that's all.'

'You know what is, *Monsieur*.' She picked up a brass ashtray and gave it an extra rub with her duster. 'It is *le bon Jésus, Monsieur*,' she said.

'Oh, for Pete's sake, madam, not that again. Christ, if he existed at all, was an ordinary man who died as ordinary men do for perfectly logical reasons which have nothing to do with the supernatural.' He shook his head at her. 'All the rest is myth and superstition. Do you really not know that?'

Just as well I hadn't told *him* about my mother materialising in the orchard.

Pascale's face took on the stubborn expression that I knew only too well. 'You believe what you like, *Monsieur*. Me, I know what I know.' She looked up at him for a long moment, then moved away and began to dust again.

Felix pursued her. 'So what is it that you know? Do you hear voices? Do you see visions?' His head jutted forward, the slope of his neck uncharacteristically belligerent. Oh dear. Whisky. I recognised the signs.

Pascale said calmly, 'I believe, *Monsieur*. Simply it is that I believe.'

'Ah well. Evolution, no doubt.' Felix nodded as if his suspicion was confirmed. 'It serves the species in some way for you to believe these things. There'll be some good scientific reason. Perhaps it's necessary for some of us to have a conscience to prevent us from ending this benighted human race once and for all.'

The study door opened and Luke came out. 'Hello, Felix. What's going on?' He looked from Pascale's peaceful face to Felix's irritated one.

'Hello, old chap.' Felix thrust his hands in his trouser pockets. 'Just trying to get Pascale here – asking her how – what makes her so – full of faith, etcetera. My argument is that there is a rational explanation for everything.'

Even my music and lights in the orchard? Maybe I actually did have to have a talk with Felix.

I sensed rather than saw Luke smile. 'It's no good trying to talk Pascale out of her beliefs, you'll be here all night and you still won't have got anywhere.' He turned back to the study. 'Ready for a game? I'm free now if it's a good time for you.'

'No, but – look at babies,' Felix persisted. 'Damn nuisance most of the time. But there they are, looking up at us with their charming little faces and big, wide-apart eyes – and why? To arouse our protective instincts so that we won't smash their heads in when we can't stand their crying – getting on our nerves – there's a good evolutionary reason, you see.'

The atmosphere below froze instantly into an ice-like stillness. Felix's voice died away. Pascale stood like a statue, her hand over her mouth. It was like the coming of the Snow Queen in Narnia. The hairs on the back of my neck prickled.

Luke cleared his throat and suddenly things were normal again. He turned back into the light streaming from the open study door. 'Well,' he said. 'Ready when you are.' He nodded to them both and strolled into the study, leaving the door ajar.

Pascale said, turning away, her voice a little shaky, 'Is no good, *Monsieur*, it make no matter what you tell me.' She looked at him for a long moment. 'I pity you, *Monsieur. Oui.* I pity you and I will pray for you.'

I stood up, suddenly conscious of eavesdropping, and called down the stairs, 'Just off to bed now. Goodnight!'

They looked up at me, their pale faces shadowed in the lamplight.

'Goodnight, my dear,' Felix said.

Nothing from Pascale. I turned to go, my heart beating extra hard. What was all that about, that sudden creepy silence and stillness as though someone had walked over someone else's grave?

Chapter 16

Silver Service

'Hello, Milly. On time again. Well done.'

'Hello, Mrs Booth.'

'Amy, please. How are you?'

'Fine thanks.'

'And the family? Luke – and—'

'We're all fine.'

'Oh *good*.'

This got us into the hall. I looked down at the gleaming parquet then at Amy who was surveying me with a pleased look as though I was a favourite child or pet. Today she wore tight blue jeans, high heels and a silky top like the one she'd had on last time only in turquoise instead of pink. Perhaps she had a whole drawerful. I looked down at my plain school shirt and sighed. Clothes were so unfair.

'Now I don't need you to do any actual cleaning today.' She turned to lead the way into the kitchen. I trailed after her. 'Can't have Luke accusing me of taking advantage.'

I'd been there about a minute and a half and she was talking about him again. 'He seemed a little surprised when

I reminded him you were working for me,' she said. 'I assumed he must know.'

'Oh, he knew,' I said. 'He was probably thinking about work. He gets a bit vague when he's thinking about a design. He's so busy at the moment.' And doesn't spend his entire time thinking about you.

'Perhaps he's worried your mother might not have approved. You doing a cleaning job, I mean.'

'My *mother*?' I trotted after her.

'Well, he is *in loco parentis*, isn't he? He feels very responsible for you.' She turned and gave me a soulful look. 'He feels that responsibility very deeply, you know, Milly.'

I pressed my lips together and turned away. So Luke had been talking to her about me, had he?

'Now – the silver,' Amy said, her heels dancing on the cold stone floor. 'For my dinner party on Saturday. I told you, didn't I? It could do with a polish. Luke's coming, of course.' She indicated the kitchen table on which, spread out like a burglar's haul on a dark-green cloth, was what looked like a whole canteen-full of silver, arranged in neat piles. Beside the cutlery sat a silver sugar bowl, a cream jug and two sets of salt, pepper and mustard pots with blue glass linings. My eyes widened.

'There is rather a lot of it, I suppose.' Her eyes shining, Amy picked up an enormous fork and examined it as if she'd never seen it before. 'See the crest? *Ever upward.* The family motto.'

'Cool. I'll get started then, shall I?' I picked up a tin of silver polish and shook it vigorously.

'I've commissioned him to make me a chair,' Amy said. 'I expect he's told you.'

'He did mention it.' I took a piece of cloth from the neatly folded pile on the table and tipped some polish onto it. 'He's not just any old furniture-maker, you know,' I reminded her, annoyed by her casual manner. 'He's an artist. A craftsman.' Deliberately I breathed in the sharp polish smell to calm myself.

'Oh, my dear, I know,' Amy said. 'I wanted the very best and obviously Luke Merryweather is it. I don't care what it will cost. Nobody else I know will have anything like it. Of course they will all be wanting him to make something for them now. This could be big for him, Milly. He takes his time, doesn't he? But he's such a charming man. He pops in quite often now and of course I've been out to his place at Leigh.'

I knew Amy had been out to the workshop but she made it sound as though she was there all the time. I picked up a large fork and looked at it. It felt more than ever as if things in our formerly quiet, contented life were changing. My spirits sank.

'I have sometimes wondered about Juno,' Amy said, pacing about. She seemed nervous. 'I haven't spoken to her about it but I gather from Mrs Murchison that she and Luke were – well – an item once.'

What? *Juno* and *Luke?*

'She says they used to do everything together. Quite a couple they were, she says. At the beginning, when he first came.'

'Really? You mean after my mother died?'

She nodded.

I rallied. 'Juno was probably just showing him the ropes,' I said. 'You know how people gossip in villages.'

I couldn't help noticing that she looked relieved. She leaned her hip against the table and watched as I worked. She seemed inclined to chat.

Juno and Luke? I polished feverishly, my heart thumping. I wasn't sure why I found the idea so upsetting. Maybe because neither of them had ever mentioned it? They weren't even particularly friendly now, not so's you'd notice. But perhaps I wasn't very good at noticing. Look at Izzy and Rob, I'd had no idea it was so serious till Izzy told me. But *Juno*?

'I'll just get on then, shall I?' I put down a massive fork and picked up another one. I was not going to be interrogated anymore about Luke.

'I'd better leave you to it,' Amy said. 'I need to look at my post. Oh and by the way, be a dear and make me a cup of coffee, will you? You know how to work the machine?'

'Sure,' I said gloomily. It couldn't be rocket science.

Chapter 17

The thrill of the chase

THERE HE WAS, WALKING PAST THE WINDOW. JUNO gave him a minute or two then slipped out of the office and across the road into Rennie's the bookshop. Luke was standing at the pay-desk, a book in his hand. She picked up a packet of batteries from the bin by the door and went to stand behind him. Aware that her hands were balled into fists by her sides she took a deep breath and consciously relaxed them. She touched him on the shoulder. 'Hello, Luke.'

He turned in surprise. 'Oh, hello. Not at work today?'

He didn't look particularly pleased to see her. Her spirits slumped. 'Just popped in for some batteries. How's things?'

'Fine. You?'

'Fine. You're looking well.' A pause ensued while Luke waited for the girl behind the counter to be free. She wasn't anything to look at: Juno dismissed her with a glance. The girl put a paperback book into a paper bag and gave it to the man in front of Luke in the queue. Juno blundered on. 'I made some cupcakes.'

'Cupcakes?'

'I made too many. I wondered if you'd like some for the workshop. For elevenses tomorrow. Jean-Paul too, of course.'

'Well ... that's very kind. Jean-Paul has a sweet tooth, he'll be delighted. Thank you.'

'I'll bring them over. After work maybe.'

'Right. Thanks.'

He moved forward and put the book he was holding on the counter. Juno moved up and stood close to him, close enough to smell the musky aftershave he always wore.

'Thought I'd get this for Milly,' he said over his shoulder and moved away slightly. 'Anything to encourage her.' He took a note out of his wallet and handed it to the girl behind the counter.

'What is it? Oh! A cookery book. That's nice. *Alice B. Toklas ... Cookbook*. I haven't heard of that one.'

'I think this will suit her. American, but she was born in France, the writer, so it's quite cosmopolitan, I think. Recommended by a friend.'

A friend? What friend? A woman friend? 'Ah ... I mean, good, if ... Milly could help with the cooking a bit more.' I mustn't be too obviously critical, he won't like that, she thought. All the same it was a bit much. There was absolutely nothing for Milly to do with Babe and Pascale running around after her. She was spoilt rotten.

'She does help,' Luke said as if reading her mind. 'She skivvies in the kitchen when she can get a look in. Peels things – you know. Lays the table. She pulls her weight.'

Juno felt reproved. 'Oh, of course, I wasn't saying – anyway, they're hopeless at that age, aren't they? Izzy's the same. Hopelessly impractical.'

He looked surprised but said after a moment, 'I must

admit, it's more in hope than expectation.' He accepted his change. 'Thanks.'

He'd hardly glanced at the girl. Juno forced her stomach to relax. Her jaw clenched. It didn't matter. Not any longer.

'She doesn't get much chance to be creative with Babe trying to get to the Aga and Pascale determinedly underfoot. It's cooking wars in there. Thanks, I'll manage without a bag.'

Juno laughed as though she understood and sympathised. 'Teenagers,' she said. 'Dreaming about. Heads in the clouds. Izzy's the same. Well, they're young, aren't they? Children still, really.' And don't you forget it, she thought, her heart pounding, as Luke wished her a casual goodbye. She was shaking. Milly is a child in your care. You have no right. If that is the way your mind is working.

She paid for the batteries which she neither needed nor wanted, thinking as she left the shop that she needn't have bought them, she could have just said she'd changed her mind and thrown them back in the bin. Stupid. Depression hit again. Her heart was thumping. She wasn't sure what she'd hoped for but whatever it was it hadn't happened.

Thinking about Milly she found herself shrivelling up inside with jealousy and what felt perilously like hate. It couldn't really be hate ... not for Milly ... but the fact was that from the sallow, skinny little girl she had been, all long legs, big eyes and temperament, over the last year Milly had filled out, calmed down and blossomed into a confident, beautiful young woman. And she was living in Luke's house! Juno simply couldn't bear it. They all dote on her, Juno thought. Even funny old Felix. They think she's God's gift.

But what about Luke? That's what was the important thing. Was Milly the one he wanted – his heart's desire?

The person without whom, if he was deprived of her, his heart would break? That was what she wanted to know.

Anyway, it would be wrong for him to be with her, her frantic thoughts darted off in the opposite direction. He was her guardian, someone could report them. Child abuse or something. Hmm, she thought, her jaw set. That could be an option, if all else failed.

Pam looked up from her desk and hissed, 'Where the hell have you been? Porky Pie's been in and she wasn't best pleased to find you away from your desk. I said you felt faint and went out for a breath of air but I don't think she believed me.'

'Oh, blow her,' Juno said. Cheered by the prospect of delivering cupcakes to a grateful Luke and Jean-Paul, the prospect of facing an annoyed supervisor paled into insignificance.

JUNO BANGED on the workshop door with her free hand. Nothing. She rapped again and heard Jean-Paul's voice. 'Coming. Hang on a sec.'

He opened the door and stared at her as though she was a stranger. His dark eyes moved to the plastic box in Juno's hand.

'Cupcakes,' Juno said with a big smile, her heart sinking. 'Didn't Luke say?'

'No ... sorry. We've been busy.'

Not too busy to buy Milly a cookery book. She strained her ears for any sounds coming from behind Jean-Paul. 'Is Luke here?'

'Sorry, no. He's just popped out to see Mrs Booth.'

'Amy? Whatever for?'

Jean-Paul looked surprised. 'She's a new client. And he's on his lunch break.'

'Oh, right.' She held out the box. Of course. She'd told Luke she'd come after work. That was before she'd remembered she had a teaching afternoon. Her spirits lifted a little. He might have waited for her if she'd kept to what she'd said.

It all seemed pointless now. Bloody Amy Booth. She was probably feeding Luke coffee and shortbread right this minute. Or lunch.

'Thanks. That's great. Fabulous.' He took the box and stood smiling at her as though she was a child to be placated.

'Well ... bye then.'

'Luke'll be really chuffed,' he said, taking a step back. Thanks again.'

You're a nice man, Juno thought, turning away. Trouble is, you're not Luke. I wonder, she thought. I don't seem to be getting anywhere. It might be time for Plan B.

SHE STOOD on the front doorstep. It was nearing the end of a long day and she was exhausted. Also annoyed, as she'd got back late from her half-day at the office, because of delivering the cupcakes, and had had to move almost immediately into teaching mode.

'Goodbye, Fiona. Well done. Thank your mother for the sweet peas, they're gorgeous. So kind. Now when you practise, remember your diaphragm. Put a belt around your ribs the way I showed you, not too tight, then when you need to breathe just relax your stomach. Ribs up all the time. You'll find all the breath you need. Good. Well done.' She closed the front door behind the girl and headed for the kitchen.

'Mum.' Izzy was standing in the doorway to the sitting-room. 'Can we talk? I thought she'd never go.'

'We did run over a bit but she's worth the trouble, I'm really pleased with the way she's coming on.' Juno started towards the kitchen. 'I'm just grabbing a coffee, would you like one? I'm gasping. I've only got ten minutes before Julia comes.'

'No. Can't you come and talk? I need us to talk.'

And I need a coffee. Juno sighed inwardly. At least Izzy was speaking to her. Perhaps this was going to be an apology and an explanation. Something worth hearing, anyway. She turned towards the armchairs in front of the glass doors. Izzy followed slowly. Juno threw herself into a chair and looked at her daughter, perplexed. Why were the young so selfish? She could just go and make herself a coffee anyway but Izzy was so prickly, if she turned down this olive branch she'd probably take umbrage and storm out. Maybe that's just what she should do. Maybe she shouldn't encourage Izzy to be so thoughtless. Honestly. All this mental energy wasted on a measly cup of coffee. Good God, she was seventeen, not seven.

Izzy perched on the arm of the chair opposite. Juno gazed at her unpeacefully.

'I need to ask you about my father.'

Suddenly breathless, Juno looked out of the window into the sunny garden. 'Of course you do,' she said after a long pause. 'I want us to talk about him too. I'd like to explain if I can. But not now, Izzy. Julia is due in five minutes. I can't cancel her lesson at this short notice. You do understand, don't you?' Izzy's expression was not encouraging but she nodded reluctantly. 'Come back when she's gone and we'll talk. And Izzy.' She pulled herself to her feet and looked down at Izzy, keeping her expression carefully neutral. 'I'm glad you've brought this up – no, honestly. We should have talked about it a long time ago.'

The doorbell rang. 'There's Julia now. Go and do something else for an hour and we'll talk when I'm finished.' She watched Izzy slope dejectedly out of the room. The doorbell rang again. She went through the kitchen and into the hall. As she put her hand on the door-latch a vivid image of Izzy's father came into her head and pain gripped her stomach so that she had to wait a full minute, and the doorbell had rung again, before she felt ready to open the door.

Chapter 18

Awfully like Mr Knightley

AFTER TEA, I LEANED MY BACK AGAINST THE SINK waiting for Pascale's next instruction. Babe had given up and left her to get on with prepping supper. I watched, fascinated as always by the dexterity of her knotted fingers neatly trussing the chicken we would eat that night. It was like watching people who knit. Their fingers know.

Now she was chopping onions at arms' length and blinking away the resulting tears with fierce grimaces.

'Shall I do that?'

'Is quicker to do myself. You peel potato. I make *galette*, ver' good. Also the beans. *Voila.*'

'Okay.' I sighed, tipped the potatoes into the sink bowl and reached for the peeler. I ought to make Pascale go and sit down but it would annoy her and I didn't want to disturb her good mood especially as Babe had given in and taken the afternoon off.

'Always your *maman* she tell you the stories,' Pascale said uneasily. A faint rosy pink flushed her cheeks. She slid a sly glance sideways at me, wiped her hands on a cloth, picked up the trussed chicken and toddled over to the fridge, talking quietly to herself. Or to André. Who could tell? It was a wonder we didn't all die of salmonella poisoning. While her back was turned I seized the cloth and threw it into the washing-machine. 'Ah, the story she recount,' Pascale said, slamming the fridge door. 'She sit you on the knee and she read you – *Barbar et Pierre Lapin et Madame Tiggiwinkle*. Again! Again! you cry.' Pascale's hands flew dramatically upward. I bit my lip. 'And again she read. *Quel bon coeur. Si gentille*. So kind heart, no? S*i altruiste*, give up her life, *aucune plainte* ... you understand?'

Although I sensed something backhanded behind these remarks, I loved it when Pascale went on like this because when she started on about Miranda she forgot to snipe at me and became quite human. But there was something strange and feverish about these forays into the past. It never felt quite real. I sometimes felt quite strongly that she was making it up. And then I would think, but that's crazy. Why would she do that?

LATER THAT EVENING, sprawled face-down on my bed with a pillow over my head, I tried to stop agonising about the awful way human beings went on – about their cruelty and greed and general nastiness. Of course it had only been a butterfly and a damaged one at that ... but the problem was it wasn't always just a butterfly. Human beings did this kind of thing to each other all the time the world over, and sometimes I just couldn't bear it.

I felt a tiny movement, like the brush of an eyelash, on the back of my hand. I lifted a corner of the pillow and looked down at my hand. A large bluebottle was walking across it. I was about to shake it off – as Babe always said, you never knew what it had been sitting on before it came and sat on you – when a ray of evening sunshine, gleaming out from behind a cloud, beamed in through the window and shone directly onto the fly.

Just look at that! I sat up on my elbows and leaned forward, enraptured by the beauty of the blue-green luminescence of its back, the blackness of its legs and face. The fly was rubbing its hands together as if about to set to and beat someone up. The pillow fell onto the floor.

Perhaps the universe was trying to tell me something. Maybe someone was trying to say that given half a chance, everything, everyone was beautiful if you looked at them in the right light.

Even Pascale?

Leonie? Because from the moment I'd seen the photograph in Felix's room I'd been haunted by the contrast between that smiling, rosy face – the person whom Felix remembered as a sweet, affectionate little girl – and the angry, flint-eyed little horror I'd met in town.

Self-delusion, that's what it was. But was it better for him to go on thinking of her the way he remembered her than to discover the truth? Was knowing the truth always the best outcome?

It was so tempting to think I might be able to do something about it ... get them back together. Felix missed her so much. For a moment I let myself indulge in a fanciful dream where noble Milly discovers lost Leonie, reforms her and brings her back to her waiting grandfather's loving arms.

Oh, for goodness sake! I jumped off the bed and stood for a moment, thinking. I mustn't be an Emma. She wouldn't mind her own business and look where that got her. Come to think of it, what would Jane Austen advise? She'd obviously thought about this kind of situation a fair bit or she couldn't have written the novel. Then there was Izzy. Ought I to do something to help her? And what about Esme and her lost love? Maybe I should try to find out more about that, see if there was anything that could be done there.

I wished I could ask Luke. Luke was a bit like Mr Knightly, wasn't he? Mr Knightly was almost like a guardian to Emma and he loved her but he didn't tell her, not until she'd almost given up hope. Only that wasn't right because I didn't love Luke and he didn't love me. But Mr Knightly wasn't afraid to tick Emma off, put her in her place when she got too full of herself, was he? That was like Luke, I thought uncomfortably, remembering the episode in the kitchen earlier that day.

Luke had come home early for once and had stood in the kitchen, leaning one arm on the dresser and listening while Pascale complained about Felix. Pascale was upset because once again Felix had insisted on cleaning his room himself. 'How can he clean a room, a man like that?' she moaned, hobbling over to the sink holding the colander full of runner beans. 'He not know how to clean a room! For what use if he not let Baby do the work? Is not her job? And now Madame Esme say there is a mouse. A mouse! A mouse is not like cat or dog – *bien alors*, they are not domesticate, these mouses. The room will be very bad, not good at all, And why he stay in the room so long every day, no hardly go out?'

'It is his room,' Luke said mildly. 'He can stay there all day if he wants to.'

Pascale banged the colander down on the draining board. 'Baby she come soon,' she said. '*J'ai changé d'avis.* Tonight she cook.'

It was true that Felix clung to his room like a field mouse to its nest. He much preferred, he had told me, to climb into an unmade bed. It was cosier, he explained, somewhat defiantly, when I'd remonstrated with him in the early days before he'd managed to make me understand that when he said he wanted to be left alone he really meant it.

'He does go out on his bike,' Luke said placatingly, taking a bottle of wine out of the wine rack. 'And he's extremely fastidious personally, whatever his room may be like. I've never thought it was my business to intrude on his personal space.'

'He not think Baby she clean the room properly?' Pascale huffed. 'He take the vacuum up there, is true,' she said, subsiding onto a chair. 'But he got too many book. What he want with all these book?' She waved her hands in a gesture of despair.

Arranging flowers in the sink, I hoped they would forget I was there and carry on talking. Pascale was on a roll, she'd probably start on about me next. I glanced sideways at Luke who was uncorking the wine. He turned around and caught my eye. 'Those are nice, Milly, very attractive, I like those yellow ones. I thought we'd have some wine with our dinner, to celebrate.'

I turned around. 'What are we celebrating? Has *Amy* found you another commission? Honestly, that woman, she's like a teenager with a crush—'

'Milly,' Luke said sharply. 'Show some respect. Don't talk about Mrs Booth like that. Anyway, wouldn't you be better doing the flowers in the scullery? Babe will be in to cook supper in a minute, she'll need the sink.

'Sor-*ry*.' Shocked and embarrassed I turned back to the sink. Luke knew I would have moved the moment Babe needed the sink. He knew I was thoughtful, considerate. What had got into him? Flushing, I lifted the tall glass vase with the shrivelled flowers in it and carried it slowly and with dignity through to the scullery. I shall ignore that remark, I told myself. I shall pretend it never happened. I shall be pleasant and calm and dignified, just to show him.

I came back into the kitchen to collect the fresh flowers, walking pleasantly and calmly and with dignity, but it was wasted because Luke had gone.

Chapter 19

The other other woman

'I know it isn't reasonable,' Juno said. 'I don't expect you to understand.'

'I'm trying,' Izzy said. She sat on a stool near Juno's feet, a soaked cotton handkerchief clenched in her fist. 'Honestly, I am. It's just – how could you do it? How could you keep all the stuff he sent me, leave me thinking he'd forgotten about me, that he didn't care. How could you? Look – I know he hurt you, yeah? I know how you feel.'

Juno turned stony eyes onto her daughter. 'Please don't insult me by telling me you know how I feel. You have absolutely no idea how I feel. You were a little girl when your father left, far too young to understand. I loved and trusted him and he went off and found somebody else.'

'Who? Who was she?'

'I can't tell you that.'

'Why not? Why can't you? I'm not a child, why do you always have to treat me like a child?'

Perhaps because you behave like one, Juno thought. 'I can't tell you, Izzy. There are reasons, good reasons.'

'Do I know her then?'

Juno swallowed. This was turning out to be even more difficult than she had imagined it might be, lying in bed at night visualising the day when she would have to say all this to Izzy, because of course she had known that day would come. 'It's not important, now, who it was. It wasn't Claire who he's with now. He met Claire after he left us.'

'What happened to the other one, the person he—'

'It wasn't love,' Juno said bitterly, as much to herself as to Izzy. 'He never claimed to love her.'

'What was it then?'

'Oh, for goodness' sake.' She sighed. 'Attraction. Novelty. You know what men are like. Or perhaps you don't, not yet. You'll find out.'

'You make it sound as though they're all like that. They're not.'

'You mean Luke I suppose. Well. Luke is a one-off. It didn't seem to make much difference to your father at the time, that it wasn't love.'

'Do you think men often ... sort of stray? Take up with people who aren't the person they're married to?'

'It happens. It doesn't make it any less painful at the time, when you're the one left.'

Izzy was silent for a while. Then she said, 'What happened to her? If Dad isn't with her now? Did they break up?'

Juno looked up at the ceiling, then out of the window. After a long pause she said, 'She died.'

Izzy drew in her breath. 'Jeez. How?'

'I really don't want to talk about this.'

'But I have to know. Can't you see I have to know? It's my father we're talking about. I have to know if there was a good reason for why he did it—'

'A good reason?'

'No ... I'm sorry ... you know what I mean. If he really fell in love with her ... but you said he didn't ... it's just if I knew who it was ...'

'It was Miranda.'

'Miranda who?'

'Milly's mother. The girl next door.'

Izzy's mouth fell open. '*What?*... Oh sugar.'

'Now do you see why I didn't want to tell you? What good does it do, your knowing? Does it make you feel any better knowing about it? It was a long time ago. I don't want it to make a difference to you and Milly. It's not her fault.'

'Does Milly know?'

'Of course not. You *must not* say anything. No – Izzy, listen. She mustn't know. There are enough—'

'Enough what?'

'There are things. About Miranda.' She shook her head irritably. 'Look. This is all in the past. It won't do any good to go raking things up.'

'What things?'

'Izzy, *stop*. Don't keep pushing.' Here I am, she thought, begging Izzy to let things be, when I've spent the last ten years trying to get Luke to tell Milly the truth.

'Milly deserves to know the truth. Honestly, the way she goes on about her perfect mother ... She'd hate not to know.' She twisted the soaking handkerchief around her finger.

'Izzy, don't you dare. You mustn't tell her. Let it alone.'

'Okay, okay, keep your hair on. Does Luke know?'

Juno blinked. She said slowly, 'I don't think so, unless Pascale found out and told him. But even if Pascale did know, she was so besotted with Miranda she would probably have kept her secret. I can't see her telling Luke.

Remember that Luke and Miranda were very close as children, almost like brother and sister.'

'How long did it go on for? Dad and – Miranda, I mean.'

'About a year, I think. Up until the time she died.'

'Golly, poor Dad. I mean I know it's awful, but her dying like that.'

'I don't think you need spare any sympathy for your father.'

'Of course not. No. But all the same.'

Juno closed her eyes. It's not deliberate, she told herself. She's young. She hasn't a clue.

'I still think Milly ought to be told.'

Juno leaned forward. 'Izzy, think how she would feel. You're not thinking. You're upset, and when you're upset somebody's liable to get hurt.'

'That's not a very nice thing to say.'

'I'm sorry. I happen to know you rather well.' Juno sat back, exhausted.

'I didn't mean to upset you.'

'Look, Izzy. When Mike left, you were a child. I tried not to let you see how much I was hurting. You're seventeen now, practically grown up. Do I really have to explain how I'm feeling about this? Out of the blue you announce that you've found some letters from your father that you insist you didn't know about and accuse me of concealing them from you.' She stopped, struggling for breath, hearing the self-pity in her voice. 'I'm sorry. I'm finding it hard to do this. It's so – so unfair.'

'I'm sorry, Mum.' Izzy scrubbed her eyes with her balled up hanky. 'I didn't realise you were so – hung up about it still. I'm sorry. Perhaps you did tell me about the letters.'

'I can assure you that I did. You didn't want to know.'

'What?'

'I put the letters to one side because I didn't want you to be upset. You reacted so violently to them. You were so angry with him.'

'I'd forgotten.'

'It was a long time ago, Izzy. Look, I could do with a cup of tea. I expect you could too. Would you make some, please?' She had to have a few moments on her own.

She heard Izzy moving about in the kitchen, filling the kettle, the chink of mugs on the table. She felt the beginnings of a headache. She got up. 'I'm going for a walk.'

'Mum.' Izzy stood at the kitchen door. 'What about your tea?'

'I'll have it later. We'll talk in the morning.'

'Mum.' She came into the room holding a tea towel. She looked miserable. She seemed to have shrunk. My little girl, Juno thought. What am I doing? Izzy came and put her arms around her. 'Mum, I'm sorry. I didn't mean to hurt you. Mum.'

Rigid with tension, Juno relented at last and held her lightly. After a moment or two she gently pushed her away. 'It's all right. I'm not angry with you. I need to think.'

'Do you have to go out? It's getting dark. Where will you go?'

'I won't be long. An hour. I promise. We'll talk again tomorrow.'

She'd managed to control herself so far but she was weakening, the desire to reveal growing by the minute, the temptation to blast the complacency off Izzy's face. They thought they knew everything, the young. Well, they didn't. If this conversation went on she'd let it all out, she'd tell everything. She'd never been good at keeping secrets.

What she needed was to see Luke.

. . .

He was sitting in the pool of light from the standard lamp, in the lumpy old chair with the stuffing coming out of the arms that was always on the verge of being thrown out. Once it had even got as far as the front door, waiting for Sam the rag and bone man, but somehow the next day there it was back in its place again.

Watching him from outside the window, from the garden where moths fluttered and the darkness gathered around her, Juno thought how typical it was of Luke to be sitting in that old chair. Two much newer, pale-blue damask-covered armchairs sat on either side of the old grey stone fireplace. Along the polished wooden mantle-shelf over the fire Milly's grandparents' china ornaments were arranged, the order unchanged during all the years he had been here: the pair of orange china greyhounds on their blue bases in the centre, the Dresden shepherd and shepherdess at each end, and galloping along the length of the mantle the set of Chinese carved wooden horses that had been her grandfather's favourites.

Luke's head supported by his hand was tilted sideways, his elbow leaning on the arm of his chair, his book balanced on his lap. He was wearing the heathery wool sweater Juno had always loved and his old brown corduroys. She recognised the purple socks as a pair Milly had painstakingly knitted for him one Christmas: it had taken her for ever with frequent visits to Juno for help when things went wrong. Luke's shoeless feet, neatly crossed at the ankles, rested on the wide square stool with the curved painted legs and tapestry top that Cathy, Milly's grandmother, had made.

Juno knew that Luke preferred this small sitting-room to the more formal drawing-room across the hall. Nothing much in the house had been altered or moved since Milly's grandparents' deaths apart from some slight adjustments for the convenience of the lodgers. Despite eleven years of occupation the situation still had a temporary feel. Luke was like somebody house-sitting, waiting patiently for the owners' return.

Juno leaned forward and tapped gently on the glass. Luke lifted his head and looked towards the window. She opened her mouth ready to call out but he turned his head back again and resumed his reading. He hadn't seen her.

She felt that she had become a ghost, invisible. She turned her back on the window and leaned against the wooden frame, trembling. It had grown dark and moths flickered, attracted by the lighted window, blundering against the glass. She would have to go in through the kitchen if she couldn't attract his attention this way. But that might mean running into Babe who would take a dim view of this late visit. Honestly, you would think she owned the place. Owned Luke.

She felt so confused. Despite everything, she still wanted him. If only she could melt through the glass and appear miraculously in front of him, climb onto his knee and find herself enclosed within those long, strong arms as once she'd seen Milly be when she was a little girl. She still longed for the right, that once so briefly she had known, to kiss his eyelids and his mouth and to bury her face in his neck. For him to look at her again with love instead of kindly indifference.

Except that it had never been love, had it? Not on his side. And whatever it was, he had withdrawn it and left her swinging in the cold, changed for ever, wretched for ever, now she had known what love was, and longing. Knowing that one person and one person only could make her feel the way she had felt for that brief period, and that that person was for ever denied to her, was shattering. A sort of death.

She was turning away from the window when a crack of bright light appeared in the shadows of the room and a door opened. Milly stood there in the doorway, slender and tall in jeans and a purple jersey. The passage light cast a golden nimbus of light over her auburn hair, turning it extravagantly rich and alive. She smiled and spoke but Juno, straining to hear, could hear nothing. Luke said something in return and Milly threw back her head and laughed, the long pale column of her neck gleaming in the soft light. Juno held her breath, her heart pounding.

Milly lifted her hand in a little wave and left, smiling around the door until the last moment. When she had gone Luke stared at the door for a few seconds then closed his eyes and let his head drop back. Juno, about to turn away for a second time, turned back, caught by the expression on his face, plain and undisguised. No one could doubt that look of pain, of turbulent emotion.

She turned away, her heart thumping heavily, coldness in the pit of her stomach. It was true then, the proof she had been looking for. This was what he wanted, his heart's desire. Milly. She hardened her resolve, sure now what she had to do. Luke to have his heart's desire? No. Absolutely not. That could never be.

Chapter 20

Could this be what he's looking for?

'I WANT EVERYTHING TO SPARKLE TODAY,' AMY SAID. We were standing just inside the front door. 'Because of Saturday evening. Luke's coming, you know of course. The floor in here,' she said, ticking off on her fingers. 'And I'd like you to vacuum the drawing-room. Dusting, of course, and the second bathroom for my guests, and coats will be going in the spare room so if you could give that a quick going-over. Just a quick whip around, it shouldn't be too bad, nobody's been in there since you did it last. What have you been up to since I saw you last?'

'I had some papers to finish for college,' I said, walking purposefully towards the cupboard under the stairs.

Amy trotted after me. 'Papers?'

'Preliminary reading. Critical essays. That sort of thing. For university in September.' I opened the cupboard door.

Amy stood watching me. 'Oh yes, you're off to St Andrews. How exciting for you. The world opening up at your feet.'

'I'll start upstairs, shall I?'

'I'd like you to do the drawing-room first. Luke's

popping in this morning and he always likes to have coffee in there.'

Really? I thought. This didn't sound like the Luke I knew. In the kitchen leaning against the draining-board was more his style. The woman was delusional.

'He's bringing the plans for the chair he's making for me.' She spun around, her fingers laced under her chin, her eyes flicking again and again to the vast, gold-framed hall mirror in which no doubt her ravishing image was reflected.

'Well, I'll get on then,' I said, diving into the cupboard. 'Lots to do.'

'Righto! If I think of anything else I'll let you know ... oh yes!' But with my head buried among the brooms and mops I decided not to hear.

You don't really like her, Luke, do you? Hardly aware of what I was doing, I vacuumed the pistachio-green carpet in the drawing-room as though my life depended on it. It was an elegant room, with green walls, green and white chintz covers on the three-piece suite and flowers everywhere. I thought about the study at home in which Luke virtually lived, and Grandma's little sitting-room where for a change he sometimes went to ground. Half Moon wasn't his home really, the home he would have chosen; it was still Grandpa and Grandma's house. It was as if he was treading water, it occurred to me suddenly, waiting for something.

Perhaps this was it.

Oh help.

The front doorbell rang as I was polishing the hall parquet with the mop and special floor polish Amy kept in a can under the kitchen sink – she had decided she didn't approve of our Glo-Coat. Mop in hand I went to open the door. Luke stood on the doorstep with a cardboard folder under one arm. He looked for a fraction of a second completely dumbfounded to see me, then his face smoothed over and his expression turned to surprise and pleasure. 'Hello, Milly. I'd forgotten you'd be here. How's it going?' His eyes were warm. Perhaps he was sorry for snapping at me. We'd hardly spoken since.

Amy's heels clicked urgently across the parquet behind me. 'Luke! There you are. Bless you for coming.' I stood aside and she put out a hand and drew him in. She bent her cheek towards him. Luke, I was glad to see, neglected to take the hint.

Amy said, 'I've got coffee ready for you in the drawing-room. You've brought the designs! That's wonderful. You know I've spoken to Annabel,' she said, ushering him away and completely ignoring me. 'Annabel Exton? Husband's the oil chappy. Pots of money, of course. She's dying to meet you.' She was lit up like a neon sign.

With a comical look at me over his shoulder Luke allowed himself to be led away. Amy's high voice fluted all the way down the hall, the drawing-room door closed and peace reigned once more.

I went back to my mop and finished the hall floor. The mop had a ducky little tin you sat it in when it wasn't in use but even that couldn't entirely cheer my dark mood.

In the kitchen I helped myself to a mug of Nescafé and slumped into a chair. I bit gloomily into a Jacob's butter-cream sandwich (not for the staff the glories of shortbread) and wondered how things were going in the drawing-room. I couldn't stop thinking about Amy and Luke closeted in there. '*Merde,*' I muttered. It didn't sound so bad in French.

The drawing-room door opened as I was lugging the Hoover over to the stairs. 'I'll just get them,' Amy said, bustling out into the hall.

I put my foot on the bottom step, seized the Hoover by

its handle and braced myself to take its weight. I heard rapid footsteps, felt a hand cover mine and the weight of the Hoover suddenly lifted. 'This is far too heavy for you,' Luke said impatiently. 'Where d'you want it?'

Honestly! Of course it wasn't too heavy for me. But I couldn't help feeling pleased all the same, if only because of the expression on Amy's face. She was standing by the drawing-room door looking irritated. 'I'm sure Milly can manage,' she said crossly.

'Yes, I can – honestly—'

'Nonsense.' His hand was warm over mine. I let go. 'Only take a moment. Now, where?'

'Upstairs.' I leapt up behind him two at a time, my face hot. 'Thanks. That's lovely.'

'Be sure you give the bathroom a good clean,' Amy called up the stairs as Luke strode into the drawing-room again.

Yes, ma'am.

Chapter 21
Being a bitch isn't as pain-free as you might think

JUNO HAD SLEPT BADLY, DREAMING OF MIKE. THE bitter anger she'd felt over his affair with Miranda had faded over the years to the dull ache of hurt pride, an ache that had vanished in the white heat of her unrequited passion for Luke. But she could still, sometimes, most often in sleep, feel again the sadness and disappointment of that betrayal.

In her dream she'd been on-stage, singing. There was a barrier across the middle of the stage and Mike was on the other side of the screen; not only could he not see her, he couldn't hear her either. She was singing her very best, liquid gold pouring from her throat the way it only did in dreams, better than anything she could achieve in real life. The sounds she was making were heavenly, heart-breaking. If she could only make Mike hear her voice he would love her again, he couldn't help it, he would be enchanted despite himself. But he couldn't hear her. It was all for nothing, all the effort, all her genius, all for nothing.

She woke in tears and the ache stayed with her all morning. She mooched around the house, desperate for company. Even Izzy, prickly as she was at the moment, would be better than nothing but Izzy was nowhere to be seen.

She decided to take some things to the charity shop to give herself an excuse to go out. Walking along the high street she glanced over her shoulder and saw Milly, the last person on earth she felt she could face at the moment, rapidly catching her up on the other side of the road. And oh joy, she'd seen her and was crossing the road, smiling her wide, joyous smile. She was always so fucking *happy*, for goodness' sake.

'Hey, Juno!'

'Hello, Milly.' I've been so off with her lately, Juno thought. I don't deserve that big smile. 'What have you been up to?'

'Oh, doing a bit of college work. Not much, to be honest. Enjoying the summer.'

'So you're getting ready for college. That must be exciting.'

'Yes, they've sent quite a long reading list. It's going to be strange, leaving home. I've never been away before, not for any length of time. Is that bag for the charity shop?'

'Yes. I thought I'd have a bit of a clear out.'

Milly fell into step beside her, slowing her pace.

You don't have to slow down, Juno thought, irritated. I can race along too, if I need to. It's just I'm not in a particular hurry so there's no need. 'It will change things, won't it?' she said a little sharply, 'your starting to be independent. Quite a relief for Luke, don't you think?'

'Sorry?'

'Oh, you know what I mean. Luke will start to feel free to live his own life again.' Once he's fulfilled his obligation to your daft mother, was what she didn't add, but she could see from Milly's face that she'd got the implication.

Milly's face was a picture.

'Well. I expect he'll give you plenty of warning before making any big changes.'

They came to the Sue Ryder shop and Juno disappeared inside, leaving Milly waiting. When she came out again Milly said, 'I don't think anything can really change until I come of age. I won't be twenty-one for a while. Anyway, gosh, Half Moon is Luke's home now. Where would he go?' They set off walking again.

'I should think the world will be his oyster, don't you, once he decides to make a move?' Juno decided that she'd gone far enough for the moment. A shadow had come over Milly's face. 'Anyway,' she said, 'where are you off to?'

Milly's face cleared 'Doing some shopping for Babe. She's run out of Carnation. And of course, Pascale can't stand Carnation so there's bound to be a stand-off.'

'Luke was saying,' Juno said. 'He says Pascale does tend to interfere.'

Milly registered surprise. 'Babe is very patient.'

They had come to a stop outside Pete's Coffee and Milk Bar. 'Um,' Milly said, 'have you time for a coffee?'

'Okay,' Juno said, surprised. 'A quick one.'

'Oh good. It would be nice to catch up. On me, I've been paid.' She pushed open the door and stood aside to let Juno go in first. The delicious scent of coffee and fresh croissants hit Juno's nostrils. A young girl came up to them, smiling.

'Hi, Lucy,' Milly said.

The girl's blonde hair and pretty, tanned face were set off by a cornflower-blue scoop-necked blouse that enhanced the blue of her eyes. 'Hi, Milly,' she said, smiling.

'Sit down and I'll come and take your order.' Her teeth were perfect, Juno noticed, and her bottom as she turned away was neat, round and sexy in slim blue jeans. Juno frowned. Izzy was always on at her to buy jeans. She followed Milly to a table in the corner, put her handbag on the table and settled into a chair. Milly sat down opposite her.

'How are you getting on with Amy?' Juno asked.

A cloud passed over Milly's normally radiant face. 'She's okay.'

'Only okay?'

'It's a bit embarrassing. She's so gone on Luke. She can't stop talking about him.'

'Really?'

'She is, you should hear her, it's really embarrassing.' Milly's face was pink.

Juno felt as though her heart had missed a beat. An arrow pointing forward seemed to light up inside her head.

Lucy arrived and stood by their table, pad in hand. 'What would you like?' she asked, her eyes darting around the room and back to them. Her shiny blonde hair was held back in a ponytail by a blue ribbon, and several silver rings decorated her delicate fingers.

'Just black coffee, please,' Juno said. Even that sounded apologetic. It's the way I say it, she thought, her momentary elation subsiding.

'Could I have a milkshake?' Milly said. 'Strawberry? Thanks.'

On the other hand, Juno thought, Milly didn't seem particularly upset by the thought of Amy being keen on Luke. Annoyed, possibly, but not upset. If she cared for him she'd be jealous, surely. Wouldn't she? 'Pretty girl,' she said, watching Lucy hurry away.

Milly nodded. 'She's all sorted, lucky thing, she's going to art college in London.'

'Good for her. Well, about Amy. Goodness. Poor Luke.'

Milly shrugged. 'I dunno. If he minded he wouldn't be around there so much, would he?'

'Is he? Around there a lot, I mean.'

'He was there today.' Milly did look a little unhappy. 'Do you think Luke's attractive?'

'I'm sorry?'

'Do you think he's attractive? You know. To women.'

Juno gave a little laugh. She put a hand out and moved the tiny flower vase on the table one inch to the right. 'That's an odd question.'

'Not really. It's hard for me to tell, being so – well – close. Sometimes I wonder what he looks like to other people.'

'Well ... he is attractive, I suppose. Evidently Amy thinks so.'

'Do you?'

She's heard something, Juno thought. Somebody's told her about Luke and me. 'Well, yes ... I suppose. What's brought this on?'

Milly looked away. She shrugged. 'It's not important. I'm just curious. Just Amy, I expect, being silly about him. It makes him look sort of different.'

'Seeing him through other people's eyes?'

'From a distance instead of so close up all the time.' She moved restlessly. 'Oh, well.' She glanced at Juno then away again. 'It's funny you and Luke haven't got together, in a way. Living next door and everything. I know he likes you.'

She *had* heard something. Juno felt a flush rise up her neck. 'He's not interested in me. We know each other too well, I expect.' She said fiercely, 'You know Milly, you really should try to get out more.'

'Sorry?'

Juno hesitated then made up her mind. She leaned forward to add emphasis to her words. 'I've got a lovely young fellow coming to me at the moment. Nice tenor voice. I don't get many boys of that age, it's mostly women or girls, but this lad Stephen is really talented. He's in his last year at the grammar school and they're putting on the Mikado. I could introduce you, I'm sure you'd get on.' She stopped. Milly was looking at her slightly incredulously. 'Just an idea,' Juno said, bending down to get a handkerchief out of her handbag.

'Actually,' Milly said, looking flustered, 'I haven't really got time at the moment. Too much going on. But thanks for the suggestion.'

'What?' Juno demanded. She couldn't seem to help herself. 'What have you got going on? Nothing. It's just an excuse.' Her breathing accelerated. She took a deep breath and released it slowly. Sometimes she felt that the line between control and complete disintegration was the width of a hair.

'I'm happy as I am,' Milly said. She looked puzzled.

'Luke would like it,' Juno said, euphoria flooding through her.

'I'm sorry?'

'Luke. I'm sure he would like you to be more independent.' It was the danger that gave her that buzz. Taking a risk. 'He won't always be there for you, you know, Milly.'

Milly looked horrified. Their drinks arrived in an awkward silence. Juno's heart was thumping. 'Thanks,' she said to Lucy, her voice firm.

'I don't understand,' Milly said. 'Why should it matter to Luke if I go out or not? What are you trying to say?'

'I just mean it might share the burden a bit. If you saw other people sometimes, not just him.'

'The burden,' Milly said. 'I've never thought of myself as a burden. I mean – look, has he said something?'

Juno paused and sipped her coffee. The feeling of power lingered. The silence lengthened. She became aware that somewhere in the background Johnny Halliday was singing ...

Souvenirs, souvenirs de nos beaux jours de l'été...

'Well, has he?'

'Of course not, Milly.' Juno looked down at her cup.

Milly leaned forward. 'He has. He's talked to you about me.'

'Milly, we've always talked about you. Of course we have.'

'I'd rather you didn't, thanks.'

'He cares about you. He's concerned.'

'What about? I'm perfectly okay as I am. What's all this about?'

She was cross now. Good.

Inspiration struck. 'You have these nightmares,' Juno said.

'Ohhh, is that what this is about?' Relief loosened her face. She took hold of the straw in her milkshake and sucked, like a child. 'Golly, that's good! They're a pain, of course they are. But Luke doesn't know why I have them. Nobody does.'

'So he says,' Juno said, her voice half-muffled by her coffee cup as she took another sip. Another buzz.

'He doesn't, he'd have told me. What are you trying to

say?' She peered at Juno over the top of a mound of pink foam.

Juno shook her head. Her mood was now bordering on dangerous. 'Milly, changing the subject, do you really not remember your mother at all?' Her hand shook as she placed her cup carefully back in its saucer. 'You were six when the accident happened. I would have thought you'd remember something of your life before that.'

Milly shook her head, her face sad. 'Nothing. Sometimes there's a flash. Sometimes I kind of feel her, as if she's standing near me, but it's not like a memory, it's like – now. As if she's here.'

Let's hope not, Juno thought.

Milly looked as though she was about to continue, but stopped, eyelids lowered, then sucked up the last of her milkshake.

Juno wondered if Milly had been about to tell her about the music she'd heard in the orchard that Izzy had told her about. The lights. Milly's sense that her mother had visited her. Would she say anything? How seriously had she taken the whole phenomenon, or had she persuaded herself that she was imagining things? Juno watched her face.

'The other night,' Milly said. 'I don't know if Izzy told you.'

'About what?' Here it came. Juno's heart started beating unpleasantly hard.

'It sounds daft, I know. I was in the attic.' She paused, looked away as if choosing her words carefully, then looked straight at Juno. 'I heard this music coming from the garden. I did honestly hear it. I went down to look and I saw lights and I felt as though someone was there. I only saw a sort of ball of light, not a person or anything but the music was my mother's most favourite song ... that was the strange part ...

that was what made me think it was her, my mother. That she'd come back to tell me something ... to warn me ... something. It felt urgent, if you know what I mean. It wasn't peaceful. I don't know how to explain.'

Juno swallowed. 'How very extraordinary.' Her voice was shaking. She cleared her throat. 'Has it happened again?'

'No, but I think it will. I can feel something building up. Like before a thunderstorm.'

'Well,' Juno said. 'You must say if it does.' She remembered that when Milly was a small child she had sometimes had intuitions about people. She had made, Juno remembered now, some strangely prophetic remarks. At first they had put it down to coincidence, but as time went on it had become almost a matter of concern. And then when she was around five years old it had stopped, and everyone had forgotten about it. But maybe there was something there, an ability, something left over from that childhood gift.

It was thought by some people, usually the rather wacky ones – but hey, as Luke always said, it took all sorts – that some children came into the world, as some poet said, *'trailing clouds of glory,'* still with the down of other worlds on them, before developing feathers of their own. Juno remembered some intense conversations with Luke on this subject. Of course, he tended to believe unbelievable things; his openness to new ideas, some might say his gullibility, was part of his charm. 'Well,' Juno said again.

'I wish you would tell me about her,' Milly said. 'I've been wanting to ask you. It's so awful that I can't remember anything about her. Babe says it's the shock of what happened, and it was a shock, of course, but I so hoped it would wear off and that I'd remember her, a bit.' She shook her head, her expression suddenly desolate.

'I didn't know her that well.' Juno's mind was still on the extraordinary story Milly had just told her. Surely ... surely this was all down to her imagination, wasn't it? It couldn't be Miranda, back from the dead. For heaven's sake, it was impossible. It was just that Milly seemed so convinced. Anyway, even if it was Miranda, she couldn't do anything. She wasn't real.

This was ridiculous. It was important not to panic.

'But Amy says you were best friends. According to Mrs Murchison.'

'How would she know? She didn't even have the post office then.'

'Someone told her, I think.'

'Oh, village gossip, what do they know? I knew your mother, of course. We used to chat sometimes. We went to the cinema together once or twice when Mike and I first came to live here but that tailed off. She loved the cinema, theatre, anything like that. Of course she was a performer. Or had been. She was good fun. Attractive, of course.'

'I know, I've got photos. But what was she like as a person? Did you see her with me?'

Juno said, after a pause, 'Not often, no. We hadn't been here long ourselves, remember. It takes time to get to know new neighbours, doesn't it?'

'S'pose so.' She looked so disappointed. She sat back and looked around the small café. Several people had come in, mostly couples. It's always couples, Juno thought.

Retiens la nuit pour nous deux, sang Johnny Halliday, *jusqu'à la fin du monde ...*

'Better go soon, I think,' Milly said. 'Babe will be fretting.' She smiled but her face had lost its animation. She got up, almost wearily. 'I'll just pay. Won't be a sec.'

'Are you sure?'

'Course.' She stood up and hooked her handbag strap over her shoulder. Rummaging in her handbag for her purse she went to find Lucy.

Her mood had definitely changed. Juno tried to relish what she was sure was her handiwork but for some reason as she followed Milly out into the street, all she seemed able to feel was an indecipherable kind of pain.

Chapter 22
Having a go

Walking away, I bent my head back and looked up at the sky. Iris blue, almost purple at the zenith. I wished I could fly up into it, soar like a bird so that all this would become very small, then tiny, then far away, and nobody could reach me. Nobody but Luke.

I wandered down the high street. Nowadays every time I saw Juno she said something vaguely upsetting. Nothing I could put my finger on, it was just a feeling I got. For two pins I'd ask her straight out what she was after. Was it Luke? Was he special to her, despite what she'd said just now?

I stopped in front of Pollyanna and stared in. The colours were lovely, there was a lot of yellow about this year, my favourite colour. I wondered what Luke liked.

I crossed the road by Rennie's the book shop, resolutely not going in, and was nearly at the chemist when I heard raised voices. Outside the Home and Colonial a man was standing with his back to me, arguing noisily with a younger lad. The man with his back turned was tall and skinny with shoulder-length black hair which looked as though it could do with a wash. He had on a black tee-shirt and black jeans. A black motorbike helmet dangled from one hand.

The tall guy seemed mad about something. I skirted them, trying to pretend I hadn't noticed anything, but suddenly the tall guy started pushing the younger one, shove, shove, first one shoulder, then the other, so that the younger lad staggered and almost fell.

'So she yo sista, yeah?'

'Ease up, man. So what? Why you freakin', man?' the younger lad said, his eyes sliding away.

'Look at me when I'm talkin' wichu. That girl is naff, man.'

'Why, wha's it to you, man?'

'This time she gone too far. She think she so fine, she think she so sweet, she can act bougie wit' me. Yellin' at me. You tell her next time she puttin' me on blast you better be ready 'cos it's you gonna get hurt, nah mean? I gonna jump right through you.'

'Hey, don' you be all salty wit' me, man.'

'She ain't nuttin' but a bumpsy skap, man.'

'Hey man, dat my sista you bad-mouthin'!'

'So? Fuckin' nigga-boy.'

'Hey, hey, hey,' I said without thinking, stopping alongside.

'Eh?' The tall guy turned and glared at me. He was older than I'd thought, with a thin, mean face like one of the weasels in the Wild Wood.

'You can't go talking to people like that. What you just said. No.'

'Who says? What's it to you?' Incredulity turned to resentment. 'Hey, fuck off, you interferin' cow.'

'No I won't – what you said.' I stood there, hands on hips, angry now. 'You can't talk to him like that.'

'Who says?'

I shrugged. 'Well ... I do. I'm sure there must be some law says you can't. Race relations or something. Anyway, it's bad manners.'

He made a noise like a startled horse and turned slowly to face me, his body-language exuding incredulity and outrage. 'So what you gonna do about it, eh? Sod off, nosy cow. Whassit got to do with you, anyway? What's the matter wiv you?' There was a pause while he peered at me more closely, his expression more puzzled now than angry. 'Are you nuts or summing? Are you looking for trouble?'

'No,' I said on a rising inflexion. Might be, I thought.

'Who are you, his momma or summing?'

'What if I was? You wouldn't give me any more respect than you're giving him.' I glared at him. I was that close to losing it completely and yelling at him, calling him an ignorant lout. Better still, bopping him one. Except he was a lot bigger than me and it went without saying nobody would butt in and help. I crossed my arms and took a breath. I could feel my cheeks burning. 'You can't just demand respect, that's not how it works. If you talk to her the way you're talking to him, no wonder she doesn't respect you. His sister, I mean. I must say, your manners are – well, they're basically rubbish, aren't they?'

He jutted his head forward until our foreheads were almost touching. I winced and tried not to recoil from the smell of curry exuding from his skin. Curry and something disgustingly sweet. Hair gel, I thought.

The young guy seized his chance and melted away after giving me an astonished look. He seemed more amused than anything. Well, blow him, I was only trying to help.

The tall guy and I glared at each other for a long

moment. He shook his head, slapped the back of his neck and started to laugh. 'Do you know who you're talkin' to?'

'Haven't the faintest idea.' Don't want to either, I thought.

'Well maybe one of these days you'll find out. Man!' He moved off, still shaking his head.

'I hope not,' I said. I was so mad, I wished I had a gun, or a sword, or did kick-boxing, like Jean-Paul. Then I could have said, as I longed to have done, now it was over, 'Huh? Huh? I don't like your face,' and squared up to him, and then we could have had a terrific fight, and I would win, and he would go away chastened and a reformed character.

As if. Idiot, I told myself, walking away, starting to shake. Clot.

'Hey, Milly.'

I turned. Old Flint was hobbling towards me, leaning on his walking stick.

'Hiya, Mr Flint. How are you? I'm sorry, I haven't anything on me today.'

'Nah, nah, nah. 'Snot about that. Saw you talking to that there Jonny Sullivan.'

'Oh, is that who it was?'

'Yeah, yeah. Lookee 'ere. You wanna look out for 'im. 'E's no good. You wanna keep out of 'is way.'

'I will. Thanks. It's just he was roughing up some lad.'

'I saw, I saw. But that young 'un, 'e can look after hisself. Don' ee be worriting your head about the likes of 'im. Them blackies, they got their own way of doin' things. You keep out of the way.'

Oh dear, I thought. Oh help. He's old. I do wish he wouldn't. I ought to say something.

I felt worryingly close to tears. It wouldn't do to show

weakness. Anyway, I hadn't got the Carnation yet. 'Bye then, Mr Flint,' I said. 'See you soon.'

'Now you mind what I says,' he said. 'Off you go now then. Run along.'

At home again, standing at my bedroom window drinking a glass of water, I caught sight of Izzy at the far end of the orchard standing by the gate. I could just see her through the trees. I put the glass down on the windowsill and legged it down the stairs as fast as I could.

She was standing in the long grass on the other side of the gate, holding on to the top rung. White cow-parsley frothed around her knees. 'I told him,' she burst out the moment I arrived. She didn't look particularly happy. Her hands clutched the gate so hard that her knuckles were white.

'What? What did you tell him?'

'What you said. We'd had an awful row.'

'What about?'

'Can't remember, we always seem to be rowing. We always make up but – anyway I told him. I told him,' it came out in a rush, 'I said I was only pretending to be cool about him being married and him thinking it was okay to have us both and all that.'

'Whatever did he say?' I put my hand on the gate beside Izzy's. I noticed how sun-burned mine was against her pale one.

Izzy looked away and thought for a bit with her mouth open. 'He seemed a bit stunned actually. He said I always look as though I don't give a damn about anything and it was the last thing he expected me to say. Do I really come across like that?'

'I know you're not really the way you pretend to be. He ought to realise that by now though, if he loves you like he says he does.'

'I s'pose it's not wanting to make myself vulnerable, or something.' She wasn't looking at me but down at her hands. Her face was pink. She nodded. 'I am like that when I'm with him.' Her fingernails were gold today, matching the glitter scattered down the sides of her jeans. I'd never seen the jeans before. I must remember to tell her I liked them. 'I suppose I always thought – that was the kind of person he'd like me to be. I think it is actually. He once said that looking as if I didn't give a damn was what attracted him to me in the first place.'

'Oh. Oh dear.'

Izzy smiled, suddenly more cheerful. 'I think he thought I was going to say I was pregnant or something. He's always as nervous as hell about that. He says he and her only have to do it once for her to get pregnant.

'Yuck. I can't believe he says that kind of thing to you. Don't you mind?'

'I suppose he thinks I don't care.'

'Oh Iz, that's heavy. And you do.'

Izzy looked at me sadly. 'Of course I do. He even took me to help him buy her a dress once. It was only Marks but I felt awful. I couldn't believe it.'

'He's an insensitive—'

'No! No, he isn't. He just didn't realise how I felt about him.'

'Well, he knows now.'

'Yes. Yes, he does. It feels funny.' She changed her position, relaxed against the gate. The wooden strut pressed against one of her breasts so that it bulged above the scoop neck of her tee-shirt and for a moment I saw her as a man might see her, as a desirable young woman instead of the scatter-brained girl I knew her to be. 'We're going out in a minute,' she said. 'I'm a bit nervous about seeing him, I don't know why. It's being honest with him, I suppose. It feels like it's made this huge difference. For starters we're going out to dinner tonight to a proper restaurant. She'll be away. We've never done that before.'

'You'll miss *Top of the Pops*.'

She gave me a withering look.

I tried again. 'And *The Man from Uncle*. Anyway, what if someone sees you?'

'It's in Kingston. That's miles away. They won't. I hope he's going to say he's made up his mind to tell her. He's always saying he will. Maybe now he knows how I feel—'

'I expect she knows already.'

'What? What do you mean? He'd have told me if he'd told her.'

'No, I mean Esme says wives often do know. Even if they pretend they don't.'

'Yuck, that's disgusting!'

I shrugged.

'What does Esme know about it, anyway? I've been so miserable,' Izzy said, not really listening. 'When we first started going together it was all so exciting, I never thought about the future or what would happen to us, I sort of got swept along. Then I started to feel really sad. I don't know why, it just seemed so hopeless, he has this wife and these kids and I couldn't believe he loved me enough to leave them. He's hacked about making me unhappy, really he is. Sometimes I wish I was in contact with Dad. It would be so cool to be able to ask him what he thinks, what I ought to do.'

'Have you thought about getting in touch with him?'

'After finding those letters, yeah, I have. Dunno what Mum would think though.'

'Ask her.'

'Might. Once she's calmed down. She got so upset the other night when we talked about them. Honestly, major trauma. Scary. You know, about Rob, Milly. I know you've never thought much of him but honestly, he didn't have a clue how I felt. I'm sure everything will be okay now he knows. Everything will be different.'

''Course it will. Love the cool jeans,' I said.

'Yeah, me too. Mum actually gave me some money to buy stuff. Jeepers, look at the time, I'm going to be late.' She let go of the gate and set off, half-running, across the lane towards her own back gate. 'Rob hates it when I'm late. He'll be all grumpy. See ya.'

I leaned my back against the gate, my arms crossed, frowning. I had a bad feeling about all this. I should have kept my mouth shut. Now something had been set in motion, and I had no control over how it might end.

Chapter 23

Some people have no mercy

ON FRIDAY LUKE WAS LATE FOR SUPPER AGAIN.

'She's here again,' Babe said, doling out fish pie. 'Locked up in the study with him. Honestly. I've told him twice his supper's ready.'

'Why doesn't she join us?' Felix said. 'If you mean Mrs Booth. Seems a charming woman, to me.'

I rolled my eyes.

'She's off out,' Babe said. 'I did ask. Seemed only polite. But oh no. She's off somewhere posh. Doesn't seem to care that his supper's ready and he's hungry after a full day's work. No mercy, some people. And he came home early especially. Said he hadn't spent enough time at home recently, and then she turns up and spoils it.'

'Do you dislike Amy?' Esme asked, taking a plateful. 'Thank you, Babe, this looks excellent.'

Babe considered. 'It's not that so much, it's more that she doesn't seem to have any consideration for other people. This is going to be ruined if he doesn't come soon. Put it in the oven and it'll all dry up.'

The doorknob rattled, Luke came in and threw himself into his chair. 'Sorry Babe.' His face was flushed.

'Here you are. Help yourself to veg. Well?'

'Well, what?'

'What's so important it can't wait while you eat your dinner.'

Luke sighed. I picked up the dish of broccoli and offered it to him. 'Thanks. She's on her own, things get on top of her ... you know. She worries.'

'Third time she's made you late this week.'

'She does tend to drop in to the workshop just when we're packing up to go home,' Luke said. 'Thanks, this looks wonderful. Doesn't seem to have much concept of time. Ah well.'

'She's angling for an invitation,' Felix said. Everyone looked at him in surprise.

'As a matter of fact,' Luke said, 'I am taking her to dinner one evening next week. That new Chinese restaurant in Kingston. The *Kam Tang*? Never heard of it, but she seems keen. I'll have to look it up.'

'Kam Tong,' Babe said coldly.

'Ah, is that it? Thanks.'

Babe seemed to change her mind. 'About time you had a bit of fun,' she said.

Whose side was she on?

'Must repay hospitality,' Luke said. 'Oh, and I'm off out again later, Amy's invited a friend round for a drink who's interested in commissioning a piece.'

Babe looked at him. 'Hasn't she seen enough of you for one day?'

'Apparently not.'

The fish pie seemed to have lost all its taste. I sprinkled

salt, but it didn't help much. I wasn't sure what it was about the idea of Amy taking over Luke's life that I was so uncomfortable with. I mean, I did want him to be happy, of course I did. Perhaps it was because I didn't think she was the right person. Or maybe it was the disruption to our happy life I didn't like, in which case I was a selfish, horrible person. After all Luke had done for me, surely I didn't begrudge him happiness?

I began to feel the onset of a headache. I got them sometimes and if I didn't take care it could turn into a full-blown migraine. I managed to last about ten minutes more, not hearing a word of the conversation batting to and fro around me, then put down my fork and pushed my chair back. 'Would you excuse me?' I said. 'I've got the most awful headache. Feels as if my head's going to explode. Might go up if you don't mind. Sorry, Babe. Lovely pie.' They were all looking at me. I blundered towards the door and found myself in the hall. I set off up the stairs, clutching the bannister rail for support.

The kitchen door opened and Luke's voice said, 'Milly. Stop a minute.'

I stopped and half-turned. He came and stood at the foot of the stairs. 'Are you okay? You're very pale. Is it a migraine?'

'I'm fine, honestly. Just this head – I thought if I could catch it ... you know.' I was finding it hard to look at him.

'Oh – right. Well, if you need anything. There's nothing wrong, is there, apart from the headache?' The concern in his voice weakened me further. In two seconds I was going to cry, which would be an utter disaster.

I forced myself to sound normal, in control. ''Course not. Well, I'll just—' I stepped onto the next stair.

'Milly. Can't you even look at me?'

I tensed. No, was the honest answer. I couldn't. He would probe. I had to get away.

I heard him sigh. 'Goodnight, then. I'll see you in the morning.' I waited till the kitchen door closed, then I turned and looked for a long moment at the place where he had stood before setting off again up the stairs.

LATER IN THE evening when the house was quiet, I tiptoed down the stairs. Passing Felix's room I paused; strange sounds came from inside. It sounded as if some large animal had got in and was blundering about, knocking into things. I said in a low voice through the door, 'Felix? Are you okay?'

More clumsy movement. The door handle rattled.

'Can I come in?'

The door opened and he stood there, blinking. I looked past him into the room. The heavy curtains were drawn over the windows and the room was dark. In the light from the passage I saw that the small table that usually stood beside his armchair lay on its side on the carpet and a book lay splayed open, some of its pages bent underneath. A blue and yellow embroidered bookmark lay beside it.

'Are you okay?' I said. 'I came down to get a drink and heard you. I was worried.'

The room reeked of whisky. He stood back to let me in. I righted the table then reached up and switched on the standard lamp behind his armchair. I picked up the book, smoothed out the pages and put it face down on the table with the bookmark beside it. 'Come and sit down.' I took his hand and led him to his chair. 'I'll make you some coffee.'

He sank into the chair with a sigh, pulled a hanky out of his pocket and wiped his forehead lengthily. 'Sorry. Stupid. Had a bit too much to drink.'

'Oh dear.'

'Had her on my mind, d'you see? Been thinking about her. Leonie. My granddaughter.' He looked towards his desk. The photograph was no longer there. He lifted his hand and gestured vaguely. I looked around, and down. The blue edge of the photo frame was just showing under the edge of the chair. He must have been holding it, then he'd stumbled into the table in the dark, and dropped it.

I picked it up and gave it to him.

'Ah!' His eyes gleamed in the lamplight. 'There she is.' He looked as though he might start to weep.

'I'll get you that coffee.'

'Been thinking about relationships, you know. About love. All that. I thought about that at supper. Luke and that Mrs Thing. Amy. He's not had a girlfriend, not since I've been here. Lives like a monk. Nothing but work. And chess, and his music, loves his music. But a lonely sort of chap. Well. Something going on there and about time too.'

Oh, I thought. Please don't.

'Hope she'll make him happy, that's all, not mess him about. Women. Play havoc with your peace of mind.'

I went and filled the kettle, found Felix's favourite mug, the one with the Spitfires on, put in sugar and Nescafé and waited for the kettle to boil.

'Make a good couple. Saw them together in the town. Both of them good-looking – good people. Right for each other.' He looked straight at me, eyes intelligent and sincere, as I handed him the mug. 'Ah well, never mind. Hearts, eh? Hearts.'

I didn't want to talk about Amy and Luke. I handed him his coffee, pulled up the small embroidered stool, the one that had come from his mother's house, and settled down at his feet. I was so tempted to tell him I had seen Leonie. 'You shouldn't drink so much. It's bad for you.'

'I know. I know.' He took a gulp of coffee. 'It dulls – you know, takes the edge off. When things are bad. Usually more sensible.' He put the mug down on the little table and picked up his book. I glanced at the title: *These Islands* by Norman Davies. Felix riffled through the pages until he seemed to find the one he wanted. He took another sip of coffee, keeping his finger in place. Then as if he thought this might look as though he hoped I wouldn't be staying much longer, he reached for the bookmark, put it in place and closed the book.

'Why can't you get in touch with her?'

'Not sure if she'd want me to. They've gone from the cottage. That boy moved in with them, that jackanapes—'

'Which boy?'

'Black as anything.'

'Black? African, you mean? Indian?'

'No, no. Clothes. Motorcycle. Black from head to foot. All of them. Young enough to be her son.'

'Whose son?'

'My daughter. Gill.' He looked at me reproachfully as if I ought to have known all about it. 'It's his influence, bound to be, Leonie not getting in touch. She was always such an affectionate little thing. A good girl.' He said almost to himself, 'I'm sure she's a good girl. And Gill is a good mother. Mothers, you know. Important to a child. Mean everything. Mind you.'

'What?'

'My mother, different story. Couldn't please her when she was alive. Never could please her.' He shook his head. 'Could have killed her.'

'Sorry?'

'What was that?' He roused himself and turned to look at me.

'I mean ... what did she do? Why could you have killed her?'

He leaned back in his chair and said, after a long pause, 'Came home from school one day. Fifteen I was, thereabouts. She'd cleared out the cupboard in my room. All my things, gone.' His voice shook. 'My tin soldiers. My stamp album. Mouth organ. My collection of medals I'd searched for and saved up for, for years. Can't describe the fury I felt.' He shook his head. 'At least she'd left me my books.'

I was so shocked that at first I couldn't speak. After a while I said, 'What a dreadful thing to do.'

'Never felt such murderous rage before or since. Went down to the kitchen and challenged her. Swore at her. Vile language coming up from God knows where. Can see her now, her mouth hanging open with shock and disapproval. Honestly sometimes I wish I'd got up the courage to kill her.' He got out his handkerchief and wiped his forehead.

'Oh, Felix.'

'Worst of it was, she never gave me a satisfactory explanation. Any explanation, really. Seemed to have no appreciation of the enormity of what she'd done – the taking and disposing of my precious possessions without my knowledge or consent.' He seemed to have forgotten I was there. 'It was a completely unjustified, outrageous act of cruelty for which I've never been able to forgive her.' He began rubbing his hands together over and over; they were dry and cracked with too much washing. 'Some mothers, you know, better off dead. The whole of my growing up, all I wanted was to protect myself from her anger and domination.' He was almost wringing his hands.

'Why? Why was she angry?' I thought of my own

mother. I desperately wanted him to stop, but at the same time I was curious.

'Never knew. Don't think she knew herself. Nag, nag. Only way I could blot out the sound of her voice in my head was by sitting absolutely still. Armchair in my bedroom. Hours at a time. Lost. A kind of self-hypnosis, now I think it was, absolute stillness of mind and body, thinking about nothing. I could do that at will. My secret weapon.'

'Where was your father? Didn't he help?'

'Died when I was a child. If he'd been there things might not have been so bad.'

'I'm so sorry.'

'Of course it's different for Leonie. Wonderful woman, her mother.'

He still seemed on the verge of tears. I said, 'Perhaps you should try harder to get in touch.'

'No use.' He took another gulp of coffee. 'Beating my head against a brick wall.'

'What if Leonie wants to get in touch and doesn't know where you are? P'raps they haven't told her. She loves you really, I'm sure she does.'

He almost smiled. He put the mug down. 'You're a romantic, Milly – an optimist. Life isn't like that. You'll find out.' He looked at me, blue eyes wide. 'I'm afraid you will find out.'

'Did you and Gill quarrel? Is she angry with you?'

'We never quarrelled. I can't quarrel. What's the use?'

'You just let them go.'

'She told me she had feelings for him.' He shook his head. 'Feelings, hah! I would have put up with anything to keep them with me but no. Dazzled, she was. Motorcycle, you see. Leathers and suchlike. Macho. Used to take Leonie riding on the back. Worried me to death. Took Gill too, in the end. She was determined to leave and set up house with him.'

'Why did you come here? What happened to your cottage?'

'Oh ...' He shook his head again. 'I told them they could stay there and I would leave. I wanted Leonie to stay in her home. She loved that house. Well, cottage really. She loved it.'

'But—'

'They've gone. Sold up and left.'

'But that's awful. Without saying anything to you? What about the money?'

'It was him, I'm sure. Young jackanapes. Didn't care. Used to laugh at me behind my back. I knew. Thought I was an old fool. I couldn't stay. Had to leave. Don't care a jot about the money. What does it matter? Let them get on with it.' He bent his head back and rested it against the back of the chair, closed his eyes. 'At least here I get some peace.'

He seemed almost asleep. Quietly I stood up to go and as I did I heard the music again. Distinct and persistent, as before. The same tune. I said, 'Will you be all right? Are you sure you don't want anything to eat?'

He shook his head. I tip-toed out of the room and quietly closed the door. I ran down the rest of the stairs and let myself out through the side door. The music was still around, somewhere in the air. It was hard to tell where it was coming from, like the whiff of scent you get suddenly when you're out for a walk and you can't tell which bush it's coming from.

It was pitch dark, there was no moon and the sky was cloudy so there wasn't even starlight. I tiptoed towards the orchard and moved in among the trees and then I saw it, the orb of light rising out of the grass and upwards into the branches. The music came again, louder this time, insistent. Why now? What was she trying to say?

The orb of light vanished and abruptly the music stopped.

'Mother?' I said out loud. 'Is it you? What are you trying to say? Can't you speak?'

Nothing. A light wind blew up, fanning my hot face. Whoever, whatever had been there was gone as if they'd never been.

Chapter 24

The smell of gunpowder

Luke wasn't at the breakfast table when I burst into the kitchen on Sunday morning, fresh from my shower. Sleeping it off, I thought, sawing a vicious slice off the loaf. I wonder what time he got back. From the door to Babe's sanctum (Luke's word for it) the jaunty refrain from Gerry and the Pacemakers lowered my mood even more.

How do you do what you do to me, if I only knew ... then perhaps you'd fall for me like I fell for you ...

The kitchen smelt deliciously of fried bacon but I wasn't hungry. Suppose he really liked Amy? I slammed a bit of bread into the toaster.

He came in when I was drinking my second cup of coffee. He pulled out his chair and sat down, rubbing his hand over his face. Serve him right if he was tired, he shouldn't have stayed out so late.

Babe bustled in. 'Well, mornin' everybody.' She looked sideways at Luke. 'Had a good time last night?' She went over to the cooker and whisked a plate out from under the grill. 'What you find to talk about at these dinners that take half the night I don't know. It's not as if you're doing something interesting like – well – dancing.' She plonked eggs and bacon in front of Luke and stood looking down at him, pushing up the neck of her blouse which had slipped off her shoulder.

'How do you know?' Luke said rather sourly. 'We might have been tripping the light fantastic till the wee small hours.'

'It was the wee small hours all right, you didn't get in till three,' Babe said, patting his shoulder.

You give me a feeling in my heart, like an arrow passing through it ... s'pose that you think you're very smart, but won't you tell me how do you do it ...

Luke looked up at her wearily. 'Give me a break. I've got the most awful headache.'

He reached for the coffee pot. I folded the newspaper and handed it to him across the table.

'Thanks. Are you sure you've finished with it?'

'Quite sure, thanks.'

'Anything interesting?' He looked at me with reddened eyes, even sleepier than usual. From drinking and debauchery, no doubt.

'Apart from the government banning cigarette advertising on TV?'

'They haven't, have they? Why? I thought smoking was supposed to be good for you.'

'They seem to have decided it isn't.'

'Well,' Babe said, turning away. 'You'll wear yourself out with all this gallivanting. You said you had to get into work today, Sunday or no Sunday. Jean-Paul rang, by the way. Says he'll come in too. How are you going to get your jobs finished if you're dead on your feet?'

Luke rolled his eyes at me. I tried to smile, but it was difficult. *Three in the morning?*

'If you must know,' Luke said, pouring himself a cup, 'I had to drive somebody home. She arrived in a taxi because there was something wrong with her car, so obviously at the end of the evening I had to offer her a lift. Only decent thing to do.'

'Who?' I couldn't help myself.

'Oh, just some friend of Mrs Booth's. Annabel somebody. She's interested in commissioning a piece, which is good. I'll have to start giving Amy a rake-off, at this rate.'

'Was she nice?' Bet there wasn't a thing wrong with her car.

'She was okay.' Bet he liked her. I took a huge bite of toast and nearly choked.

'Steady,' Babe said, passing behind my chair. 'What's up with you?'

I took a swig of coffee to avoid having to speak. When Babe had gone I pushed my chair back and got up.

'Going already?'

'Thought I'd go for a walk.'

'Have fun,' he said, opening the paper.

How could I have fun when I didn't have a clue what was going on in his head? For once I left the room without a smile for him.

He didn't deserve a smile.

My feet took me towards Midsummer Meadow. For once I didn't feel the sunshine or take any notice of my surroundings but plunged ahead through the dewy grass. Of course it was obvious Luke was going to want to get involved with some woman someday. It was surprising he hadn't already. I suppose he's been too busy being responsible for me, I thought, coldly. I've stopped him.

He'd always been there for me. When I was little and got thrown by scary TV or if it was stormy outside and the wind was rattling the windows and spooking me, he'd put his head around the door to see if I was awake and if I was he would take me downstairs in my dressing gown and sit me in the rocking chair by the Aga and make us both a snack. His snack of choice was invariably cheese on toast with sliced-up tomato underneath and Worcester Sauce sprinkled on top, and because I was hungry and scared and missing my mother even more than usual I couldn't have imagined a more wicked taste.

My memories of the time my mother died were vague and confused. I remembered a strange atmosphere in the house, a sense of menace like the smell of gunpowder. If I really tried I could almost taste it.

I remembered a sensation that I recognised now as a feeling of unthinkable disaster. I remembered seeking Pascale out, looking for comfort, and finding her huddled in a chair by the Aga. I remembered climbing onto her lap and looking up into her face at the alien, scary tears running down, the damp handkerchief clutched in her shaking hand. I'd never seen her cry before.

I remembered Pascale pushing me away. 'Cannot you even let me grieve in peace?'

I had crept away, mortified. The sentence that burst out of Pascale in her misery haunted me for years. What other offences had I committed, things I couldn't remember, that explained that 'even'?

The word left a painful scar I returned to again and again over the years.

'Cannot you even let me grieve in peace?'

Was that what she'd said? Or was it, 'Cannot you let me even grieve in peace?'

Did altering the position of the word rob the sentence of its sting?

The coming of Luke made a dramatic sea-change. Now there was someone to pull the household together, to bind our wounds and tell us what to do. Luke was cheerful, he didn't behave as though the world had come to an end. He gathered me up and brought me in from the wilderness, sat me by the fire and warmed my chilled spirit.

'Courage, brother,' he would say, when I was upset. I liked that. I'd pretend I was a soldier in the field, Luke my commanding officer.

'Courage, brother,' I would mutter to myself, waking in the night to a wet pillow, my rib-cage aching. So there must have been tears. Why couldn't I remember?'

'Luke had a lot to put up with at first, no doubt about that,' Babe told me. 'Getting you to eat, for a start. Then you got mad and started smashing things.'

'What kind of things? Why did I get mad?'

'You'd just lost your mother, Milly,' Babe said gently. 'And your Granny and Grandpa. You had a right to be angry. One day you broke a bowl, the best fruit bowl it was, belonged to your Gran. Luke thought you'd done it on purpose. Thought it would be better to give you something legit to smash, so he went out and bought a load of old china plates and let you smash them.'

'How awful. I sound like a right pain.'

'No you weren't, lovey, you were a confused, unhappy little girl.'

'I can't imagine it now.'

'Shows what a good job he did then, doesn't it?'

He was still doing a good job. And what was it that made him so special, when really you could see that he was just an ordinary sort of bloke, though better-looking than most?

For one thing he was good at answering questions like:

Why is it good to be like a rock but not like a stone? I always went to him with difficult questions, and he was the person I went to when I had my big fall-out with Izzy.

Izzy had always been untruthful. I knew this and it never stopped me loving her even though it shocked me sometimes. But before the summer when we were fifteen, Izzy had never, to my knowledge, lied about me. So when Izzy borrowed a pair of Juno's best Lilley and Skinner court shoes without asking and broke the heel off one of them and put them back in the cupboard without saying anything, and when challenged lied about it and said that I'd done it, I was flabbergasted.

I wouldn't even have known about it if Juno hadn't started talking pointedly about shoes and borrowing things without asking. A horrible suspicion began to dawn. I went to Izzy and asked her straight out what had happened.

'I'm sorry, Milly,' Izzy said cheerfully. 'I don't know why I said it was you, I just did. Anyway, I knew she'd be madder with me than she would be with you, so it seemed the sensible thing to do.'

'But now she thinks I'm a liar and borrow things without asking.'

'Yup,' Izzy said, smiling.

'It isn't funny, Izzy.'

'Oh go on, you don't really mind, do you? She's forgotten all about it, it happened weeks ago.'

'D'you mean to say she's been thinking all this stuff about me for weeks and I didn't even *know*?'

Izzy shrugged.

'I'm going to tell her.'

'No, you're not, you love me, you'd never drop me in it. Anyway, she's perfectly happy feeling cross with you.'

I looked at her in stupefaction. At the earliest opportunity, which came that evening after supper, I poured it all out to Luke.

Luke sat and heard me out without interrupting. He was a really good listener, he never finished your sentences for you like some people – and they usually get it wrong.

'You've got two options, haven't you?' he said when I'd finished. We'd been relaxing, Luke listening to *The Songs of the Auvergne* and me half-listening and attempting the crossword at the same time, so we were both feeling reasonably calm. 'You either drop Izzy in it or you don't.'

'That's what's so difficult. Of course I don't really want to drop Izzy in it, but now I'm embarrassed whenever I'm anywhere near Juno. I mean, what must she think of me?'

'It's always possible she's guessed the truth. She must know what Izzy's like.'

'But she'd have said, wouldn't she? And if I don't say anything—'

'If you do decide not to,' Luke said, 'you could always choose to look at the situation in a different way.'

'What sort of way?'

'Well ... you could accept the situation, forgive her and move on. Good for the soul?'

'Oh bother, I knew you were going to say something like that.' I fell into a long think. 'Do I have to? It doesn't feel little, it feels huge.'

'You don't *have* to do anything. You have a choice.'

I pulled a face. 'No, I don't, not really. Of course you're right.'

Luke raised his eyebrows and stayed looking thoughtful, his chin resting on his hand. The trouble with Luke was, he just waited until you realised you'd known all along what you had to do.

'If you look at it like that,' he said eventually, 'how does it look then?'

I thought a bit more, then nodded. 'It looks okay. It looks different.'

A week or so later Izzy said, 'By the way, I told Mum.'

'What?'

'I told her it was me who took her shoes.'

'You didn't!'

'I did. You were so ace about it I felt bad, and anyway Mum's got the heel mended now and she isn't cross about it anymore.'

'Right. Thanks.'

'Sorry, Milly.'

'S'okay.'

AFTER MY MOTHER DIED, I didn't feel anything very much for a bit, but a while later – I must have been about eight – I stormed into Babe's room one afternoon and wailed amid floods of tears that I was a bad person because I couldn't remember feeling sad when my mummy died.

Babe had only been with us for about a year. She set Catherine Cookson aside without a moment's hesitation and put a comforting arm around me. She tutted a bit, the way she does when she's thinking hard, then she said, 'But of course you did. Don't you remember the sofa?'

'What sofa?'

'The one in your Gran's sitting-room. When Luke brought you home from Izzy's house, where you stayed for a bit, you remember – after – well, before he got here – you went behind the sofa and you wouldn't come out for two whole weeks. Do you remember what he did? Luke?'

I clung on, sniffing. 'What? What did he do?'

'He slept on that sofa in a sleeping bag every night until you felt safe enough to come out. Slept like that the whole of the first fortnight he lived in this house. Wouldn't let anybody make you come out. Mind you, don't know if anybody could have, you had a right temper on you in those days and no mistake.'

I was silent. I was beginning to remember now in flashes, plates of food, on the floor and then on a little table. A child-sized chair hoisted over the back of the sofa into my fall-out shelter, my safe place. 'Where's that little chair?' I said, suddenly seeing it in my mind's eye. It was bright blue with little white daisies with orange centres painted on the back.

'He made that chair,' Babe said, pleased that I could remember. 'Made it in a day. And the little table. D'you remember the little table?'

'I think I do.' I was beginning to feel better.

Babe gave me a hug. 'Don't you fret. You've got nothing in the world to feel bad about. You're a great little kid and we all think you're wonderful.'

'Luke too?'

'Luke most of all.'

And now here we were, all these years later, and Luke was still here, still doing his best. And I didn't want to get in his way, I wanted him to have a life, he deserved it after everything he'd done for us all, and because he was a good person. But what should I do?

I sat down in the grass, my elbows on my knees. A beetle ran over my leg and I ignored it. Did setting Luke free mean I had to leave him? I couldn't imagine life without him.

Idiot, I thought. Suppose he falls in love and decides to import some – woman – someone like Amy, I'd have to leave him. They wouldn't want me hanging around, for a start. And anyway I couldn't stay. I couldn't bear it. I wasn't sure why, I just knew it would be out of the question. If that happened I was off. I'd have no choice.

My God, I thought, talk about living in a fool's paradise. How could I have been so idiotic as to imagine our life would go on for ever, that nothing would change?

Things always change. That's life. I looked up at the bright sky. It felt dark, suddenly. Even the sunshine seemed to have lost its warmth. I shivered. I felt unmoored, my safe harbour threatened.

This was something I couldn't ask his advice about. This time I was on my own.

Chapter 25

Putting the boot in

'How did your drinks party go?' I asked Amy on Monday morning, dragging the Hoover out of the cupboard.

'Do take care, you'll break it, it does have a handle, you know. Oh, it went *fine.*' Amy was in a real strop this morning.

'Oh good,' I said, fitting the extension pieces together. Amy wandered around the hall looking preoccupied; she picked up the telephone directory from the hall table and put it down again, opened and closed a drawer. She stopped beside me and fidgeted with the belt of her tight-fitting jeans. 'I hope Luke enjoyed himself?'

'Oh, he had a high old time. He didn't get home till goodness knows when. Babe was awfully cross.'

Amy frowned. 'That's odd, I wonder what happened to him. He left the same time as the others, about one. Oh, of course, he took Annabel home.'

'He said.'

'I expect that accounts for it. She lives in the other direction.'

'She must live an awfully long way away,' I said, plugging the Hoover in at the bottom of the stairs. 'Or else he went in with her for ages. He must have,' I said mercilessly. 'He didn't get home till after three.'

The slam of the drawing-room door was audible even through the roar of the Hoover. Naughty Milly. But Amy was just so obvious. I shook my head as I pushed the Hoover backwards and forwards over the rug in the middle of the hall. Honestly. People.

LUKE CAME HOME for lunch and afterwards, when it had stopped raining, I went and sat on the bench in the rose garden. Luke followed me out.

'Look,' I said. Two goldfinches swung on the bird-feeder, attacking the niger seed. 'They're so beautiful.'

'Exotic,' Luke said. 'Un-English, somehow.'

I made room for him on the bench. 'It's a bit damp.'

Luke sat down and looked around at the burgeoning green. 'I really should spend more time in the garden.'

'You're busy. Anyway, it looks great. Sort of jungly.'

'Is that meant to make me feel better? Felix is seriously helping now. He has a go before breakfast most days. I've taken a good bit off his rent.'

'Oh good. He doesn't seem to have much cash.'

Luke stood up and walked about, his hands in his pockets. He'd washed his hair and it kept flopping over his forehead. He pushed it back irritably. 'Need a cut. Milly, we haven't had a proper chat about St Andrews – what you'll need, that sort of thing. It will be cold up there, I imagine.'

'Mandy who's there at the moment says we live in our gowns. We do something called the pier walk after chapel on Sunday. The wind whistles in off the sea, she says, and it's enough to freeze your ears off.'

'That's the kind of thing. We need to get things sorted.'

Watching him closely, I said, 'It's the first time I'll have been away properly, isn't it?'

He glanced at me, his expression business-like. He said, almost as though he was thinking about something else, 'I'm sure you'll be fine.'

This wouldn't do. 'I'll miss home.' I didn't want to sound pathetic but enough was enough. Wasn't he going to miss me at all? 'Everyone here.'

He gave a sigh and came and sat down beside me. 'Milly. Of *course* we'll miss you. But you'll be back, and we'll still be here.'

'But will you?'

'Will I what?'

'Be here. I mean ... once I've left home, won't you want to move back to London?'

He sat up. 'Leave Half Moon? You must be joking. Anyway, what would become of the others? There's Pascale to consider. Babe. What about Esme and Felix?'

'But – in London—'

'Milly, I don't miss London one bit.' I could sense him looking at me but for some reason I couldn't meet his eyes. 'Best thing I ever did, moving down here.'

'Really?' I turned to look at him.

'Really. Why, do you think I ought to move back to London?'

'Of course not. *No.*'

'Well, then.'

'I was just thinking, you must have some plans of your own.' I swallowed. 'I don't want to get in the way of them.'

'Get in the way – you?' He put out his hand then snatched it back again. 'Milly,' he said. I looked at him. He looked angrily at the bird feeder, then at the flower bed.

'I'll be okay, you know,' I said, trembling inside. Everything that was being said had suddenly taken on a huge significance. 'You don't have to look after me for ever. You're a free agent.'

He stood up and put his hands in his pockets. 'Right,' he said, 'I'll remember that. And by the way, Juno tells me – I gather – one of her pupils, Stephen somebody? About time you had a boyfriend. Ask him to supper, I'd like to meet him.' He strode away across the lawn, his footsteps leaving green patterns in the wet grass.

What? I watched him go, frowning. That boy Juno had talked about wasn't my boyfriend, I hadn't even met him. What had Juno been saying? Perhaps she'd been trying to make Luke feel less – how had she put it – burdened?

I desperately wanted to put him straight. Then I thought, perhaps I really ought to go out with him. This boy. Perhaps that was what Luke wanted, perhaps Juno was right. And there was always Jean-Paul, he'd made it clear he'd leap at the chance.

But Juno, what was she playing at? Why was she so odd at the moment? I stood up. The sun had gone in and grey clouds were gathering again. More rain.

Chapter 26
Earthquake insurance

'What's up, Izzy?'

'Got something to tell you.'

'Well, I gathered that.'

On Tuesday morning Izzy had suddenly appeared, sitting astride the gate, just visible from Esme's window, and Esme had called up to me. I was in the attic, reading. I came flying down.

'To hear is to obey,' Esme said as I flew past her open door. But she said it in a friendly way, not nastily. I registered in that moment before leaping down the last two steps that Esme would never be deliberately unkind.

'Well,' I said. 'Spit it out then.'

'It's Rob,' she said, coming to stand in front of me. I was leaning against a tree, my arms folded.

'No!' I said, but kindly. Then I thought, here we go again, you're not the only one in the universe with problems, you know. There's Esme, for a start, and Felix, and Luke's got his own problems, me and stuff. And I've got my worries too. The only person without a care in the world is Sapphy. And I used to be able to talk to you but now you're never listening. All you ever think about nowadays is yourself.

Then I met her eyes and saw that they were not troubled, but sparkling. I watched as Izzy's face started to heave with something ominous.

'You're not going to start all that again, are you?' she said.

'All what?'

'You know.' She turned away and started trampling about, head down, as though she was thinking, wondering how to start.

'What about Rob?' I said helpfully.

'Oh, Milly,' she said in a muffled voice.

'*What?*'

She turned and looked at me. Her blue eyes blazed in a face so pale she looked as though she was about to throw up, or pass out or something. 'I just have to tell someone,' she said.

'And that lucky person, hopefully, is going to be me.'

'We met up early this morning and went for a walk.'

'But it's Tuesday. Isn't he working? And where was his wife?'

'Asleep. Never mind that. He took the morning off. He's going to leave her, Milly. He really, truly is. He's going to tell her about us and get a divorce. Is that far out or what?'

'But. But. What about her? What about the children? Oh, Izzy, you can't.'

'Can't *what*? Oh, I knew you wouldn't understand.'

I slid my back down the tree, which hurt because the bark was rough and knobbly in places and my tee-shirt rucked up as I slid down, exposing my skin. I reached the ground with a thump.

'I told you,' Izzy said. 'She doesn't care about him. She

won't mind. I'm sorry about the kids, of course I am, but he'll see them sometimes. A lot. I don't know, we haven't talked about it.' She shrugged. 'It doesn't matter. What matters is I have to be with him. I did try to tell him I wanted to stop but it came out all wrong. It's up to him anyway, isn't it? It isn't my fault.' She was still plunging about like she was trampling grapes.

'Are you going to live with him?'

Izzy stopped in front of me. 'You know that flat he borrowed from Max we've been going to? Well, Max is going off abroad somewhere and Rob's going to rent it from him. Just think.' She squatted down so that her flushed face was level with mine. 'Our own place, so that we can be properly together. Our own place.'

'But he's got that huge great house. And you can't cook.'

'So what? We can get takeaways. I can learn. What does it matter?'

'Well, food's important. Men need food.'

'God, you sound like my mother. I'm talking about moving in with Rob. This is the most important thing that's ever happened to me and all you can talk about is food!'

'But what about university? I thought you wanted to be an architect. It's all happening so quickly, you only met the guy in April.'

'He isn't *the guy,* he's Rob. And we'll think about all that stuff later. It isn't important.'

'I won't ever see you.'

'Yes, you will.' Izzy's voice was gentle. My eyes filled with tears. I looked down at my feet in their muddy trainers, angled in front of me. Whatever I did, I mustn't cry.

Sapphy came silently out of the long grass and rubbed her chin against my knee. Her long smoky fur was smudged with patches of cobalt blue and bright orange.

'Oh, Sapphy, you've been painting again! Clever girl! Yes, you are.' Sapphy stood up on her hind legs and put her front paws on my knee. I hugged her respectfully, feeling better. 'Where's this flat then?' I asked Izzy, not looking at her in case the trickle of tears showed. Surreptitiously I wiped them away with the back of my hand. Izzy had stood up again and turned away and was striding about again.

'In the high street. Not far. It's a bed-sit really. I'll show you.'

'You'll have to start clearing up.' I thought of Izzy's bedroom, every square inch covered with discarded clothes, makeup, papers, mugs, shoes, tights, books, the whole paraphernalia of her life. She was the untidiest person I'd ever met.

Izzy laughed. 'I will, won't I?' She stopped laughing. 'I'm not looking forward to telling Mum. She'll have seven fits.'

'Fifteen fits.' I smiled shyly at her. I couldn't think what more to say. Izzy seemed to have turned into someone else, Cinderella into the beautiful princess whose every dream has come true. She had been chosen. She was special. 'Does he give you money?' I said.

'He buys me things. Underwear and things. He gave me that flower necklace and the pink handbag. And this brooch. Look!' She hunkered down again, twisted towards me and pointed to a brooch pinned to her blouse.

'Oh, I love that!' Two pink and red cats pressed together against a background of flowers, making a leaf shape. It really was pretty. I felt a moment of longing which I squashed. 'What's it made of?'

'I think he said some kind of resin? It's an Erstwilder, whoever that is. Rob seems to rate him. And ... he gave me this.' She held out her arm. A silver link bracelet was clasped around her wrist.

'That's pretty.' The sight of her pale, narrow wrist moved me almost to tears again. I longed to put my arms around her and hug her, tell her I loved her, but somehow I couldn't. I hugged Sapphy instead. Sapphy, sensing unease, struggled like an eel and jumped away with a backward look of reproach. Just when I need you, I thought.

'Wish I could come and see what she's done this time,' Izzy said, diverted, watching her streak away through the grass. 'I've got to go though. Mustn't be late again. I like *Yellow Rhapsody* best so far.' She looked up at the bits of sky visible through the apple branches and screwed up her face. 'Bother, it's going to rain.'

'She's getting better and better. I'll show you tomorrow. When she's done ten good ones we're going to have an exhibition.'

'Oh, Milly, you are funny.'

'No, really, they're wonderful. Luke's going to make frames for them. He says he'll hang some of them in the workshop. They'll probably make his fortune.'

'Sapphy's fortune.'

'He's her agent. Her fifteen percenter. It'll make his too.'

'Honestly, Luke's as daft as you are.' Izzy struggled to her feet and stood smiling down at me.

She's so beautiful, I thought. Her face had a softness and radiance I'd never seen in it before. She looked overwhelmingly relieved, like someone whose house has just collapsed in an earthquake and who's just discovered they do have earthquake insurance after all.

Chapter 27

Let me rattle your cage

Juno heard tapping on one of the long glass doors Mike had built onto the back of the house, that opened out into the garden. A narrow path ran along the back of the cottage to the kitchen door, below the shallow bank that sloped up to a little lawn. Mike had planted bulbs along the bank so that in the spring IZZY appeared, spelt out in daffodils.

Milly was standing on the path, a shadow against the bright sunlight that had come after the rain. Feet together, head bent, she shaded her eyes with her hand to see better through the blinding glass.

'Milly. Hang on a minute.' Juno went through from the kitchen, unlatched the garden door and flung it open. 'Come in. What a surprise.'

'I wasn't sure you'd be free,' Milly said, stepping inside.

'I was making coffee. Perfect timing,' Juno said. Keep your friends close, she thought, and your enemies closer.

'Actually I'd prefer a glass of milk if you've got enough. Is it all right my coming around like this? Oh, Sapphy.' Milly turned and looked down at the cat who was sniffing delicately along the bottom of the doorframe. 'You'd better stay outside.'

'She can come in if she likes.'

'Are you sure?'

'Of course.' Juno turned and led the way into the kitchen.

'Thanks. I've been at Amy's. She let me go early because she's going out to lunch. I think with Luke. Come on, Sapph, you can come in. She's so clever, she comes on my walk with me now.'

'Aren't you afraid she'll get lost?' Juno unhooked a cherry-patterned mug from the built-in, cream-painted dresser and set it down beside the kettle. She reached up and took a glass out of a cupboard and spooned Nescafé into the mug.

'Sapphy won't get lost, she's far too clever. Aren't you, Sapph? She's turning into a wonderful painter.'

Juno poured milk into the glass and hot water into her mug. 'Are you seriously telling me that cat is painting and *knows* she is painting?'

'Of course. Come and watch some time, she absolutely loves it.'

'But what does she paint *on*? And how does she put the paint on? Come on. Milly.'

'No, honestly. We spread the paint out and she dabs it on with her paws.' She grinned. 'We do cheat a bit. I use a torch. She chases the beam. Her favourite support is sheets of acrylic. Luke gets them for me. Or cardboard. Anything, so long as it's rigid and flat.'

'Hmm.'

'Luke's going to give her an exhibition. He's got stacks of room at the workshop. We're thinking of having a proper private viewing and everything.'

'Milly.' Juno led the way back into the garden room. 'Sometimes I simply can't tell when you're being serious.' Milly was smiling mischievously. Not a serious proposition then. Juno motioned her into one of the comfortable, linen-covered armchairs nestled into the corners on either side of the long glass doors. The midday sunshine flooded the room.

Milly curled herself into a chair. 'Are you sure you've got time to stop?'

'I've got an hour before the next one comes.' Juno settled herself in the chair opposite.

'I saw a picnic hamper by the door.'

'I've just dug it out. I'm having a picnic with Esme tomorrow.' It gave her such a boost to be able to say this. Gosh, I'm pathetic, Juno thought. It was just so nice to feel – well – in demand.

'Oh, what fun! Esme's nice. I didn't know you were friends.'

'Oh, we don't really know each other. It was just an idea, you know, Esme suggested it.

It'll be nice to relax for a bit. I seem to be getting more and more pupils, which is good for the finances but it can be exhausting sometimes.'

Milly was looking at her gravely and sympathetically. There was something uncanny about the girl, Juno thought. It was hard to remember that she was still only seventeen.

'I couldn't stand teaching, I wouldn't have the patience.' Milly's eyes narrowed in a cat-like smile and she started to stroke Sapphy who had jumped onto her lap, settled down and was purring loudly, her green eyes half shut. 'I do love your house,' she said, looking around. 'This room is really groovy. Like the inside of a thrush's egg.'

Charmed despite herself, Juno thought, that makes it

sound so pretty, instead of the way it is, which is just old-fashioned. She sighed. 'Everything is so old. I love nice things, I'm afraid. I've had all this stuff for ever.'

'I prefer older stuff. And I love blue, it's so peaceful.'

Did she mean it? She was always so encouraging. Did she really think all this old tat was 'lovely'? Juno fought down an impulse to express her real feelings, for once, to blurt out in great gulping sobs her dissatisfaction with her life, her misery and loneliness and fear. What on earth would Milly do? The maddening thing was she would probably cope extremely well, the way she always did. There was a strong element of the nursery-nurse about Milly, a side of her that was never happier than when sticking plasters on cut fingers or comforting troubled spirits. She would make a wonderful mother, Juno suddenly thought, and with the picture that this idea conjured up in her head came a wave of dislike so strong that she caught her breath and inhaled sharply, as though a spasm of actual pain had shivered through her body instead of through her soul.

'Are you okay?' Milly said.

Juno hardly heard her. I hate her, she thought. Amy, my foot, it's Milly Luke loves. Look at her, sitting there with that cat, as pretty as a picture, sweet and innocent and young, blast her ... completely unaware of her power. Her eyes filled with tears and she choked on a sob.

Instantly Milly was at her side, touching her shoulder. 'What's the matter? What's wrong?'

Juno flinched. 'Nothing. Nothing.' She fished for a handkerchief tucked into her sleeve. She could smell the faintly soapy smell of Milly's skin. Milly's hair brushed her cheek. She went rigid. 'No,' she said fiercely, pushing Milly away. 'It's all right. I'm all right.' She heaved great sobs, unable, now she had started, to stop.

'Let me help.'

Not you. 'You can't help.' Only by going away, she thought. Far, far away.

'Shall I get Izzy?'

'No ... wait a minute.'

'Was it something I said?'

'It's just – hormones.' Juno blew her nose. 'Nothing to worry about. Sorry, Milly. Where were we?'

Milly moved away and relaxed back into her chair, her face troubled. 'I wish I could help.'

'I'm okay. Really.' Juno took a breath and sat back, trying to calm down. 'How are you, anyway, Milly? We haven't had a proper chat for a long time. How are the nightmares?'

Milly shrugged. 'Sometimes I wonder if I fell in the river or something. Something must have happened, it can't be normal to have the same sort of nightmares over and over again like this. I'm sick of it. If I knew why I had them they might stop.' She subsided back in her chair. 'I'm talking too much.'

'No, you're not.' Juno sipped her coffee, heat rising up her face, her heartbeat quickening. Milly was looking at her curiously: she'd noticed her agitation. 'There might be something behind them,' Juno said slowly. 'Perhaps you ought to see a hypnotherapist or someone, see if they can dig out what's bothering you. It could be something quite innocuous, like – if you dream all your teeth have fallen out. That's supposed to mean something.' It means death, she suddenly remembered. Death.

Milly was looking out of the window. Now she looked at Juno again. 'You're right, I haven't made enough of an effort to find out.' She hesitated, looking as if she wanted to confide. 'I've had other dreams too, recently. There's a lot of violence and anger. Bad things. I'm running along a corridor ...' She stopped. 'I don't know where it's coming from.'

Juno said, frowning down into her mug, 'Does Luke ever talk to you about when you were little? About your mother?' Right, she thought, worry about that, why don't you. She said more gently, 'Men never seem to believe in digging into the past, do they?'

'Oh but Luke's different from most men.' To Juno's annoyance the hint seemed to have gone right over Milly's head. Her face cleared and a dreamy look came into her eyes that made Juno want to slap her.

'He is, isn't he?' she said, unable to keep the edge from her voice. 'Perhaps you should talk to him about your nightmares again, tell him how much they're bothering you.'

'Perhaps I will. I haven't, really. I haven't wanted to worry him.' After a pause Milly said, looking more cheerful, 'We saw you in town.' She sipped her coffee.

'Who did? When?'

'Luke and me. I. The other day. We went to the hardware place to get some washers for the cloakroom tap. You were on the other side of the road and Luke said, Is that Juno? She's had something done to her hair. He said how pretty you were looking.' Milly was beaming at her with apparent pleasure.

She hasn't a clue, Juno thought. God, I am so confused. Anyway, how could she know? I never give myself away, not for an instant. She's just pleased because she loves Luke and his approval means everything to her. How dare he say I look pretty? He still won't come near me so what's the use? 'Well, that's good,' she said, forcing a smile. 'Compliment duly noted. I was worried I'd let her cut it too short.'

'It suits you. You must come round, you haven't been over for ages.' Milly began stroking Sapphy with long, voluptuous strokes which Juno found vaguely disturbing. The cat sat with her front paws tucked under her, her grass-green eyes staring at Juno with an unnervingly fixed, cold gaze.

'I wish my students would concentrate like that,' Juno said. 'She looks almost on the point of speech.' Luke had said she looked pretty! Oh God, no, she mustn't swerve, mustn't weaken.

Milly was looking at her, her expression grave. 'Juno,' she said. 'You didn't tell Luke I was definitely going out with that boy, did you? The one you told me about, whom I haven't actually met yet?'

'Ah. Oh dear, have I put my foot in it?' Juno sat back. Careful now. 'Sorry, Milly. I suppose I did rather jump the gun. Luke was looking so worried I wanted to set his mind at rest.'

'Worried? What about?'

'Well ... you, I suppose. You know he's become very – close – to someone, don't you?' God. Where did that come from? What am I doing?'

'I'm sorry? Who? What d'you mean, close?'

Juno smiled. 'Amy, Milly.' She paused to let this sink in. 'You must have realised they were seeing a lot of each other.'

Milly was frowning. That had rattled her cage. Wiped the smile off her face.

'This is rather private, Milly. Luke knows he can confide in me, that I won't break his confidence.'

'So now you're telling me.'

Hmm. She was upset. Good. 'Only because you're bound to have picked something up. Am I right?'

Milly got up and walked around the room. She sat down again, lifted her glass, looked into it and put it down again.

'More milk, Milly?'

Milly shook her head. 'I really should be going.'

Juno decided that she didn't want her to go. Not yet. 'How are you getting on with Pascale?' she experimented, beginning to breathe more quickly.

'Well,' Milly said as if grateful for the change of subject. 'You know how she is with me. Ratty. It's as if there's a subtext I know nothing about. I know not everybody can get along, but it's more than that, it's as if she really hates me.' She shrugged and looked hopefully at Juno. 'I wish I knew what it was I did to make her dislike me so.'

Just because Pascale doesn't fall at your feet like everybody else, Juno thought.

'I know you've noticed. And I notice more, now I'm older.'

Juno let her face assume a thoughtful expression. 'Look, Milly. You know how devoted she was to your mother. Miranda was the only person Pascale ever seemed to truly connect with, apart from her husband of course. She worshipped her. She never wavered, wouldn't have a bad word said against her, everything Miranda did was perfect.' She heard the bitter tone creeping into her voice and corrected it quickly. She forced a laugh.

Milly was gazing at her as if hypnotised.

'And then Miranda died.'

'Are you saying she blames me? Is that what this is all about? I feel her antagonism so strongly.'

'Oh, Milly.' Feel it then. If it's the only thing wrong in your perfect life.

'I did rather ruin my mother's life. By being born, I mean.'

'Everything isn't always about you,' Juno said before she could stop herself. Milly looked surprised, then immediately penitent. 'You think Pascale blames you,' Juno blundered on, trying to gloss over her sharpness, 'somewhere deep down? It's possible, I suppose.' She felt excitement begin to churn in her stomach, the dawning thrill of euphoric pleasure at the precipitating crisis.

'But that's not fair. I didn't ask to be born.'

For two pins, Juno thought, she'd tell her the whole truth. That really would wipe the smile off her face. Not that she was smiling at the moment.

But of course she couldn't. Not the whole truth.

The doorbell rang.

'Oh, there's Alex. She's early, surely.' Juno glanced at her watch. 'Goodness, look at the time. I didn't hear a car, did you? It's Alex Ferguson, do you know her?' She got up, wiping her hands, suddenly sweaty, down her slacks. Just as well, perhaps.

Milly shook her head. 'I know her vaguely. I'd better go.' Juno watched as she unwound from her chair, her face troubled, and bent to retrieve Juno's mug from the floor. She followed Sapphy who was strolling ahead of her into the kitchen. She put the mug and her empty glass down on the wooden draining board and her hand on the hot tap.

'Leave those,' Juno said. 'I'll do them later. I must go and let Alex in.' She let Milly, still looking unhappy, and the cat out of the garden door, closed it behind them and went to open the front door. She opened it just in time to prevent Alex – a large, imperious-looking girl, now slightly annoyed – from ringing the bell again.

Chapter 28

Are we dancing?

'There's a dance or two,' Esme quoted, walking ahead of Juno with her long, rather shambling stride, '*in the old girl yet.*'

'Not so much of the old,' Juno said dutifully, slightly breathless. The picnic hamper was heavy and the rug she carried over her other arm was heavy too. The day was fine which had come as a relief, but she was unhappily conscious that as usual she'd made far too much food, and that all too soon her folly would be revealed. She and Izzy would be finishing things up for weeks. She'd made sausage rolls and sandwiches, she'd brought ham and cold chicken legs and mounds of salad. Artichoke hearts and olives and coleslaw. Basically she'd gone completely over the top.

Why did she always do this? She never seemed to learn. Why couldn't she be like Gina? Gina and Ted were a couple she and Mike had been to dinner with several times in the old days. Gina, on each occasion, had made a point of producing next to nothing, elegantly and with conviction, and surprisingly by the end of the meal they'd felt perfectly satisfied. Whereas whenever she and Mike gave a dinner party the table groaned under the weight of far too much food, a good deal of which was left over at the end of the meal.

'This looks like a good place,' Esme said, pausing by a blackthorn hedge on the river bank. She'd been to the library, she'd told Juno, and a carrier bag laden with books swung from the end of one long arm. 'We don't want to stray too far if you have to get back to work.'

'Actually I don't, thank goodness,' Juno said, dumping the hamper on the grass. 'I've taken the afternoon off. Here, let me put this down.' She spread the rug on the ground. 'This is nice. Good spot.' She looked around. It was a beautiful day, sunny and warm. The river flowed past, serene and peaceful. Moorhens pecked about. In the distance a pair of swans dipped their long necks under the water, searching for weed. She felt herself beginning to relax.

'Do you not enjoy your work?' Esme lowered herself onto the rug and Juno joined her, setting the hamper down between them.

'I love my teaching.' She still felt a little shy of Esme. 'The building society is just to keep the wolf from the door. It's not the kind of thing you get excited about. What about you? What do you do?'

'Oh ... red-hot romance, my dear,' Esme said, stretching out her long legs. She wore workaday brown leather sandals and seemed to feel easy inside her clothes and skin. Juno envied her composure. 'I translate romantic novels into Esperanto. It's fun. I enjoy it. A kindly aunt left me a legacy, in the nick of time I may say, so I don't have to work as hard as I would have had to, had she not.'

'How lovely. I wish somebody would leave me a legacy. Were you ... were you married?'

She nodded. 'For a number of years. It foundered, as so many do. One of life's shipwrecks. You?'

'Oh, the same. He found someone he preferred to me.' She opened the hamper and handed Esme a paper napkin and a plate.

'Oh, my dear. I am sorry.'

Juno shrugged. 'That's life.'

'Yes. Still ... *it's cheerio my deario that pulls a lady through....*'

Juno looked at her, mystified and unsure how to reply. Esme really was rather odd. She eased the lids off the plastic containers and laid them on the rug like offerings before a shrine.

Esme gave a quiet guffaw. 'Sorry,' she said. 'I've been re-reading *Archy and Mehitabel* and I can't get their voices out of my head. Do you know Don Marquis? I find him quite irresistible.'

'What's it about?'

'Well. Archy is a cockroach who writes by tapping the typewriter keys with his chin. His friend Mehitabel is a cat. I'll lend it to you, if you like.'

How peculiar! She is odd, Juno thought, but I do like her. She watched as Esme helped herself liberally from the containers.

'This is wonderful,' Esme said. 'What a treat.'

Suddenly it didn't seem too much after all.

'Would you ever consider marrying again?' Juno asked, helping herself to a sausage roll.

'Hmm. I used to think not ... but then a year or so ago I met someone. I was on holiday in Cornwall. He was there with his very sick wife. We fell in love.'

As simple as that. Juno looked at her, intrigued.

'So, of course ... actually, he wrote recently to tell me

she had died.' She made a little grimace and wiped a spot of dropped mayonnaise from the front of her anorak with her finger. 'Have you noticed how fate has a way of throwing a spanner in the works just when you think you're back in control? I'm agnostic, of course, but you know what they say. If you want to make God laugh, tell him your plans.' She smiled wryly and licked the mayonnaise off her finger with a complete lack of self-consciousness.

'Oh dear, how sad.' I don't want her disappearing off to Cornwall, Juno thought.

Esme shrugged. 'Too late. Too late. Come on, let's change the subject. Your turn.'

Pitying her but feeling like a girl again, Juno said, 'Teach me some Esperanto.' I need friends, she thought. I've shut myself away too long. I wish I could confide in her.

'Esperanto. Right then. What shall I say? *"Konfesado kuracas la animon."* "Confession is good for the soul."'

Juno's hand stopped halfway to her mouth. She looked at Esme who, apparently oblivious, took a huge bite out of a thick slice of olive ciabatta. She knows, Juno thought. But how could she? Who would have told her?

Nobody. Guilt was making her paranoid.

But she's right, she thought. Esme was still speaking but her voice seemed to come from far away, as faint as though a closed door stood between them.

I can't go on like this, Juno thought. She's right. I need to confess.

JUNO RAN hot water into the sink and began scrubbing the stuck-on bits around the inside of the scrambled-egg pan with a Brillo pad. The last of her two afternoon pupils had gone and the evening stretched ahead, devoid of interest.

Izzy, as usual, hadn't eaten the lunch Juno had left for her in the fridge. She'd refused breakfast and had gone rushing off somewhere, she hadn't said where.

For two pins if it wasn't so late she'd pop down to Guildford again. Losing herself in shopping seemed the only way she could relax. But she mustn't, she was spending far too much money. Every so often she got this reckless feeling and then she just didn't care what she did. She gave the saucepan a shake and put it upside-down on the draining rack.

This wouldn't do. She had to pull herself together, go for a walk or something. She couldn't stay here alone, with nothing but lurid images going around and around in her head. The terrible screech of a lorry trying to brake, the scream and crackle of metal tearing and buckling, the sight of a hank of blonde hair caught in a lorry's wheel and torn from a head, the impact of bodies on tarmac, the smell of blood and burning tyres.

She put her hands up to her ears to block out the sound. She scrunched up her eyes and opened her mouth in a silent scream. Sometimes she felt that the guilt she was carrying might be slowly sending her mad.

Chapter 29

Some enchanted evening

Juno said, 'Did you mind meeting here?'

It was Saturday evening. On impulse she had invited Luke to join her for supper at Mr So, the Chinese restaurant that had just opened in town.

'Not a bit.' Luke's expression calmed her a little. He looked tranquil, even a little amused. He'd washed his hair so that it flopped over his forehead. Perhaps she ought to feel flattered that he'd bothered. He pulled out a chair for her.

'Thanks.' She sat down. He had such nice manners; she'd always liked that about him.

He sat down opposite her at the square, black lacquered table, set with red placemats and plain white china, and looked around with interest at the bright interior of the restaurant, at the red lacquer screens, the red tasselled hanging lanterns and the waitresses in their brocade Cheong Sam. He sat back with his arms folded and smiled. 'Nice place.'

That was a plus but Juno felt anything but relaxed. She wasn't at all sure the invitation, offered on the spur of the moment, had been a good idea. She had intended to talk to Luke about Milly, but now, looking at his closed face, she was afraid she might have caught a tiger by its tail. It alarmed her a bit, the way he looked at her sometimes as though he could see right through her.

'I was surprised by your invitation.' Trust Luke, straight for the jugular.

'I thought it would be nice to meet away from home. Spur of the moment thing. I hope you don't mind. My treat. I felt we hadn't had a proper chat in ages.'

'Of course I don't mind and I shouldn't dream of not sharing expenses. I did wonder if you wanted to talk about Milly.'

'Milly?' Was she really so obvious?

'Well.' He leaned back in his chair and crossed his long legs. The fingers of one hand tapped a little dance on the table top. 'We've always been at loggerheads about the way to handle things.'

Was this a chance? 'She did – say something, but that wasn't why I wanted to meet.' She looked at him with her head on one side. 'Does there have to be an ulterior motive?' Immediately she regretted her choice of words. 'I mean – a reason? Maybe I just thought we might enjoy each other's company.'

'That's a kind compliment. May we have five minutes?' he said to the waitress, a tiny Chinese girl wearing a red and gold Cheong Sam, who had come up and was standing silently by. Juno wondered if Luke thought she was attractive.

The girl bowed and retreated.

'You were saying?' There was a glint in Luke's eye.

'Oh, it wasn't anything special.' She daren't risk it. They hadn't even ordered. He might walk out. Luke's anger was something to behold. When he was angry his grey eyes flashed and turned silver, scary.

'I'd rather you told me what was on your mind, Juno.'

She gave what she hoped sounded like an exasperated little sigh and said with genuine reluctance, since she was now terrified of messing up, 'It's just, Babe told me that Milly was still having these awful nightmares and that you still go into Milly's room when she has them, to – help – you know.' Babe hadn't, but he wasn't to know that. 'Luke, she's seventeen. People will talk.'

'Will they?'

'You know what I mean. These things have a way of getting out.'

'I'm not going to tell anyone. Are you?'

'Of course not but – oh, you know what I mean, it isn't appropriate. You being in her room in the middle of the night—'

'But we're having a passionate affair, didn't you know? It's entirely appropriate.'

'Luke!'

'Yes?' Perfectly straight face, not a glint of humour. Lips tighter than usual.

'*Are* you – I mean—'

'Look here, Juno. How could you even imagine such a thing? Having made that quite clear, whatever does or does not go on between Milly and myself is none of your business. Right? Now, change of subject, please.'

'I was only—'

'No. None of your business, Juno.'

But it was. It was. Oh, Luke, Juno thought. She bowed her head. 'Sorry.'

He nodded. 'Now that's settled, shall we order?'

Juno picked up the menu and pretended to scan it, her

heart thudding with humiliation. For two pins she would have got up and walked out, but she couldn't, not yet. There was another reason she'd asked Luke here. Another little turn of the screw.

And there they were coming in from the street, Jean-Paul and Milly, talking nineteen to the dozen. No doubt about it, Jean-Paul was an attractive young man. Surely Milly could see that? Luke really was too old for her, whatever he might think. Milly was glowing, happy. She looked carefree, instead of burdened, as she sometimes looked when Juno had caught sight of her deep in conversation with Luke about some ridiculous subject – poetry, or chess.

Luke, who had his back to the door, hadn't seen them come in. Juno looked forward to the moment when he would catch sight of them and realise that his gorgeous pet Milly was being wined and dined by another – much younger – man.

Sure enough, Milly's voice dropped clearly into a momentary lull in the quiet hum of other diners' conversations. 'Look, you do know this is just mates, don't you?' The rest of the sentence was drowned in a renewed buzz of conversation.

Luke had heard. In the same moment that he turned his head and saw them, Milly said, 'Oh look, there's Juno!'

Jean-Paul looked across at them and said something to Milly.

'Good lord, there's Milly,' Luke said. 'And Jean-Paul.'

'What a coincidence,' Juno said.

'I think I'll have a word.'

For goodness' sake, Juno thought. 'Hadn't we better order?' she said.

'I didn't know she was meeting Jean-Paul,' Luke said.

'She doesn't tell you everything, Luke. Did you tell her

you were meeting me? Exactly,' Juno said as he shook his head.

'It was rather last-minute,' Luke said.

'I expect her date was, too. Now, what do you think? I rather fancy their Kung Pao chicken. Or there's always dim sum, to start with.'

Their waitress came over, smiling. 'Ready to order now?'

As soon as she'd taken their order and left, Luke stood up without a word. Slightly anxiously Juno followed him over to Milly's table.

'Hello, you two,' Luke said. 'I didn't know you were meeting Jean-Paul, Milly.'

'I told Babe,' Milly said. 'It was kind of last-minute.'

'It's okay,' Luke said. 'Just saying.'

'I didn't know you were meeting Juno.'

'That was kind of last-minute, too. Oh well, enjoy yourselves.'

Jean-Paul was leaning back in his chair, watching this exchange with bright, knowing eyes. Don't say anything, Juno thought.

Too late. 'Great suggestion, Mrs—'

'Juno,' Juno said.

'Juno. Thanks. This is perfect.'

Milly looked puzzled.

'Mrs ... Juno ... recommended this place.'

Luke frowned. 'When was this?'

'Day or so ago,' Jean-Paul said.

'I didn't know you two had met,' Luke said.

'She brought those cakes to the workshop,' Jean-Paul said.

'Of course.'

'Then we bumped into each other in the street, we got

talking, I said I was taking Milly out tonight and wanted somewhere we could get some good food, and she recommended here.'

'Thanks, Juno,' Milly said, beaming. 'I've been longing to come here. Juno's our next-door neighbour,' she told Jean-Paul.

'Ah,' Jean-Paul said. 'So your friend Izzy—'

'Is my daughter,' Juno said. She didn't dare look at Luke. 'I quite forgot I'd told you about Mr So,' she said. But she knew Luke didn't believe her.

I wonder if I can think of anything else I can do to sabotage this evening, Juno thought. 'Have you worked with Luke long?' she asked Jean-Paul.

'Couple of years now.'

'Couldn't do without him now,' Luke said. 'Oh, and Jean-Paul?'

'Sir?'

'For goodness' sake. When have you ever called me sir?'

'It seems appropriate. I have a feeling I'm about to be told off.'

'Nonsense, of course you're not. Of course not. Only get her home by eleven, right?'

'Right. No point in arguing,' Juno heard him mutter to Milly as Luke went back to their table. 'He had steam coming out of his ears.'

'No, he didn't.'

'Yes, he did. He looked the way he does when someone's cocked up in the workshop. Good and mad.'

'How sweet,' Juno said. They'd reached the coffee stage. The conversation had been sticky but they'd managed to find enough to talk about to get through the meal although by now Juno, at the point of despair, was feeling that this whole idea had been one of the worst she'd ever had. 'They make a handsome pair, don't they? How old is Jean-Paul?'

Luke shrugged. 'Twenty-four? Twenty-five?'

'Ah. A bit old for Milly but she's quite grown-up for her age in some ways.'

'In other ways disconcertingly child-like.' He had his fierce look.

Juno said, 'I suppose they see quite a lot of each other, Jean-Paul being your right-hand man.'

'I hope she knows what she's doing. He's a bit of a charmer and she has such a kind heart. I thought I ought to have a word.'

'Oh, Luke.'

'What?'

'You can't keep her wrapped in cotton wool for ever, you know. She'll be off to university in a couple of months. She'll have young men buzzing around her like bees. And now there's Stephen as well.'

'Hmm.'

'Of course she will, she's very pretty, haven't you noticed?'

'Of course I've noticed. She's exactly like her mother. Miranda was one of the most beautiful women I've ever seen.'

So Milly was beautiful. Juno's lips tightened. She looked at Luke under her eyelashes. He was looking moodily over to where Milly, obviously relaxed and enjoying herself, was talking animatedly to Jean-Paul. She was wearing a dead simple, long, sleeveless dark blue dress which showed off her womanly figure. She looked stunning. And very grown-up.

Juno shifted in her seat. She felt the quick anger with

Milly that seemed to lie just below the surface, welling up at the slightest prompt. She leaned down to where her handbag rested against the table leg, pretending to look for a handkerchief, desperately searching for a topic of conversation that would distract him and shift his attention away from the girl across the room.

She had thought her plans were succeeding. He had seemed to be keen on Amy, but honestly, it was hopeless. Milly just had to lift her little finger. It was sickening.

Jean-Paul and Milly had finished their meal. They were getting up, Jean-Paul holding Milly's cardigan, solicitous, attentive, while she slipped her arms into the sleeves. Jean-Paul had paid the bill and now they were thanking the smiling waitress and coming over to say goodnight.

'Bye then,' Milly said. Her cheeks were flushed and her eyes sparkling.

'We thought we'd go for a stroll,' Jean-Paul said. 'Enjoyed your meal?'

'Very much,' Luke said.

'The Peking duck was yummy,' Milly said childishly.

'Good,' Luke said, smiling. 'Thanks, Jean-Paul.'

'What for?' Jean-Paul said, his eyebrows going up.

What for, indeed? Juno thought. Luke didn't own her.

'It's entirely my pleasure,' Jean-Paul said with a lift of his eyebrows.

Milly was looking grave, too. Good. She wouldn't like him being proprietorial. Give him enough rope and he'd hang himself as far as she was concerned. Perhaps the evening hadn't been a complete disaster.

'Don't let her get cold,' Luke said.

For heaven's sake!

'I won't.'

Milly smiled her sweetest smile at Luke, looking at him with what – regret? – apology?

They'd gone, and a stillness settled over the table. Juno racked her brains for something to say. What had possessed her to think this would be a good idea? Around them voices rose and fell, glasses tinkled, knives and forks clattered lightly. A while back, the waitress had come and put a small, lit candle in the middle of the table. The music had changed from gay French *chansons* to dreamy and slow. Romance was in the air.

And inside Juno, a desolation. What was the use? Even if her plans came to fruition and she achieved what she had set out to achieve, what then? Would it make her any happier?

She looked at Luke's abstracted face with a feeling of near-despair. He had withdrawn again and obviously didn't feel like talking. In anyone else this lack of effort might be thought ill-mannered but Juno couldn't bring herself to blame him. This was all her fault. She noted surreptitiously the expression on his face. He looked bereft. Hopefully, if her plans worked out, this was only the start of it.

She must face the fact that she was never going to win him back. It would have to be done through someone else. Amy looked like the best bet at the moment. Oh well. She sat up and straightened her back.

Her heart might be broken but her will was as strong as ever. Whatever happened, Luke was not going to get Milly. Juno's plans would succeed, one way or another. Just watch.

Chapter 30

When hope flies

'What's the matter, Izzy? What's wrong?'

Izzy, hunched in a heap in our favourite spot in the orchard, was crying so hard she could hardly speak.

'I had to talk to someone.' She twisted around, her breath shuddering, and sat up, her legs crooked up, ungainly. For once she didn't care what she looked like. Her face was a swollen mess and she hadn't brushed her hair or bothered with makeup, unless she'd cried it all off.

She looked so broken I was almost afraid to touch her. I crouched down and put my hand on her shoulder. 'Has something happened to Juno?'

She shook her head.

'Robert?'

Izzy's head bowed even lower. She nodded.

'Oh, Izzy, what's happened?'

She blew her nose and dropped her hanky between her legs into the grass, still damp with dew. 'I can't see him anymore.'

I looked at the slump of her shoulders, her bowed head. 'Why not?' I said. 'Has your mum found out?'

'That wouldn't stop us.' Her contempt scorched. Of course it wouldn't.

'What is it? What's happened?'

'It's her. His wife.'

'She's found out?'

'That wouldn't stop us either, dummy.' She started crying again. 'She doesn't know anything.'

'Well, what then?' She seemed to be calming down so I plonked myself down beside her and waited.

She heaved a sigh dredged up from her very depths. She leaned her head back against the tree behind her and closed her eyes. I thought that if this was a scene on telly there would be snot running down her upper lip which she would make no attempt to remove. They always overdid it. Izzy's face by contrast was puffy and wet, but clean. 'She's ill. She's got cancer. He says we can't go on because it wouldn't be right, with her being so ill. With the children and everything.'

I refrained from commenting that he hadn't seemed so bothered about the children before. 'Is she going to die?'

'I don't know.' Izzy turned her head and looked at me and in her eyes there was a glimmer of hope which I did my best not to notice. Then she started crying again.

I sat and waited. I examined my feelings and was relieved to note that there was not one spark of gladness in my heart. Not one.

Izzy left after only a few minutes, looking terrible. She was going home, she said, she couldn't face anybody, all she wanted to do was crawl into bed and sleep. Her life was over; she would never be happy again.

Feeling I hadn't helped a bit, I walked down the hill to

the river. It was weird to think that Robert's short but potent reign was over. I stopped by the stone bridge to watch a pair of swans move languidly over the still, dark water under the overhanging trees. It was a lovely day, the sky gentian blue, the sun warm on my back. The serene surroundings made Izzy's pain seem worse somehow. Like when someone dies in the spring, I thought, leaning my elbows on the parapet.

I had been tongue-tied in the face of Izzy's grief. Of course Rob couldn't leave his wife if she'd got cancer, Izzy wouldn't want him to, not once she was in her right mind again. It was just such a dreadful shock. But at least they were breaking up for a proper reason, not because he'd gone off her or anything. She'd see that once she'd calmed down. Of course it was awful that he'd been going to leave his wife but after all, that must mean that he had really loved Izzy, and she'd see that too, eventually.

The memory of Felix slid into my mind. Felix, grieving over Leonie, getting it all wrong about the way she was now. Wishful thinking. We seemed to do rather a lot of that in our house. All of us dreamers, wishing for the moon. Well, apart from Luke.

I remembered Jean-Paul saying that Leonie's mates hung around by the river sometimes. Might be worth whizzing down there to have a look. Perhaps I could persuade her to come and see her Grandpa.

I left the bridge and ran down onto the towpath. Roses spangled a high hedge on my left and purple balsam crowded the banks of the river. I dawdled, enjoying the lushness and isolation of the river bank. It was very quiet. Heat rose from the sun-baked ground and I felt too hot in my jeans. I should have put shorts on, or a skirt.

I brushed past fronds of willow overhanging the path and turned a corner. The path opened out into a clearing. I paused in my onward rush and stood still, watching. A group of lads were clustered around a rackety bench by the weir. Between them and the water was a stout wooden barrier against which they leaned then moved away and milled around, then leaned again. All of them were smoking. All held cans in their hands.

A girl's flag of almost-white hair shone out against the universal black of leather jackets and jeans. Tiny among her much larger companions, she leaned against a tall man in a black Graveyard Blues tee-shirt, nuzzling and stroking, pushing her face into his side. He smoked, ignoring her. Could that possibly be Leonie? Ought I to say something about Felix to her now I was here?

There was a mess of litter lying around. A smelly rubbish bin leaned nearby, full to overflowing. All around the base more rubbish had fallen: fast food containers, pizza boxes, drink cans, newspapers. Even, incongruously, a collection of chipped and cracked, once-white cups and saucers and an old metal tray, scratched and worn. The grass around the bench and the rubbish bin was worn through to the earth by many feet, and around the group by the bench, beer cans littered the ground. I could smell the booze from here, mingling with the smell of fags and mouldering food.

Don't be a coward, I told myself. Take no notice and walk on. You don't have to speak to them, just walk past. But they were all over the path, I would have to go through them. I frowned, looking harder.

My heart began to beat faster. I was scared. There were so many of them and three of the group were men, taller than the boys in the town.

The sensible thing to do would be to turn back, just turn back and go back to the road. I hesitated. It would be obvious then that I was trying to avoid them ... they might come after me. Perhaps the best thing would be to go straight on, say hi and walk on. They wouldn't stop me, surely? It was broad daylight. I mustn't be a wimp. But then I remembered the murder there'd been on this very towpath only a couple of years ago. Gruesome, pointless, a woman strangled in broad daylight by a group of boys very like this lot. Of course it had nothing to do with this gang and the police had made a point of saying how incredibly rare that sort of thing was. The perpetrators had been caught and were now in prison.

What I had to do was hold my head up and not show that I was scared. Treat them as I would anybody else. It was fine, I must stop letting my imagination run away with me. I couldn't bottle out now. Come on, one foot in front of the other. Walk on.

The sound of rushing water seemed to echo the hard pounding of my heart. The sun shone into my eyes. It was mid-afternoon on a perfect summer's day. Nothing was going to happen: this was Surrey, for Pete's sake, not Chicago.

I put my head up and marched straight towards them, my heart beating so hard I could feel a pulse throbbing in my throat. Even the birds seemed to have stopped singing; everything seemed to be holding its breath. Except for the sound of the water falling over the weir, rolling on and on like Niagara. The nearer I got to them, the louder grew the rushing of the weir and the greater my fear.

Some of them had spotted me. Actually they didn't seem interested, they just kept on smoking and milling around. I relaxed a bit. If I kept my cool and walked on it would be okay.

A bird flew squawking from a willow branch over my

head. I jumped, sending rose petals scattering from the hedge. The man in the Graveyard's tee-shirt turned his head and saw me. I stopped walking and became deeply interested in the hedge, then dawdled on. He dragged on his cigarette, exhaled and watched me through the smoke. He lowered his hand and went on staring.

Two of the taller lads turned to look. One was tall and thin, his ginger curls bushed around his pale face giving him a look of clownish sadness. The other was thick-set and hard-faced, his black leather jacket armoured with studs. Uninterested, they turned back to their cigarettes, but Graveyard kept on staring. The girl who I was now almost sure was Leonie seemed lost in a world of her own.

'What you want, girl?' Graveyard said at last as I came nearer.

My tongue seemed to be stuck to the roof of my mouth. I shrugged. 'Just walking.'

'Wait a minute,' he said after a pause, looking more closely. 'Don' I know you from somewhere?' He dragged on his cigarette and knitted up his forehead, trying to remember.

Leonie, who'd ignored my approach, suddenly woke up and turned to look at me. 'Christ, if it ain't Miss Butterfly. This is the bim we was tellin' you about, Jonny.'

She turned towards the man and put her thin arms around his midriff, nuzzling his chest with her face. He pushed her away, leaned back against the barrier and tilted his head to one side as he stared and stared. His cigarette, between drags, dangled from fingers stained with nicotine and what looked like engine oil.

I sincerely hoped he had a really bad memory, because I had just realised who he was and the last time we'd met he hadn't been at all pleased with me. After our last encounter

I'd walked home from town with the heartfelt desire never to set eyes on him again. Instead of which here I was facing him in the middle of nowhere, and he seemed rather drunk, definitely sinister and on the point of remembering who I was.

'Hey, Leonie,' I said at last in desperation. If only he'd stop staring.

Leonie frowned. 'How d'you know my name?'

One of the younger lads threw his cigarette butt on the ground and stamped on it, reminding me forcibly of the butterfly episode. I swallowed, increasingly nervous.

'What you want?' Leonie said, pushing away from the barrier and sauntering over, looking half-asleep but determinedly belligerent, to stand in front of me.

It's like dogs, I reminded myself. You mustn't let them see you're scared. Leonie was right in front of me, but I couldn't introduce the subject of Felix just like that, could I? No. 'Just out for a walk, that's all. Saying hello.'

''Well, don't bovver. She just saying hello,' she said, imitating my voice. 'Well, say hello to my bruvs then. Come on. Say hello.'

'Hello,' I said, trying to stay cool.

'She don't like you, bruvs,' Leonie tossed over her shoulder. She took a swig from the can in her hand, looking at me through slitted eyes.

'Well, that's a shame,' said Jonny. 'Because we've met before, ain't we, Miss *all up in other people's biznezz?*'

Oh bums, he'd remembered.

He detached himself from the barrier and ambled forward. It was his voice I remembered, light, tenor rather than bass and rough, almost as if there was something wrong with his throat. You felt a sense of strain, listening to it.

He tripped over a clod of dry earth and stumbled. Somebody laughed. It was the boy called Micky I remembered from the town. Jonny rounded on him. 'Shurrup, you.'

There was a long pause during which it flashed across my mind that I might actually faint from terror, and then what would happen? 'This beezy,' he said at last, turning to his audience, 'Came interferin', disrespectin' my space.'

They shifted and murmured and nodded their agreement. Scared as I was, I had a strong feeling that this was all an act. I was sure he could speak perfectly good English if he chose. Surprisingly this conviction took the edge off my fear and I looked back at him with something like equanimity.

'In she comes,' he went on, looking hard at me. 'Like she my momma or summing, choppin' me up in front of that panty-waist Denzil cat.' He turned to the others. 'We was just coolin', thassall.' He turned back to me. 'You're buggin', man. You owe me an ap-ol-gy.'

'Um – do I?' I bit my lip and tried to remember to breathe. I tried to think of something to say that wouldn't annoy him, but I was starting to feel pretty annoyed myself. 'Look,' I said. 'I'm sorry if I hurt your feelings or bugged you or whatever, but you were really rude to him, this Denzil guy. You called him an effing nigger-boy. I think that's awful.'

'What? He is an effin' nigga-boy.'

The others nodded in agreement.

'But that's racist,' I said earnestly, then felt embarrassed about my voice which suddenly seemed stuck-up and prissy. 'You're white. He's black. What's the big deal? And all that about his sister. You were pretty rude about her.'

'What? *What?*'

'Jonny,' Leonie said, throwing me a warning look.

'Shurrup,' Jonny said. 'Christ, this beezy is just asking for a slap. You one crazy bitch, you know that?' He was breathing hard.

'You don't wanna rile him,' Leonie said anxiously.

Jonny threw his cigarette butt on the ground. He came slowly towards me until he was standing so close that our fronts were almost touching. 'Ap-ol-gise,' he said. 'Now.'

A murmur of agreement rose from the audience.

I recoiled. He'd been eating curry – again. I turned my head aside to deflect his dragon breath and put my hand up over my mouth. He was scowling, his eyes flinty. My fear had come back, magnified, my whole body shaking with the thundering of my heart. Any minute now I was going to turn around and bolt.

I decided to cough. I coughed and coughed, bent over as though in the throes. He took a step back and stood looking at me, frowning.

'Come on, rudie,' Red Head said calmly, tapping ash from his cigarette with one finger onto the ground. 'We need to split soon. Does she look like she gonna apologise?'

I stood upright again. 'I do apologise, if I upset you,' I said. 'But I still think you shouldn't treat people like that.'

Jonny looked around at his following and made a gesture of incredulity. He shook his head, turned back to me and said, 'You're asking for a smack.'

'Aw, what is it with you?' I said, my own temper rising. 'I've apologised, haven't I?'

Scowling, he made a move towards me. Leonie grabbed his arm. 'Jonny,' she said.

Jonny threw Leonie off. She staggered and almost fell. 'Shut it,' he told her, glancing at the others. 'This ain't none of yours, so cool it.'

Bonar Ash

'Hey man,' Red Head said. 'Leave it, yeah? What you flippin' for? She's just some candy-ass tart.' He inhaled and looked on in a detached way.

Tension had crept into the group. I could almost smell the adrenaline flowing. My heart was pounding so hard I was sure the front of my tee-shirt must be bouncing up and down. I thought of Luke. His normality, his sanity seemed a long way away. They're like a pack of dogs, I thought. The two youngest ones were staring at me with their mouths hanging open. Another choke of laughter from somewhere.

Red Head appeared to have woken up at last. As if at some subtle signal from Jonny he moved around to stand behind me. I just managed to stop myself turning around to look at him.

'Yeah, clear off you, and you,' Jonny said, indicating the two younger boys. His dark eyes under their thick brows were fixed on me. 'Plans have changed. You can stay, Beaver,' he said, his eyes flicking to the thick-set man in the black leather jacket who, I saw now, had red-rimmed eyes and several days' growth of stubble.

The atmosphere had become charged, and in a snap my terror returned. A hush fell. They're like a pack of jackals, or a shoal of fish in the deep ocean, I thought, my anger draining away, my mind racing, looking for a way out. Infinitesimal signs show them which way to go, then they all move together.

The two younger boys moved off reluctantly. Perhaps they would tell someone. But I knew they wouldn't, they were too much in awe of Jonny.

'Here,' Jonny said, pleasantly enough. 'Let's see if you got any dosh.' He stepped up to me, pulled my rucksack off my shoulder and emptied its contents onto the ground. Out fell a comb, a hanky, my leather-bound copy of *Emma* and my small red purse. He opened the purse and spilt the contents onto the path.

He hunkered down and shifted through the coins with a look of disbelief on his face. 'Christ, this all you got? You ain't got much, have you?'

'I have to get home,' I said.

'You ain't goin' nowhere, mate. Five bob. Christ. How come you ain't got no bread?' he said disgustedly, standing up again and pushing the coins around with the toe of his boot. 'Posh bird like you.'

'I'm not a posh bird.'

'Look,' Leonie said.

Jonny rounded on her. 'I ain't tellin' you again. Fuckin' shut your gob.'

'You can't talk to her like that,' I said before I could stop myself. 'You really do need to mind your manners.'

He looked at me in disbelief. 'What's the matter wiv you? You got a death wish or summink?' He looked over my shoulder at Red Head and nodded towards the river. 'This bimbo needs teaching a lesson.'

They're going to drown me, I thought. My mind seemed to have gone numb; I hardly seemed able to think at all. I wouldn't turn to look behind me. Instinctively I kept my eyes on Jonny.

'Right,' Jonny said, back to staring at me again. He was smiling now, a kind of unconscious half-smile. Things did not look good. He said coldly to Leonie, 'You can clear off now.'

'No ... look ... Beaver, do something.'

I wondered if it was any use shouting for help.

'Hey, Jonny,' Red Head said behind me. 'Leave it now, hey?'

He shook his head. 'We ain't started yet. We're goin' on the island. Nobody ever goes there.'

'How we get across?' Beaver asked.

'Low tide. You can cross easy. There's that place by the bridge.' He looked at me again. 'You're comin' with us.' He sounded deprecating, almost contrite. 'Look, you like me, don't you? You'll enjoy yourself, promise.'

No way, I thought, my heart roaring. I closed my eyes and prayed. Help me. Please.

'Wait a minute,' Jonny said, looking behind me along the towpath.

I turned my head and saw, lurching along the towpath, a motley group of ancient-looking men. Some held bottles in their hands, some walking sticks. They were all talking and gesticulating widely as they marched, reeled or hobbled towards us.

'Fuck,' Jonny said. 'I'm off.'

The others moved off after him. None of them looked back. Leonie stayed where she was. The expression on her face almost made me laugh except that I felt too swollen with relief and the tears wanting to burst out of me. 'For Christ's sake,' she said, turning to run after the others, 'scarper before he changes his sodding mind.'

'No, wait,' I said. 'Leonie, your grandpa. He really misses you.'

'What?' She stopped and stared at me as if seeing me properly for the first time. 'How the fuck you know my grandpa?'

'He's living in my house. Our house. He has a room there.'

She was still frowning. 'Where's that then?'

I told her and she moved off, throwing me a last look

over her shoulder, a mixture of astonished discomfort and irresolution. She went a few paces then began to run.

I picked up my rucksack, my hands shaking so badly they could hardly function. Slowly I stuffed everything back into it and set off, walking fast, back towards the men. Approaching them I saw Old Flint at the head of the group.

'Hiya, Milly!'

'Mr Flint!'

'We saw you was in a bit of trouble there. Benny 'ere went back and got the other boys. Couldn't not come and see's you was all right. All ready to do battle, wasn't we, lads?'

'Sure we was.'

'Hear, hear.'

'Oh, Mr Flint!' Tears, not far from the surface, prevented me from continuing. I smiled and wiped my eyes.

'You get on home now, girl,' Mr Flint said. 'We'll make sure they's gorn. Off you go now. And don't you go walking down here on your own again. Ain't safe, pretty wench like you.'

'I don't know how to thank you.'

'See ya!' They lurched on, waving and smiling and calling me darling, love and beautiful. I wanted to hug them all individually, drunk or sober. They must be from the night shelter. Did they realise they had saved me?

Thank you, thank you, I said inside my head. I jogged on to the road bridge and halfway across I stopped to get my breath. My heart was still pounding, my legs felt weak. Luke. I had to find Luke.

Chapter 31

Eat your heart out, Fanny Cradock

JUNO, CARRYING A LARGE YELLOW CAKE, POKED HER head tentatively around the kitchen door. 'Babe? That you?' She was sure it must be Babe banging about in the pantry, but it was always advisable to announce her arrival, Babe being ridiculously proprietorial about Half Moon. You'd never think Juno had been coming here since long before Babe's time; if anything, Babe was the interloper.

Babe put her head around the pantry door. 'Oh, hello,' she said. 'What's that you've got there?' As always when you were anywhere near Babe some pop song or other was warbling out from her radio, practically drowning out her voice.

'I've been baking,' Juno said. 'I thought I'd make a cake for you all. Can't have too much cake.'

Just listen to the music of the traffic in the city,' Pet Clarke sang. '*Linger on the sidewalk where the neon signs are pretty ...*

'Well, that's nice,' Babe said. 'I'm sure they'll appreciate it.' She disappeared into the pantry again, raising her voice. ''Course at Milly's age they're always worrying about their weight, aren't they? Madness I call it, it's only a bit of puppy fat.' She came back into the kitchen, wiping her hands on a towel.

'I don't think Milly bothers her head about that kind of thing,' Juno said, looking around for somewhere to put the cake down. 'She's far too sensible.' She gestured towards the table, looking for a space among the cooking debris. Babe obviously didn't believe in clearing up as she went along. 'Shall I put it here?'

'That'll do.' Babe came back into the kitchen, went to the sink and started running water into a saucepan. From the scullery a man's deep voice boomed, 'Hope you're not feeling this way, but just in case, here they are, the Animals, with *We Gotta Get out of This Place*.'

'Luke about?'

'Not home yet. He's often in late nowadays. He's that tied up with that Amy Booth, always on the phone to him she is, and going around to the workshop again today, so Jean-Paul told me. Sweet on him she is, he says. She's around here every opportunity she gets. Comes into the kitchen without a by your leave asking for coffee or cups of tea for them both. Even suggested he teaches her chess. Can't wait to get her feet under the table.'

Girl, there's a better life for me and you, sang the Animals. *Believe me baby, I know it baby, you know it too....*

'Is he keen, do you think?' Juno said, leaning her back against the table and folding her arms. Be careful what you wish for, she reminded herself. It still hurt. She was torn between satisfaction and pain. Why couldn't it have been her?

Babe was scrubbing a saucepan vigorously with a Brillo pad. 'Hard to tell. Doesn't seem able to stand up to her.' She turned and gave Juno an appraising look as if wanting to confide. 'If you ask me he isn't in love with her. It's almost like ... well ... never mind. None of our business.' She turned back to the sink and banged the saucepan upside down on the draining board. Juno winced. Babe always had to make such a row about everything. 'Lamb curry tonight. Milly's favourite.' She chuckled. 'Well, one of her favourites.'

Juno tried and failed to think of something disparaging to say.

'She's a real homebody, I will say that for her. She'd rather be in the study reading or playing chess with Luke than off out somewhere.'

'You'd think she'd want to be out with friends her own age, at the youth club or somewhere.'

'Not Milly. She's not interested. Anyway, she's got Izzy.'

'Well, it seems rather unhealthy to me.'

'Yes, well, spending time with Luke is what she likes. It's nice, the way they get on. He's going to miss her dreadfully when she's away at St Andrews.'

'I suppose he will.'

Babe turned to the twin-tub and started hauling clothes out of the washer and dropping them into the dryer. 'Better get on.'

'Let me help.'

'I can manage, thank you. You've made a nice cake, that's quite enough.' She slammed the lid down and stayed for a moment, thoughtful, her hand on the lid. 'You knew her, Miss Miranda, didn't you, Juno? Pascale was on about her earlier.'

'Of course. We moved here just after Izzy was born.' Why was it Miss Miranda, Juno thought, and just Juno? Who the hell was Miranda, after all? Just the spoiled only daughter of doting parents who didn't know her at all.

'Course you did, you being neighbours and all. I was

forgetting.' She nodded. 'Ah well,' she said, bending to put the dryer on. 'She was only human, like the rest of us.' She hesitated as though she wanted to say more but changed her mind and went into the scullery again, returning with a colander full of runner beans.

What did she say that for? What did she mean? She couldn't possibly know, could she? By the time Babe came on the scene, Miranda was dead.

'Let her down badly, that choreographer fellow,' Babe said, depositing the colander on the sink drainer. 'Mad about him, she was. So Pascale says.'

You're fishing, Juno thought. You don't know anything about Miranda. Her spirits rose slightly. She stood there feeling redundant but unwilling to leave. Luke might be home any moment.

'If you just leave it there,' Babe said over her shoulder, 'I'll see it's put away somewhere out of sight. Thanks for your trouble.'

'It's no trouble. I hope they enjoy it. Well, I think I'll just pop up to see Esme for a minute.'

'She's working,' Babe objected, still with her back turned.

Juno's eyebrows went up. 'She can't work all the time. She must have tea breaks.'

'Suit yourself.' Babe dried her hands on a tea towel and started putting crockery away into the vast pine dresser.

She didn't need to make such a bloody awful racket doing it. I don't know how Luke stands it, Juno thought, going through into the hall. And it was none of Babe's business if she wanted to pop up and see Esme.

The point was, Esme was bound to chat with Luke sometimes, and, you never knew, the subject of Milly might come up, and it would be all to the good if Esme wasn't quite so starry-eyed about her. Juno hadn't liked the way Esme had sung Milly's praises the other day on their picnic. She wasn't sure how to lower her in Esme's estimation, but she'd think of something disparaging to say. Not too much: a seed of doubt was all it took. Just a seed.

Chapter 32

Sanctuary

I stumbled along the pot-holed lane and across the cobbled yard and threw myself at the workshop door, hammering with both fists, calling for Luke, then when there was no reply, for Jean-Paul. Nobody came.

I turned and leaned my back against the door, shaking. Stupid, there was no van in the yard. And I remembered now that Jean-Paul had gone to visit his father in Norwich.

I sank down onto the step. A strong wind had got up and was bending the tops of the silver birches in the small copse opposite the workshop. The familiar trees and bushes seemed peopled by ominous shadows; I became aware of threatening creaks and rustles. A twig broke.

I looked up at the sky. The sun had disappeared and the sky was laden with grey clouds. Luke wasn't coming. He was probably with Amy somewhere. He didn't care. I began to shiver. The day was warm but I was so cold. It must be shock.

Then I heard the van. I'd know the sound of that engine anywhere. It came slowly around the curve in the lane and pulled up in the yard. Luke's long legs emerged slowly, almost reluctantly, as though he was tired. I sprang up from the step and began to run.

It seemed to me that the gap between us was so great that it would take days – weeks – years for me to reach him across what seemed to me now a desert – a plain – an ocean. An unbridgeable divide. As if the faster I ran the further he would retreat from me, fading backwards with a rushing sound like the wind bending the branches which were starting to lash to and fro. I ran and ran. A sob caught in my throat.

He held out his arms to catch me. 'Milly! What's wrong?' A drop of rain fell.

'He ... he—'

'Who? What's happened?' There was something in his face. 'Tell me.'

'The river. I went. I was walking. I was upset about Izzy. There were too many of them. Oh, Luke, I needed you ... he was so scary.'

'Who was? *Who?* For God's sake, Milly, what's happened?' He seized hold of my upper arms and shook me. 'Are you hurt?'

'No.' I shook my head. 'It's all right. It was just some boys. Mr Flint came. He saved me.'

He pulled me to him and wrapped his arms around me. He held me tight against his chest and the pounding of his heart reverberated through my body. 'Are you hurt?' he said again over my head. 'What happened?' His whole body shook with the thunder of his heart. He smelt of rage.

'I got away. Mr Flint came. It's all right. He didn't.'

'Who?' He pushed me away from him, still holding on, so he could look into my face. 'Who are you talking about?'

'It was just some boys,' I said again when I could speak.

'They got a bit aggressive, that's all. But the men came and scared them off.'

'Who were they?' He pulled me to him again. 'Oh, Milly. My darling. My God, I'll kill anyone who hurts you with my bare hands. Look at me.' He tipped up my face with his finger-tips and the look on his face sent a shiver down my back. 'Oh, my Milly,' Luke said. 'My sweet Milly.' He bent his head and kissed me on the lips and my whole being became suffused with joy. I put my arms around his neck and kissed him back.

After not nearly long enough he raised his face from mine. 'Oh God, what am I doing?' he said. He disentangled my arms from around his neck and folded his arms around me, holding me tight against the thunder of his heart. I relaxed against him, trembling with shock, glued to him as though by some magnetic force.

The rain had started coming down hard, drowning the sound of a car coming around the bend in the lane. 'Oh!' I said and pulled away, feeling his impatient intake of breath. The noise of the wind in the trees was now almost deafening.

'Damn,' Luke said between his teeth. It was the first time I had ever heard him swear. 'Amy.'

We stood side by side like two children, hand in hand, as the rain poured down and Amy's blue Volvo pulled into the yard. She pulled her raincoat hood over her head and climbed out of the car.

She isn't real, I thought. One puff and away she will fly like thistledown. None of it felt real, perhaps I was dreaming. Maybe they had raped and murdered me after all and I'd died and this was my longing, which I hadn't even realised was there, making strange things happen, and I wasn't really real either.

'What on earth is going on?' Amy said, running to the workshop door with little pattering steps. 'What are you two doing standing out here in the rain? Let me in, Luke, for goodness' sake.'

We're busy, I wanted to shout. Go away. But Luke pulled me with him to the door, fishing the key out of his pocket. 'You need to get dry,' he said, not looking at me. 'Go into the washroom and change. There are some spare overalls there. Put them on and come back and I want to hear what happened. Everything,' he said as I blundered towards the washroom. 'Milly.' He called me back. 'It wasn't Jean-Paul, was it?'

'Jean-*Paul*! *No!*'

'Okay. Hurry back. Hello, Amy. Sorry. Urgent – urgent problem.'

You don't have to apologise to her, I muttered in the washroom, all thumbs. She would come and spoil it. But Luke called me his darling. He did! He called me his darling. He's Luke. He's my guardian, my friend.

But he called me his darling.

Everything was different. Everything was changed. I'm a woman, I thought, fumbling with buttons. Nothing will be the same. It was as if some protective shield around me had fallen away and shown me myself as I really was.

I love him. I love him.

When I got back Amy was sitting sideways on a bench, looking up at Luke, looming above her with his hands in his pockets. He turned quickly towards me. His face was pale, his black hair scuffed as though he'd been running his hands through it.

'Ah, Milly.' Hands out of pockets, body tense. 'Come and sit down. Amy came to see how the chair was getting on.' He walked towards me.

'It's okay, I'll go,' I said, radiant. 'I'll see you later at home. I don't want to interrupt.' I didn't care. Amy could stay. I would go. I was impervious, floating.

'Wait, I'll give you a lift home.'

'No, I will,' Amy said, standing up. 'I'll see you later, darling. This child needs to get home.'

'No – look—'

'I'm going that way anyway. We can't interrupt your work a moment longer, I'm sure Milly understands that, don't you, Milly? Come along.' She ushered me towards the door, like a sheep dog watching for signs of escape. I smiled. Everything was amusing, lovely, like champagne. Bubbles. 'I'll see you later, darling,' Amy said, giving a little wave over her shoulder.

Darling? (Twice.) Damn her, all the same. Why didn't he say something instead of just standing there? He'd looked – shell-shocked. Not particularly happy. Oh, darling Luke, I love you.

(What was that look on his face? Resignation?)

'What was all that about?' Amy said in the car over the sound of the rain on the car roof and the clicking of windscreen wipers. The car smelt of her scent.

'Oh, just some boys ... nothing. Things got a bit out of hand, that's all.' My hands were tight fists.

'Luke seemed quite concerned.'

'No – really?'

Amy glanced at me sharply. So she recognised sarcasm. That was something. 'Well, of course, he is responsible for you.'

As you, and Juno, never tire of reminding me. 'Excuse me, Mrs Booth, but I'd like to get out here. I'll walk from here.'

'But it's miles! And it's pouring!'

'I'd like to walk. It's only a couple of miles. I don't care about the rain, I like it. Stop the car, please.'

'Well – if you insist – but—'

'Thanks.' I got out and set off along the road, not looking back. I don't care, I don't care, I thought, not waving as the car drove slowly past me then away. I wanted to be rude. I wanted to be honest instead of polite all the time when I didn't mean it. Luke, I thought, when the car was out of sight.

I wanted to turn around and walk back. What would he say to me? What would he do? I paused, irresolute. No. I walked on through the driving rain.

Chapter 33

You can push some people too far

'Talk to me, Izzy,' Juno said. 'Tell me. What is it?'

'You wouldn't understand.'

It was Tuesday afternoon. Juno had come home from work and opened the front door to the sound of sobbing coming from Izzy's bedroom. The room was stuffy, the window shut and the curtains closed. Izzy lay face down on the bed, her face half-buried in the duvet. The small section of cheek Juno could see was scarlet and sodden. Strands of hair stuck to her damp forehead.

'Izzy, what's the matter? Whatever it is I'll understand.' A terrifying thought struck her. 'You're not pregnant, are you?'

Izzy gave an animal wail that struck Juno to the heart. She recoiled. 'Are you?'

'Of course not, how dare you, trust you to think of that, you would!' She turned her head away.

'If you won't tell me, what can I do but guess? Please, Izzy. I can't bear to see you like this. Let me help.'

'Nobody can help. I wish I was dead.'

'Don't. Please don't.' Ineffectually Juno stroked the duvet beside Izzy's shoulder.

'Why, because it makes you feel bad? It's all about you, isn't it? It's always about *you*.'

Was it? How was it?

'Just because you hated your dad, you never wanted me to get to know mine.'

'Izzy, that's rubbish! We've been through all this. Is that what this is about?'

'No. No! I'm just saying ...'

'I don't understand.'

'Why couldn't I have a mother like Milly's? Someone who really loved her. I know Dad had an affair with her but I'm beginning to see why, perhaps you didn't understand him either, perhaps he had to turn to her for understanding ... sympathy ... I mean, *you* weren't ill, *you* didn't have some awful disease, so it didn't matter, did it, if you didn't really care about him?'

'What in God's name are you talking about?' Juno began to shake. 'What do you mean, I wasn't ill? And don't you dare say I didn't care about your father. That's a terrible thing to say. I loved Mike, you know I did. Till he went and – what's the matter with you?'

'At least Milly's mother loved her ... cared about her ...'

And Juno burst, like a bottle of cider that's been shaken too long, Izzy's words piercing her careful control like a needle going into a balloon.

'Loved her! Cared for her! If you only knew.' Struggling for control she got up and strode over to the window and stood with her back to the room, holding onto the windowsill for support. The shaking was worse now, a hot rage creeping up her body to her head. There was a mist in front of her eyes.

'What d'you mean?'

Juno turned around. Izzy was sitting up on her elbows, staring at her. 'I don't think Miranda was a good mother to Milly,' Juno said, her face red, then white as the adrenaline leached away with the supreme relief of letting it all out. 'I think she was unkind to her. I know you two were always up trees and standing on your hands but there were too many bruises ... Milly came to me sometimes, crying, but I could never get her to tell me what was the matter. You were too small to notice how nervous and jumpy she was, but I'm sure you remember how terrified she was of the dark? I had to practically beg Miranda to let her have a night-light because Milly told me she was so scared, she couldn't sleep. Do you remember that time she had a broken arm? Miranda said she'd fallen down the stairs. Bruised ribs and a broken arm. And there were really dreadful bruises on her back one day when we changed her clothes in our house. She was only five. She was black and blue. I was horrified. Whenever I said something to Miranda, there was always some excuse.'

'You're lying,' Izzy said, twisting around and sitting up.

At least she had her attention. Juno shook her head. 'I think Miranda was completely selfish and Milly was just a nuisance who had ruined her life, so she took it out on her. Look—' as Izzy opened her mouth to speak. 'I can't take it anymore, Milly's daft illusions about Miranda and you going on and on about what a great mother Miranda was and how you wish I was like her. Believe me, you don't. And that isn't the worst of it. It's time you knew the truth. There's something else.'

Chapter 34

The blind side of the heart

I LAY ON MY BED, FACE DOWN, MY HEART THUDDING. I tried to think about Izzy and her sadness, to ignore the sensations pouring through my body like a river, unstoppable, my heart pulsing in my throat so that I felt I was suffocating.

How would I face Luke? Had I imagined what had happened out there in the yard outside the workshop? How should I behave? It was nearly time to go downstairs and I was lost, it was all so huge. I must behave like a grown-up. I must show him that everything was good, that I could cope.

But I loved him ... I loved him! A whole new world was opening itself up in front of me. Joy powered through me like a tidal wave, carrying me, aching with longing, along with it.

I had a frantic game of Catch the Tie with Sapphy to calm myself down, then ten minutes later set off down the stairs.

Passing the study door I heard voices. I stopped. Luke – it was Luke! I hadn't heard him come in. My heart set up its now familiar roar ... I must control myself ... I mustn't let them see ...

But who was that with him? Not Amy again so soon, surely? She'd been on her way home an hour ago. Actually it sounded like Izzy, but what on earth would she be doing here, and with Luke of all people? It couldn't be Izzy. I went closer to the door and listened.

It was Izzy. How come she'd made such a rapid recovery? She'd been in pieces. Shattered. But here she was and – well – shouting. At Luke. What was going on?

'You've got to tell me,' Izzy said. I grinned. At least she'd stopped crying. 'Sorry, Luke, but you're not fobbing me off, not anymore. I want the truth. I need to know if Mum's finally flipped, saying all this stuff.'

'Izzy, please calm down.'

'No, I won't calm down. Is it true? Is it? About Milly's mum ill-treating her – and actually – actually trying to – Mum says Pascale stopped her. Is that true?'

Luke cleared his throat and said something indistinct.

'But why?' Izzy wailed. 'It doesn't make sense. Why on earth would anyone want to kill their own child?'

I STOOD BESIDE MY BED. I climbed under the blankets fully clothed and lay on my back, staring at the ceiling. Two lines from a poem Felix had shown me ran through my head, over and over:

> *But we shall lie still as the night*
> *And know that at last we are dead.*

And know that at last we are dead. I thought it might be by Eiluned Lewis. *Music in the Garden*. I loved that poem.

I lay as if frozen to a block of ice. I was shivering from head to foot, like that time I had rigors with pneumonia, when I was little. It came back to me suddenly then, the memory of lying there shuddering, shadowy figures moving about the room. How old had I been? Was my mother there?

An intense sense of harm kept me anchored in one position, frightened to move even a finger. Gradually the light faded and seen through the window, across which I hadn't drawn the curtains, a crescent moon floated on its back in the pale evening sky. Complete silence lay over the house, as though someone had cast a spell over it and all its inhabitants so that they, like me, could neither move nor speak.

At some point somebody tried the door but finding it locked they went away again, and silence returned.

After I've no idea how long I pushed back the duvet and rolled out of bed. I hauled down an old airline bag of Luke's from the top of the wardrobe, pulled a spare pair of jeans out of a drawer, found a tee-shirt, my brush and comb, a notebook and biro and my green leather hardback copy of Persuasion. I unpeeled my flannel off the hand-basin and bundled it into my sponge bag with my toothbrush, toothpaste and deodorant. I had no clear idea in my head why, I just knew I had to gather together the minimal needs for survival and get out of there.

I left the room, closed the door silently and set off down the stairs. I met no one on my way to the side door, the door no one used because it opened into the bramble patch. I'd beaten a way through it. As I passed the orchard I heard it again, the little tune I knew so well, melancholy, compelling ... perhaps the only true memory I had of my mother.

Despite everything the pull was too strong: I paused and peered through the trees. There it was, the glimmer of light, a feeling of movement like a breath of wind, and the music. My heart set up its clamorous rhythm in response but this time my reaction was no longer longing or sadness. This time I thought quite coldly, why? Why is she doing this now? What does she want, this woman who apparently hated me? Whom I've got wrong all these years, wasted hours of emotion and regret on, all of it on a fantasy, a chimaera, a will-o'-the-wisp. The mother I regretted and longed for had never existed.

Miranda, I said to her inside my head, my jaw set. What do you want?

As if she'd heard me the music became louder and the lights came nearer. Several orbs this time, dancing up and down as though on strings, agitated, almost, I thought, enraged. Low branches swayed. For a moment I felt afraid. Did she wish me harm? What if I actually saw her, my mother, her actual form? What would I do? My breath was coming so fast I felt a bit sick. Was I scared? Surely she couldn't hurt me now?

The orbs floated up rapidly and one after another disappeared. Abruptly the music stopped. I advanced a few feet into the orchard. 'Miranda?' I couldn't call her Mother. The word stuck in my throat. 'What do you want?' I demanded. 'What are you trying to say?'

No response. Nothing. I gave up, shook my head and dashed away around the side of the house and towards the lane. My feet took me on my usual route, down through the village and onto the common. Landmarks looked different in the dark: pale colours shone out, everything else sank back into oblivion. I remembered Sapphy and wished I had brought her with me.

I ran till I was exhausted. I spread my jacket on the ground under a tree and sat down. I had no idea where I was. It was deep night now and black. Clouds had extinguished the moon. My brain didn't seem to be working properly. I didn't feel upset or angry. I didn't feel anything except cold. I leaned back against the tree trunk and closed my eyes.

'Milly.'

I opened my eyes and struggled to sit up, disorientated, shivering, my body aching. Around me were trees and dead leaves and the smell of earth and grass and cold morning and there was Luke standing in front of me, his hands in his jeans pockets and his work boots on.

I'd fallen asleep at an awkward angle and I felt stiff and sore where nobbles of tree root had pressed into my side. It took a moment or two to remember, and then I did. I moved away from him.

'What's happened? What are you doing here?'

'Milly?' he said again.

'I heard you talking in the study,' I said. 'To Izzy. I heard what she said.'

'Ah. I thought that might be it.'

Was that all he could say? A robin cascaded into song somewhere nearby and above, and beneath the song's riotous sweetness I could hear Luke's ragged breathing.

I felt ill. Everything had changed. It was like being inside a kaleidoscope, mirrors were everywhere and the truth was nowhere.

He squatted down in front of me. 'Milly. Look at me.' His voice was ragged and strained.

I bent my head. I couldn't meet his eyes.

'Nothing's changed,' he said.

'You have.' Everything's changed.

'How? How have I?'

'You should have told me. I thought you would always tell me the truth but you haven't been. Nothing's the way I thought it was.'

You were my soothsayer, my magician who made my life wonderful. My Merlin. I looked around wildly, terrified that I was going to cry.

'You've had a shock.'

I looked at him as if to say No! in my most sarcastic voice, but he looked so pale and tired, his chin dark with stubble, that I couldn't. For the first time in my life he looked unkempt. And I'd given him all this worry.

My head was clearing a little; things were shaking down. I began to recognise where I was and to remember how I'd got there. Then in the distance I saw him, my friend with the red setter. He passed across my line of vision, almost as far away as I could see but it was him, I would know him anywhere, and of course the unmistakeable dog. He stopped for a moment and raised his hand in greeting, and then he disappeared into the trees.

What was he doing out so early, my friend with the red setter? He always seemed to be there at times of intense emotion or trouble. I frowned, thinking. I wondered if there was significance to the times the music came. If I could work that out I might be able to work out what Miranda wanted.

'What's the time?' I asked Luke. I was still only half-awake.

'Six-thirty. Time you came home.'

I took a breath, stretched and yawned. I staggered to my feet, arched my aching back and rubbed my hands down my jeans. 'How did you know I was here?' I was still cold but at least my brain was beginning to work.

'I heard you call out and went up to see if you were okay and you had gone.'

'How could I call out if I wasn't there?'

He shook his head as if he was as bewildered as I was. 'Anyway, your mug from last night was on the chest in the hall and I reckoned you must have brought it down with you on your way down to supper. And then you weren't there.' He paused. 'Why didn't you come and talk to me? It's not like you to run away.'

'It isn't, is it? I don't know why I did, it was instinctive I suppose, like an animal knows when it's going to die and goes away somewhere all by itself. That's what it felt like.'

'Don't be so melodramatic. You're not going to die. And I've been looking for you all night, so if anybody's going to die, it's me.'

'Luke,' I said. 'You have to tell me what happened. Why did my mother try to kill me? And how did she? I mean, what did she do? Attack me with a kitchen knife? Did she really hate me that much?'

'Of course she didn't attack you with a knife.'

'There's no of course about it.'

'Sit down, Milly. Wait.' He shrugged off his jacket and spread it on the ground. 'Sit there.' He settled me, then sat down beside me on the ground, his hands linked around one bent up knee. 'I visited your grandparents quite often after my parents moved away from next door. I was always tremendously fond of them, and I'd known Miranda all my life: we were in touch all through her pregnancy. I was twelve when you were born. Although she was older, she used to confide in me. We were mates.'

'Was she upset about getting pregnant? It stopped her dancing, didn't it?'

'Yes. That was a blow, but she was really excited about

having a child, more and more so as the time grew near. You were very much wanted, Milly. I hope you believe that.'

Well, you would say that, I thought, but I said, 'So what went wrong? Did she just get fed up with looking after a child? She was awfully young, wasn't she? Younger than I am now.'

'Your grandmother told me that after you were born your mother became ill with post-natal depression. It took her a long time to recover. The episode ... we're discussing ... happened when you were about eleven months old. According to Pascale, what happened was, she came into your nursery one evening because you'd been crying, and found Miranda leaning over your cot, pressing a pillow down over your face.'

'What? No. *No*.'

Luke paused. I sat there, finding this almost impossible to take in. I felt numb.

'Pascale took the pillow away,' Luke said at last. 'She made sure you were breathing. I've sometimes thought that the feeling of being suffocated might be the cause of your drowning nightmares. According to Pascale, Miranda was in a terrible state, shaking, crying, saying that she couldn't look after you. Basically having a meltdown. She didn't know what she was doing, Milly.'

'So Pascale saved my life.'

'According to your grandmother, yes, she did.'

'Whew.' I straightened my back and drew in a deep breath. I'd always taken breathing so much for granted. I tried to square this information with my experience of Pascale who'd been pretty horrible to me for as long as I could remember. I wondered if she regretted not letting my mother go ahead and finish me off.

No, that was daft. There must be some other reason she found me so objectionable.

But she had saved my life, and that was huge.

'I do have other quite scary memories,' I told Luke, thinking I might as well get it out in the open, now that we were talking about it. 'I wonder if that was my mother too, being unkind. Did she hurt me? Did anybody know? Perhaps I've suppressed the memories or something.'

Luke was silent for a long time. 'Of course I wasn't around then, apart from brief visits, so I can't honestly say I know, first-hand. Juno knew about the suffocation thing. Pascale told her. We could never agree over whether you ought to be told about it. She thought you should, I thought you would be better off not knowing. Only you,' he said, looking at me at last, 'can be the true judge of that.'

'I could ask Juno about it. Maybe.'

'Juno did once tell me that she didn't think your mother treated you well. Various little clues: some bruising, your fear of the dark. A burn on your arm.'

'A *burn*? Jeez, why didn't somebody do something?'

'Juno did try. She told Pascale, and Pascale said she would make sure that you were safe. There was no proof, apparently. They don't seem to have considered telling your grandparents. After that, Juno says, Pascale hardly left your side. Milly, that's enough for now, you look exhausted. I think I ought to get you home.' He got up and stood looking down at me.

'It's a lot to take in.'

'Of course it is, sweetheart,' Luke said. 'I don't know whether to be glad or sorry that it's come to light.'

'Glad,' I said. I put up a hand for him to pull me to my feet. 'Better out than in, as Babe would say.' My knees wobbled as I tried to stand. I brushed myself down.

'You're a brave girl.' He put his arm around me and gave me a brief hug. For some reason, all the passion, the emotion that I would have thought a touch of his hand would have induced in me, had gone. How could that be? Was I still in shock?

Luke picked up the airline bag. I couldn't remember for a moment what on earth it was doing there. I had a vague memory of packing, but I couldn't think why on earth I had bothered. Had I planned on actually running away? How stupid. What had I been thinking? That wouldn't have solved anything.

'There's something else I need to say,' Luke said, as we turned towards home. 'This is a little difficult.'

'What is?'

'I owe you an apology.'

What for? I felt a twitch of anger. For not telling me the truth about my mother? All these years? For not helping me work through something that might have helped me get over those ghastly nightmares? I shook my head. It all seemed like a dream, unreal. I reached for the bag but he shook his head and transferred it to his other hand. He set off and I followed.

'About when you came to me at the workshop,' Luke said. 'I reacted badly – inappropriately, when I thought you'd been hurt. I apologise. It won't happen again. Of course it won't. I'm sorry.'

'Oh, don't worry about that,' I said airily, tramping along by his side. 'You can't be there every time something difficult happens. After all, I'll be in Scotland in a couple of months.'

He was silent. I wondered how he was feeling, if he felt as numb as me, if everything felt meaningless to him, too. I wondered if I would go on feeling like this or if it would wear off and I would love him again. I felt a bit lost, to be honest. In a kind of limbo. None of my usual emotions seemed to be working. Did this mean we were back where we were before he kissed me? Perhaps it was easier this way. I mean, where would we have gone from there? Had it meant anything to Luke or was he telling me how it really was, that he'd reacted instinctively, that it hadn't meant anything deep or lasting? That he'd reacted a little bit like a man, too. After all, he was a man. A young man still, really.

But then the memory of the kiss returned and a little bit of the ice inside me melted. Oh gosh. I closed my eyes and fell over a tree root. Luke put out a hand and caught my elbow and this time, oh dear, this time I felt it again, the magnetism that had glued me to him yesterday. He let my arm go as if I was red hot.

Back home we parted without a word and I ran upstairs, tore off my clothes and fell into bed, thankful for the comfort of a proper mattress instead of damp turf with bumps in it. I closed my eyes and tried to relax but I couldn't. I had a horrible suspicion that all this numbness was wearing off, fast. Also that Luke was regretting his momentary lapse. That kissing me hadn't meant anything at all and that once again I was putting two and two together and making five. Just like I had about my mother. Wishful thinking.

But where did that leave me?

Chapter 35

Let the pain begin

Woken by the alarm I dragged myself out of bed and got dressed. I'd slept for two hours. Luke I assumed had gone off to work, zombie or not. I tried not to feel guilty. He deserved to suffer a bit, surely? He ought to have told me.

I tip-toed downstairs and let myself out of the house through the bramble-patch. It was too early for Amy but I'd walk around until it was time. I needed some peace. I couldn't face seeing anyone, not even Babe.

At five to nine I headed for Grange Road and trudged up the drive. I rang Amy's bell feeling detached and spacey, as though fainting might not be completely out of the question. Nobody came. I waited, rang the bell again and waited some more.

Where was she? It was nine, the time I was supposed to start. Then I remembered that I wasn't supposed to be there, I'd finished at Amy's. She'd rung and told Babe to tell me that Gill was out of hospital and back at work and I wasn't needed any more.

I stumbled down the drive. Luke had known the truth

about Miranda all this time. He'd been living with this huge lie, all this time. Would he ever have got around to telling me? Or would he have gone on letting me believe all the rubbish Pascale liked to feed me about what a wonderful, loving person Miranda had been? Would he have let me go on thinking myself cherished and loved by her, like a normal person? What had all this done to my feelings for him?

And now there was Amy, poised for action. Did I care still? Did it matter? Why couldn't I trust my feelings? It was all a huge muddle. Was I still in shock or was it real?

What should I do? Did I wish I didn't know the truth? Was it always better to know the truth, however painful? I thought about Robert's wife not knowing about Izzy. Suppose she had found out. Wouldn't she have been devastated?

I thought about Juno not giving Izzy her dad's letters, letting her think he didn't care rather than letting her know he did care and allowing her to make up her own mind about how she felt about his desertion. Taking it upon herself to make that decision, just as Luke had taken it upon himself to make the decision not to tell me the truth about my mother.

What you don't know can't hurt you ... but in my case not knowing *had* hurt me. I thought of my horrendous nightmares. Also the vague sense I'd always had that something was wrong. The difficulty I had in believing myself loved and wanted, despite all the evidence given to me daily by (almost) everybody at Half Moon, that I was.

I had to get over this somehow and move on. Back home I ran up the stairs and into my room. I sat on my bed and stared at the wall, my eyes heavy with sleep. It was so quiet in the house. Did they know what had happened between

Luke and me? Esme's old typewriter was rattling away as usual. Babe must know something was up: she'd left a breakfast tray outside the door.

Footsteps trudged up the stairs. Babe had a special way of walking, she put her left foot down more heavily than her right; you could always tell it was her. She tapped gently on the door.

I swallowed. 'Hello?'

'Can I come in?'

The door opened. I half-turned my head then turned away to hide the tears beginning to well up. I bit my lip, resenting my weakness but unable to control my sobs. Babe sat down beside me and put her strong arm around me. I smelt the faint whiff of her sweat, the mask of deodorant. 'Luke told me.'

I turned my face into her solid shoulder and wept. Babe sat in silence. After a while I fished under my pillow for a hanky and blew my nose. 'I went to work and I've finished there and I forgot. Would you believe that? Oh Babe, why didn't he tell me? And Juno has known all this time. My nightmares. Everything.'

'I know.'

'I can't believe it. I don't know who I am anymore.' My mind skidded off. 'I wonder if this is how people feel when they're suddenly told they're adopted.'

'You're a brave girl, that's what you are. You went to work in spite of everything. That's good.' She gave my shoulders a little approving shake.

'Do they know? Esme – and Felix?'

Babe shook her head. 'Only Pascale. Never says a dicky bird, mind you. Daft she may be but she knows how to keep her mouth shut.'

'And she won't have a bad word said against Miranda, Juno always says. Come to think of it that sounds as though there were bad words that could have been said. But it never crossed my mind.'

Babe shook her head. 'This was all before my time.'

'I can't face him. I can't trust him.'

'It's the shock. It will pass. He was only doing what he thought was best for you, lovey. I know it's hard for you to believe that now but it's the truth. You know Luke, not an unkind bone in his body.'

'It wasn't kind. I'd rather have known.' I thought again of the shrine, of all the wasted hours.

'Difficult though, to know when to tell a child something like that.'

'It's all different now. I don't feel like myself.'

'Think of all he's done for you.'

I started crying again. 'That makes it worse. I can't explain. I'd rather he'd been horrible to me, instead of being so lovely all the time. I respected him. Honoured him.' I loved him, I thought. Where's it all gone?

Babe took her arm away and put her hand on my shoulder. 'What you need is a good sleep. Now just you lie down there and I'll send Sapphy up to you. Things will look different when you've had a good sleep.'

Then maybe I wouldn't have loved him so much, I thought, still sitting on the edge of the bed, rocking, my arms around my stomach, staring at the floor. Even if I didn't know it. Not until yesterday. I stopped, frowning, confused. Did this mean I was beginning to feel it again?

From the door Babe said, 'There's something else might be worth thinking about. When you've had a rest and all.'

'What?' I didn't turn my head.

'All the resentment and hurt,' Babe said. 'Are you sure it's Luke you're mad at? Are you sure it isn't meant for your mother?' The door closed.

What? I tipped sideways and pulled the duvet up over my legs. After a few minutes the door cracked open and a moment later Sapphy's soft weight landed on my legs. I heard the sound of her purring and her cold nose touched my chin. With a sigh she flopped down into the curve of my body. I slept.

I OPENED my eyes to grey light and the sound of rain falling on the roof. I looked at the clock. Half-past four! I rolled out of bed and pulled back the curtains to a soggy afternoon, overcast with a steady rain falling. Still half-asleep I trod barefoot down the stairs. I needed something hot. Coffee.

Crossing the hall I heard voices coming from the study. Luke's voice and a woman's. Amy's. I paused. I felt a slight quiver of dread. Why wasn't Luke at work? She'd probably gone into her "poor little me" act and he'd come rushing home.

They hadn't shut the door properly. I stood still.

'Oh, darling,' Amy said. 'I don't know what to do. I'm at my wit's end.'

Rumble, rumble. Indistinct.

'He's gone for good this time. He's met someone else. He wants a divorce.'

Silence, then sobs. 'I didn't know whom to turn to. You've been such a good friend. So kind.'

More silence.

'Such a sweet man. Thank you, thank you, darling Luke. I know I'm just a silly woman. I shouldn't be so weak.

If only he was more like you ... kind ... and understanding. Oh, Luke. Hold me, just for a moment. Please. Oh, darling.'

Oh God, Oh God. I closed my eyes, opened them again, turned and went back up the stairs. When I reached my room, I closed the door, went to the window and opened it.

And from the orchard below, I heard the music again.

Chapter 36

The art of fencing

'Oh yes,' Juno told Amy the next morning, manoeuvring her trolley briskly around a hole in the tarmac outside Fine Fare. 'He adores her. She's terribly pretty, don't you think? It wouldn't surprise me a bit if they got together one day. He'd have to wait till she's eighteen, of course. She's still very young.'

'What – *Milly?*' Amy said, trolley-less (she hadn't even started), hurrying to catch up. 'You're not serious.'

'Never more so. Don't tell me you didn't know? I thought you and Luke were such good friends.'

'We are, of course we are. That's just – but wait a minute, Juno – I mean, *Milly?* She's never said a word to me. Nor has he.'

Juno paused beside her car boot and leaned forward, rummaging in her bag for her keys. 'Is she still working for you? You could always ask her.'

'No, Gill's back. She was only in hospital a short while. You're wrong, Juno, you must be. Luke's – I mean, his attitude to me is – he's very fond, very caring. If he felt like that about Milly I would know, I'm sure. He's hardly mentioned her name.'

'Ah,' Juno said, unlocking the boot and starting to unload her trolley. 'There you are then. Dead give-away. It's when they don't talk about them you know they've got something to hide. And Luke – well! He's got a bit of a reputation, you know. You mustn't take him too seriously.'

'*Luke?*' Amy stood, uncertain for once, fiddling with the strap of her handbag. 'What on earth do you mean? He's bound to have had some experience at his age, you'd wonder if he hadn't. Goodness, I don't listen to gossip, it's probably made up by a lot of jealous women. I wouldn't take any notice of that.'

'Well, don't say I didn't warn you.' Juno laughed, starting to wheel her trolley to the trolley-bay.

'Oh my goodness,' Amy said, following her. 'He was kissing her. Outside the workshop. I didn't think anything of it at the time. She was upset, you know, that business with the girl, that gang – Luke said something – I didn't pay attention. But he definitely was … oh, this is awful, I must talk to him, I must make him see what a mistake—'

'Kissing her?' Juno said. '*Kissing* her?'

'Well, there's no need to look so flabbergasted. You were the one who said he – who said – oh, and by the way, we saw that daughter of yours in Delillo's in Kingston when we were having dinner the other evening, Luke and I. She was with my sister and brother-in-law as a matter of fact. We didn't see Sylvia but she must have gone to powder her nose. I didn't realise Isobel was on such close terms with them. I must ask Sylvia about it.'

. . .

WHEN SHE GOT home Juno picked up the phone and rang Half Moon house. Milly picked up.

'Milly. It's me. Coffee? The kettle's on.'

'Thanks, Juno, but not just now. I woke up terribly late and I've got so much to do—'

'I'm sorry I let the cat out of the bag. I'm really sorry, Milly. Are things okay between you and Luke?'

'Of course.' From the tone of her voice she was lying. My spirits rose.

'It's just, I have wondered for ages what would happen if you found out. Luke ought to have told you.'

'Everything's fine.'

'Can I have a word with him?'

'He's at work. You'll have to ring him there.'

'Of course. For what it's worth, I think he was quite wrong not to have told you the truth about your mother years ago. I always—'

'I can't talk about this now. Goodbye.'

WELL! That's not like polite little mouse Milly, Juno thought, put out but exhilarated. She put down the phone. Her heart beat hard with excitement.

It's really happening, it's working, she thought. Milly sounds upset with Luke and I've given Amy a prod: she'll up her game if she sees Milly as a challenge. Let's see what happens now. It was a good move to tell Izzy about Miranda. In any case it's time Milly knew the truth about her mother. Luke deserves to lose Milly. Milly won't push, that's the thing. She's too young. She wouldn't know how.

She sat down at the kitchen table, hardly knowing what she was doing. All this talk from Milly about Miranda turning up in the orchard, having returned maybe to tell them all something, her with her music and lights and carrying-on – she never could bear not to be the centre of attention – had brought memories, so long suppressed, flooding back into her mind with absolute clarity, almost as though she was under some kind of hypnosis. It was as if news of the accident had only just come.

Her hands gripped the edge of the table. She sat stiffly upright, rigid with tension. The scene, vivid in her mind in contrast to the present-day darkened skies and the drumming of the rain on the dustbin in the yard, opened with Miranda sauntering up the path to the back door, the way she always did when she came visiting.

It had been a warm, sunny June morning. A Thursday. Miranda was wearing that cornflower-blue shirt she was so fond of because she knew it brought out the blue of her eyes, and a pair of white slacks with white tennis shoes. She looked like Grace Kelly in High Society – and she knew it. She was slim as a blade, so slim, you'd never believe she'd ever given birth to a child.

Miranda knocked on the window, a series of rapid little knocks, rat-tat-tat-tat-tat, the way she always did, and at the sound Juno froze in her chair. Miranda would never have come calling if Mike had told her – as he'd promised Juno at the weekend that he would right away, the next day – that Juno knew about the affair.

Or perhaps he *had* told her, and she was just going to brazen it out, the way she always did. She thought because she was so good looking she could get away with anything, like some film star. Well, she couldn't.

Juno walked slowly to the door to let Miranda in. She heard her own voice, friendly, deceitful. 'Hello, Miranda. This is an unexpected pleasure.'

As usual Miranda breezed in without waiting to be

asked. 'Hi Juno, just thought I'd come in and say hello. I'm off to Heathrow in a bit, to pick up Mum and Dad.'

'Oh, today, is it? I hope they've had a good time in Greece. Do sit down. Have a drink. Oh, I suppose you'd better not, if you're driving.'

Miranda hesitated, and that's when the idea came to Juno, straight out of nowhere. If Miranda hadn't hesitated, if she'd been firm, resisted the temptation to have just one drink ... then maybe ... Juno bowed her head over her clenched fists, allowed the pain to enter her stomach, her midriff, her chest. Allowed herself to acknowledge her guilt.

She went on. 'Still, it's after six, isn't it? One won't hurt, will it? I hate drinking alone. Sit down and I'll get it. You like whisky, don't you, like Mike? I'm a gin and tonic girl, myself. Second thoughts, come into the sitting room, it's more comfortable in there.'

She left Miranda settling herself to best advantage on the sofa – there didn't have to be a man present for her to feel the need to show off – and went into the dining-room, collecting a tray from the kitchen on the way. The cheerfulness of the tray, white melamine with a gay bouquet of bright red and blue flowers ornamenting its centre, contrasted noticeably with the blackness of her mood. Her heart had started to pound with a weird excitement: she'd embarked on an adventure. She didn't allow herself to think about the consequences. It was down to Miranda, wasn't it? She wasn't forcing her.

Mike kept the bottles in a drinks cabinet some client had given him that had come off a yacht somewhere. It was shaped like a double bass and he was so proud of it. She reached into the cabinet, took out the almost full decanter of his best Glenfiddich and set it on top of the cabinet. She hesitated, then reached in for a bottle of Smirnoff and a bottle of Gordon's. She set all the bottles on the tray and carried it through to the kitchen table. She reached up for two glasses from one of the wall cabinets, then went to the fridge for ice and a bottle of tonic and a lemon. She sliced the lemon carefully with her favourite kitchen knife and arranged the slices on a saucer. And all the while she was thinking.

She poured a stiff whisky, added a big dollop of vodka, paused then added some more. She mixed herself a gin and tonic, added ice and lemon and carried the laden tray into the sitting-room. She set it down on the low coffee table and handed Miranda her drink.

'Here you are.'

'Hey, that's a big one,' Miranda said. 'Oh well, I've been told more than once I've got hollow legs.' She laughed and raised the glass to her lips: lovely, curved, full lips. White, even teeth: the two front ones with a slight overhang, giving her a pouting look in repose, adding to the sensuality of her face. Her eyes slanted under eyebrows shaped like circumflexes, the accentuating eyeshadow expertly applied.

Juno found herself metamorphosed in her imagination into Mike, imagining Miranda's mouth on her own, the full lips, the inside of her mouth wet and welcoming. Her lips tingled. She wiped her mouth with the back of her hand, staring, staring.

She pulled herself together. 'Well, chin chin.' She sat back, her anger gathering. She'd decided on shock tactics. 'I gather you've been seeing quite a lot of my husband recently. I've been meaning to ask you over for a chat, actually.' She looked at Miranda over the top of her glass with bright, calm eyes.

Miranda blinked and set her drink down on the coffee table. 'I don't—'

Juno leaned forward, took a small blue and white tile from the shelf under the coffee table and put it under Miranda's glass. 'Don't look so shocked, did you think he wouldn't tell me? He always does, you know.'

'Excuse me?' The complacency on the pretty face had vanished. She looked positively shocked.

'Standard behaviour from Mike, I'm afraid. No,' she said, putting a hand out to Miranda, who was starting to push herself up from the sofa, 'don't go, I'm not angry, I promise. Not in the least.'

'I don't know what this is about, Juno, but I can assure you—' She stood there uncertainly. She wasn't looking so confident now. Actually she looked quite scared. Perhaps she thought Juno had put poison in her drink.

Mustn't frighten her away. Juno gestured towards the sofa. 'Oh, sit down, Miranda,' she said impatiently. 'Finish your drink. You mustn't think I mind. I don't, honestly, I'm used to it. Ought to be, by now. This isn't the first time he's had a bit on the side, won't be the last either, it's just the way he is.'

'I don't know what's going on, you're in the most peculiar mood, Juno, I don't know who's been saying—'

'Mike told me himself. He always does, in the end. I saw you together in the orchard. I was looking for the cat, as a matter of fact. He's weak, you know, never could stand up to pressure. Mike, I mean, not the cat.' She laughed. 'Oh, I'm not blaming you. Poor old sod can't help himself, it's been going on for years, it's pathetic, the old goat.'

'No!' Miranda said, and sat down again. Good. Even though it was because she looked as though her legs wouldn't support her. Juno fought down an image of those slender legs wrapped around her husband, the head thrown back, mouth wide, eyes closed in extremis;

mentally she blocked her ears against frenzied gasps of sexual pleasure ...

She watched the lovely, expressive face protesting, refuting, and hardly heard a word. She was consumed by the physical aspect of Miranda. Nothing else seemed relevant. Who cared what she thought, what she felt? She was, that was all that mattered.

'This is ridiculous,' Miranda said, taking a large gulp of her drink. 'I don't know what's got into you, Juno, why are you talking like this? It isn't Mike's fault if people make things up. I bet it's that Mrs Murchison, she never could stand me, the old battle-axe. Couldn't hang onto her husband, so she's jealous of anyone who can attract a man. No, I don't mean – you know what I mean. I bet it's her been saying things about me. Is it? Well, if it wasn't her, who was it?'

Juno smiled, friendly, elder-sisterly. 'You aren't listening, I told you I saw you together, and when I challenged Mike, he confessed all. Now, drink up and let's be friends. I haven't quite decided what to do, I mean I can't be expected to put up with this kind of thing happening under my very nose, but we're both women of the world, aren't we?'

'Look Juno ... my goodness, it's really decent of you to take it like this – perhaps I did have a little bit of a thing about Mike—'

'And he about you.'

'God, I wish I didn't have to do this drive. That was awfully strong, I'm feeling a bit dizzy, do you think I'll be okay? My goodness, this has all been a bit of a shock. Look, we never meant for you to find out, we never meant to hurt you. You've been a good friend to me, Juno, I wouldn't hurt you for the world ...'

God, Juno thought, she's getting maudlin on me. What kind of a fool does she take me for?

The police came to Half Moon to report the accident. There was nobody in the house apart from Pascale and six-year-old Milly. A hysterical Pascale had phoned Juno to tell her the news. No control, absolutely typical, going on as if it was her personal tragedy and hers alone. What about Milly, for fuck's sake? It was her mother who'd died. Her grandparents.

And Juno listened coldly to Pascale sobbing down the phone and commiserated with her, and expressed her horror and surprise, and refused to think about the earlier part of the evening and Miranda sitting there on the sofa, sipping her mammoth drink.

When the police came and asked her if she could tell them anything, she said yes, Miranda had called in that evening, but they'd drunk nothing but coffee. (She'd washed up the two glasses, because she always washed up a glass the moment she'd finished with it, it's just the way she was, that's what she did. Still did.) The bottles of whisky and vodka were safely back in the double bass. Yes, she'd known Miranda was due to set off for the airport. No, of course she wasn't the worse for wear at that point in the evening. Well, mightn't she have stopped at an off-licence on the way? Perhaps she had a secret stash in her room – had they looked?

So convincing. She'd almost convinced herself.

LATER THAT EVENING Juno opened her bedroom window and stood looking out into the night, away from Luke's house and over to the left above the allotments to the hills beyond. She shoved her hands deep into the pockets of her cotton skirt, trying to control her anger. If she let herself get really riled up she wouldn't be able to sleep and tomorrow would be hell.

Early that morning she'd seen Luke and Milly walking back to the house through the dawn light. She wasn't entirely sure they hadn't been holding hands. She had no idea where they'd been. She hadn't been able to get the memory out of her head all day.

I'm jealous, she admitted to herself. I'm jealous of a seventeen-year-old girl who has absolutely no idea of the power she has. I hate him. I hate him for abandoning me, but he can't have her. He can't.

She sighed, uncrossed her arms and leaned her elbows on the sill, gazing up at the little moon. That terrible row with Izzy yesterday ... she still felt bruised. They'd hardly spoken since. Izzy had come in earlier today, in the middle of Jenny Barker's lesson, but she'd gone out again and she hadn't come back ... she glanced at her watch. Nearly ten o'clock. She'd be starving. It wasn't like her to stay out this late without saying anything.

Footsteps came up the stairs, light steps, a little slow.

She turned her head, but the steps passed her door without stopping and went along the passage. Izzy's door closed softly. Juno's eyelids flickered. She turned towards the door, then checked herself. What if Izzy would rather be left alone? Was she still mad at her? It was becoming increasingly difficult to gauge the teenage barometer. All too frequently she seemed to be getting it wrong.

And you had to remember that Milly was only a little younger than Izzy. I'm the nearest thing to a mother she's got, Juno thought miserably. I oughtn't to be feeling like this ... oh God, I thought I was over Luke. I thought I could just hate him, concentrate on getting my own back. Making him suffer.

Her lips tightened. She wasn't going to abandon her plans because of a moment of weakness. She'd planned revenge and revenge was what she was going to get.

Chapter 37

The truth will set you free – but first it will piss you off

I stood at the attic door with a black rubbish sack in my hand. The place looked the same but to me it felt different, as though haunted by the ghost of my former persona, the innocent one, the one nourished by the idea of a loving mother taken from me too soon, regretting her death and wishing for her still to be alive.

I walked slowly over to the bed and knelt down. I pulled out the suitcase, opened it and began to pull out the contents, stuffing everything into the plastic bag, hardly glancing at the green silk petticoat, the theatre programmes, the scent bottle. When the suitcase was empty I slammed it shut and stuffed it into the bag with everything else. Miranda's ballet shoes had gone in already.

'There you are, Mummy dearest,' I said aloud. 'All gone. And good riddance,' I said, sitting down on the floor, breathless all of a sudden. 'Dust to dust, ashes to ashes. In sure and certain hope of never having to set eyes on you again.'

I got up, hauled myself to my feet, brushed myself down and went to the door, dragging the sack behind me. At the door I stopped and looked back. I'd never come up here again, not unless I absolutely had to. All that wasted sadness, that self-delusion, was over, gone.

All the things that had made sense, didn't make sense any longer.

He would be there at supper. If he wasn't out with Amy again. I'd just have to act as though nothing had happened. I'd talk to him if I had to, if he spoke to me. It didn't matter either way, I thought, angry again. I didn't care anymore; he could do what he liked.

'WE WERE so sorry to hear you weren't well,' Esme said. 'Fancy having to miss Babe's lamb curry, what a shame. We missed you.'

'Are you feeling better now?' Felix asked, helping himself to ketchup. 'Luke said—'

'I'm fine now, thanks,' I said, having noticed the small headshake Babe had directed at Felix, stopping him midstream. Well, blow them, I didn't care anymore. I bent my head over Babe's cottage pie. 'This is fab, Babe.'

'You've hardly eaten a thing,' Esme said some while later. 'Are you sure you're all right?'

'It's delicious,' Felix said. 'Is this cheese on top?'

'Gives it a nice crust,' Babe said briskly.

'Poor Luke,' Esme said. 'Missing this. Where is he, did you say?'

'Eating out, he said, with friends. Didn't say who, but it's not hard to guess.'

'Like that is it?' Felix said. 'Major changes about to take place?'

'*Non, non et non,*' Pascale said. '*Toujours tu fais des bêtises, André. Toujours c'est la même chose. Laisses-moi tranquille, alors, pour l'amour de Dieu.*'

'Pascale, would you mind asking André to wait until we've eaten?' Babe said. 'It's not fair on the rest of us when we can't hear what he's saying.'

Pascale relapsed into silence, darted a look at me and looked down at her plate. Did she know that I knew?

Esme winked at me and I tried to smile back, but I could see that she was uncomfortable, she knew something was up.

Luke came in as we were having coffee. He pulled his chair out and sat down without a word. Babe passed him a cup and he tipped a splash of milk in and looked at the cup as if he wasn't sure what to do with it.

'Well, things to do, people to see.' Esme pushed her chair back and stood up, smiling around into the charged silence.

Felix, clearing his throat, stood up too. 'Got a letter or two to write, if you'll excuse me.'

'Milly,' Luke said, as the door closed behind them.

'Did you know Amy was getting a divorce?' I said, pushing my chair back. I felt reckless and childish and as though at any moment I might cry.

'Yes, I did, as a matter of fact,' Luke said. He was pale and had blue shadows under his eyes, I noticed, now that I looked at him properly. Really almost cobalt.

'I suppose she told you, Mrs Booth. Well, that figures. Excuse me, please.' I stood up. 'I might go and see Juno, she probably knows somewhere I could stay, get out of your hair.' I left the room without looking back. So what if I was being rude and infantile? I didn't care. Then I remembered that I'd been rude to Juno too and wondered if after all I would be welcome at the Carltons. It was beginning to feel as though I wouldn't be terribly welcome anywhere.

. . .

At Juno's I knocked on the door and rang the bell. Whether I was welcome or not I was going to see Juno. I'd been a bit off with her earlier but she would understand. They'd arrange everything, then I'd go back and tell Luke – and Babe ... that wouldn't be so easy. It wasn't going to be easy, leaving Babe.

I had to find somewhere to go. To make matters worse it had begun to rain, a drizzle that quickly turned into a downpour. It had just occurred to me that possibly Juno might let me stay here with her, when the door opened and Juno stood there.

Chapter 38

Careful what you wish for

Juno blinked at the sight of Milly standing there, soaking wet. It was tipping down and she had no mac on and no umbrella.

'Can I come in?' Milly said. 'I need you to help me. I have to go away.'

Juno stood back to let her in. Milly looked half-demented. Her face was pale and her hair looked as though it hadn't had a brush through it in days. 'I'd better get you a towel,' Juno said, seeking the triumph her head told her she ought to be feeling. Milly, at last defeated, broken; Milly, removing herself from the scene, leaving Luke broken-hearted, with any luck. Leaving the way clear for Amy, or for anyone, just not Milly, to be with Luke.

But whether it was a hangover from the pain of revisiting the day of the accident, or a newly-discovered sensitivity to another's distress, all Juno seemed able to dredge up was pity and a feeling of wrongness. This wasn't how she had visualised it, planned it – wished for it. Luke, demolished, diminished ... less than.

She returned with the towel and watched as Milly wrapped her hair in it and rubbed some of the wet out.

'You'd better change, you're soaking. I'll get some of Izzy's clothes.'

'No, it's okay, I can't stay long. Where is she? Izzy?'

'Out somewhere. Listen, Milly, about all that – your mother—'

'Don't want to talk about it. It's okay. I had to find out sometime. I'm grateful, honest.' She sketched a smile but there was something wrong with her eyes. 'The thing is I need to find somewhere to go. I can't stay – there.'

'Why? What's the problem?'

'It's Amy,' Milly said. 'I think she's about to move in.'

'Really?' Juno's heart began to pound. Careful what you wish for, she thought. But I'm glad, aren't I? It's what I wanted.

'I need to get away for a bit.'

Juno thought rapidly. Her momentary weakness had evaporated. As far away as possible, seemed a good idea. 'You could go off with Izzy. She's going to look for her father.'

'Sorry? Is she? When did she decide this? She hasn't said anything to me.'

'She's been thinking about it ever since she found her father's letters. I think it's made her realise that he'd welcome a visit.' She tried and failed to keep the bitterness out of her voice. 'She can't wait to be gone.'

Milly hardly hesitated. She said, 'Would it be possible – I mean, I couldn't go with her, could I? It would help to get away for a bit, till things sort of calm down.'

'Well ... you could ask her. I'd be happier if you were with her, to be totally honest.

She's determined to go. In a gipsy caravan, of all things.

Honestly! With a horse. Mr Bradley at the garage says he'll lend her Samson. Her father's in Cornwall somewhere, caravanning with his family, we're not sure where.'

'I wonder if she'd mind. I think she's upset with me about something but I can't remember what it is. I can't remember anything much at the moment.'

'Milly ... have you told Luke about this?'

She lowered the towel. 'No, but he'll understand.' An expression of desolation came over her face.

'Well ... if it's just for a holiday. But you're not eighteen yet. You have to tell him what you're doing. And you've got St Andrews in September.'

'I'll make a more permanent plan when I've had time to think.' But she gave Juno a look so bleak that Juno blinked and mentally recoiled. She hadn't reckoned on this degree of pain.

'Got to go now,' Milly said, standing up. 'Thanks, Juno. Thanks for everything,' she said as she turned towards the door. Her voice cracked and she looked as though she might cry, but she didn't, thank goodness. Some people knew how to cope with random outbursts of emotion, but Juno didn't. She never knew what to do. She didn't have Milly's gift of empathy.

Chapter 39

First the blow, then the bruise

TIME PASSED. THE NIGHTS WERE THE WORST. I WAS frightened to close my eyes because if I slept I would have to wake up and remember all over again. The numbness had gone and the anger was fading which left nothing for me to focus on, it was just me, floating like a jellyfish in a sea of uncertainty and disillusion. It was as if I had ceased to exist.

At meals I was quiet and polite. It seemed the easiest way to make myself invisible. Everyone treated me gently, as though I'd been ill. Babe must have said something, it was obvious from the way people left me alone as if they were waiting for something to happen. Or for an explanation.

I'm punishing him, I thought, but I couldn't seem to stop. All the wisdom I'd hoped I'd accumulated over the years had simply disappeared.

I tried to meditate. I tried to pray. I went through the motions, tried to offer blessings and praise, but I couldn't feel it, it was like pretending you love someone when you don't. I wondered if I really was ill and that was why I felt so terrible.

I kept remembering things. It was as if the certain knowledge of what my mother had done had unlocked a door. Images flashed into my mind, isolated scenes I didn't understand passed through my head like dream sequences:

I was standing on a fire escape; it was night, and dark and cold, and I was frightened, calling for someone who didn't answer.

I was beating with sore fists on the door of a locked room. My head was on a level with the door handle so I couldn't have been very old. Nobody came.

Someone was screaming at me. I cowered in the corner, my hands over my face to hide the sight of the contorted face, the black hole of the mouth, the glaring eyes. Something was broken, I heard the tinkle of breaking china, saw the shards of something white and pink around her feet; I felt an inexplicable grief.

I STOOD DOING nothing in the middle of the kitchen. Along with everything else, time seemed to have lost its meaning. Faintly from the scullery came Wilson Pickett's grating, soulful voice ...

I'm gonna wait till the stars come out, and see that twinkle in your eyes ...

Babe came in, went over to the sink and started running the cold tap. 'Hello, ducky,' she said with her back to me.

I jumped. 'Babe. Thanks for – well, you know. Hanging in there.'

Babe turned and looked at me. 'Feeling better?'

'I think so ... I'm sorry, Babe.'

'You had a shock. People act funny when they've had a shock. Well, Luke's back.' She squirted some Fairy Liquid into the washing up bowl.

'Back? Where from?'

'He's been in London the past week or so. Staying with friends. Don't tell me you hadn't noticed.'

'I – I realised he wasn't around much ... I thought he was probably out with her.'

'That Mrs Booth?'

I nodded.

'There's been a lot of that, but not this last week.' Babe turned off the tap, came over and pulled out a chair. 'Milly.'

'Yup?'

'Sit down a moment.'

'I guess there's a lot to talk about. Actually, I need to talk to you.'

'First I need to tell you something.'

'Why – what is it?'

Babe waited while I pulled out a chair and sat down.

'It's Felix,' she said, watching my face. 'He's had an accident. He's okay, but he's in hospital.'

'What? What kind of accident?'

Babe was silent.

I leaned forward, frowning. 'What?'

Babe said, not looking at me, 'They think he tried to commit suicide. He'd been drinking ... it seems he went into the river down by the bridge. There's a weir—'

'I know the weir. What? *No*. Felix wouldn't do anything like that.'

Babe shrugged. 'You tell me, ducky.'

'But how is he? Who got him out? Is he okay? Does Luke know?'

'Luke's at the hospital with him. They think he's going to be all right. Two men were passing and pulled him out, just in time. One of them was a stranger out walking his dog. He's having trouble with his breathing, but other than that—' Babe sighed and pushed herself to her feet, her hands on her knees. There were shadows under her eyes. I felt a great relief, that Felix was okay, and a pang of remorse which rather delighted me because at least it meant I wasn't going to be this frozen for ever. At the same time it reminded me how selfish I was being. I'd been completely wrapped up in myself, and Babe had had me to worry about, and now this. But Felix, whatever could he have been thinking?

'Where is he?'

'FELIX PALFREY?'

The nurse looked up, unsmiling. A round face, navy-blue uniform. She looked worn out. 'Along the corridor there, third on the left. Lovely flowers.'

'Thanks!' I tiptoed across the expanse of highly-polished floor. My heart began to thump. What do you say to somebody who's tried to commit suicide?

I passed two small wards, peered into the third. People were lying in beds everywhere. I put my head around the door and there, in the far corner by the window, was Felix. Alone, thank goodness. Luke must have left.

Felix was sitting up in bed, reading. He looked pale, but otherwise the same and thank goodness, alive. I realised suddenly how fond I was of him and my eyes filled up as I padded across the room, holding the bouquet of flowers like a shield. I swallowed hard as I approached the bed. Whatever I did I mustn't cry.

'Felix.'

He looked up. 'Milly! How nice.' He was actually smiling. 'What lovely flowers. I'm so glad you've come.'

How could he look so cheerful? He ought to have

thought about the effect on all of us before throwing himself in the river. My eyes filled with tears. I lowered the flowers onto the bed, came closer. 'How are you?'

'Very well, considering. I'm a lucky man.'

I stared at him. 'Why didn't you talk to us?' I burst out. 'Why didn't you say if you were feeling that bad? Why do you have to be so damned independent? Don't we matter at all?' Sadness and frustration tipped me over into fury. 'How *could* you? You didn't give a hint. You didn't even say goodbye!' Tears began to slip down my cheeks.

Felix looked at me as if I'd gone mad. 'What are you talking about? Good heavens, I didn't do it on purpose,' he said in a scandalised voice. 'My dear child, how could you even imagine such a thing? I'm hardly the suicidal type. No ... I fell in, I regret to say. The rail had been vandalised. Cut right through then propped up. Not my idea of a good joke.'

'What rail?' I dug in my pocket for a hanky and blew my nose. More tears, this time of relief, welled up.

'The barrier above the weir. I leaned on it and it gave way. Went straight in. Hit my head on something and would have sunk without a trace if a kindly chap out walking his dog hadn't happened to be passing. And then a gentleman from the night shelter, your friend I believe – Mr Flint? He came and joined in. Took the two of them, I have to admit. Water-logged, you know. Of course I'd have been all right if I hadn't hit my head. Must have been on the weir. Knocked me out cold. The last thing I saw was the kingfisher, arrowing over my head like a harbinger of doom. I'm a lucky man. Are those for me? Now, pull yourself together and come around here and sit on the bed and tell me all about it. Kill myself indeed. Whatever next?'

. . .

'PASCALE, I want to ask you something.'

It was the next morning. Seeing Felix lying there in that hospital bed and realising how near we had come to losing him had galvanised me into action. Something about life being short and never knowing what's around the next corner, I suppose. I'd decided to have it out with Pascale.

Startled, Pascale turned, staggering a little. She put out her hand to the Aga rail for support, and at the sight of her face I flinched, my resolve weakening. Her eyes peered out from the brown folds of her face like broken flints glinting in a furrowed field. Her expression was cold, unwilling. She pulled a handkerchief from her sleeve and wiped her right eye, which often watered. The leakage of old age.

'Come and sit down.'

'I sit.' Slowly she lowered herself into the rocking chair. She looked so small, sitting down, like a little pile of leaves that the least puff of wind would blow away. I hardened my heart, pulled a chair up close and sat down. Pascale looked at me apprehensively.

I repeated slowly, leaning forward, 'I want to ask you something.'

Pascale looked down at the gnarled old hands lying in her lap. I blinked. I must focus. It was hard; I was so tired, all I wanted to do was sleep. 'I want us to speak the truth from now on. No more concealments. There's something I want you to tell me. Why have you always disliked me? Is it because of my mother? Is it because you think I ruined her dancing career? Is it me? I really want to know. Please, just tell me.'

There was a long silence. Pascale's head was still bent, the corners of her mouth down-turned. My lips tightened. I would wait till supper time if I had to.

Slowly Pascale lifted her head and raised her hands to

her face and began to shake. I put out my hand and touched her thin arm. 'Pascale.'

Pascale lowered her hands, swallowed. She shut her eyes and opened them again. '*Non*,' she said. '*Non*. Is not your fault.' She leaned back in the chair and the words fell out of her. 'I say now. You are little baby. Your mother she is – *distraite*, she cannot manage. My André at the same time he become ill, with the heart. Then on the last day, he ask me to make him the tea. Simply the cup of tea. Your mother have leave you, you are crying, crying. I have to attend you. I am your nurse, no? Because your mother, she cannot manage. So ... so I do not make my André the tea he ask for. Just the little thing, the cup of tea. I go up the stairs to attend to you and André ... while I am gone, André he fall to sleep.'

Shivers ran up my back. I felt a coldness in the pit of my stomach.

'Never he wake again. Soon, a few minute maybe, he is gone, and now he ask me for nothing more. Such a little thing, the cup of tea.' Her hands flew to her face again and she began to sob. 'And always, I blame you. Is a sin. Is not your fault. But I cannot help. I blame you.'

'Oh no.'

'Is wrong. I know that.' She sobbed, fished in her sleeve for the handkerchief, blew her nose. 'I ask you to forgive.'

'Oh Pascale ...' Was that all it had been? A lifetime of ill-treatment and slights and withholding of affection – for that? It didn't seem possible. 'Well,' I said, looking down at my lap and feeling an easy anger gathering. 'There's nothing I can do about it now, is there?' I pushed my chair back.

Pascale had dried her eyes and was looking at me

lugubriously, her expression wary. I looked at her coldly. 'Thanks for telling me, anyway.'

'*Je suis désolée,*' Pascale whispered.

'And I'm sorry about André, and the tea, and that I was a baby who cried,' I said, my voice rising. I stood up.

Outside the door I stood still, gritting my teeth. I banged my head rhythmically against the wall. Bad girl. Bad, bad girl. Henry Hamblin would be ashamed of you.

But it was a bit much. Not just a mother who hated and resented me – why? – but her ally resenting me too. It was a miracle I was so normal.

I sought refuge in my room again. The phone rang in the hall as I passed and automatically I picked up.

'It's all your fault,' Izzy's voice stormed into my ear. 'If I hadn't listened to you and told Rob the truth about how I felt we'd still be together. I never want to speak to you again. *Ever.*'

What? It wasn't my flaming fault his wife had got cancer. What was the matter with Izzy?

'And I thought you'd like to know,' Izzy went on, 'Rob told me some dreadful things about Luke. In the restaurant. Luke was having dinner there, being all lovey-dovey with that woman if you want to know. They saw us. You think he's so wonderful, well he isn't the person you think he is. Rob says he did something terrible, he got some girl pregnant and then dumped her. She had to have an abortion. I just thought you'd like to know that.' She slammed down the phone.

I flinched. What? What? For a whole minute I sat frozen. Then I shook my head. Luke? No way. I didn't believe it for a minute. He couldn't. Not Luke. It was just Izzy, getting her own back.

Jeepers, just one more senseless onslaught to add to all

the others. So who cared? All the same her fury did rather put paid to any idea I might have had of Izzy welcoming me on board her gipsy caravan.

Which didn't help when it came to trying to get off to sleep.

ANOTHER DAY. Another night. I opened my eyes, suddenly wide awake, and looked at the luminous dial on my clock. Two a.m. Rain pattered on the roof, cooling the air. I pushed back the sheet, rolled out of bed. A drink might help.

I tiptoed down to the next landing and stopped. From inside Esme's room came the sound of low voices. I waited for a moment, then knocked.

'Come in,' Esme said after a pause.

Izzy was sitting huddled in a blanket in one of the armchairs, her hair all over the place, her face swollen with crying. Esme was perched on her desk wrapped in a brown poncho, her legs neatly crossed at the ankle. Both of them were holding mugs. The room smelled of Ovaltine.

'I found her in the orchard,' Esme said. 'She's had a bad shock.'

'Izzy?'

'I'm okay now.' Izzy held her mug against her wet cheek. Her breath shuddered. She didn't look at me.

'She'd got rather wet.'

Something had happened and Izzy hadn't told me; she'd gone to Esme instead. Because she was still angry with me. 'D'you want me to go?' I said.

'Of course not,' Esme said. 'Sit down, dear. Take the pouffe.'

'I know you're only trying to make me feel better,' Izzy

said to Esme, ignoring me. 'But if he'd really loved me he'd have told me the truth, even if it meant admitting he didn't have the guts to leave his wife.'

'I don't think you should tell yourself he didn't love you,' Esme said. 'Love isn't exclusive. It's quite possible that he loved both you and his wife. I've met her, you know. Sylvia.'

'She's beautiful.' Izzy blew her nose. I sank down on the pouffe beside Izzy's chair.

'And she loves him,' Esme said. 'Although this may be painful for you to hear.' She looked at Izzy with her head on one side. 'Also, if I've understood you correctly, the premise under which he first entered into his relationship with you was a false one.'

'Sorry?'

'You gave him to understand that you were happy for the relationship to remain on a certain footing. When he realised that this was not in fact the case, he panicked.'

'That was her fault,' Izzy said, still not looking at me. She said to Esme, 'Milly said I ought to tell him how I really felt. Then look what happened.'

'Ah.' Esme looked thoughtfully at me, then back at Izzy.

'He lied,' Izzy said, turning her head and looking straight at me. Her eyes, normally so bright, were small and dull. 'She doesn't have cancer at all, his wife. She's fine. I saw them together, bold as brass. I made him tell me. He just said that to get rid of me.'

My mouth fell open. 'No! *No!* Oh, Izzy, that's terrible. That stinks.'

'All the same,' Esme said, 'I do wonder how long you could have gone on maintaining the pretence.'

'What pretence?' Izzy leaned her head back. She looked exhausted. 'What d'you mean?'

Esme looked at her kindly. 'In your heart of hearts,

didn't you want him to know the truth about how you felt about him? Honestly?'

There was a long pause during which Izzy looked down at her empty mug. Then she leaned forward and plonked it down on the desk and said, 'You're right, I did want him to know.' She glanced at me again and this time there seemed to be a softening, the beginning of forgiveness. I let my breath out.

Esme nodded. She slid down from the desk, patted Izzy on the shoulder, picked up Izzy's mug and took it with her own over to the sink. 'Now, my dear,' she said over her shoulder. 'What's your next move?'

Izzy blew her nose. 'I'm going to look for my dad. I'm taking to the road in a gipsy caravan. It's all sorted. Pete Bradley's got one he says I can borrow. And a horse.' She looked at me. 'You know Pete. Luke takes the van to him for the MOT and servicing and stuff. He's lending me Samson.'

I thought with longing of the gipsy caravan. 'Are you really, Izzy?'('Can I come too?' I wanted to say, but this wasn't the moment.)

'Tell us more,' Esme said. 'What are you having, Milly? Tea? Izzy? We seem to have run out of Ovaltine.'

'I'd better get back,' Izzy said. She heaved herself out of the armchair and began to unwind herself from her blanket. She seemed calmer. 'I'm sorry I yelled at you,' she said, not looking at me. 'On the phone. I'd only just found out about Rob lying. I was upset. I didn't know—' She glanced at me and looked away again. 'I mean it's awful for you what's been happening, all that about your mother. Sorry.' She staggered as she pushed herself upright and moved slowly towards the door. 'My legs have gone to sleep. Thanks, Esme. You've been amazing.'

'Hang on a minute,' I said. 'Before you go. What you said about Luke. In the restaurant.'

'Oh. That.' She picked up the blanket and began folding it.

'Yes, that. Tell me again.'

Izzy looked at me. 'I shouldn't have spouted off like that. It was just – okay – Rob said Luke got this girl pregnant and then wouldn't help her. She was very young, sixteen or something.'

'Oh, he said that, did he? Well, I don't believe a word of it. Luke would never do that.'

'Perhaps you don't know him as well as you think you do.'

'Just a minute,' Esme said.

'What?' Izzy said, defensively. 'That's what Rob said. Sorry.'

'I think some wires have got crossed.'

'What d'you mean?' Izzy said.

'Juno and I had lunch with Sylvia last week,' Esme said. 'We'd drunk wine and were all a bit mellow, you know how it is. She told us what happened. With that girl. I'm sorry, Izzy, but it wasn't Luke who got the girl pregnant, it was Sylvia's husband. It was Robert.'

'What?' Izzy said.

'And the girl wasn't quite sixteen,' Esme said.

'No,' Izzy said. 'No. Rob wouldn't do something like that. And why would he try and make me think it was Luke—'

Esme said, 'It was fairly common knowledge at the time, Sylvia said. It wasn't that long ago. Perhaps Robert was afraid Luke knew and would tell you about it. Perhaps he thought if he maligned Luke you wouldn't believe him.'

'Amy could have told Luke,' I butted in. 'She must have known. Sylvia is her sister.'

'Oh my God,' Izzy said. 'Is she?'

'Didn't you know?'

Izzy shook her head. 'We never talked about things like that ... families.' After a while she said, 'How could Rob do that? Oh, bananas. Maybe I was wrong about him. Maybe he makes a habit of picking girls up. All those things he said. Like I was the love of his life.' She looked at Esme. 'D'you think Sylvia will stay with him?'

'I have to say I rather hope not. He got into a lot of trouble over the girl. They managed to hush it up. A pity, in my opinion.'

'I wonder if she knows about me,' Izzy said, looking stricken. 'His wife, I mean.'

Esme looked at her for a long beat. 'I can't believe she'd have invited your mother to lunch if she did know, unless to interrogate her, and she didn't do that, on the contrary, they seemed to get on very well. Of course, Amy may well tell her. She was with Luke, you said, in the restaurant.'

'Oh jeepers, I'm dished,' Izzy said. 'She'll tell Mum.'

'Well, it *is* over between you and Robert,' I said.

'I don't think that's going to help much. The sooner I'm off the better. P'raps it will all have blown over by the time I get back. How could I have been such a fool?'

'Because you loved him?' I said.

'I did. I did love him. Oh crumbs, I'm so confused.' She clutched her head with both hands and circled on the spot, her elbows two triangles.

'I wonder if making a clean breast of it might not be the most sensible solution,' Esme said, 'as far as your mother is concerned, that is. If she's going to find out anyway.'

'You could be right. Oh gosh!' She set off for the door.

'Before you go,' Esme said, 'there's something I'd quite like clarification on, while I've got you both here. This isn't necessarily a criticism, but I would like the truth.'

Izzy stopped and turned around. We both said together, 'What about?'

'Juno said,' she stopped. She gave a little laugh, shook her head and said, 'Juno called in on me the other day. Not something she's done before so I do think she was genuinely worried. She said that you two – Milly in particular – are in the habit of taking bottles of vodka from the supermarket without paying for them. That you regularly drink a lot more than is good for you.'

'*What?*' said Izzy.

'But I loathe alcohol,' I said, truthfully. 'I hate being beside myself and out of control.' Unless, I thought, it's the kind of feeling that happens sometimes when you're lying in the orchard looking up through the apple blossom at the blue, receding sky, and the sheer, wild, inexplicable wonderfulness of life descends on you and your insides fizzle and you feel like crying with the wonder of it, only you couldn't have said why.

Feelings like that seemed a very long way away at the moment; they seemed to belong to another era.

'Why on earth would Mum say something like that?' Izzy said. She stood looking down at the floor. She looked at me. 'I think she must be having some kind of breakdown. What are you grinning about?'

I gave up and started to laugh. 'It's the idea of us creeping around Sainsbury's stealing bottles of booze. It's hilarious.'

'It bloody isn't. I won't be able to go away if she's having a breakdown.'

'We did get a bit – wasted – once,' I told Esme, still

giggling, 'to be fair. After our O-level results. We were sick. It was horrible.'

'That's the only time,' Izzy said. 'I don't like booze much either,' she said to Esme.

'Your poor mother,' Esme said.

'She shouldn't tell lies,' Izzy said. 'Especially about Milly. On the other hand,' she said, perking up, 'this is going to make it a whole lot easier for me to come clean to Mum about Robert. When it comes to telling lies and deceiving people, she hasn't got a leg to stand on.'

Chapter 40

Some people need a kick up the backside

IN THE MORNING I CAME DOWN LATE AND BLEARY-EYED into a kitchen heavy with the scents of sugar and vanilla.

Babe opened the oven door and slid a cake-tin into its interior. 'Morning, Milly.'

'Hi. That smells good.'

'Felix phoned. He wants you to pop over to the hospital with some books he wants. He gave me a list. I found all of them but one. I'd go but I'm behind with things as it is.'

'Sure.' I glanced over to the pile of books on the table. 'Is that cake for tea?'

'If you're still here.' Babe hung the oven glove back on its hook by the Aga. 'Since you seem so keen to abandon us. Have you told Luke your plans?'

'I don't think I'll be going anywhere, actually,' I said, going over to the table to look at the books. 'Izzy's going but not me. Running away won't solve anything. I'd have to come back. And I'll be off in September anyway.' I turned them over. 'D.C. Somervell's *The Reign of King George the Fifth*, *Zuleika Dobson* ... Max Beerbohm ... *Queen Victoria* – Lytton Strachey ...'

'Well, thank goodness you've seen sense at last.'

'Anyway, fat chance, we spend most of our time avoiding each other.'

'Milly, please,' Babe said, going into the scullery.

'What?'

'I wish you'd come down off your high horse.'

'I'm not on any horse. Oh the contrary my feet are firmly on the ground, at last. No more rose-coloured specs. No more believing in unicorns.'

'Well, I want the old Milly back,' Babe said through the door. 'I liked her better.'

Well, tough, I thought, putting Felix's books into the string bag Babe had left beside them. She's gone for good. Like it or lump it.

Come here mama and dig this crazy scene, sang James Brown. *He's not too fancy but his line is pretty clean ...*

'Jean-Paul rang for you,' Babe said, coming back into the kitchen carrying a cabbage. 'He says he'll give you a lift in, he's got some business in Reigate.' She dumped the cabbage on the draining board and reached for her favourite chopping knife. 'By the way, Milly, did you put the bin out?'

'Yup, done that. Jeez, I could do with something fizzy. The pop man hasn't been around this week, did you notice? Hope he's okay. I could just do with some Cherryade.'

'If that's all you need to cheer you up I'll go out and find him personally. Better get a move on lovey, Jean-Paul will be here in five minutes.'

'That's good, it's too hot for the bus.'

'Weird stuff Felix reads, doesn't he ever relax with a good detective story? Oh – and Milly,' she said over her shoulder, her voice brightening, 'Guess who popped in yesterday looking for Felix? I forgot to tell you.'

'Who?'

'His granddaughter, would you believe? Leonie, I think she said her name is. She said she'd been talking to you.' She turned around to face me and leant against the draining board, brandishing the knife. With her hair standing on end and her petticoat hanging down she looked like a demented serial killer.

I was so amazed I couldn't speak.

'Funny little thing,' Babe said. 'Not what I'd have expected.'

I found my voice. 'I think she's changed a bit from when he last saw her.'

'Oh?'

'Not sure how they'll get on, to be honest. Is she going to visit him in hospital?'

'She said Gill would take her. Her mum.'

'Right.'

'You don't sound too sure.' She turned back to the sink.

'No, I'm thrilled, it's just … I don't want Felix to be disappointed,' I said to her back.

Here we go again, I thought, looking out of the window at the sunny garden. Would it have been better to leave him with his deluded idea of what Leonie was like rather than face the person she's become, warts and all?

But Felix is a grown-up. And isn't it better to know the truth, even if it hurts? Then I thought, well, hark at you.

And then Babe told me to stop dreaming and I scurried off so as not to keep Jean-Paul waiting.

HE ARRIVED in his old red Fiesta, pulled up and came around to open the passenger door for me.

'What a gent you are,' I said, climbing in. 'Thanks for the lift.' I settled back in my seat.

Jean-Paul got in and switched on the engine. 'Ready?'

We set off and after a moment I said, 'Jean-Paul?'

He glanced at me. 'What is it?'

After a longish pause I said, 'I was thinking I might move out soon.'

'What? Out of Half Moon, you mean?'

'Yeah. I'm thinking I need my own space.'

'You what?' He took his foot off the accelerator and the car slowed to a walking pace. Fortunately there was no other traffic on the road. 'What are you talking about? You've got all the space you need at home. Look at you, rattling around inside that big old house. What's brought this on?'

I glanced at him. 'Keep your hair on.'

'Well, what's all this about then?'

'Luke wants me to go.'

'What d'you mean, he wants you to go?' He leaned back, waiting for my answer.

'Well, maybe not now, not immediately but – when she moves in, he won't want me around then. It's for him, Jean-Paul. I'm thinking of him.'

'When who moves in?'

'Amy. Mrs Booth. She's – they're – well, you know.'

He didn't seem to have heard me. 'Is this because of what happened between you and Luke, because of that thing with your mother?'

'He *told* you?'

'Of course he told me, he's my friend. He needed someone to talk to.'

'Don't get mad. Why are you getting mad?'

'I'm not getting mad, I just want you to know how he's been since all that blew up.'

'I told you, it's because of Amy.'

He shook his head. 'No, it isn't. He's been doing his nut. It's because he's bothered about you. He knows he's upset you. He cares about you, you muffin. You know that. He made a little mistake, so what? Haven't you ever made a mistake?'

'This is different.'

'Why? How is it different?'

'It just is.'

'Look.' We were coming to a pull-in area by the side of the road. Jean-Paul indicated and moved into it, pulled on the hand-brake and switched off the engine. He turned in his seat to look at me and his normally amiable eyes were stern. I felt a flutter of disquiet. 'If you're going to start messing about like this, I've got to say something. Luke's a decent bloke. You can't go upsetting him and taking advantage.'

'*Me?*' I said indignantly. 'Me taking advantage? You don't know the first thing about it. What did he tell you? This isn't my fault, none of it is my fault.' My temper rose. 'How dare you? Just get off my back and let me get out of here. Hell's teeth, why does everybody always blame me?' I scrabbled for the door handle.

'Hang on, Milly, calm down.' Jean-Paul put his hand on my arm. 'Wait. Nobody's blaming you. All I'm saying is that Luke *cares* about you, all he wants is for you to be happy. The only person who doesn't seem to realise that is you. Look, whatever's gone wrong between you, you can sort it out, I'm sure you can.' His voice softened. 'Come on, Milly, you're not a child. Stop fighting him. Do the decent thing and put the guy out of his misery. I can't stand to see him suffering like this.'

My mouth fell open, I turned my whole body around and glared at him. 'Suffering?' I said. '*Suffering?* You don't understand. He's going to marry Amy and when he does I'll have to go away. Don't you see? I love him, you idiot. I'm mad about him. I don't think I can live without him.'

Oh sugar, I thought, hearing myself say the words out loud, it's true. Luke doesn't love me but I love him and I always will and I'm going to get my heart broken.

I turned to face Jean-Paul. 'But don't you dare say anything to him, Jean-Paul, just don't you dare. If you say one word I will never, ever, speak to you again.'

FELIX HAD BEEN MOVED into another ward. There were eight beds in the ward and as I walked in the other patients, mostly elderly and frail, turned their bleached faces towards the door like sunflowers towards the sun. I spotted Felix in the far corner bed and hurried towards him, then skidded to a halt. Luke was sitting beside him. I started to back away but too late, Felix had seen me. He raised a hand and waved, beaming.

The walk towards them seemed to take for ever. I swung Babe's string bag with Felix's books in it and saw, as I approached, Luke getting to his feet, the relaxed smile that had been on his face wiped away by the sight of me. 'Hello, Milly,' he said.

'Hi,' I said, not looking at him.

'Well, I'll be off if you've got another visitor,' Luke said.

'*No*,' Felix said with unexpected force, but Luke had gone, striding away down the ward. He didn't look back. Several people turned their heads and watched him leave. 'Oh Lord,' Felix said. 'Sit down, Milly. There you are, pull that chair up and sit down. Now, look here. It's time we had a proper talk. I don't know what's been going on, and you can tell me to mind my own business if you like, but, and I speak not only for myself but for all the residents of Half Moon, this has got to stop.'

'I—'

Felix held up his hand for silence. 'This is how wars start,' he said. 'With people refusing to talk to each other. It won't do. Look here. I could have drowned in that river. It's only by sheer chance that I didn't and one thing this experience has taught me is that life is too short and unpredictable to make enemies. You and Luke can't quarrel. Or at least, if you absolutely have to, then you might at least have the courage to try to sort your disagreements out.'

'He'd rather I was out of the way,' I muttered.

'What gives you that idea? I should think it's the last thing in the world he wants.' Felix lay back on his pillows and closed his eyes. 'Now, please, child, go home and sort this out. This is bad for my blood pressure. I'm far too exhausted to care about the whys and wherefores but I do care about the outcome. Now off you go. Vamoose. I'll be home in a few days and I want things back to normal, please.'

It isn't just up to me, is it? I whined to myself, crossing the hospital forecourt. But good old Felix, I thought a moment later, my mouth twitching despite myself: a glimpse of the old schoolmaster there.

No sign of Luke. He hadn't even waited for me. That was how much he cared. Showed how much Jean-Paul knew.

AT HOME I sat on the edge of my bed and cried. Again. At this rate I'd drown in a sea of tears like the mouse in Alice. I'd simply got to stop crying. It was just that my emotions kept being jangled and pushed about, this way and that.

Jean-Paul had better keep quiet. I couldn't believe I'd let it all out like that, all my misery and frustrated love, my despair.

Perhaps Luke really had only been doing what he felt was best for me. And Babe was right too, look how he'd cared for me all these years.

I was so confused.

Felix had said we needed to talk but by the time I got home Luke had shut himself up in the study. An unbridgeable chasm seemed to lie between us.

What have we done? I thought, blowing my nose, glad he wasn't there to see me all red and blotchy and out of control. We both did it. He by concealing the truth and me by reacting the way I did. We were both at fault. *And* he hadn't waited for me, so I'd had to come home on the bus.

I banged my feet against the side of the bed, feeling like a child again. I felt wronged but I was beginning to feel guilty too.

If we could just forgive each other, everything would be okay again. But could we? And it wouldn't be, because there was still bloody Amy.

But we couldn't walk around each other like this for ever, not touching, worrying about hurting each other all the time. I looked out of the window. Overhead the sky had darkened. It was starting to rain again.

Chapter 41

Growing pains

I stood outside the study door. The rain had cleared and a watery sun gleamed on wet trees and flowers in the garden.

'Wish it would make up its mind,' Babe had grumbled earlier, bringing in the washing for a second time.

Luke was sitting in his armchair with his hands linked behind his head and his eyes shut, listening to a Gorecki symphony, one of his favourites.

I picked up the record sleeve and looked at it, then plonked myself down onto the floor cushion. I waited quietly until the end of the piece and then said in a small voice, 'I've been really, really stupid.'

Luke opened his eyes, lowered his arms and looked at me, his eyes guarded.

'Felix said we have to talk.' I flexed my bare feet and fiddled with a thread hanging loose from the hem of my jeans. 'So I think we ought to.'

The silence closed around us, soft, enveloping us like a cloud. I'd like to stay like this for ever, I thought. Words are so difficult.

Luke looked at the gramophone, at the ceiling, over at the window and then at me. After a long while he cleared his throat and said, 'You have every right to be angry.'

I gripped my hands together in my lap. The air prickled with tension.

'It's my fault,' he said after another long pause. He sighed. 'My mistake.'

'Anyone can make a mistake,' I said. I looked up at him through my hair. I took hold of my toes and pulled my feet in so that the sole of one foot was pressed against the other. I said, looking at my toes, 'What I said about the nightmares, that was unfair. I'm sorry, I didn't mean it. It mightn't have made any difference, my knowing. It wouldn't necessarily have cured them, they might even have got worse.'

Luke put his head back and laughed.

'What?'

'That's my Milly. Trying to let me off the hook. That's so you.'

'Well, I have been a complete pig to you, you must admit.'

He leaned forward, his elbows on his knees, his hands clasped. His dear face was so near, I could see the small vein throbbing in his temple. I looked at his mouth and remembered how it had felt, closed over mine. I felt sick with longing, wanting to feel it on mine again. I longed for the scent of his skin, the smell of his sweat. I closed my eyes, then opened them again.

'Milly, if you had any idea how wretched I'm feeling, you wouldn't feel you had to apologise for anything. I'm devastated. I can't think how I came to make such an error of judgement. It's humiliating.'

If only I could hurl myself onto his lap and hug him, the way I used to when I was a child if we'd fallen out over some little thing. If only. My face felt hot, my lips swollen with longing.

'Juno was right. I should have listened to her. Milly.' He looked at me and I saw the pain in his face, the dark hollows under his eyes. 'What can we do to make things right again?'

'Can't we just forget the whole thing?'

He looked astonished. He sat back. 'Is that what you want?'

'It's boring, being a drama queen. It was a terrible shock, I can't pretend I'm happy to know my mother loathed me and tried to kill me but honestly, life's too short. It's over. Done and dusted.' I looked down at my feet again. 'And I'm really grateful to you for putting up with me getting the hump. I had no right. I'm sorry.'

He looked down at his hands, resting in his lap. 'Oh, Milly,' he said. 'You're more generous than I deserve.' After a long time he said, 'I won't make any excuses, for thinking the truth about your mother was best kept from you. It was an error of judgement. But I can't pretend I'm not relieved. However hard it is for you, it's usually best to face up to things, however difficult. We can't change what happened, and if we can move forward from this, it can only be good that the air is cleared. Now,' he said, turning his head to look at me. 'Is there anything you want to know – about your mother, about anything? I promise that anything you ask me, I will try to answer truthfully.'

I thought for a bit, then shook my head. 'No. Although —' I stopped. I'd been going to say, although I think there's something she's trying to tell me. Until I remembered that Luke knew nothing about the music in the garden, the manifestation, apparently, of Miranda. Was now the time to tell him? Perhaps it would be better to sort this out now and tell him later. I drew in a deep breath and smiled at him. 'I feel better.'

'Do you?' He looked at me and smiled back. Tentatively. But a smile. At last. 'Milly,' he said with infinite tenderness. He put out his hand and I took it and on an impulse put it to my mouth and kissed it. My heart was pounding. Did he know? Could he tell? I forced myself to smile to make light of the gesture, swung his hand a little, and said, 'Friends?'

How could we get back to where we were before? And was that what I wanted? What did I want? All I knew was that whatever it was, Luke was an essential part of it.

'Friends,' he said. 'And you won't run away, will you? Not until term starts, that is. Let's at least enjoy the time we do have left together.'

And then I knew for certain that I couldn't run away from whatever was coming. I couldn't let him see how much it would hurt if he got together with Amy but if he did decide to bring her to Half Moon to live, then we would decide what to do. But I must be brave, I had to let him go free.

'Perhaps I won't,' I said, my head on one side, teasing. I'm flirting, I thought. I love him. Oh, I do love him.

Perhaps it was up to me to heal us both. Make it possible for us to go on living together in peace. I was a woman, after all; women did that kind of thing. They were the peacemakers. Men would suffer in silence, maybe wait for difficulties to pass, but did they ever actually make the first move to sort things out?

If I could just pretend nothing had changed for me, that that incredible kiss hadn't made any difference; if I could just hide how I really felt and wait until he thought I was old enough – a year? – I'd be eighteen – perhaps he would own up. Perhaps then he'd admit he loves me.

And then I remembered Amy again.

I had so little experience. Perhaps this feeling in my bones I had that there was something real between us, that it wasn't Amy but me he liked, me he wanted – was completely wrong and that kiss, the kiss that had changed everything for me, had just been from relief that I wasn't hurt, and meant nothing. I mean, if he did love me, why didn't he just get on with it and kiss me again? Was he regretting kissing me?

Maybe he thought I was too young and that loving me would be wrong because he was in loco whatsit for me and it would be breaking some kind of rule.

He still hadn't let go of my hand. We both seemed to be pretending he wasn't holding it. But neither was he making any move to do anything more. Was he was waiting for me to show him how I felt? Couldn't he tell by the way I was clinging to his hand, my palm and fingers hot with longing?

Maybe I had a choice. Either to tell him how I felt, and risk disaster, or keep quiet and just wait.

Could I do that? Ought I to?

And how ironic was that? If I did go on pretending, I would be doing what I seemed to have spent my whole life telling everybody else, and that included Izzy, not to do – living a lie.

Was this what growing up was? Learning to compromise, learning that telling the truth was not always the most obvious or best solution?

Luke decided for me by abruptly letting my hand drop and practically leaping to his feet. 'Well,' he said, looking down at me and putting his hands in his pockets. 'Thank

God for you, Milly. Thank God for your common sense and your sweet nature. Whoever manages to sweep you off your feet will be a very lucky man.'

What? *What?*

'Only I don't think you ought to encourage young Stephen too much. You're very young and you're on the verge of spreading your wings and flying off to university and a life you can't even imagine at the moment. Well,' he said, as though nothing unusual had happened, 'I'm off out for half an hour. See you at supper.' He touched me lightly on the shoulder as he passed, flung open the study door and strode off.

I leapt to my feet. I heard him whistling in the hall, the front door slammed and still I stood there as though I'd looked over my shoulder at something I shouldn't have seen and been turned, like Lot's wife, into a pillar of salt.

AGAIN I WENT to find Pascale. She was in the kitchen, unsuccessfully trying to drape a drying- up cloth over the Aga rail. It kept slipping off and she fumbled with arthritic fingers, muttering to herself.

'Pascale, come and sit down. Please. I have something to say.'

I pulled out a chair for her and she lowered herself unsteadily onto the seat. I sat down opposite her again, like before, and waited till she was settled and still, apart from the old hands which wound themselves together as if playing with an invisible ball, betraying her nervousness.

I said, 'I owe you my life.'

'*Mais non,*' Pascale said. She looked at me, frowning.

'*Mais oui,*' I said. 'Look here, Pascale, I was angry before because I felt you'd been unfair, blaming me because I'd prevented you from being with André at the end. But this is something different. You saved my life. Luke did tell me but it hadn't sunk in. I know now that my mother tried to harm me. And I know that it was you who saved me. And I am really, really grateful.'

Tears filled the old eyes, which looked at me still, to my discomfort, with a kind of horror. She shook her head fiercely. 'Do not thank.' She fished in her sleeve for a handkerchief, blew her nose. '*Non*. Do not thank.' She gripped the handkerchief tight in her hand. 'It is *le Bon Dieu* who watch over you,' she said, looking away. After a long pause she went on, 'It is He who wake me and carry me to that room, so that I help Miss Miranda.'

'If it were not for you, I might not be here – and I'm so glad to be alive.' And I was, I realised. 'I'm sorry I didn't know. I didn't realise – what I owed you.'

Pascale shrugged, her lips tightening. '*Monsieur* Luke, he feel it is best. Now you know.'

'Yes. It's been a big shock.'

She nodded, her eyes clouding over. All this was almost too much for her.

I hardened my heart. 'There's something else. Those things you told me about my mother, her being such a loving person. That wasn't true, was it? Luke – says – he thinks she was not kind, she was cruel. And she did not behave as though she loved me.'

Pascale looked down at her hands again. Her fingers moved as though telling her rosary. The hanky fell on the floor. I picked it up and returned it to her. When at last she looked up, her tortoise eyes were swimming with tears. She shook her head. She said in a faltering voice, 'Perhaps she blame you. All she want is dance.'

'But why tell me all that stuff, Pascale?' Frustrated, I put out a hand, then withdrew it again. Pascale still looked stony-faced. What was the matter with her? Perhaps I shouldn't hold back, perhaps I should be yelling at her.

I was upsetting her, but I felt ruthless, justified. All those lies.

Pascale shrugged, still avoiding my eyes. 'I do not know. I do not know.' Her head lowered, her shoulders began to shake.

I pulled my chair closer and put my arms around her. I rocked her gently. Pascale didn't object. She cried, repeatedly wiping her eyes. At last she twisted her head to look at me piteously. 'May God forgive me.' She shook her head.

'You didn't mean any harm. You have suffered too. I just wanted to know why you kept telling me what a wonderful person she was, that's all. But it doesn't matter. I suppose you did it for the best. From now on we will speak the truth.'

Pascale closed her eyes and sat for a long time as though wrapped in thought. Now and then she nodded her head, afterwards resuming her trance-like silence. I didn't interrupt her but sat and waited. In retrospect it was as if I knew that some momentous decision was taking place inside that troubled head, that I had to give her the chance to make the right choice.

I waited while the minutes passed, until I realised that something was happening. I watched as at a snail-like pace, as though propelled by some force too strong for her to resist, her hand moved to fumble in the pocket of her dress. I watched, my mouth falling open, as she brought out a small book bound in green leather and without a word held it out to me. On the cover a date was stamped in gold: 1954. The year of my mother's death.

I took it from her. 'A diary,' I said, my heart beginning to beat fast. 'It's a diary.' I opened it and flipped over a few pages. 'Oh my God. It's my mother's diary.'

Pascale nodded. 'I keep,' she said in a low, harsh voice, dredged up from somewhere deep inside. 'I keep for you one day. Now I tell you the truth. Now is the day.'

An hour later I was sitting cross-legged on the floor in my bedroom, my back against the chest of drawers, the diary open on my lap, looking in complete disbelief at the words written on the page in front of me. They couldn't be true, could they? Could my mother have been lying?

But lying to herself? In her own private diary which it was unlikely anyone else would ever read? No. Surely not.

I scrambled to my feet and went to the open window. The rain had cleared at last and the sky was that wonderful washed blue that sometimes follows rain. A few white clouds sat pensively on the horizon. My heart was pounding, hope rising as my mind tried to make sense of what my mother had written. There it was, scribbled in her writing and surely, surely the truth at last.

Was this why Pascale had kept it hidden away all these years? To prevent the truth from coming to light? I shook my head, imagining her desperation as she ferreted about in Miranda's room after the accident, trying to find the diary.

Was this what Miranda had come back to tell me?

'What is it, Milly?' In the kitchen Luke threw himself onto a chair and started heeling off his work boots. He looked tired. He'd gone to work in the afternoon to finish Amy's chair and I'd been waiting on tenterhooks all afternoon for him to come home. I couldn't settle but fidgeted about until Babe, unable to stand it any longer, ordered me to 'Get out of the kitchen, for heaven's sake, Milly. Go for a walk or something. What on earth is the matter with you?'

I'd heard the music again, on and off all afternoon. Agitated music, louder than usual and going on for longer. Whatever it was out there sounded frustrated, annoyed, instead of relieved, which I would have expected.

I couldn't understand it. Did that mean that it wasn't what was written in the diary that Miranda was trying to make me understand? The shattering, bewildering truth that I would have thought must be the most important thing to any mother. The truth that was causing my cheeks to redden, my eyes to sparkle as I waited for Luke to be ready to focus on the little book in my hand which I held behind my back.

'You're looking particularly bright-eyed and bushy-tailed,' Luke said, sighing with relief and wriggling his toes. I handed him a mug of tea and he nodded thanks. I'd made the tea the moment I heard the van's wheels scrunching on the gravel. 'What's up? I can see you're dying to tell me something.'

I gave him about three seconds to lean back in the chair, relax and take a long swallow, then brought my mother's diary from behind my back and held it out to him. 'There's something here you've simply got to see.'

'What's that?' he said, looking at the little book. He put his mug down on the table and took it from me. He opened it, flipped over a few pages and looked up at me. 'Good grief, where on earth did you find this? This is Miranda's diary. But it's private. I can't read this.' He closed it and held it out to me.

I shook my head. 'I think you're going to have to. Pascale

had it. She's had it all this time. She gave it to me. It's important. You need to read all of it, especially the end. It explains everything. Then we need to think what we're going to do.'

Chapter 42

Crunch time

'She has to go,' Luke said. 'She can't stay. Not after this. What was Miranda thinking?'

We were sitting on the bench among the rose bushes gilded now by the evening sunlight. Luke's face was pale, his fist, resting on the wooden struts between us, clenched. I had never seen him so enraged. I'd had to restrain him from marching up to Pascale's room there and then and ordering her out of the house.

'She's too old,' I said, with the magnanimity of the reprieved. 'Where would she go? Perhaps she's a bit mad.'

'But you can't be expected to live in the same house as Pascale. Not now you know.'

'Luke, I'm used to her. And it was so long ago. I know she still gets at me whenever she can but it's nothing to speak of now. It's bearable.'

'Well, that's stopping, right now.'

'And I'm no longer a small, defenceless child.' I tried not to sound self-pitying but it was such a relief to voice my sense of unfairness.

'Oh, Milly. I've noticed her barbs, but I thought that

was just the way she was. I am so sorry, I'm at fault as much as Miranda was. If she had told her parents about Pascale when she found out what was going on then maybe the woman could have had treatment.'

'Pascale was probably as nice as pie when anybody was around. I expect she was careful to reserve her most bizarre cruelties for when she and I were alone. She's still pretty good at keeping her sniping in check when you're around. Miranda caught her out, that one time, didn't she, and began to realise what was going on. It wouldn't have occurred to her until then.'

'When I think – she could actually have—' He shook his head. He was having difficulty even mentioning Pascale's name. 'If Miranda hadn't come in to your nursery at that moment.' He put out his hand and grasped mine briefly, then let it go. 'Milly, aren't you angry? If I was in your position I don't think I'd ever want to see her again. She hurt you, Milly. She abused you. It's frightful. I wonder if you're in some kind of denial.'

'Of course I'm angry. I've had all afternoon to be simply furious. But we've been living in the same house for years. I'm used to her. And I'm grown up, she can't hurt me now. I feel quite sorry for her, actually.'

Luke shook his head. 'I'm not sure I should be listening to you.'

'But where would she go, if we threw her out? What would Grandpa say if he were here? Grandma loved Pascale, and so did my mother. She must have done, to want to protect her so badly that she risked goodness knows what happening if she wasn't there to stop it.'

'But at the expense of her own child?'

'Perhaps she thought Pascale was ill. Or a bit peculiar or something. Perhaps she thought she couldn't help it.'

'Come on, Milly. There are no excuses. Not from where I'm standing.'

'She says in the diary that Pascale was depressed. Did you read that bit?'

He shrugged. 'That's all very well but it's no excuse. It was criminally negligent of Miranda to cover it up. And that was quite early on. How old were you – two? And it seems to have gone on until—'

'Until the accident. And then Juno took me in, because you couldn't just drop everything and come that minute. No wonder I was confused ... I remember being so conflicted about my mother dying. Of course losing her was terrible, but it also meant going to stay with Juno and Izzy for that year I was taken out of Pascale's reach, and that was such a relief. This explains such a lot.'

We sat in silence for a while. I said, 'And then you came.' After another long pause I said, 'I wonder if my nightmares will stop now. Did you read about the bathtimes? I think that's at the back of them. I wonder if she's a sadist. Sort of water-boarding for infants.'

Luke sat forward and put his head in his hands. 'Don't joke. Milly. She can't stay.'

'But where will she go?' I touched his arm and when he looked up I managed a smile. 'Do you think we ought to just forget about it and carry on?'

Luke sat back and looked at me. 'Do you mean that? Could you do that?'

'Well, I've had the best training. You've always said we should forgive people.'

'Within reason. You can forgive someone but that doesn't mean you have to fraternise. If she stays you'll have to see her every day.'

'But in a way it's a relief, don't you see, Luke? At least it wasn't my mother hating and terrorising me. It's a gift, after thinking that. I can't tell you how awful that was, it sort of made everything seem pointless. Knowing it isn't true is—' I shook my head, feeling near to tears. 'It's the most wonderful thing you can imagine. I think I could forgive Pascale a hundred times over now I know the truth.'

Luke shook his head. 'I don't know. I'm not at all sure about this.'

'I can't tell you what it means to know that my mother did care about me, that all she did was try to help and protect me. She rescued me over and over again.'

'She should have told somebody. I can't think why she didn't.'

'Okay, yeah, she should, but Luke, she loved Pascale. Pascale had been her nurse all my mother's life, she was more of a mother to her than Grandma was, because Grandma was not very well a lot of the time. I suppose it would have been like shopping her own mother. It must have been really stressful having to be on her guard all the time, wondering whether Pascale would crack again and do something really terrible.'

'She did. For heaven's sake.'

'Yes.' After another long pause I said, 'If Pascale stays I won't have to see her very often, only at mealtimes really. It's a big house. And everyone else is around then. It won't be so bad.' I glanced at Luke's stony face. 'She really does seem to be sorry, unless that's all an act too. I'll be going away to university soon anyway.' I glanced at Luke again as I said this but he gave nothing away.

'Things are beginning to come back,' I admitted. It was such a relief to be able to talk about it. 'Memories ... things I think I've suppressed. I wake up in the night and remember her raging at me, saying I'd ruined my mother's life, telling me I was worthless, useless, that I'd be better dead. She was always threatening me with dire consequences if I told. She liked locking me in cupboards in the dark, I remember that.' I pressed my lips together. I felt a surge of anger again. After a while, I muttered, 'Look, it's all in the past. She can't hurt me now.'

Luke stayed for a long while, sitting back, staring down at his long legs stretched out in front of him. Eventually he said, 'I can't bear to think about it. But I will leave the decision to you. If you want Pascale to go, out she goes. It must be your decision. For what it's worth I think we should send her packing.'

'I think it would be a worse punishment for her to stay,' I said. 'She's still got to live with her conscience.'

'If she's got one. She doesn't seem to have shown much sign of one so far.'

'Everybody's redeemable. Didn't you say?'

'Milly, I do wish you wouldn't keep reminding me of my rather sanctimonious homilies. I was trying to teach you to be a good person. I think I've succeeded. Please shut up.'

I really did laugh this time.

LATER ON THAT day Izzy and I stood facing each other in the orchard, in the fading light. There was something different in Izzy's face. She looked older, there was a new sadness in her eyes.

'I'm going to miss you.'

'I'll miss you too. I'll be back in good time for the start of term.'

'Are you okay?'

'Surviving. Mum's been cool actually. I've told her the lot, everything, and she took it really well. No hysterics.

Almost as if she understood. It's a bit of a relief, not to have to carry on telling all those porkies.'

'When are you off?'

'Tomorrow morning, first thing. Are you sure you won't come with me?'

I shook my head. 'I can't, Izzy. I thought I wanted to get out but I was wrong. I need to be here.'

'Will you be okay?'

'Me? Goodness, yes.'

'Is everything cool?' Izzy was peering at me. 'You look—'

'I'm fine! Sad to see you go.'

'I'll be back before you know it.'

'Are you really not still cross with me?'

''Course not. You were right, you can't keep living a lie, it's too big a strain. Honestly, it's a relief not to feel guilty all the time.'

'Did you feel guilty? I'd never have guessed.'

'Well, there you go. Even managed to hide that from myself. No, it's out in the open at all times from now on. Like you. No more secrets.' She looked at her watch. 'I'd better go. Mum and I are having supper out, kind of a bonding thing before I go. I read all the letters, you know. He's really missed me. He only left because—'

'Because?'

'Oh ... I'll tell you another time.' She was walking away. 'It was because of a woman.'

'The one he's with now?'

'No.'

'Poor Juno. I never realised.'

'Yup. Poor Mum. Keep an eye on her for me, will you? She's a bit – I dunno – low, I suppose.' She turned back. 'Oh, and by the way, she's really sorry about lying about the booze thing. She says she wanted to get you into trouble with Luke.' She pulled a face. 'She says she thinks she went a bit bonkers. Can you believe she was jealous?'

'*Jealous?*' My heartbeat accelerated.

'Yeah, of you and him. The closeness – you know. She says she's been soft on him for years. Thing is, Milly, she's lonely. She's still sad about Dad. The other thing is, Luke and Amy. She's upset about that too. All this change I suppose. Oh, but one bit of good news, meant to tell you, she's got this new student!' Izzy grinned suddenly. 'He's way cool; quite old – I mean, as old as Mum – most of them are really young – and I think she likes him. Really likes him. His name's Jack. Jack—'

'Oh! The man who wanted to sing!'

'Sorry? Marmaduke, that's it. Jack Marmaduke.'

'That is really, really good news. That should cheer her up.'

'What are you grinning about?'

'Nothing. Not a thing. Pleased, that's all. We'll keep in touch, promise. We'll invite her to supper. Or them. Don't worry, Izzy. You just go and find your dad. Come here.'

We hugged for a long time, in silence, and when we separated Izzy's eyes were wet too.

'I'll ruin my makeup. What are we like? You'd think this was for ever.'

'Come back safe.'

She's changed, I thought, watching Izzy climb the gate and jump down the other side. She walked slower. She was calmer. Happier, actually.

I hadn't told her about the diary. It was all too new, the truth needed time to settle and I needed time to come to terms with a new reality.

Chapter 43

Lemon drizzle

I WAS LATE FOR SUPPER. ESME WAS SITTING IN HER place at the table looking thoughtfully at the awful cock-and-hen salt and pepper pots I'd given Babe when I was eight. Babe stood by the Aga with her oven gloves on, holding a pile of plates.

'Ah, there you are,' Babe said. 'Not like you to be late.'

'Sorry, Babe. Just saying goodbye to Izzy. She's off first thing.'

Luke stood behind his chair, seemingly lost in thought. I glanced at his face and for a brief moment our eyes met. My breath quickened and I looked away. I caught sight of Felix.

He was standing behind Pascale, holding her chair. Pascale, bent forward, seemed to be making up her mind whether or not to sit down.

'Felix!' I exclaimed. 'You're home! Are you okay?'

'Champion,' Felix said. 'Brought me back in an ambulance, would you believe. Dismissed without a stain on my character.' He nudged Pascale's chair into the backs of her knees to persuade her to sit, which she did, slowly and with much protestation. Felix patted her shoulders and stumbled back to his own place.

'Come on lovey, food's getting cold,' Babe said. 'Sit down, for goodness sake and let us get on. Jambalaya, in case anyone's interested.'

'Before we begin,' Felix said, not sitting down, 'I have something to say.'

We all looked at him in surprise.

'When I was laid low in hospital,' he went on, 'I had a visitor. Well, two visitors to be more accurate. My daughter Gill and my granddaughter Leonie.' He looked at me. There were tears in his eyes. Oh heck, I thought, he's seen Leonie for what she is. But he went on. 'I have Milly to thank for getting us back together again.'

I looked down, holding on to the back of my chair. Was he being sarcastic?

'My granddaughter has changed beyond recognition,' Felix went on, pulling out his chair and sitting down. 'She's grown up. She's not the child she was, the child I remember, and she's got into unhelpful company, but the great thing is that she has reconciled with her mother. That is what matters. Gill is a sensible woman. Milly,' he said and nodded towards me, 'I cannot express adequately how grateful I am for your intervention.'

'That is very good news, Felix,' Luke said into the slightly stunned silence that followed.

'I'm awfully glad, Felix,' I muttered, pleased but embarrassed. Luke helpfully pulled out my chair and I sat down, aware that my face was burning. 'Where's Jean-Paul?' I said, anxious to change the subject, 'I thought he was joining us tonight.'

'He's on his way,' Luke said. 'Got held up in traffic.'

The lobby door banged.

'Here he is now,' Babe said. 'Now perhaps we can get on.'

'Entrez!' I called. 'Hello Jean-Paul! Sorry, I think I'm a bit hyper.'

Luke smiled to himself. Jean-Paul came in, rubbing his hands and looking pleased. 'Hello, everybody. This is very nice.'

'Sit you down,' Esme said, patting the vacant chair on her right.

'This will have to go back in the oven at this rate,' Babe said.

'It's fine, it's fine,' I said.

'Well at least the plates are hot,' Babe said.

'Should we start?' Felix said, looking lovingly at the jambalaya. 'Sorry to have held you up, everybody.'

'What's happened?' Jean-Paul said, pulling out his chair and sitting down.

Esme spoke to him in an undertone. Jean-Paul said, 'Cool. Great news. Happy for you, Felix,' and Felix actually smiled.

'This is so great,' I said. 'I just wish Izzy was here.' Everybody was smiling at me. Love swirled around the room and my eyes wandered shyly to Luke.

I was in a daze. People chattered, chairs were pulled out, everybody sat down and I looked sideways at Luke and thought, I love him. I love him! What am I going to do?

Pascale conveyed a small forkful to her mouth and chewed thoughtfully. She swallowed. 'More the garlic,' she said.

Luke gave her a look which said as plainly as though he had spoken, *How you have the nerve to contribute one word to any conversation in this house defeats me. You should be out on the streets, tarred and feathered and in the stocks.* He was going to find forgiving Pascale more difficult than I was. To my surprise I seemed able quite easily to separate the terrifying Pascale of my childhood from the grouchy old woman of today.

'D'you think so?' Babe said, chewing. 'P'raps you're right. I was thinking more paprika.'

Pascale, apparently oblivious to undertones, nodded. 'Per'aps,' she said, 'Still, is ver' good.'

'Jean-Paul, be a love and pass those beans around,' Babe said. 'Eat up, everybody. Especially you, Milly. Your job is to sit still and eat as much as you can. You're looking thin. Have you been losing weight?'

'I'm not, am I?' I said, looking down.

'Of course not,' Jean-Paul said. 'You're just right, isn't she, Luke?'

'I'm sure she's practically perfect,' Luke said, not looking at anybody. He handed me a dish of cauliflower and carrots. 'This is a conversation I don't feel qualified to participate in. I'm so thrown I'm forgetting my manners.'

Perhaps I'd imagined the way he'd looked at me. It all seemed normal again, apart from my heart which was refusing to believe it and thumped away so remorselessly that it seemed impossible people wouldn't hear it. I took the dish of vegetables from him and offered them to Felix on my other side.

'None for you?' Luke said. I shook my head and passed him the beans. The table was laden with food. I looked at it and felt sick. I couldn't eat a thing. 'Are you okay?' he asked quietly. 'You're rather pale.'

What I needed was not food, but to get up and dash off onto the common. Find Sapphy. Anything to distract me from this new feeling I couldn't cope with.

If only I was down at the other end of the table, instead

of which if I wasn't careful my leg would fall sideways and my knee would touch Luke's, so I couldn't relax for a moment. I was so aware of him and concentrating so hard on not giving myself away that the next thing I was conscious of was Babe staggering in from the pantry with a tilting cake, glowing with a mass of lit candles.

'Just look at that!' Esme exclaimed.

'This is a non-birthday cake,' Babe said.

'Splendid!' Felix exclaimed, actually smiling. 'I do like a bit of cake.'

'It's your favourite,' Babe told me. 'Fuller's walnut. With the funny icing. I found a recipe in one of those old Cordon Bleu cookery mags.'

'Oh, Babe.'

Luke was frowning. 'I thought Juno said she was making a lemon – sorry, Babe?'

'Went the way of all flesh,' Babe said rapidly. 'Now who's going to blow them out? Milly. Come on. You do it. Where's that knife? You can cut it too.'

'But it's not my birthday.' They were being so nice. So kind. They were trying to make me feel better. Because they didn't know about my mother's diary. They didn't know that they didn't need to feel sorry for me anymore.

Only Pascale knew.

'I think Pascale should blow them out,' I said, with malice.

'No, no, you do it,' Babe said. 'Come on. And make a wish.'

I took a deep breath amid clapping and laughter and blew out the candles. Luke handed me a knife and I saw that his eyes were resting on my face, again with that strange expression in them. Grazing suddenly sprang into my mind. His eyes are grazing on my face, as if he can't drag them away. For a moment I saw myself as he must see me. It was a strange, out-of-body feeling, bringing a flush to my cheeks. I cut deep into the cake amid cries of 'Make a wish! Make a wish!' I closed my eyes again and wished.

'I'll do this now.' Babe took the knife from me and started cutting slices. I passed the plates around. I felt dazed, everything was at a remove, as if it was happening to someone else.

'Hang on a minute,' Luke said, getting up. 'We must drink a toast.' He went to the fridge and took out a bottle.

'Champagne!' Esme said. 'Just what the doctor ordered.'

Oh glory, I thought, my dreams falling in shards all over the table cloth. He's going to make an announcement. He's going to announce his engagement to Amy.

'I'll get the glasses,' Babe said. 'They're in the scullery on a tray.'

So they'd prepared this, he'd planned it. Babe too. Babe had known and she hadn't warned me. And that special feeling I'd imagined between me and Luke was just that – my imagination.

'I'll get them,' I said, springing to my feet. I mustn't let them see.

Glasses were circulated.

'To friendship,' Luke said. 'To truth.'

Oh. Well, maybe he was going to wait a while.

People got stuck into their cake and hubbub broke out again, everybody talking, laughing. Seizing my chance I touched Luke's elbow to attract his attention. He turned towards me and I marvelled, as my hazel eyes met his grey ones, that in the past I had so easily, so painlessly, borne their level gaze.

And I felt it again, something intense building between us, a force-field, emotions skating across from him to me and back again, so strong nothing could stop them. It was like being on the big dipper, at the top of the plunge, everything slipping out of control.

Was I imagining it? Was my longing for it to be true so strong that I'd started making stuff up?

I said, 'I've never thanked you for the things you did for me when I was little. This seems – kind of like the right time.' My voice shook a little. Suddenly I felt like crying. His hand was resting on the table, inches from mine. I felt an almost irresistible urge to seize hold of it and cover it with kisses. What on earth would he do?

Something came into his eyes, something like pain, or sorrow. Not embarrassment, quite. Demurral.

I moved my hand away. 'Like the little table you made for me, and the blue chair with the daisies on it. The green mince. D'you remember? You chopped up the veg I wouldn't eat and mixed it in with the mince so I wouldn't notice – that was in my anti-green veg phase. Babe reminded me. All the times you came up when I couldn't sleep because of thunderstorms. The snacks in the rocking-chair.'

He kept his eyes on me and I knew he was remembering. One corner of his mouth twitched and he reached out his hand and covered mine with his own and squeezed it. Quite hard, as if he meant it.

But meant what? My heart thundered. Slowly he let go of my hand. If only we were alone.

'Wait a minute,' Jean-Paul said. 'Wasn't that the doorbell?'

'Was it?' Babe put down her half-eaten slice of cake. 'I'll go.'

The bell rang again.

'Perhaps it's Izzy,' I said. 'Maybe they didn't go out. Maybe they changed their minds.'

'Hope not, I only catered for seven.'

Luke pushed his chair back and got up. 'I'll go.'

The bell rang again as he left the room.

'Someone's keen,' Felix said.

And I knew. Unsurprised, I watched as the kitchen door opened and Amy stood there, framed in the doorway, Luke close behind her. Maybe this was what he had planned. Maybe he'd asked her to come, so that she could be there when he told us.

'Oh!' Amy said, smiling around. 'Have I barged in in the middle of something?'

'Not at all,' Esme said, since nobody else spoke.

'How do you do? I don't think we've met,' Felix said, pushing his chair back and rising.

'Come and sit down,' Luke said. 'Milly—'

'Have my chair,' I said, jumping up. I couldn't look at Amy. One glance had been enough; she looked stunning, and, worse, Luke was looking stunned. It was hopeless.

'Here, Milly,' Jean-Paul said quietly, pushing an extra chair in between Babe and Felix. Thank goodness he'd had the tact not to put me next to Amy.

'Thank you,' Amy said, looking up at Luke who was pushing her chair in. 'What a lovely welcome. I only wanted to have a word, but you're all being so nice. Sylvia told me,' she said quietly to Luke, as if nobody else was in the room. 'But she doesn't know who the girl is. I wanted to ask you if you thought I ought to tell her.' She looked around the table. 'I did wonder what I would do if the little tramp was here, but thank goodness,' she said, making a rueful face, 'she isn't.'

I straightened up. The room fell silent. 'What little tramp?' I said, heat pouring up into my face.

'I'd expect you to defend her,' Amy said, 'being as you're such bosom friends. I'm sorry, Milly, I've had a shock.'

'Are you talking about Izzy?' I said. I looked at Luke, then back at Amy. 'She's not a tramp! How dare you!'

'Steady on, Milly,' Luke said, but mildly. He looked as if he couldn't believe his ears either.

'I don't know what else you can call someone who decides to have an affair with a married man.'

'It takes two,' I said hotly, after an electric pause. Everyone seemed to be holding their breath. 'And I can assure you that if she'd known what kind of man he was she wouldn't have touched him with a barge-pole.'

Amy looked as if someone had slapped her in the face with a custard pie. 'I beg your pardon?'

'You heard,' I said, pushing my chair back and standing up. 'Your precious brother-in-law—'

'Milly,' Esme interposed gently.

'No!' I said, hot-faced and furious. 'He can't go around slandering people and getting away with it. He said it was you,' I said to Luke, almost in tears. 'He said it was you raping people and getting them pregnant and then dumping them.'

'What?' Luke said, frowning.

He looked so shocked that I almost regretted my outburst. Almost but not quite. Enough was enough. 'All I'm saying,' I said, my temper fading, leaving me feeling nauseous, and I didn't think it was due to too much champagne, 'is that Robert is not exactly as pure as the driven snow himself.'

'What are you talking about?' Amy's face, I noticed with wicked pleasure, had gone pale. Sweat beaded on her forehead and her nose had gone pink. She didn't look half as pretty as she had when she walked in.

I looked at Esme. She looked back, her eyes warning me not to say any more, but I was far too incensed to obey. I said to Amy, 'I don't know who the girl was, but your sister told Esme – go on, Esme, help me out.'

'Is this about Gill?' Babe said, to my surprise. What had it got to do with Gill? 'Oh sugar,' Babe said, closing her eyes, then opening them again. She turned to Felix. 'Felix, I'm sorry. I don't think Gill ever wanted you to know. I've known Gill a long time, she's a good friend. And yes, she told me just the other day who it was who had got her into trouble. I didn't know at the time that that was why she left.'

'Left what?' Esme said. 'Left who? Oh my. Gill was the girl?'

'Yes,' Babe said. She was doing a holiday cleaning job for Sylvia and Robert when she was a teenager. Fifteen, she was.'

Felix's face was ashen. 'I am her father,' he said. 'I think I have a right to know. Do you mean to say – Babe, are you saying that Robert is the baby's father?'

'She told me that she was pregnant,' Babe said. 'With Robert's child. And that he had forced himself on her. I'm sorry, Felix, but that's the truth.'

'What?' Amy pushed her chair back and stood up as though someone had rammed her in the rear with a cow prod. She looked at Babe. 'What on earth are you talking about? Rubbish. She's just saying that. It isn't true.'

'I'm sorry, Amy,' Babe said, 'Gill doesn't tell lies. And she thinks this recent attack on her, the attack that put her in hospital, was instigated by your brother-in-law to warn her of what would happen if she told anybody that he was having yet another affair with a girl less than half his age.

Gill had found out, how, she wouldn't say, and she was threatening to tell his wife. She was worried about Izzy.'

Amy pushed her chair back. 'I am not staying here to be told lies like these. Luke, are you going to let her—'

'I think it would be best if you left,' Luke said. 'Come on. I'll see you to the door.'

'Come home with me, won't you?' Amy said in a low voice, audible to everybody in the room. She took his arm. 'Please. I'm very upset. Sylvia's only just told me. And now all this ... it can't be true, what she says. It can't be.'

'You should ask your sister,' Luke said, opening the door and ushering her into the hall. The door closed. Oh God, I thought. He's gone with her. He'll be consoling her.

Felix cleared his throat. 'Well, I'll be damned,' he said. He took out his handkerchief and blew his nose. 'What a terrible thing,' he said.

'Felix,' Babe said. 'Look. I did help her as much as I could. She wasn't alone. I want you to know that. And she never even considered not having the child.'

'I'm glad of that,' Felix said. 'And she adored Leonie. We both did.'

I felt so sorry for him.

Esme said, studiously avoiding my eyes, 'What a shame, we were having such a good time. Perhaps we should talk about something else now.'

'I think we'll clear the table and get on,' Babe said, getting up.

'Luke hasn't finished his cake,' I said in a small voice. It was my fault this had happened. I should have kept my temper. Luke would not be pleased.

'He won't notice,' Felix said. 'Other fish to fry.' Stowing his handkerchief away in his pocket he said, remarkably calmly I thought, and as if deliberately changing the subject, 'By the way, Milly, I got the ambulance to put me down by the shops instead of bringing me here so I could do a little shopping and I came across that nice man who helped pull me out of the river. A gentleman of the road, from the looks of him. I gather he's a friend of yours. Mr Flint? He introduced himself and asked after you, and he said to thank you very much for the cake. Lemon, he says, is his absolute favourite. There was enough to delight everyone in the shelter, apparently. Extremely chuffed, I think was the expression he used.'

'Cake?' I said. 'But I haven't made it for him yet. It isn't his birthday for another week.'

'Er, that would be me,' Babe said. 'Couldn't have it going to waste, could I? Since Milly was going to make him one anyway. Nice man, that Mr Flint. Very fond of you, he is, Milly, and very appreciative, he was. Now, if you've all finished—'

Luke still hadn't come home when I dropped into bed later that evening, exhausted with waiting.

Chapter 44

Jane and me, sisters under the skin

Days passed. 'Babe,' I said one morning, coming into the kitchen, having wandered aimlessly about town since breakfast, unable to settle to anything. 'D'you think – he is seeing her an awful lot, isn't he? I saw them just now, standing outside the post office. I thought he'd gone in early to work. I thought he was supposed to be busy.'

Babe sighed and started collecting soup spoons and bowls.

When you snap your fingers or wink your eye, sang the Four Tops, *I come running to you.*

'I'll lay,' I said.

'Thanks. I dunno, Milly. Honestly, I don't.' She leaned on one arm, watching as I laid the table for lunch. 'She came in here yesterday, bold as brass, starts criticising my kitchen. Lots of potential she says but everything's in the wrong place. Needs *rationalising*, according to her.' She shook her head, her eyes fierce. 'Over my dead body. That's what her job was, she says, some kind of interior designer. Stopped working when she married Mr Booth, apparently.'

'What does Luke say?'

Babe shook her head gloomily and shrugged. 'She said she'd brought him a present, some biscuits she seemed to think he liked. Left them for him in the sitting-room.'

'Oh, really?'

'Came into my kitchen without a by your leave. Stood right there where you're standing, looking around at everything. Started poking about, even looked in the cupboards. Good thing Pascale wasn't down, that's all I can say. I managed to hold on to myself while madam made herself at home.'

'Oh glory.'

'Anyhow, I dunno what she's talking about. I don't see anything wrong with it, do you?'

I looked around at the two enormous dressers, the long table, the Aga, the wood-burning stove, the quarry-tiled floor, the old sofa on which Izzy and I had spent many a rainy afternoon playing whist. 'Absolutely nothing.'

Babe sighed and shook her head again. 'It does look as if things might be getting a bit serious. Well,' she stood upright and folded her arms. 'If she comes to live here, I'm off. Can't be doing with that high-handed manner. I know the type. She won't give him a moment's peace.'

'Oh, poor Luke.'

'He's making a big mistake.' She went into the scullery and started running water into the sink.

Roger Miller was singing now: *Trailer for sale or rent, rooms to let fifty cents ...*

I sighed. Rather appropriate in the circumstances.

At least Babe was on my side, I thought, filling the kettle for after-lunch drinks, my stomach knotted with tension. Despite our reconciliation, things between Luke and me had gone from bad to worse. Normally cool and relaxed, he seemed more than ever restless and distracted. At home he seemed unable to settle but wandered about the house picking things up and putting them down again. He would get up suddenly and leave the house, saying he was going for a walk.

'What's the matter with him?' I asked Babe, who shrugged and shook her head.

He stayed long hours in the workshop, sometimes not coming home until late in the evening.

'What's he doing for food?'

'Don't ask me,' Babe said, furiously kneading dough at the other end of the kitchen table. 'Over at hers, maybe. Here, Milly, you take over, I've got my steak and kidney to see to.'

When we were together, Luke's attitude towards me veered between the old jokey intimacy and a new reserve. I found it almost impossible to concentrate on the work I ought to be doing for my English Literature degree. I had set myself a lot of reading to get through: critical essays and articles about texts and key theories and so on. I was conscious of the passage of time, and not just because I was dreading being away from Luke.

Perhaps he's angry with me, I agonised, lying on my bed with Sapphy or plunging through the woods trying to walk myself into peace of mind. I wished I could turn back the clock. I wished I'd behaved better, been more dignified about everything instead of showing him I was so upset.

If we could even just be friends like we were before, it would be better than this. Something had gone wrong. I thought we'd made up, that everything would go back to how it was, but no. Everything was different now.

It was ever since that kiss, I thought. Maybe it was because I let him see how I felt and he was embarrassed.

Now he was steeling himself to tell me something he knew I wouldn't want to hear.

And if he did marry Amy, what would I do? Where would I go? I didn't want to have a life that didn't have Luke in it. If I had to leave him, how would I bear it?

We were all on edge. Even Esme and Felix had retreated to their rooms, only emerging at mealtimes. It was as if we were all waiting for something to happen.

Then one day, another change. Luke came home to supper in a cheerful mood, everyone relaxed and we had a friendly and pleasant meal. It was almost like old times.

'Game of chess?' he asked me as we sat around drinking our coffee.

'Sure.' Perhaps he'd been ill and now he was feeling better.

'Do you have to go to bed?' he asked me a couple of hours later. 'Can't you stay a bit longer? Give me a chance to get my own back? You're getting rather good at this.'

'I only beat you because you're not concentrating. Did you have a good time last night?'

'Last night?'

'Didn't you take – You went out to dinner.'

'Oh yes. Amy. Her divorce is coming through.'

'So she'll be free.'

'I suppose she will.'

You know she will, I thought. I stood up. 'I'll go up now.'

'Milly.'

'Yup?'

'Sit down a minute.'

I sat back down, my heart going into overdrive again. Was this it? Was he going to break the news to me now?

'What would you think of me if – if in pursuit of

personal happiness I behaved in a way that would make people disapprove – of me. Think badly of me.'

'What kind of way?' I frowned, completely at sea. 'You'd never do anything really bad, I know you wouldn't. What do you mean?'

'Would you stand by me?'

'Luke.' He was looking quizzically at me, his eyes intent. He was waiting for my answer. 'Happiness is important,' I said slowly.

'Is it? Is it, Milly? Even if it involves doing what might be considered to be a bit – iffy?'

'What kind of iffy? In whose eyes?'

'Society's?'

'Society's! Are you saying it would be wrong? I mean, morally?'

'N-no. Not exactly.'

'Is this about Amy?'

'Amy might be involved, but only peripherally.'

'You've lost me.'

'Have I? Ah.' He started to gather up the chess men, his movements brisk. Discussion over, then.

I felt somehow that I had failed him. 'Luke. Look, if you'd just explain. All I can say is that whatever you did I would stand by you. What I mean is—'

I looked away, tongue-tied. You're the air I breathe ... you're whom I think about the moment I wake, the person I'm thinking about when I fall asleep. My heart beat so hard I felt I was suffocating.

Watching him leaning back again in his chair now, his eyes closed, as if he'd suddenly tired of the conversation, images of my life with him flashed through my mind like a film unreeling.

So many memories of Luke. His beloved face, the sleepy eyes as changeable as flowing water, silver-grey with tiny golden-brown flecks in them, that Babe said reminded her of a Welsh mountain stream; the kind mouth; the dusty black hair which always seemed too heavy and had a tendency to slip sideways and often had to be swept back with his hand which was strong and bony and good at using things like chisels.

Luke coming home from work late in the afternoon, covered in a fine layer of sawdust and smelling of wood and beeswax and turpentine; heeling off his leather work-boots in the lobby and stretching his toes with relief; unfolding his long, strong body into an easy chair and stretching out his legs, so that you noticed how long they were and how big and consoling his feet; rubbing his hand over his face to wipe the tiredness away like Sapphy washing her face; padding around the house in his socks in the winter and barefoot in the summer.

Luke laughing; sitting at his desk in business mode, his brow furrowed, working out bills; weeping in front of *Brief Encounter* and pretending he'd got hay fever.

As long as I could remember he'd been my north and south, my east and west; and now he was behaving so oddly that I felt unmoored, as if something catastrophic had happened or was about to happen. Like really, really bad news; something you couldn't change and you were going to have to be brave about. Amy, I thought. Amy.

'So that's a yes then. That's your answer.' He had opened his eyes again and was looking at me, again with that curious intentness in his face. His beloved face.

There was a strange feeling in the room, a feeling you sometimes get at the changing of the seasons. A feeling of the ending of something, held within it the possibility of something else. Something you might not want, but you couldn't stop.

'THERE's something we need to ... discuss,' I said to Luke a few nights later, pushed beyond endurance. 'I'd quite like to talk about it now, if that's okay.'

He looked up from the paper. 'Sounds serious. Everything okay?'

I looked at him. Sometimes it was difficult to credit the density of men. He couldn't possibly really think everything was okay, surely. Nothing was okay. Nothing was normal. Everything was up in the air still. 'Look,' I said, closing my eyes and opening them again. 'I know you've been seeing a lot of Amy.'

'Are you still working for her, by the way?'

'No.' He sounded distracted. Surely he must know I wasn't working there anymore? What on earth did they talk about when they were together? Perhaps that was it, perhaps they didn't talk. 'Amy only needed me while her regular cleaner was in hospital.'

'Ah, yes. I expect she did mention it.'

'I expect you have more important things to talk about,' I said.

'She does like to chat.'

I looked at him in surprise. I persisted: 'It's just – if you do – get together, and she moves in here, I don't think I can stay here. Nothing personal, it's just it would feel a bit awkward. I'm sure you understand.'

Luke, his face turned away from me, was silent for a long, long time. At last he said, 'What d'you think would be best in that case, where would you like to go? Would you stay with Juno, do you think? I'm sure they'd have you. Izzy would love it.'

I looked at him, dumbfounded.

'I did think you were happy here,' he said, raising the paper again, 'but I do realise you must be longing for independence and a life of your own. Don't worry, we can talk about all that nearer the time. Goodnight, Milly.'

What's come over him? I thought, frozen, climbing the stairs to bed. Who does he think I am, to be shoved aside like that, as if I've got no feelings, as if I don't matter? What's got into him? He doesn't seem to care a bit how I feel.

I paused on the landing. Anger welled up, drowning sadness and fear. How dared he treat me like that?

I turned right around and clattered back down the stairs. I burst into the study without knocking. Luke was standing by the window, his hands in his pockets, looking out into the dark garden. I stood in the doorway, seething. Luke turned, looking surprised.

'Hello, back again?' he said. 'Something you've forgotten? Well?' he said, as I continued to stand there, looking at him. 'I'm not psychic, Milly. You will need to put whatever it is into words.'

'I'm beyond words,' I said finally, and went out again, slamming the door.

How does he expect me to sleep one wink, I thought, going on like this? Acting as if him importing Amy won't affect me. He knows – he knows – how I feel about him, he just won't admit it. He could at least be kind about it, instead of treating me with such – contempt. That's what it felt like – contempt.

I lay awake, unable to settle, burning with outrage, sadness, regret. I couldn't even go and get a hot drink in case

I bumped into him downstairs. And then what would happen?

I wouldn't trust myself, I thought, and then I fell asleep.

'Come for a walk,' Luke said the next evening, getting to his feet. 'You don't want to go to bed yet, do you? I thought we could try and find the nightingale.'

I looked up from my book. 'A nightingale! I've never heard a nightingale.'

'Jean-Paul says people have heard one singing in a garden at the end of Drove Lane. I thought we could see if we could find it.' He held open the sitting-room door. 'D'you need a wrap – a cardigan or something?'

'It's warm. I'll be fine.'

We walked along Angel Road and turned into the unlit lane. I looked up. 'The stars are so bright! And look at that moon. Is it full?'

'Very nearly.'

'Lovely, isn't it?'

The trees along the lane reared up around us, black against a sky encrusted with a million stars. Why isn't he with Amy? I thought. Why is he with me on a night like this? I glanced at his profile, just visible in the starlight.

I stumbled and Luke put out a hand to steady me and caught hold of my hand.

'Sorry,' I said. 'It's the potholes.' Don't let go, I thought. Please don't.

'Okay now?' He gave my hand a quick squeeze, then let go. We walked in silence for a bit. 'Milly.'

He was going to break it to me now. This was it. I steeled myself. My heart was thumping.

'You must be longing to get out into the world, spread

your wings,' Luke said. I sensed rather than saw him watching my face. 'Ready to soar,' he said. 'The whole of life in front of you.'

'I'm living my life now,' I said. My insides had started to quake again. What was he trying to say?

'You're very young, Milly,' he said gently. 'You've seen nothing of the world.'

'I've seen enough to know that I'm happy here with you.' Don't plead, I thought. You sound as though you're pleading.

'Milly,' he said.

He knew. He had guessed how I felt and he was letting me down gently. I swallowed hard to hold back tears. He was trying to tell me that my place was not here, by his side, but out there, somewhere else.

'We're friends, aren't we, Milly?' he said.

'Of course,' I said, not looking at him.

'Good friends. We know each other well. I hope – I hope I've not let you down in any way. You know I promised – your mother – if – of course one never thinks these things will happen. But it's been – you know I told you that coming here was the best thing that could have happened to me. I meant it. I don't want you to feel—'

'What?'

'Well – beholden. That you owe me anything. Your life is your life, Milly. Being with you all this time has been a joy – a privilege. But that doesn't mean you have to feel – that there are things – that—'

'Are you trying to say I can't stay with you?' I stopped and faced him. 'Look. I know about Amy. I know – if – when you. You don't have to tell me. I'm not stupid. When she comes to live in our house, I know I can't stay then. I couldn't anyway, I couldn't bear it. Is that what you're saying, that your life is here and I must go and make my life somewhere else?'

'Of course not.' He made a gesture of hopelessness. 'I'm putting this very badly.'

'Come on,' I said, setting off rapidly. 'We'll never get there at this rate.'

'You're shivering. Here, take my jacket. You're cold.'

'I'm fine. No. Oh, well ... thanks.' I felt the warmth of his hands under my chin. He arranged the jacket carefully around me and buttoned it up under my chin. I could smell his aftershave, faintly his sweat. I closed my eyes. If you don't kiss me right now, I thought, I'll die.

He moved away and set off again. 'We're nearly there. Look. Here we are. Now listen.'

We stood in silence and listened. Minutes passed.

'There it is.'

Into the soft air the throbbing notes of the nightingale's voice poured like honey from a jug. Again and again it sobbed its song to the stars, to the trees, to the night. To us. And I cried. Surreptitiously, pretending nothing was happening, turning away and walking a few steps away from him so that he wouldn't see.

'We should go,' he said after a long while.

'Do we have to?' I said. 'Does it have to end? I wish we could stay here for ever. I wish I was dead.' I started to walk away, rapidly, back the way we had come.

At the corner I looked back. Luke was standing where I had left him, his head bent.

I can't bear it, I thought. He's going to marry Amy and I'm going to have to leave after all.

. . .

When we got back from listening to the nightingale, both of us wordless and awkward, we stood for a moment in the hall. Luke looked down into my face with grave attention, touched my cheek briefly and disappeared into the study without even saying goodnight. I went up to my room and sat on my bed with the door open, waiting until I could be sure that he had gone up and the house was quiet. At this moment only one thing could have distracted me from the numb misery I was feeling. There was something important I'd forgotten in my preoccupation with Luke. One thing I had to do.

After a couple of false starts, mostly down to Felix characteristically making a couple of trips to the loo – once to go and once to make sure – I crept downstairs and felt my way across the hall and out of the side door, through the bramble patch and onto the gravel path. Even though it was after midnight it wasn't fully dark. The light from the moon and from a trillion stars cast a gentle glow over the sky, just enough to light my way to the orchard.

I wanted to reassure my mother that now we knew the truth. I felt in my bones that this was why she had come. It was because of the diary. She had wanted me to read her diary, to know that it was not she who had hurt me. I needed to apologise to her for ever believing that she could. I wanted to tell her that I was in love with Luke and needed her as never before.

I hurried, full of dread. I couldn't bear the thought that she might have disappeared without giving me the opportunity to say these things to her, to say goodbye.

'Mother?' I went in under the trees. I stood listening to the leaves rustling, felt a light wind fresh on my face. The air smelt of apples and damp, mown grass. 'Oh Mother,' I whispered. 'Where are you? Come back. Just for a moment or two. Just to say goodbye.'

Nothing. Nothing. She had gone, mission accomplished, and I had a horrible feeling that this time it was for ever.

I put my hand on the gnarled trunk of the nearest apple tree. 'I love you,' I whispered aloud. 'I love you.' And there it was, the faintest strain of music, and far away between the trees a single orb floating just below the lowest branches of one of the trees.

'Mother,' I said. 'I came to say goodbye.' The music faded away and the orb began to move towards me, slowly, almost hesitantly. I held my breath. It came closer. I began to feel a little afraid. Would my mother appear? Would I see her at last, the mother I remembered, the mother from the photographs? Would she be able to touch me, hold me, would she be there in person or would it be like a hologram, a mirage?

The orb stopped moving about three feet away from me on a level with my head. It seemed to be pulsating, like a heart, and from it came the strongest feeling of energy, of goodwill, of love. I bathed in this energy, I let it surround me and support me for a length of time which I can't recall. I closed my eyes and surrendered to it and felt all my doubts, my misgivings, slowly dissolve and disappear. When I opened my eyes again it began to move away. It lingered at a distance for a long moment and then moved upwards and disappeared into the dark branches above it, and I knew that my mother had gone.

Tiptoeing back to the house I was surprised to see light spilling from the kitchen window onto the gravel path. I pushed my way through the bramble-patch and let myself into the house. The kitchen door opened as I was stealing across the hall, and Esme stood there in her blue silk dressing-gown, holding a mug between both hands. 'Milly. Can you spare a moment?'

'Of course.' I wondered why she had come downstairs to make herself a drink, instead of using the little gas ring in her room.

As if reading my mind she said, 'I had to get out of my room. I felt too agitated to stay.'

'What's happened?' I followed her into the kitchen, which smelt of cocoa. She closed the door and we sat down at the kitchen table.

She sipped her cocoa and composed herself. 'I won't keep you too long, Milly. I know it's late,' she said. 'You know I told you about the man I met on holiday, the man with the sick wife?'

'The man you fell in love with.'

She nodded. 'His name is Charles Bannister. And yes, I did fall in love with him and we did have a brief ... affair. It was wrong, we knew it was wrong, but his wife was – no, no excuses. It happened.' She paused and took a sip of cocoa. I waited. She resumed. 'I haven't told you this, but recently he wrote to tell me that his wife had died and consequently he was now free.'

I leaned forward. 'Esme, that's wonderful!'

'Wait. I wrote back. I told him that it was too late, that I had moved on, was settled in my life here. The truth is, I was afraid.'

'Was he upset? Did he understand?'

'He did seem genuinely very upset. I hardened my heart and stuck to my guns, despite a second letter from him.'

I sensed that more was coming.

'Milly,' Esme said, 'I've made a decision. I have changed

my mind. I wrote to him. I have some holiday due and I'm going down to Cornwall to see him. It's a risk, of course, a risk I've been too cowardly to take.'

'A risk?'

'I risk having my heart broken again. I risk having what I believed to be love shown to be a mirage. I have no idea if we will still love each other. If indeed what we thought we had was real.'

She looked at me with large, scared eyes. She looked about fifteen, instead of forty.

I laughed. I couldn't help it. 'But Esme, that's wonderful,' I said. 'Okay, so it's a risk, but you've gone for it, you've done the brave thing. I'm sure Luke would say you've done the right thing.'

'But suppose,' Esme said. 'Suppose ...'

'Of course you're scared. But isn't it better than always wondering if you missed the opportunity to find love again? What's he like, this Charles? Is he nice, Esme? Does he deserve you?'

Esme's shoulders relaxed and she laughed. 'He's wonderful. He's a really nice man. A good man.'

'Well, there you go. You're doing the right thing. And what's the worst that can happen?'

'The death of a dream?'

'Yes. But maybe facing the truth is a good thing. I think it's better to know, however much it hurts. Then you can move on.'

Chapter 45
Things are falling into place

LUKE GOT UP FROM THE TABLE AND WENT INTO THE hall to answer the phone. 'Merryweather here. Hello? What can I do for you? Say again? Ah, I see. No, I'm sorry, you've been misinformed. Felix is back home in full working order. No suggestion of his room becoming vacant. Sorry. If you'd like to give me your name and telephone number we can certainly contact you if a room does become vacant but at the moment that's a remote possibility, I'm afraid. There's already a long queue. Hang on, I'll just get a pen. No? Ah well. Thank you for calling.'

He came back into the kitchen where the others carried on eating their pasta, pretending nothing had happened. Pascale, who seemed genuinely not to have heard anything, chewed carefully and swallowed. 'More pesto,' she said.

'D'you think so?' Babe said. 'P'raps you're right. I was thinking more black pepper.'

Pascale nodded thoughtfully. 'Per'aps.'

We were all in a cheerful mood. Several days had passed and things had fallen into a pattern Luke and I seemed to be managing to cope with, both of us pretending the kiss and the nightingale hadn't happened, and more or less avoiding each other. Izzy had been gone for nearly two weeks now, we were well into September and thoughts of university were beginning to play seriously on my mind. I was tormented by the thought of having to leave Half Moon with things between me and Luke still so unresolved. If only he would give me some sign, I moaned to myself ... some hope.

This evening Luke for some reason had decided that a glass of wine at supper would be a good idea and astonishingly we'd moved on to a second bottle. I discovered that I was enjoying the wine; I knew now that I liked Sauvignon Blanc but didn't much like Chardonnay. We all welcomed the second bottle with enthusiasm but at the same time I was slightly bothered when Luke suggested it: he was definitely beginning to let his guard down. Was he building up to telling us something?

'Luke,' I said, 'I didn't know there was a queue for Felix's room.'

'There isn't.' Luke sat down and picked up his fork. 'We'd better not let that gentleman find out I lied. He's in urgent need of a room so he won't wait.'

'Luke!'

'Just covering all the avenues.'

'You're not thinking of leaving, are you, Felix?' I asked him.

'Not I. The food is far too good around here.'

'Oh good. I've got used to having you around.'

'You won't let out my room while I'm away, will you?' Esme said. 'My plans are somewhat fluid.'

'Esme, of course we won't,' Luke said.

'It's just that the rooms seem suddenly to be very much in demand.'

'When are you off?' Felix said. 'Who will look after the cat?'

'I'm in charge of that,' I said. 'Don't worry, Felix.'

'In a day or so. I have a couple of projects to finish first. I must say I'm quite excited now. Cornwall! It's many years since I was there.'

'Jean-Paul is interested in a room,' Babe said, looking up. 'Seemed very keen, too.'

Luke looked at her sternly. 'Well if either Felix or Esme happen to leave and there's a room free, Jean-Paul can't come and live here. I won't have it.'

There was a charged pause.

Babe cleared her throat. 'Actually,' she went on. 'I bumped into Juno in town yesterday and she expressed an interest in Felix's room, too. I told her I'd mention it.'

'What?' I exclaimed. 'What's the matter with everybody? She can't come and live here, she's got a perfectly good home of her own. She's not thinking of selling, is she? And what about Izzy, she'll be back from seeing her father, she's not staying up there, I sincerely hope. Luke, you won't let—'

Babe leaned back in her chair and exploded into laughter.

'*Babe!*' I said, reddening.

'You two, you should see yourselves! Your faces!'

'You are a bad, bad woman,' Luke said, trying to suppress a smile. 'Giving us a fright like that.'

My heart lifted.

'No Juno, and no Jean-Paul, delightful as he is,' Luke said. 'Is that understood?'

'And no Amy either,' I said firmly. 'Even if she has divorced her husband.'

Luke looked at me very hard, and I looked back at him

with new daring. There was something funny going on in his face. I couldn't stop looking at him, and he didn't seem to be able to stop looking at me.

Perhaps it wouldn't take as long as I thought.

'Actually,' Luke said, tearing his eyes away, 'I do have some news.'

What? Oh no.

'About Amy. Her divorce has indeed come through, and she's put her house on the market. She's leaving the area, going to live near her mother in the Cotswolds.'

My mouth fell open.

There was a stunned silence. My heart was racing and I felt sick.

'Well,' said Babe. 'That's that then. More chicken, anyone? No? Well, if Esme does leave, and Felix does decide to go, get someone reliable,' she said, getting up and starting to remove plates. 'Then maybe I can go off and have a nice holiday. About time I had a break.' She glanced over her shoulder. 'You know what people are like. Minds like sinks.'

I blushed. I didn't dare look at Luke.

Babe's right, I thought. Pascale's so old, she doesn't count. There needs to be someone else here with us, or goodness knows what I might do. I might creep into his bed at dead of night.

'Milly,' Babe said sharply. 'Curb those thoughts.'

I'd always known Babe could read my mind.

'That's me done,' Luke said, pretending nothing was happening. 'No pud for me thanks, Babe.'

'But it's lemon meringue pie,' I said.

'Exactly.' He patted his flat midriff. 'Will you excuse me? Got a bit of paperwork to do then perhaps we could have a game of chess or something. Up for it?'

'Sure. Love to. Chess would be great.'

'Ah, she's too good for me now,' Luke said, going to the door. 'Much too good for me.'

Babe looked at the door and raised her eyebrows, then returned to the matter in hand. 'That's how he keeps so trim,' she said, putting the pie in front of me. 'Here. You be Mum. And yes, please, can't resist a slice of pie. Pascale?'

'I just go ask André,' Pascale said, holding on to the edge of the table and struggling to her feet.

'Pascale,' I said gently, cutting Babe a generous slice. Was it worth trying to convince Pascale that hanging onto her illusions about André wasn't a good idea, either?

Was I living under an illusion too?

'For goodness sake, Pascale,' Babe said, 'sit down and eat your pud.'

When we'd finished I helped clear the table then ran up to my room to wash my hands before going to the study. I sat on my bed, drying my hands on my towel, staring out of the window at the roof of Izzy's house, just visible through the trees.

Luke loved me, I knew he did. He just didn't think he ought to be in love with me, because I was too young and because he was my guardian and therefore in a position of responsibility. It was down to me to show him that it was okay, that he was allowed and that I would wait for him for as long as it took. If it meant being patient for a hundred years then that's what I'd have to be.

I allowed my thoughts to wander and got a bit silly and giggly, wondering how long it would actually take. How old would I have to be – twenty-five? Thirty?

Chapter 46

Confession is good for the soul

JUNO STOOD ON THE PORCH OF THE PARISH CHURCH IN Shere. She'd gone further afield than she'd intended, looking for somebody who would understand, to whom she could make her confession. She wasn't a Catholic, she wasn't anything really, but the need to confess her contribution towards three deaths had become too urgent to resist.

If she could find the courage to share the rest of it – her painful jealousy of Milly, her resentment towards Mike – and Luke – for the way she felt they had treated her – and be offered absolution, then perhaps she could forgive herself, clear out all the emotional clutter and start again. Make room for new feelings. Because now there was Jack.

Perhaps with a clear conscience she could start to live a new life and stop wasting her time in useless longings and dreams and crippling bitterness. Even maybe start to sing again.

It was nearly time. She was dreadfully nervous. Father Peter might tell her she had to go to the police and tell them, about the drink. About what had been in her heart. Well, maybe she'd have to. She was beginning to think that anything would be better than having to go on carrying the load of guilt she was lugging about with her. It was exhausting.

She hadn't told Jack about Miranda and the accident because she didn't want to lose him. Was this to be her punishment? To lose this lovely man she was falling in love with?

She'd phoned the parish office and spoken to Father Peter, and he had said that of course she could come and of course he would hear her confession. Not enough people took advantage of this invaluable service, he had said, making it sound like having your fireplace swept. She would be most welcome. He wasn't at all alarming, he'd said, hearing her nervousness down the phone.

'Konfesado kuracas la animon.' In her head she heard Esme's voice and the memory of that moment of revelation comforted her. She pushed open the ancient, heavy oak door and ventured into the dim interior of the church.

Chapter 47

A waiting game

I SAT READING ON THE STAIRS. IT WAS A FEW DAYS later, ten o'clock in the evening and I was beginning to yawn. Izzy would be back tomorrow. She'd rung to say that she had found her father and had spent the last fortnight staying with him and his wife Celia and their two little girls, Izzy's half-sisters. She'd sounded happy. She had so much to tell me. I couldn't wait.

Luke had gone out to supper with some clients, more friends of Amy's, also interested in commissioning a piece from him. No doubt Amy would be there, fluttering her eyelashes at him to the last.

I was reading *Persuasion,* my favourite Jane Austen, and had almost got to the best bit – where Anne Elliot begins to suspect that her beloved Captain Wentworth actually does return her love – when the phone rang in the hall, making me jump. I put my book down, sprang up and leapt down the stairs to answer it. 'Hello?'

A man's deep voice said, 'Could I speak to Esme, please? Er ... Mrs Landower?'

'Who's speaking, please?'

'My name's Bannister, Charles Bannister.'

I gave a squeak. 'Didn't you get her last letter?'

'I beg your pardon? Who is this, please?'

'I'm a friend of Esme's, Milly Redmayne. I posted it myself, about a week ago. First class. It ought to have got there by now.'

'Could I speak to her, please?'

'Well, no, that's the point, she isn't here. She's on her way down to the West Country as we speak.'

'Is she? My goodness. Do you know where to, exactly?'

'Well, to St. Ives. You can't have got her second letter. Oh dear.'

'Is she really on her way down?'

'She is. She *is*.' I held my breath. Now did he sound pleased, or not?

'Well. That's – that's very good news. Goodness. No, she did write, to say she was thinking of coming, but she didn't say when. Perhaps the letter got lost. Or delayed somehow. Well, I'm absolutely delighted.'

He did sound genuinely awfully pleased. 'Oh good!' I said. 'When she didn't hear back from you she was a bit worried. She'd booked her vacation, you see, with the company she works for. So she thought she'd go anyway. On spec, so to speak.'

'Well, that's wonderful. Really wonderful. Do you know when she thought she might get here?'

'She left this morning. She thought she'd stay the night in Devon rather than doing the whole journey in one go. There's a Highwayman's Inn she was talking about. Or somewhere on Bodmin Moor. She says she's always wanted to visit Jamaica Inn. I wasn't sure if it actually existed.'

'I think it's some kind of museum now. I'm not sure they

take guests.' His voice was full of energy and cheerfulness. Full of hope.

'Oh well. She'll find somewhere.'

'I say, I'm terribly sorry it's so late. It took me a while to nerve myself to make this call.'

'I'm so glad you did. I guess she'll be in St. Ives tomorrow, perhaps by the afternoon?'

'That's good news. That really is good news.'

He sounded so nice, the sort of person you could tell things to. 'If she rings here, shall I give her a message?'

There was a pause, then he said,

'Just tell her – tell her – I'll be waiting.'

Just like me, I thought, putting down the phone. Oh Luke, my love. Just like me.

Before you go...

I hope you enjoyed reading **_Now I Can See the Moon._**
Would you mind leaving a rating or short review?

Your feedback would be very much appreciated.

Rate this book!

Discover more

Please visit **Bonarash.com** to learn more about me, my writing life, and my forthcoming novels.

Printed in Great Britain
by Amazon